Sarah Jost was born and grew up in Switzerland in small yet stunning Montreux against the backdrop of Lake Geneva and the Alps. She studied medieval French, modern French and history of art at the Université de Lausanne and worked part-time as a publishing assistant alongside her studies.

She has been living in the UK since 2008 and works as a housemistress and French teacher at a girls' school, which she considers an immersive course in character study. Sarah lives in Buckinghamshire with her husband, Luke, and their adorable and goofy golden shepherd, Winnie.

One Last Chance is her debut novel.

Sarah Jost

One Last Chance

PIATKUS

PIATKUS

First published in Great Britain in 2023 by Piatkus

1 3 5 7 9 10 8 6 4 2

A CIP catalogue record for this book
is available from the British Library.

ISBN 978-0-349-43153-6

Typeset in Bembo by M Rules
Printed and bound in Great Britain by
Clays Ltd, Elcograf S.p.A.

Papers used by Piatkus are from well-managed forests
and other responsible sources.

Piatkus
An imprint of
Little, Brown Book Group
Carmelite House
50 Victoria Embankment
London EC4Y 0DZ

An Hachette UK Company
www.hachette.co.uk

www.littlebrown.co.uk

*To Dora Kislig, beloved grandmother
and vanilla pretzel queen*

Monday 15 July 2019

Baby elephants can die of loneliness.

I'm hiding at the darker end of the room, in this village pub erected so close to the church that either would crumble without the other. I sneaked out after the service; now, at the wake, while I wait anxiously for somebody to come and ask how I knew Nick (I didn't, not really), I'm reviewing my life and regrets, basking in the proximity of death like a chicken roasting in its own juices. Compressing the past four years of my life into my brain, trying to figure out where it's all gone wrong.

'Time is a funny thing,' I tell Yuki when she returns. She went to offer her condolences to the family, all huddled together in the bay window.

She leans next to me against the bar. The voices around us are muffled, the carpet dappled in burning puddles of sun. There's a garden out there, full of grass and flowers and cats, but it must have been deemed too hot, too cheery for the

1

occasion. Or nobody could stand to be judged by cats today, and I can't blame them.

Yuki checks her glass, which still stands empty where she left it. Was I supposed to get her another drink? Be her funeral wing-woman? She sighs as she orders, the tips of her fingers drumming on the bar. Her nail polish is unusually flaky, like the paint of those neglected houses by the seaside. That's all I seem to be able to see in England nowadays. The crumbling plaster, the burst fast-food bags, the electric wires threatening to come loose.

'Yeah, I know what you mean, Lou,' she says. 'If only we could go back and see Nick again.'

'Of course,' I say. Yuki's eyes are deep, slightly swollen, ringed with eyeliner gone blurry. 'I mean, this is such a tragedy.'

'But …? Go on, I know you have something on your mind.'

'I … I can't stop thinking I've messed up my life.'

'Ah, mate. You and me both.'

When she called me last week saying her friend Nick had died, asking me to go with her to the funeral, I was surprised. We hadn't been in touch much the past two years, since she'd put an end to our flat share to move in with her best friend Lucy. We had got on well when we lived together, had been lucky given the randomness of our pairing, but it had fizzled out.

I was desperate when I met Yuki. The end of my teacher training year was in sight, I'd got my first job, had to leave university accommodation and was terrified of setting out by myself in a foreign country for the first time. I'd gone on SpareRoom, scrolling through a world of bachelor pads, rehabilitated cupboards and dark bedrooms brimming with spooky dolls. When I found Yuki's advert, I kept thinking there had to be a catch. Even after she'd let me into the neat top-floor flat padded with soft furnishings, even after she'd called me *mate* and asked eagerly about types of fondue. We only lived together for a year, and I know now, retrospectively, that it was my best year in the UK. My best relationships always seem to be short-lived.

During that out-of-the-blue phone call, I remember hearing Yuki only faintly over the sound of a lawnmower, as if her voice itself, normally pure and confident, was being chopped up in small blades. 'But you and Nick have friends in common,' I tried to argue, thinking of her clique from uni and work, their house parties and big nights out. Panicking at the thought of intruding where I didn't belong. 'I hardly knew him at all. Will Lucy not be there?'

'Lucy's in Barcelona for work,' Yuki said. I could tell she was upset, and I'd never known her to be upset, not really. Her mood and direction were meant to be constant, like a shiny boat. 'I'd like someone with me,' she continued. 'Someone neutral.'

'Is it because I'm Swiss?' I joked.

'Lou, please, matey. I don't want to be there alone. My other friends will all have babies to wipe or whatever.'

So I said yes, and she seemed to want to say more, but changed the subject, and we talked about how glad we were to be childless. It was like those old conversations we used to have, sunk into the numerous cushions of her sofa. It made me realise how much I had missed them.

I never had enough time to get to know Nick, however, which made the funeral today rather uncomfortable. As I sat in the hushed silence before the beginning of the service, in the rustle of tissues and quiet sobs, hiding my phone between my knees, I felt like one of my pupils, waiting to be caught out. The church was packed, and the doors had been wedged open to allow people to spill outside. There was an older lady in some kind of hiking trousers and a chunky necklace, who had to stand by our pew; whoever she was, she must have known Nick better than I did. I was checking tribute messages on his social media, cramming homework, as it were. His grin on his profile picture was wide, his face handsome and relaxed. With his sun-kissed hair tied back, his stubble and his hoodie, he looked wholesome, like he'd just been doing some casual rock-climbing.

> Nick Harper you legend can't believe your gone.
> Rest in peace wherever u are

> What a loss. Such a genuine and generous lad.
> Love to all the family. Will miss your smile so
> much, and all your wise advice. I'll never forget
> your help xoxo

> Nick, you always made us laugh. You were a
> wonderful colleague and teacher. We'll all miss
> you so much here at St Mary's, Year 5 especially.
> Love and RIP

I ended up scrolling all the way back to two days after Nick's death, when his sister, Charlotte, had written about the funeral on his page: *Close friends and family only* – she clearly didn't want to share it with the world. I clicked on her Instagram username, and there she was, sitting on a herringbone wooden floor, wrapped in a robe fluffy enough to have been spun by Cinderella's mice, one arm hugging a Bernese Mountain Dog. I felt some envy for her life, the striking quality of it, her confidence, with huge additional shame for that envy, because she had just lost her brother.

Then Yuki elbowed me hard. 'You're not stalking Romain? I thought you'd stopped,' she scolded, looking over my shoulder, her intrusion bringing my thoughts right back to him. Not that I'd stopped thinking about him, or loving him. Being at this funeral had made me realise that in all the time I'd been in England, I hadn't met anyone who mattered as much to me as he did. The loneliness of this was suddenly unbearable, a dull ache I'd been living with and ignoring for years. When sitting in a church pew surrounded by mourners, I could no longer ignore it.

Romain wasn't my first love, but he was the first one that mattered. One of those people who comes along and rescues you from all your doubts and insecurities. With them, you find yourself standing in a new landscape, holding bricks and mortar and desperate to get building – and then suddenly there's a landslide. Something due to your own negligence; you didn't protect your foundations, ignored the rough terrain, and all at once you're sucked into a gaping hole. When he broke up with me, back home in Switzerland, my grief spread to the landscape, to the towns and train stations where I might bump into him, to the cafés we'd sat in together – everywhere I looked was haunted by what our relationship would never be. And it was my fault.

So in September 2015, I moved to England, carrying his ghost with me in my suitcase, along with my brand-new ten-item wardrobe of reinvention. Leaving behind my sister, Marion, and my mother, who I thought were fine.

Romain sent me letters, making my heart leap every time I recognised his writing. I bent Yuki's ears at first, even a year in. 'Ah, Romain le Writer, what a *tristesse*,' she would sympathise. Her fake French is the worst. She has a C at GCSE – they all do here. Believe me, it's not a gauge of quality. She pronounces his name *Romaan*; I've long stopped correcting her. There was comfort, though, in acknowledging his existence, at a time when I thought I might have dreamt that we ever were together. Little by little, the distance seemed to work, the letters became more sporadic, and I stopped bringing him up, convincing myself I had moved on.

Except I'm looking back now and I realise I haven't progressed at all. I haven't got over anything; I've been stuck in time.

'You know, we met Nick exactly two years ago on this day.' Yuki's words bring me back to the present: the wake. She takes a big gulp of her fresh Diet Coke. I'm drinking lager, even if I know my stomach will be torn apart later with acidity and gas. I was hoping a pint would help me blend in, but the other women all appear to be drinking small glasses of white wine.

I turn to her – her face is so sad, still, as if made of wax.

'Was that your birthday? At the Five Horseshoes?' I ask. I only have vague memories of that night: a quick chat with Nick at the bar, perhaps about animals, which seems to be my only safe subject of conversation. Two years ago to this day; if I think back to where I was, things must have been looking up. I was just finishing my NQT year; I was exhausted, but I remember excitement, too. Yuki had moved out, but she had invited me to her birthday, and it looked like I was going to make it: I would become a real teacher, my new friendships might last the distance, it was summer . . .

'I saw you cried during the service,' Yuki says.

'Maybe. It was moving.'

I can't tell her the truth. That I have stored a programme I saw, the one about the lonely baby elephants, for these kinds of occasions. When I need something to attach my pain to, and need it quickly.

I watched the programme one evening after a particularly bad day at school, when one of the Year 10 boys had run out of the classroom and started sprinting round and round the building like a crazed firecracker, while the rest of the class cheered him from the windows. There was a tiny orphan elephant who had to sleep under a blanket and grew too attached to his keeper. The keeper knew it wasn't good; the calf loved him, but he would die if he didn't make any elephant friends. During Nick's eulogy, I allowed myself to spend some time there, in the vivid memory of the calf's story. The way he looked so small under the giant blanket. How he struggled to know what to do once he met other orphans. After a while, I realised everybody around me was crying, and I was crying too.

'It's so fucking tragic,' Yuki says, clearly referring to Nick's death.

Funerals do this to you: they are endings, but also beginnings. They point with awful clarity to the gaps in your own life. If things were looking up two years ago, that light has since dimmed. Now I'm thirty-three years old, in a country that still feels foreign, living in a tiny soulless studio I can barely afford, students rioting as I teach them the French

7

words for fruit and vegetables, my social life peppered with acquaintances and work colleagues who never quite become friends, my phone silent. Wishing it would all get better by itself, magically, with time.

What happened to me? How did it all slide downhill so slowly that I'm only now realising the extent of the damage?

I look at Yuki's profile, wondering whether she knows me well enough to explain it to me, taking in her bob of dyed blonde hair, more frizzy than usual, the Japanese tattoo on her forearm hinting at some unspoken heritage, though I know from the official-looking letters she received when we lived together that her legal name is Anna. 'Are you okay?' I ask her.

She shrugs. I'm not sure where we stand any more, what degree of intimacy we operate on. How to get back to what we once had, which I played down at the time. I keep looking at her, not knowing what I should say, and saying nothing.

And to make matters worse, Nick's sister is watching us across the room, coming our way. She'll interrogate me about my relationship with Nick and find out I have none. It will be awful.

I don't know how I know this, but I do.

My brain goes into panic mode – it is constantly involved in the anticipation of events. I play through my typical mishaps as if watching a film preview, to the point where I feel I've lived them already. Yuki used to say I was anxious, socially awkward, but even she doesn't understand to what extent. I try to steady myself by gripping the bar, but it's sticky with cider.

Italian has a word for the ring-shaped print of your drink. *Culaccino*. In the rising unease, I try it aloud.

8

'*Culaccino*. Nick's sister is coming.'

'Is that a swear word? Didn't know you spoke Italian too,' Yuki says.

I don't speak Italian. I spent my Swiss childhood reading cereal boxes where everything was written in three languages. Perhaps that counts as trilingual here.

'She's coming,' I repeat. Yuki clearly hasn't grasped the gravity of the situation. I'm praying for her to get me out of it, perhaps fireman-carry me out of the pub, but now she seems transfixed by Charlotte, who is closing in with calm purpose, silver bracelets clinking, as if she were Medusa and had turned Yuki to stone.

> We're utterly broken to let you know that Nick
> passed away on Wednesday 3 July. If you wish to
> pay tribute to him at this point in time, please do
> it here. We'll leave his page running for a while.
> Don't have the heart to pick up the phone at the
> moment, but thank you for your support.

'Hi again, Yuki,' Charlotte says, but she's looking at me.

'Hi.' Yuki comes back to life, combs through her hair.

'Where's your dog?' I blurt out, before mortification hits. That's what we call jumping from the cockerel to the donkey, *sauter du coq à l'âne*. I always do this when I'm embarrassed, put on the spot. That's why most of the time it's wiser for me not to do or say anything. Both Charlotte and Yuki startle, but Charlotte recovers first.

'Chomsky's with his borrower.'

'Borrower?'

'Yes.' She's clearly not willing to explain.

'He's really gorgeous, and so are you – I mean your photos on Instagram,' Yuki says. I thought she didn't like dogs.

'Thank you.'

There's a silence, left on purpose, I think, for me to fill with something about Nick, but I'm petrified. I go through my brain, but it has turned into bircher, and the longer the silence goes on, the more worried I become about saying the wrong thing. Yuki is of no use, and Charlotte is staring at me, while my eyes go from one to the other, not knowing where it's safer to land.

'How did you know Nick?'

I can tell she's been crying. Probably hasn't stopped for days. Everything she does or says is controlled, but her angst is raw. This is love. And seeing it so publicly displayed, so pure, makes me dizzy with heartbroken longing.

'Louise used to be my flatmate,' Yuki finally says. 'She's a teacher too.'

Charlotte nods, but her eyes are cold. 'I see.'

'Such a genuine and generous person,' I try. I hope she doesn't realise that I'm quoting Facebook. I'm not even sure how to pronounce the word 'genuine'.

'Yes, he was.'

I don't know what else to say. I don't have anything to offer. Baby elephants can die of loneliness. Baby elephants, the zoo. Capybaras. No, otters.

'I put you on the spot, didn't I?' Charlotte throws in a clipped smile, and we stand there for a while longer as I try sentences in my head, then discard them. In the end, she says, 'Well, it's nice meeting new friends of Nick's. I thought I knew them all. Bye, Yuki.'

She's made her point. I shouldn't be there, a spectator

to other people's pain. Both Yuki and I watch her turn around; she leaves us a perfume print in the air, jasmine or orange, something blossoming softly in the summer evening.

'The otters . . .'

This has come out of nowhere, even for me. But I've said something. Loud enough for Charlotte to turn and look back.

'I'm sorry?'

'Nick told me I should go to the zoo and check out the otters.' I stumble on my own accent, the words turning into pebbles in my mouth, a memory forming in my brain. Otters juggle pebbles, don't they?

Charlotte softens, though. 'He did love the zoo,' she says, chuckling to herself. 'Weirdo.'

And she goes back to her family, wrapping her long arm around her mother's shoulders, leaving me to wonder if Nick was the weirdo, or if I am.

I order another pint, and drink half of it, one tiny sip at a time, breathing through my nose. I must have gone through quite a lot of lager, I realise, as my head feels fuzzy. Yuki is still watching Charlotte's back, leaning against the bar, her elbows pointing up behind her like angel's wings.

'That's such a Nick thing to do,' she smiles, 'trying to match you to your animal mascot.'

I shrug, briefly wondering how the memory materialised. 'It must have been at your birthday. During that whole three minutes of small talk.'

Yuki leans over to me. 'That night, at the Five Horseshoes . . .' My phone buzzes in my pocket. A text. I go to retrieve it, but she stops me. 'For fuck's sake, Lou, please listen.' Her intensity is such that I freeze. 'Nick and I kissed.

Or I think I kissed him. It's so long ago, and I was drunk, a bit of a blur. Nobody else knows about it.'

'What ... how?' Among the men and women Yuki has dated these past three years, nobody has stuck.

'Thing is, it was nothing.' She shrugs, leans back again, finishes her Coke. Her fingers are trembling; a droplet of condensation runs down the glass, falls. 'Really really honestly, I hadn't given it much thought until he ... I remember bumping into him in the smoking shelter. We spent ages there, and he helped me, gave me life advice, Nick-style, and he was so, like, nice.'

'Did you ... did you, you know, like him?' I try.

'No,' she says, 'no. Actually, well, not like that. It wasn't about the kiss. We both knew I was being silly. It's more ... we talked about my life, and he had this way – things I haven't told anyone – then we ... well, I kissed him, and he said ... ' She lowers her voice, and I wait, but she composes herself. 'I just think things could have worked out differently since that night. That's all.'

Since that night. Ah, having the power to go back, rewrite our lives. Yuki's right, and I'm stunned that we're both feeling the same. I follow her gaze. Against the backdrop of the window, Charlotte is talking to the woman with the chunky necklace, the one who stood near us in church. The woman rummages in her bag to offer a handkerchief, a real fabric one; places her hand on Charlotte's shoulder, her face so close to hers that for a moment I expect their foreheads to meet, and perhaps them both to lift up, levitating in the air.

I want love. I want connection. I just don't know how to get it. How to say and do the right things. Instead, I haven't done anything. For two years, I've stood still, waiting for things to get better by themselves. And they got worse. If Chomsky were here, I would sit in a corner and hug the hell out of him to give myself courage. I also, weirdly, long for Nick. If there's one thing I've learnt about him today, it's that he gave good advice. It sounds like both Yuki and I could do with some. About who to love, how to be better friends. How to stop watching life passing us by like missed trains. Perhaps I'll go to Switzerland this summer, spend some time with Mum, help Marion. Call Romain.

As Yuki isn't saying any more, I check my phone for the message I received earlier. A WhatsApp from Marion. We used to be close before I left – especially when Dad moved away. Even in the first year of me being here, she used to send me funny memes. Now she only texts me with bad news I can't do anything about from here: *Mum didn't get up today. Mum threw away our photo albums. I got her the wrong granola and she burst into tears.* I open her message, bracing myself.

> I just saw that Romain got engaged.
> I thought you needed to know.

It's not so much of a surprise, more like a blow to the head I'd been living in fear of. It doesn't hurt any less. I close my eyes to blink away this new reality, but when I open them again, the text says the same. My browser tabs are still open; with clumsy fingers I navigate from Nick's Facebook page to Romain's, and here it is. The blue and white life event, accompanied by a plethora of photos of Romain and Aurélie-with-whom-it's-not-going-to-last by the lake, the ring sparkling on her hand laid on his chest. *Engaged – 15 July.*

I don't think. I immediately go to my texts, type his name.

13

I don't know what I want to say; I just want – I need – something to happen. I can't be left with this. The tiny text box opens, above which is the last text in our last conversation. From him. Unanswered by me. I see the date, and my breath freezes in my lungs. No.

It comes back.

'That night, Yuki.' My voice is strangled. My hands are shaking. I speak to her unable to take my eyes off the screen, glued to it by the coincidence of time, the enormity of my missed chance. 'At your birthday, two years ago. Romain texted me. He told me he missed me.'

'And what did you do?'

'I ignored it.'

My heart is beating in my throat as the memories pull me back to that night. It was the first time, and the last time, he'd said it. That he'd reached out like that. Why did I ignore it? I had felt happy, out with Yuki's friends, then the text came and I panicked. I told myself I was better off building a life here, away from the heartache; that I needed to move on. Now I know I was scared. I was scared of opening myself up to him, of potentially being hurt by him again. Hindsight isn't such a wonderful thing.

It's clear now – Yuki is right. That was the point where it all went wrong. That was the point I decided to shut the door to possibilities. I feel like I'm going to faint – blood beating in my ears, my vision blurring. Is it the lager suddenly rushing to my head? I feel like I'm fading away, losing contact with reality. 'Shall we . . . ?' I nudge Yuki, securing my beloved satchel over my shoulder despite my hands shaking, despite the room closing in on me like a tunnel.

Yuki's staring at me. 'Are you okay?'

14

I nod. I've never had a panic attack, but I've seen some of my students go through one and I'm pretty sure this is what it's like. 'I ... Can we just go, please? I'm sorry ...' Black flies mottle my vision as I try to control myself long enough to get away. All that missed time – all the regrets and worries I've worked hard at keeping under a lid these past two years are spilling everywhere. I'm finally drowning.

'Well, sure. I guess there's nothing left to say – nothing to be done. It's too late anyway.' Yuki struggles to retrieve her bag, which she hung on a hook under the bar. With her other hand she ruffles her hair, and I think she's crying, so I try to help her. As I bend down, my elbow knocks over the half-drink I've abandoned, sending great splashes of pee-like liquid all over the counter and beyond.

They say change happens when something moves. As the glass crashes, the beating of my heart takes over, and everybody turns and watches us: me with my hand extended to catch it, always too slow, always too late; Yuki frozen, drenched in lager. I can't breathe with the knowledge that I've ruined the day, the funeral, everything – this 15 July, that other one two years ago, and all the chances in between that I missed due to fear, cowardness. If only I could erase them, make different decisions ...

Time accelerates, slows down, building pressure in my ears as if I were on a roller coaster or a submarine; seconds start to fizz and bubble away, until it's all mixed up, all the sour regrets – then the pub door opens and I stumble out ...

*

We go back.

15

CHANCE 1

Saturday 15 July 2017

I'm standing on the threshold. I have to blink, as the pub is dark, my pupils not dilated enough. It's busy, with a kind of lightness I wasn't prepared for, glasses clinking and laughter erupting. For a few seconds, I'm not sure where I am – I turn away, towards the dazzling outside, the English summer, the gentle warmth pressing on me like a mother's hand on a child's head, and the smell of freshly applied deodorant mixed with chips frying through the hot vents of the kitchen. Relief comes as I'm able to take in my bearings: I'm where I should be, and everything is going to be all right.

To celebrate Yuki's thirtieth birthday, bees are buzzing around the big terracotta pots in the Five Horseshoes beer garden, a historic, sloping, black-and-white pub nestled within the row of cafés, banks and food chains of St Albans' high street. I'm struck by the memory of the bees' absence, the summer strolls spent looking for them and finding instead clouds of midges and armies of wasps – something, among many other things, I know used to pain me. Now I take in the well-trodden yet gloriously green grass, the picnic tables, an oasis against the backdrop of Saturday-evening traffic, all bathed in the gold that only British summers can give — that rare dazzling warmth that seems to reach deep into your bones and your soul. Those moments remind me how much I love it here — I've been here two years, and things are beginning to fall into place. In a week, I'll be a fully qualified teacher, Yuki has invited me to her birthday party, everything is brimming with possibilities.

I've ensured I arrive early, just after Yuki and her best friend Lucy, because I would rather not have to look for a free chair in a group of well-established friends. I know Yuki, but I don't know her mates that well, and she is fickle, easily dazzled, a fluttering butterfly. It's only the two besties for now, Lucy bending forward conspiratorially, Yuki shaking her head and smirking. I'm a bit nervous. I'm about to move forward when I realise I'm carrying a giant object clumsily wrapped in layer after layer of striped paper. I search my brain for an explanation.

Of course. My birthday present for Yuki, a two-tiered fruit basket. I can't remember when it seemed a good idea, as if I've only just landed in the body of somebody who buys awkward gifts. As Yuki was packing her things ready to move out, I noticed she didn't have one. I cringe as Lucy produces a tiny package, something pink and black with a brand I've never heard of, and Yuki squeals in delight.

Before they spot me, I step aside and drop my present behind one of the terracotta pots. I don't have a plan, except avoiding embarrassment. Perhaps the foxes can have it, to store their dusty chips and burst fast-food paper bags.

'Lou, over here!'

'Happy birthday!' I try to sound cheery as Yuki hugs me, my words 'Sorry – voucher to follow' drowning against the soft material of her top. She always smells good, like people who have their act together, and her hair is held up with a thousand pins, her special-occasion do. One of the pins nearly stabs me in the eye. Behind Yuki's shoulder, Lucy looks a little smug, but that's just her face.

'Don't worry at all, matey,' Yuki says. 'So nice you could make it. We really don't meet up often enough now ...'

Her unfinished sentence hangs in the summer air, and we all chat over its trail, pretending there isn't even a twinge of awkwardness that Yuki left me as soon as Lucy found herself in need of a housemate. We laugh that it has been a bit like a break-up, but in truth, we know she really *has* dumped me for Lucy's Victorian two-bed, her cool travelling ways, their nights spent drinking Savignon Blank on the sofa. *I'm so sorry, Lou, there's only one spare bedroom, and Lucy and I have been best friends since uni. I'll help you find a flat, I'll help you move, I'll do anything.* Although it hurt, and it was inconvenient, I did understand. Yuki and I only lived together for a year. She had her whole life here, already established. But I'm pleased she invited me tonight – perhaps we can stay in touch, find a way to continue watching the Food Network together and laughing at American salads made mainly of mayonnaise. I would like to make that happen somehow.

Other guests start arriving shortly afterwards. 'The referendum was a year ago,' somebody says, and I startle for a second, because it feels like we've been living with the build-up to Brexit for years. Their outrage seems too fresh, too energetic, almost. 'Can you believe it?' People nod gravely.

21

In such circumstances, if I don't say too much, and don't say nothing, I can ride the tiny train of the inconspicuous.

'Will you be going back to Sweden, Louise?' somebody asks.

'Switzerland, actually,' Yuki says, and smiles at me.

They insist on buying me drinks, 'while you're still able to live here'. They're all sad, it seems, a bit bereft. Me too, though I know I'll probably be okay, unlike others. I was sold a map containing only London's buzz and multicultural-ism, cream teas in Cornwall and charming moor-swallowed Yorkshire villages. When I needed a fresh start and had been watching too much *Escape to the Country*, I heard there were bursaries for students willing to become foreign language teachers in the UK, and my own mother tongue was at least something I felt I couldn't mess up. This was the one risk I took in my life, because staying put, not with Romain, was way worse. I thought I could start over in one of those novels where the heroine meets a man who repairs boats, or perhaps works with horses, but I'm now finding myself in a very dif-ferent place, and not only because St Albans is nowhere near the sea. It's a little bit like the end of a honeymoon, for me and for England – a form of mourning, when you wonder why it all started in the first place, if it's still love or if it's habit. If your partner still wants you. However, on evenings like tonight, when there's beer and warmth and hope, I want to make it work.

Yuki's getting up to go to the loo, and I find myself having to engage in small talk with the guy sitting on the other side of her, a lawyer called Ben. I don't know why he decided to speak to me, because everyone else around the table is listening to another bloke at the opposite end with a short, messy ponytail and an armband tattoo. Ponytail guy must have joined the table when I'd gone to the bar, after begging Yuki way too earnestly to save my seat. His story is obviously entertaining but I'm too far away to catch it.

'Hiya,' lawyer guy says, bending over Yuki's empty seat. 'I'm Ben.'

'Louise,' I say, wondering whether to shake hands and going instead for hugging my sides firmly. He's quite handsome, with his blue eyes, sharp haircut and loosened tie.

'Hi, Louisa,' he says.

I've met him before, I'm sure of it.

'How do you know good ol' Yuki?' he asks.

I explain the whole housemate thing, then he says he went to uni with her and Lucy in Bristol.

'Where are you from in Switzerland?' he continues. 'And don't you speak a million languages there?' I can tell he's already feeling a bit strained. I always sound so French when addressing someone new, or on the rare occasions I speak out in public. My accent, acceptable when mild, can become strong enough to make myself cringe, like an over-ripe cheese. I give Ben my slick geography lesson, my hand tracing the banana-shaped Lac Léman in the air.

'Here, I'm from here,' pointing my finger at the imaginary vineyards, the castle on the water, and further along the shore, sleepy Vevey mottled with red roofs and white boats. 'So if you imagine that Switzerland is the shape of a pig, I'm under its tail.'

He startles at the analogy, but recovers. Of course, he goes skiing yearly with his mates, and wants me to join him in shared appreciation of Zermatt – I don't tell him it's nowhere near my town and I've never been there. At least he isn't talking about Stockholm. As I listen to him, I think he's exactly the kind of man all my colleagues are engaged to or want to date, someone I'm convinced would not be interested in me. He's confident, in a suit, and smells of cologne. He seems to know what he wants and where he is headed, as if he were on skis, rushing down the slope in a straight line.

Laughter erupts around the table. The guy with the ponytail is talking about his pupils (Ellies and Millies) but, it seems, in such an endearing way that he has everybody enraptured. He looks like a PE teacher – of course things are easy for him, wandering around high-fiving kids all day and occasionally blowing a whistle. I think of my own battle to defend the learning of something out of the kids' immediate experience, and find nothing funny in it. I envy all those people who seem to have a genuinely good time teaching. This year has been tough, but the tantalising proximity of the long summer holiday erases some of the hardship. Surely next year will be better, now I know the ropes.

'How do you know Yuki, then, Nick?' someone asks, words catching the edges of my hearing while I wonder what I should say to Ben to appear interesting.

'I don't,' PE teacher Nick replies. 'I was meeting my sister for a drink, and I bumped into Max here, who's an old school buddy of mine.'

'Where's your sister?' someone else asks. 'Can't she join us?'

My pocket buzzes and I jump, snapping out of the conversation. Time spikes, two seconds of excitement and possibilities, although the text is most probably from Pizza Hut, or my doctor's surgery telling me they're closing for training. But somehow – somehow – I know this is going to mean something. There's a quality to the silence, the stillness following its reception. Like the sounds around me have been turned down as I'm diving inwards. I wriggle on my seat to extract my phone, and it almost shoots out of my hand.

'All right there?' Ben asks half-heartedly, but I ignore him. Romain's name has appeared on my screen.

The powerful whoosh of longing takes me back to the seagulls and the sweet and cool algae-rich smell of lake water, the mountains powdered in snow, the first time Romain kissed me – in the backdrop, the museum's giant fork sculpture piercing the water in its heart. 'Like Cupid's fork,' I think he said, and I laughed, because he was always clumsy when he tried one of my metaphors. Somehow, though, he was right: the kiss, and the fork, did pin me in that specific place and time. The essence of the moment, so close to the surface, has always been waiting to be revived.

I open the message. Every time I hear from Romain, an old-fashioned letter, or a text, his distinctive writer's voice embraces me like a lover.

We had a fling, I guess you could call it that, at Easter. I went back to see my family and met him for a drink, and things just happened. We didn't talk about what it was, what it meant, and I just hopped on the plane again, made a deal with myself that I wasn't going to be the one reaching out first. This text is the first rush of something I have craved for months. Time stretches and closes on itself like a circle, bringing me back, and here I am again, in love with him.

It's terrifying, having that door open. I could just ignore it; I don't think I'm ready. I could stay here at the party, celebrate with Yuki, talk about otters, and think about it all later. But I know this moment is important. I don't know how

25

I know it, but I do. I know this could change everything, change the course of my life.

I should leave. I have to be on my own to process this, read the message again and marvel at its possibilities – chewing and chewing the dream until it becomes digested reality.

Everyone is engaged in conversation. I grab my bag and nod at nobody and make for the way out, through the pub, hoping that I won't bump into Yuki, who still hasn't come back. *Filer à l'anglaise.* Take English leave. Ha.

'Hey.' I look around, and PE teacher guy is striding alongside me, as if we'd agreed to leave together. 'You going for a smoke?' he asks, nodding towards the sheltered patio at the side of the building. His grin is wide and friendly, and for a second I forget what I stood up to do. Nick, isn't it? Is this really the first time we've met? But my phone is in my hand. Romain, whispering that he misses me. Burning.

'Ah, no, I don't smoke,' I say. 'I'm just going . . . ' I nod to the pub door – it could mean the toilet, or the bar, or that I'm planning a hold-up, anything.

'No worries.' He smiles and we part ways.

The evening is alight on this long July day. My heart races as I walk past the town hall and down the tiny French row lined with stooping buildings marked with history, hosting cocktail bars full of possibilities and missed encounters. I wish I could bottle this feeling and drink it later, at my convenience, sip by sip. I wish I could mark the WhatsApp as unread, so it would pop up on my lock screen again and I could relive the first rush. It's already faded a bit, the burst of being reminded that I'm alive, that Romain is thinking of me, so I'm not opening the message again for fear of blunting it too much. I make my way through the darkening evening,

26

through the crowds drinking outside various pubs, holding the elation tight against my heart like a baby bird.

I reach the front of my block of flats. I don't want to go in just yet, into the empty box of my narrow studio. Instead, I sit on the low wall near the front door. It's a new development, all spick and span, and I wonder how long I can sit here before a neighbour reports me to the management. I'm a bit giddy, and I have an urge to ruffle the lawn like a dog's shaggy mane.

My heart beats fast as I open the text again. *Dear Louise.* Romain is the only one of my friends who doesn't call me Lou. I move eagerly to the next line: *I was thinking of you. Will I have the pleasure of seeing you at my book launch?* I translate dutifully as I read, back and forth between the two languages, trying out different outfits to see if the overall effect remains the same. But of course, something is lost in English: Romain's quirky French formality, laughable almost (*aurai-je le plaisir*), which I'm so attached to because of the rare occasions I've experienced its breakdown.

And how to translate his sign off, *Je t'embrasse?* Something a great-aunt would write, but coming from somebody who – what is it? – *French-kissed* me, it's definitely loaded with, as Yuki would say, double entendre. I'm determined to reply to him. No more waiting; something is telling me I ought to take this chance. I press reply.

Out of the blue, my phone starts ringing, bursting to life in my hand with Yuki's name.

'It's your birthday,' I say dumbly.

'Mate, I know it's my birthday! Where are you? We're thinking of moving on to—'

'I'm back home, sorry.'

27

'Can't hear you?'

There's noise around and inside Yuki, a happy slurring of drunkenness.

'Sorry, Yuki, I didn't feel . . . I came home.'

'You're kidding? Come back!'

'No, really, I—'

'Only a few of us left here. The others went home to their babies, but you don't have a babyyy or a familyyy . . . ' Is she singing? I'm losing her. I try something else.

'I got a text from Romain.'

'Ah, what? What's he saying?'

She's listening now. No more giggles. This makes me reluctant to tell her.

'He . . . he's saying he misses me, and wants to see me, I think.'

She mutters something that is drowned by the sound of people calling out to her, then: 'Just a minute!'

'Sorry, what did you say?' I ask.

'That's good, mate,' she says cautiously. 'Go home, dazzle him with your exotic Britishness, bring him back shortbread and . . . what did you say that guy Jason got again?'

'A golden fleece.' I smile.

'Yes, that. Maybe it'll all work out this time.' A pause. 'Just be careful, okay?'

'Thanks, Yuki.' I don't tell her that Jason and Medea's story was less than perfect. I don't think Yuki really listens when I go on about my beloved mythological tales. 'Have fun on your big night out,' I say, as she calls out to someone in the background. We hang up.

I should be happy, but as I go back to the text once more, the elation is weakened, lake ice under my ski boots.

28

Something in Yuki's tone – *this time*. Doubt creeps in, as it always does when I have time to think. Romain wrote, *I miss you. 22 July at La Fontaine*, our favourite bookshop. Is the text really about missing me, or about his launch? Have I misread the signals? My heart has caught a chill, a whiff of familiar worry.

'Don't get messed up by a boy.' Two blokes, clearly drunk and full of 'Wheeey', are walking past me on the pavement, their gigantic, non-apologetic laughter booming when they see they have startled me. The air has cooled a little now, and the street lights have come on. I'm sitting right under one, a lonely actor who has forgotten her monologue in the spotlight.

I stand up quickly and brush the back of my thighs. The lads are walking away, swaying like ships in a storm. *Maybe it'll all work out this time*, an unfamiliar voice in my head chimes. But I've messed up the chance of Romain and me so many times before, why would it be different now? I feel the familiar worry tap out those last beats of hope that for some reason bloomed today. I'm not ready. I need more time here to prove myself, I need something to change so I become worthy, or history will keep repeating itself. I'll get in touch with him next time I'm home. By then, I'm sure things will be better. I'll feel more equipped for whatever might happen next. Just a little time to breathe first, to get my act together.

'Oi, miss, don't get fucked up.' The lads push each other onto the road, laughing big and hard with their throats open to the sky, and carry on to the traffic lights.

Friday 18 August 2017

'Shame you only come back for funerals,' Marion says.

We buried Grandma today. In the Jardin du Souvenir, a neat little square of roses drying in the August sun, the lake and the green vineyards peeking through ancestral spruces. All the priest had to do was pull a trigger at the top of the urn, and she was gone. The whole ceremony was sober and swift, as if people had merely made the trip to admire the manicured flower beds, the marble pyramids at the corners of the square. Like an awkward family outing to a museum.

I cried behind my sunglasses as everybody was acting like it would be indecent to be upset: Auntie Sylvie turning up in bright yellow and exclaiming cheerfully that it was so lovely to see us all together for once; Marion's sad but composed face, the emptiness on Mum's, her only permitted emotions as thin as a paper mask; Fabio, Marion's boyfriend of two years, in his dark linen suit, silently handing over packets of tissues, condolence cards, bottle of water (refillable, of course), phone, as though Marion were a grief surgeon and he her nurse. My jaw still aches from clenching. A ladybird landed on my finger just where a ring would be, and I left it there, glad for the spark of life it brought to the occasion. Grandma would have liked it.

'That's a slight exaggeration, don't you think?' I say to Marion. We only met up three hours ago, and we're already at each other's throats. It wasn't always the case. When Dad left, we had to stick together. She was the wild child, four years younger than me, hitting adolescence too early, hiding her sensitivity behind broken curfews and dancing until her feet bled. I was the sensible one, shy and unsure and sticking close to the familiar, therefore deemed reliable. We bickered, but always reconciled; we were two sides of the same coin. Now we're both adults, and since I've left home, I don't know how to be around her. I don't know how to deal with her prickliness.

It's a typical Swiss August, the air about to burst with heat and water, the electricity of an approaching thunderstorm tickling the back of our ears. Grandma was made for spring: flurries of primroses and daffodils, budding apple trees, blue skies whose chilly crispness you could taste on your tongue. I think she would have rather died in March or April.

I didn't want to come back. I didn't want to go through today.

Recently I've been watching scenes of my life as if I've seen them before. In a film, a while ago, as if their characters, their development and moods, already existed on the edges of my brain. This scene I was dreading, yet I still boarded the plane. It had to be lived, even though I knew it was going to be tough. Without Grandma, the family appears depleted,

31

and I don't like being reminded that I've abandoned it too. I don't like feeling the gap between us increase with every visit, but it's so uncomfortable, I've been allowing the distance between my trips to lengthen as well.

As the plane started its descent yesterday, and the tourists pressed their faces against the windows and squealed with excitement, I watched the bottle-green lake, the marinas, the tiled roofs, the furrows of motorboats mirroring the planes in the sky, a hard knot in my stomach. I tried to spot Vevey as we turned above the water to go back on ourselves, and it was only when I remembered that Romain was there that my heart did a little loop.

'Careful, Mum.' Marion has leapt into action upon spotting that Mum's plate was drooping, threatening to drop its contents of cold meats and cheeses. She takes the plate and sets it safely on the table.

Mum is enduring yet another elderly lady babbling about her being the perfect daughter for caring for Grandma at the end of her life. 'Klara was so lucky to have you,' she says. Mum's face is closed off, her mouth a small line of a polite smile. Grandma was as lucky to have Mum as Mum was to have her. I know she got her through all the tough times. I wonder how Mum feels now the phone doesn't ring with her number any more.

Marion goes off to work the room with ease, gracefully offering her cheeks for everybody to kiss three times. She's our family's best PA, a hippy with a clipboard. Efficient, with a distinct 'don't mess with me' aura. Meanwhile, I have become a concept, 'the one who lives in England'. 'How long are you staying?' is the only thing I've been asked today, by every single person who spoke to me. They all looked pained when I said only for a few days, as if it were a betrayal of the Motherland.

'Mum,' I say. She's still standing with me by the cake buffet, overflowing with Linzer *torten* and eggy apple tarts. I have to give it to those Swiss old ladies: they can certainly bake. Mum looks up at me. 'Shall we get something to eat?' I ask, surprised by how tentative my voice sounds.

'Not hungry.'

'Okay, never mind.'

I understand that she is grieving, but there's a hollowness to her demeanour I wasn't expecting, although it feels frighteningly familiar. I find it hard that she doesn't listen to me any more; I think she would eat something if Marion asked her. Marion is the one Mum reaches out to now when she needs advice about her finances, when she needs to be driven somewhere. It used to be me, I used to be the one coming back for lunch every Sunday, but then I left, didn't I.

'Are you going to see Romain while you're here?' she asks, out of the blue.

'I . . . I don't know.'

'I always thought it was such a shame that you . . . It was good for you, having someone.'

I'm not sure what to say. Romain is wonderful, Mum is right; being with him gave me purpose. Every time I'm back, his presence imbues everything. I expect to bump into him at every corner, in every train carriage gliding along the shore, even kilometres away from where he lives. I know I was wrong to ignore his text, and I've been thinking about contacting him since I landed. There's only a little time left to give it a go – before it's too late.

I adjust my blouse on my shoulders, black with small

flowers and a cute collar. I was wearing it the first time Romain and I spoke, and I have been thinking of it as my lucky outfit since, the armour I can wear to prevent further disasters. I had noticed him many times at the university library, the young, handsome man behind the reception desk. As a newly appointed archivist, he stood out among the rest of the older librarians, his dark, intelligent eyes, his efficiency, his vast knowledge. I took to choosing a table from where I could watch him work rather than tackle the PhD in Classics I was struggling to write. I grew fascinated by the way he squinted at the computer screen, the way he stapled paper together or raked his fingers through the slight quiff of his hair whilst waiting by the printer. I never asked him for help.

One day, he came into the bookshop I worked in in Vevey. It seemed a massive sign of fate, then I remembered that he didn't know me. Except he did. As he bought *The Truth About the Harry Quebert Affair*, and I scanned it for him, worried I would do something wrong and make a fool of myself, he said, 'I know you. You're the girl who works in the Tacitus corner. How's your research going?' And because it was going so badly and he saw that I was upset, he suggested we have coffee at uni the following day, to talk some more and give me a break.

The library coffees turned into proper dates, obscure films d'auteur at the Zinéma, walks by the lake in Vevey, where he kissed me for the first time. He eventually got me through the failure of my academic prospects, morning after morning of tearful coffee when I felt I could not, would not leave the hard plastic of the café chair for the closed scowls of books that refused to cooperate with me. I used to want to show other people the relevance of those stories, share my interest for them, to eventually become an academic, a historian of some sort, but I simply couldn't make it work. I dropped out, and Romain stuck by my side during the following months of nothing but my part-time bookshop job, as I drifted aimlessly; none of this felt that bad, though, because Romain was the only future plan I needed.

I get my phone out. Stop watching life passing you by like a missed train, Lou. You don't have all the time in the world.

> Hey, sorry for the late reply. I'm
> actually around. Would be great
> to meet up. I miss you too.

I hesitate, my thumb hovering over the delete tab, but the wake and Romain's geographical proximity give me some of the courage I lacked earlier in England. I wonder why I need death to spur me on, why I can't just act every day as if it were the last one, without painful reminders. I press send.

Marion and Fabio have finished their social rounds. I don't think I've heard Fabio's voice today except to reassure Marion that yes, he remembers how to drive a car. I still don't understand how they're together – to be honest, why she is with him. Marion used to date tough men with spikes and motorbikes and break their hearts, and then she met Fabio. I can see he needs to be bossed around, which Marion has a gift for, but what does she get from his meek silence? I don't even know who my sister is any more, this hyper-efficient adult who today has almost managed to look like she doesn't want to punch Auntie Sylvie.

'Is there something wrong with Mum?' I ask, not knowing how to phrase it.

Marion scoffs. 'No shit, Sherlock.'

We both look at Mum, who is standing at the other end of the room, smiling vacantly. That is grief, isn't it?

'What's going on?'

'What, except the fact that she just buried her mother?'

'I know, I only mean ...'

Marion pinches a slice of cheese, breaks it, gives half to Fabio as though he were a lapdog, then eats the rest. 'Dammit,' she says.

'What?'

'It's mild Gruyère, not mature.'

'So what?'

She sighs. 'Mature was Grandma's favourite, Louise.'

'I know,' I say, wishing it didn't come out so defensive. There would always be strong Gruyère on Grandma's break-fast table, crunchy with flecks of salt; but after two years of English supermarket cheese, the standards of my palate have lowered.

'And you said the florist's mistake didn't matter earlier, but she hated lilies.'

'Yes,' I say, 'it's a shame we couldn't get daffodils or prim-roses. They always make me think of her.'

'*We?* Remind me, did you help organise any of this at any point?'

I understand things can't have been easy for Marion, but her abrasiveness hurts. Our relationship has been collateral damage of my escaping to England, something I hadn't anticipated. And now I don't know how to fix it. The room grows hotter, like a hammam. The thunderstorm has been building, and I wish it would get on with it and rip through the sky, relieving the pressure, which has been giving me

36

a headache. Marion takes a slice of *tresse* and stares at it. Would she understand if I explained that visiting people you miss, people you live far from, and the shock of seeing how much they've changed every time, makes living abroad much harder? Sounds like a rubbish excuse even to me, but it's real.

She starts picking at the bread, the fluffy white crumb tearing in her hands like candyfloss. 'So?'

'So what?'

'How long are you staying, now you're here?' This question again. So loaded, coming from her.

'My flight back is on Monday.'

'What have you planned for the weekend?'

I want to try to take care of Mum, but I know that as I don't live here, it'll always be not enough, too late. I can make her bircher and herbal tea, but I'm always still going to be hopping on a plane. I'm suddenly overwhelmed with worry about her fate, the shaking hands she's trying to hide. I wonder what I have missed by being away, what Marion hasn't been telling me, what exactly is at stake here.

'Well, apart from making sure Mum's okay, I might also get in touch with Romain, see if he's around. Given that I missed his book launch.' I'm tentative. Marion liked Romain, I think, when we were together. They always slid into witty back-and-forth that most of the time I felt excluded from.

Marion turns and mutters something to Fabio, who pretends for my benefit that he hasn't heard, which makes it even worse.

'What was that?' I ask.

'Nothing,' she says. 'It's been a lot, here, these past few

weeks. Grandma dying. Organising the funeral. Looking after Mum. That's all.' Her voice is clipped.

'Not now, please,' I say. 'Can't we talk about this later? Out of Auntie Sylvie's earshot?'

Plus *you* encouraged me to move away, I think. You had your life together, your job, your friends and the wild men you tamed – I cramped your style. You didn't want to have to worry about me and the state I was in after the break-up, when it was clear my life was going nowhere. When I asked you if you thought it was a good idea, you said it would be a fresh start. You can't take it back now.

'Whatever,' Marion says.

I look at the buffet, which has been both provided and depleted by the old ladies from Grandma's village, a proper swarm of white-haired locusts. I don't know what I'm feeling – dread for something that's already happened, perhaps. Is this grief too? Mum is so still she might as well be one of those living statues. I always thought Marion and Mum were made of sturdier stuff than me, an ability I didn't possess to get on with things. I didn't think they would ever struggle with anything.

A text comes in.

> Dear Louise, that's a lovely offer. I'm
> sorry, but I actually met someone
> (at my book launch) and it's all quite
> new, so I don't think the timing is
> right. Perhaps a bit more time until
> you and I can be friends. I would have
> loved to see you, though. I hope you
> have a good time back home. R

I stare at the text, feeling like an utter fool.

We watch our motherless mother shake more hands, and Marion leaves me to go and rescue her. I think about Romain's text, and about death, petrified and mute like the most rubbish Cassandra, predicting a lonely future that everybody has seen coming except me, replaying old conversations whose meaning I clearly missed at the time. I watch it all unfold before me until finally thunder and lightning burst the heavy sky open, and torrential rain starts to fall.

Sunday 18 March 2018

This morning, the potential first day of the rest of my life, I lie in bed staring at the ceiling, my eyes running along new cracks in the plaster. Everything in my tiny studio is white; I could be anywhere, even in hell, except for a packet of Yorkshire Tea and an empty bottle of milk (blue top, always) on the kitchen counter, and the deadly March draught reaching me through the closed window, a phenomenon I didn't know was possible before I moved to England. I have a feeling in the pit of my stomach telling me today is important. That I'm standing at the edge of something, unable to see what my next step will be, and I'm restless.

Through squinted eyes, I text Yuki.

> I have that date today, and he says I
> should decide where we go. HELP.

Yuki's always awake at six a.m. like me. One of the reasons we got on well as housemates was our pre-dawn weekend mornings in our pyjamas, watching the Food Network, cooking a full English when most people were still drunk. It has taken me a while to suspect that her friends don't see *this* Yuki, salivating at the sight of the biggest burger in the world, obsessed with dipping things in chocolate and cheese. Resolutely uncool. I can't imagine Lucy getting up before noon at the weekend.

Her response pings through immediately.

Ah, come on, you can do it. Cinema?

Since the bombshell of Romain's girlfriend, last August, I have found life generally hard. School did not get better. The autumn term hit me like the shock of freezing water: teaching a full timetable for the first time, the new classes with colour-coded seating plans, whole fresh cohorts of students mistrusting me and my teaching – it took two, three, five years, my experienced colleagues reassured me, an ever-moving goalpost. The slow, ineluctable shut-down of nature, the darkening of days, always more dramatic this side of the Channel, followed by a sad first Christmas without Grandma all matched the drowsiness of my mood. I retired deep into myself, surviving on buttered crumpets, struggling to get to sleep, then to stay awake in class, despite the rising chaos.

I've made some effort to stay in touch with Yuki, spurred by a feeling that I ought to hang on to her; an image of her flashing in my mind every so often, a different her, broken, sad, her nails flaky as she rolls the corner of . . . is it an order of service? It's never clear, and very un-Yuki, but enough to

41

make me pick up our lapsing conversations. She called me after I left her birthday after all, so she must care.

I told her about the Romain disaster, and she attempted to cheer me up by sending a few memes and inviting me out for breakfast a couple of times. For her, I tried a little harder not to let myself go completely.

Then one day, after Christmas, she insisted on coming to my flat. I think it was intended as an inspection visit, to check the state of my kitchen surfaces. She dunked stale digestives in her cup of tea before glancing at the pile of dirty dishes and the old jumper of Romain's I'd stolen at Easter and announcing she was going to set me up with her friend Ben. 'All it takes is one date,' she said. 'The right one. It's about time you tried to meet someone here. Gave us Brits an actual chance.'

I was terrified; I had to fight every instinct I had to agree – it would have been much easier to stay under the duvet. But I thought of funerals, of yearning for love alone; if it could work out just this once, if it could open the door to something – I silently plead with the cracks on the ceiling – if it could finally show me I'm worthy . . .

I text back.

> Not sure. I find cinema dates a bit
> suspicious because you can't really
> talk there. Also I always eat all the
> snacks and my greediness isn't
> conducive to a good first impression.

> Ah mate, you crack me up.

42

It was followed by three crying-with-laughter emojis.

A thought pops into my head. Otters – greedy otters, cracking open clams of some sort.

> Btw, did you know baby elephants
> can die of loneliness?

> Wait, what?? That's too sad
> for today – shush.

A brief pause, and she sends another message.

> I know re date location –
> what about le zoo?

> ???

> No need for conversation, just
> describe to each other what you see,
> oh there's a nice bear, and if you need
> to cut it short, say you're too cold,
> whatever. Plus you love animals so
> at least you will have a great time.

I drop the phone on the duvet, lean back on the bed with my elbows to the sky like the heroes of romantic comedies when their life is about to change. Romain and his girlfriend walking by the lake. No, no. A handsome, smiling lawyer buying me hot chocolate. What every girl wants. Ben rescuing baby capybaras from drowning, in his suit. What if Yuki is right, and there is something for me to find here?

> Won't the zoo be a bit too ... quirky?

But I'm smiling already. I'm pretty sure I've heard good things about that zoo.

> Nah, it's perfect. Quirky is cute.
> I'm sure Ben will be game. But pls
> don't wear that horrible jumper.

The zoo is bursting with noise against the vast sky. There were snow flurries yesterday – the frozen ground cracks under my boots, the nerves of my teeth hurt when I breathe in. Grey on grey, vast aviaries erected like tombstones, and sometimes, the surprise of a tiger's tail, or a yellow monkey dashing about like a will-o'-the-wisp.

This was a terrible idea.

'I've seen better lions in South Africa,' Ben says.

In his grey clothes, he blends in perfectly with the day – if we played hide-and-seek, which I daren't suggest (he's clearly *not* game), he could hide in front of a lamp post. Our first interaction was him complaining about the cold and calling this expedition 'a bloody trip to the North Pole', but he paid for our tickets online to get the 5 per cent discount, so I guess he was committed. His attitude made me feel I had messed up before we even started, and I've been scrambling to make it up to him since. We float along the paths, not looking at anything, tragic visitors whose only task is to haunt the place.

'I've never been to South Africa,' I say, because I really want to try. 'What's the best animal you've seen there?'

'What is it you do again?'

'I'm a teacher.'

'Ah.' (What does he mean? Yuki said he wanted to date somebody in a 'caring profession'; isn't that what teaching is?) 'Bad luck for the holidays.'

'The holidays are the best bit, I'm told.' I offer a smile.

'I mean you have to go away during the school holidays.'

'Yeah, that's the p—'

'*So* expensive. And so crowded. Bit of a bummer.'

I don't know how to rescue the conversation without changing my job, which I can't do, though I really wish to, most of the time. As I consider a bird in a cage, very much looking like a normal pigeon, I wish I could be what Ben is looking for, somebody Oxbridge-educated with long hair and a posh accent.

'So you like travelling?' I ask. Yuki said that travelling is always a good topic on a date. But Ben ignores me.

'State or private?' he says.

'What?'

'Your school.'

'Ah, um, mixed comprehensive.' For some reason he doesn't seem to know what to do with this information he's just asked for.

'I went to an all-boys public school,' he says.

'Ah, what was that like?' I'll never get used to single-sex education. It's so alien – sometimes you see them in London, out on a trip, an unkindness of girls all wearing the same dark blue blazer.

'A blast,' he says, looking forlorn.

We're coming up to the central area. Children are running around us, wrapped in so many layers of clothing they look like puffed-up marshmallows, prepped to bump into things

45

repeatedly. A family catches my eye: two tired but happy parents, the dad crouched down to zip up his daughter's green jacket. It's the look on the mother's face that strikes me as she watches him, holding their son's hand – tired contentment. Pride. The little boy's face is a painted tiger, and he's wearing a Superman cape on top of his winter clothes. How do they do it? How is it even possible to achieve this, when every single small decision you make can spoil it all?

My date with Ben is clearly riding on a derailed train carriage, and I feel powerless to change its trajectory. As I mentally review the topics I could bring up, I feel the weight of my responsibility for his silence. What if he is The One and I haven't managed to find our connection?

'I bet you have to do all that health-and-safety, anti-bullying and safeguarding nonsense,' he finally says.

'Not sure I understand.' Since we started our magical zoo tour, he's been keeping his hands deep in his pockets, making sure there's absolutely no ambiguity that he might want to move closer into my space.

He repeats the words, but slowly, detaching every syllable for my foreign benefit. *Safe-guard-inggg.*

'Yes, I'm a teacher, so if I weren't familiar with the concept, we'd be in trouble,' I say.

'My father was in the army. I think we should bring back corporal punishment in schools. Kids are becoming too soft.'

Not too far from us, above the other animal and child noises blending together, a bird gives a long, ominous cackle. Are you mocking me, bird? I did try to get myself out there, for all the good it's doing me. If I had replied to Romain's text last summer and gone to the book launch, I might have been in Switzerland with him, curled up in front of a log fire and reading obscure books with his head on my lap. Nobody I know back home has a log fire, but there would have been time to find one.

'They complain about everything, about online bullying, even exams. They need to get tougher, and teachers aren't helping them if they listen to everything they say.'

Who are 'they', in Ben's world? I think I have some kind of brain-to-mouth malfunction; it escalates quickly. 'Are you going to tell me next that the Nazis had some good ideas?'

Ben's face has gone red, his lips a tense line. Is he going to slap me with his thin, cold hand? Getting a reaction out of him feels good, but perhaps I misunderstood what he said. My phone buzzes loudly and, relieved, I faff about to locate it in my satchel.

'Sorry, it's my sister. I need to check . . .'

I focus hard on the screen, walking away from Ben a bit.

> Mum doesn't want to use her phone any more. She's talking about getting rid of it. Just wondering whether you'd noticed she hadn't called you in a while.

It's the first time I've heard from Marion since the Christmas I spent at home, when I started spotting things, new mannerisms of Mum's, the way she responded to us, or didn't, a certain slipping in her energy, her attention. I didn't know how to talk to my sister about it without her biting my head off, so I kept the worry to myself.

Normally I'd sit and think about what to send back, but I rattle off a response.

47

What's wrong with her phone?

She says nobody ever calls her anyway.

Ben will have to wait. Then I'll have to go back, and perhaps apologise. There must be another topic of conversation we could safely land on; there might be a way to rescue this. I should stop being so bloody awkward all the time.

Well maybe we should try
to call more often.

Genius idea.

I flinch at Marion's signature passive-aggressivity.

The truth is, what can I say to this? I know Mum isn't herself, but I can't help, not from here. Of course I feel guilty for not calling her more often, but I don't want to talk to her about my own disasters; if I said this to my sister, it would hardly go down well. Marion goes offline for a couple of seconds, but reappears as I'm about to close the tab and go back to Ben.

I bumped into Romain and
Aurélie the other day.

They're still together?

Apparently so. They looked disgustingly
happy. You told me to update you, so . . .

48

If I focus my vision, I can see some of my falling face, against a portion of sky, reflected on my screen. After Grandma's funeral, I interrogated Marion; the new girlfriend was a former schoolmate of hers. She dismissed the relationship entirely – *Aurélie is too wholesome for Romain. She'll want babies straight away, she'll cook him ragout, he'll get bored* – but she got it wrong. She was supposed to be my spy and now, seven months later, it sounds serious. My instinct tells me it's going somewhere there can be no return from. Meanwhile, I'm on the worst date of the century. Something that will be used as a cautionary tale to warn innocent Swiss girls against men with nice scarves.

Something washes over me – a kind of waxy tiredness filling all the cavities where my normal feelings would be. I yearn for something familiar, something reassuring. The capybaras. My teeth are clattering, the day freezing deep.

Grandma used to take us, Marion and me, to see the capybaras in the zoo in Bern. It was more of a farm, paddocks nestled in the loops of the deep, fast-flowing river, with wild felines looking exactly like domestic cats, and rabbits that children were allowed to pet. I long to be there again, holding Grandma's hand – Marion running ahead on her little legs, me solemn and serious, worrying about what ice lolly I was going to choose. I feel a deep sense of loss, bigger than any grief I've ever felt before: I wasted my precious childhood not realising I was happy and safe, when everything was still to play for. Not any more.

The capybaras were always my favourites. *How about we go and check out some giant guinea pigs?* I ready the words, with effort, as I turn back to Ben, but he is gone. All I am left with, once again, is the feeling of being left.

*

49

'I just feel . . . ' Romain said.

His voice was so unsure, I felt the urge to say something silly to comfort him. But my heart was already in my throat.

'I feel that you're relying on me too much. It's not healthy.'

Seagulls were positively screeching, hurting my ears. He had taken off his glasses and started cleaning them, his signature gesture, but his fingers were unusually clumsy, and he had to keep wiping the lenses. We sat on a bench along the promenade in Vevey, where we'd kissed for the first time. The lake was misty and stretched to infinity ahead of us, giving us the illusion of the absence of mountains, of the absence of other worlds to hang on to. Was Lac Léman always the same water? Did anything ever change, or move, in Switzerland? A wide, low wall ran between the quay and the big black boulders where rats plotted mischief and the water smelled like algae. That smell I usually loved was suddenly cloying, steeped with decay.

'I'm sorry, Romain, I'm . . . ' I knew what he meant, but I wasn't sure how to change. If he had told me how, I would have done anything.

'Since you quit your PhD,' he said, 'since we met, I know things have been hard for you, but I can't . . . I feel like I'm the only thing you like about your life.'

His writer's words, so carefully picked, pierced through my winter coat like knives.

'Sometimes I'm like a reverse King Midas . . . ' This was the best explanation I could come up with.

'You mean, what, turning everything into mud?' He smiled. He was so attractive when he smiled. All I wanted was to snuggle up against his dark blue coat, feel the slight coarseness of the wool under my cheek and the warmth of him seep through. But I couldn't deny it. For months, Romain had been my anchor. My reason to be here, not to want to run away, or worse. With him, it was okay if my life wasn't going anywhere – I wasn't wasting it with my part-time job and my low mood as long as he was with me.

'Yes.' My voice was so small, I wondered at him hearing it. 'I'm sorry.'

'I don't want to be turned into mud, Louise. You shouldn't be okay with it either.'

He always wanted the best for me, for us. But I was stuck in a rut, and I didn't know what to do. I knew I couldn't give him the relationship he deserved. I think that was when I started crying.

'Please don't cry,' he said, pulling me against him. 'We're going to be fine. I'll focus on my novel. And you . . .'

We stayed like that for a while, my tears wetting his coat, then he stirred gently, as if he were about to stand up, and my heart sank. I could only be balanced when we were operating at the same level. I pulled away and looked at him. He'd had a haircut. His hair was neat but still curling on top of his ears and with a slight quiff at the front. A young Colin Firth, a couple of years before *Pride and Prejudice*, with glasses. Except Romain hadn't emerged from the lake and sought me out in the pristine gardens of my sweet, sweet embarrassment. He was very much dry and about to walk away. All the boulders started tumbling on top of me.

'What about me?' I asked.

'Perhaps you should get out of your comfort zone. Explore something new. Go and travel the world. You've always played it so safe, Louise, it's like . . .'

'What?'

'It's like you're sticking to a child's sandpit when there's a whole beach out there. Look.' He pressed my hand, with the other pointing at the lake, the outline of mountains slowly emerging from the mist, the tangible limits of my universe.

'If . . . if I did, if I became more interesting . . .'

'Don't,' he said. 'Interesting is not the word. Of course you're interesting.'

This cheered me up a bit.

'Well, if I widened my horizons, would we then . . . have another chance?'

'I don't know,' he said. 'We might. Who knows what life has in store for us?'

As he stood, smoothing back his hair and giving me a small, tender smile, I felt the panic rise in me again, black and white flecks catching in my eyelashes like polluted snow. It was really happening. Romain was leaving me. The thought came to me, not of Midas, but of the Moirai, spinning the thread of my most longed-for relationship and snipping it with a swift flick of scissors.

I stand in the zoo, pinned into place by the memory of our break-up, and as I did when Romain severed himself from me, I feel precisely where my skin is exposed to the bite of the cold: my wrists, the tip of my nose, all places of absence. I was twenty-nine then by the lake, I'm nearly thirty-two now, and I have nothing to show for it. Time shrugged and carried on while I struggled between the bottom and the surface.

I stumble to the zoo map of cartoon animals and grab on

to the barrier nearby to steady myself, leaning my forehead against the wet sign, my right hand still clutching my phone, closing my eyes so that the meerkat, on whose face somebody has drawn two giant goggly eyes, will stop staring at me; I feel dizzy, as if time were both accelerating and slowing down, and—

'Hello?'

A male voice startles me, and whatever door nearly opened shimmers a little longer before vanishing. I open my eyes.

It's not Ben. I know that I know this guy, but I can't remember where from, or what his name is. I hope he's not one of those many PE teachers at school, because it would be embarrassing for me not to be able to tell them apart. They always appear so interchangeable, in their grey track-suits, with their bunches of keys, and sure enough this guy is playing with his, making them jangle between his fingers as if he's late and needs to drive off imminently.

I stare at him for a bit, then look around, blinking. We're near the penguin island. Feeding time is over, the families nearly all gone. In the calm after the storm, only a few penguins are still swimming around manically.

'Those birds are hilarious. I think they're sassing us,' the man says.

It's the grin that does it. 'You're that funny guy from Yuki's birthday,' I say.

He grins some more. 'Ah, I guess. You're Yuki's old housemate, aren't you? She told me about you.' He pauses, and adds, 'All good things, I mean.'

'I'm Louise.' I might be able to remember his name if every breath I took wasn't scooping away the inside of my head.

'Nick,' he replies, and holds out his hand. I shake it. It's dry and warm and real. 'So what are you looking for?' He nods to the map.

Am I going to have to make small talk with him? I glance around for a girlfriend or a nephew, but he appears to be alone.

'Capybaras.'

'Don't think there are any here, I'm sorry,' he says, as if he were personally responsible for the zoo's poor animal line-up.

This groan hasn't come from a cage. It came from me. I bump my forehead against the map again.

'Why capybaras?' He seems so nice, but I want to be left alone.

'Giant guinea pigs who don't give a crap.'

He laughs, bends forward to study the map. He's right in my space.

'Would red pandas be okay instead? Or perhaps otters? Otters don't give a crap either. They're evil bastards.'

Near us, the family I spotted earlier, with the tiger-faced son and the daughter in the green jacket, are the last ones hanging around the penguin pool. The daughter is having a tantrum; clearly the day hasn't met her expectations either. She heaves, puffing out to the point of imminent explosion.

Nick follows my gaze. 'Like being at work,' he says.

'You're a teacher too, right?'

'Yeah. Primary school.'

You always have to smile when you meet a fellow teacher, and do a 'hey there, you too, isn't it the worst?' little dance. I don't get to the dance, as I'm shivering, but I manage a smile.

'You sure you're all right? No offence, Louise, but you don't look it.'

Perhaps it's hearing my name in somebody else's mouth, but my words freeze on my lips, my jaws are screwed together. I shake my head. I feel a bit weird that he's here, as if the day has gone wrong somehow.

'Try me,' he says. 'I'm told I'm decent at giving advice.'

The little girl wails louder, a drill into my brain. Both parents are kneeling by her, trying to calm her down. Her cries might even have put the penguins off, because the pool is now empty. Unattended, the little boy has been pressing his nose and mouth against the glass for a while. Now he ventures further, where the barrier is made of mesh and logs, and starts climbing up.

My stomach tightens. I can't take responsibility for that child right now. I look back to Nick. He's less tanned than I remember, perhaps slightly more yellow in complexion, a bit thinner. He looks hung-over, I decide. The kind of guy who would make the most of his Saturday night, a pint in each hand with mates slapping him on the back. The kind of guy everything comes easy for.

'No,' I say, staring at the boy's booted feet, which have left the ground. 'No, I'm all right, thank you.'

'Perhaps you might consider talking to a counsellor. I know a good one,' Nick says.

I stare at him. 'That's a bit rude, don't you think? You don't know me at all.'

He looks mortified. We stand in silence for a few moments, while I look around for a way to extricate myself from the conversation.

'Louise,' Nick starts, breaking the silence, but I interrupt him.

'Should we . . . ?' I gesture at the boy, who is about to hurl

55

himself on top of the boulders, and in the blink of a frozen eyelid, Nick is off to alert the parents, in a purposeful jog that's too cool to be a run. I stand watching his efficiency, and above all his ease. The father catches the boy, the mother smiles, the little girl quietens as Nick waves at her, and I sneak away. I hate that a stranger who doesn't know me took two minutes to come to the conclusion that I needed psychological help. How bloody dare he, with his grin, his smoothness, his ability to charm parents and children and wild animals.

The zoo's exit is in sight. I stop and look over my shoulder, but Nick is nowhere to be seen. When I turn back, I spot Ben by the exit, regularly glancing up from his furious texting, like a lanky, entitled meerkat keeping watch. As I hold my breath and hope to creep by unnoticed, he spots me, bolts upright and marches towards me.

'I think you owe me money,' he says. He's at it again, clearly prepared to mime *money* if necessary. (I can hear him already, to his mates: '*They*'re invading the country, stealing our zoo fees . . .')

'Sorry?'

'I paid for your ticket. Then you called me a Nazi. Think it's only fair you pay me back.' His tone is so hard, I stumble a bit.

'I . . .'

'Let's not argue about it. You were incredibly rude.'

Something can be rude and accurate at the same time, but I don't say this, because the scene he's causing is attracting attention, and people are looking at me, clearly wondering why I've insulted such a nice lawyer with a scarf.

'Are you really—' I begin.

56

'Come on, chop chop.'

Cheeks burning, I fish my purse out of my bag, count the notes.

'Both my grandfathers fought in the Second World War,' he says, taking the notes as if they were contaminated. 'More than your fucking neutral Swiss grandparents could ever say.'

At that, he walks off. People are still staring at me, and I have to wait there a while in embarrassment, to make sure I won't bump into him at the bus stop.

Saturday 15 December 2018

'So are you doing better now, matey?' Yuki asks me in the kitchen.

'I . . . well, I guess.' I shrug. Have I been doing better? I've been merely existing, as the year crawled slowly forward: the heatwave of summer fading into autumn, the beginning of winter. Since the embarrassing date with Ben, it's all passed me by.

The omnipresence of Wham! and Mariah Carey make all English Christmas celebrations merge into one. It's the first time I've come to one of Yuki and Lucy's house parties. I found it hard to motivate myself to do it; I told Yuki I wouldn't know anybody, but she insisted I knew *her*, and promised me a tame mid-afternoon gathering of people perched on armrests under paper garlands, munching mince pies. *Right up your street, Lou. And Ben won't be here – off skiing. Nothing to fear.*

She was right: I had to try and leave the flat. I was already on my way, mentally reviewing the list of her mates and possible topics of conversation, when the thought struck me that Nick might be there. I knew they'd become good friends after the 'epic night out' I'd missed on her birthday last year.

My head suddenly raced ahead of my feet, describing to me in the most excruciating detail what was about to happen: how I would hover awkwardly in a corner of the room, watching everybody else get on like a Christmas tree on fire, laughing and slapping their thighs at one of Nick's stories; how he would suddenly turn to me and call out, for everyone to hear, 'So, madwoman, have you gone to the shrink like I advised, or have you remained a pathetic lump, someone who gets asked for a refund after a date?' And as everyone loved Nick, they would all laugh with him, at me. I felt so vulnerable at the thought of him being there that I considered turning back, but I didn't want to let Yuki down again. She'd been trying hard to look out for me after the setback with Ben, and I appreciated her efforts.

When I arrived, early as usual, the wooden floors were shining with soapy water and Yuki was sitting at the dining table sampling her own punch, wearing her favourite Christmas pudding shirt with white and red tights. 'Doesn't she look a bit naff?' Lucy asked as she walked through the room. She was wearing a figure-hugging black jumper dress and lots of make-up.

'I think she looks amazing,' I said.

'Only joking, hun,' Lucy said, blowing Yuki a kiss before going to open the front door.

'Are you going back home for Christmas?' Yuki has been looking after me since I arrived, in her own way, sending me on small errands to fetch the bottles cooling outside, refill the crisps, making sure I feel, if not sociable, useful. Why did I not notice her little kindnesses before?

'Yes, briefly. Three days are about as much as I can handle.' I open another packet of mince pies, start arranging them on a golden paper plate, aiming for a festive star shape.

'Ah, mate,' Yuki says. 'Surely Christmas in wondrous Switzerland is magical, no?'

Nothing feels wondrous about Switzerland right now. The more down I feel, the less energy I have to pour into whatever is happening over there. Marion messaged me last week:

> Mum's orchid appears to be dead and
> I don't know what to do about it.

I offered to get a new one delivered, and I haven't heard anything back since, so I guess that was the wrong answer. I don't want to think of another Christmas with Marion snapping at my every move and Mum sitting very still hoping we'll leave if she merges in with the wallpaper. I miss what Christmas at home used to be, in simpler times: making St Nicholas's bread men, scalding my palate with pea soup in the village square, the real candles on the real tree, singing carols while Grandma played the piano, our long walks between the farms sleeping under a deep blanket of snow.

'Back in a sec,' I say, leaving Yuki to stir another weird alcoholic concoction called 'Yuki's eggnog', which she promised me has no egg involved, because she's been scared of salmonella since she ended up in hospital after a trip to Stockholm's bakeries. I know so many little things about her, but I still don't know the story of her name.

As I carry the mince pies into the lounge, I notice that the atmosphere has changed. The laughter rings thicker, more forced. People have moved some of the chairs around, there's an awkwardness in the air, and I hover on the threshold, not wanting to interrupt anything. Mariah Carey is singing at the top of her voice; I can't put my finger on what has changed, or why.

I aim for the coffee table with the mince pies. People barely nod to me as I bend to put the golden plate down.

When I look up, my eyes meet those of a man sitting in the middle of the sofa, a familiar face, and the shock wipes my mind blank. He's surrounded by Yuki's hundred cushions and a circle of guests on hard chairs, or cross-legged on the floor, as though he were about to give out a prophecy.

'Hi, Louise,' he says.

'Hi,' I croak, then, incredibly embarrassed, I run back to the kitchen, where Yuki is pouring drinks.

'All good, matey?' she asks. 'Have some eggnog.' More people are coming in and out, fetching mulled wine, punch, water. Have I landed in a different dimension?

'What's up with Nick?' I ask. I must be mistaken. It couldn't have been him. He looked so . . .

Yuki's eyes widen. 'Shit. I didn't tell you,' she whispers, looking around the kitchen. 'Is he here?'

Quickly she pushes the drink into my hand, gestures for me to follow her outside.

The garden is a sad strip of land, half eaten by mossy wooden decking. It's been a damp, mild run-up to Christmas, water dripping through the absence of real cold. Yuki has hung colourful lanterns on the washing line. I miss living with her.

'Nick's got fucking cancer.'

61

A small robin is hopping around the hedge. If the afternoon weren't so drizzly, the scene could be a Christmas card. Though I've heard somewhere that robins are belligerent birds – evil bastards. Evil bastards? Like otters?

'What?' I say dumbly.

'Yeah.'

I wonder if somebody, somewhere would have anything relevant, anything helpful, to say to this.

'But . . . he's going to be okay?'

There's a silence while Yuki scratches some flaking paint off the wooden railing. Her nails are liquid golden drops today.

'Well, I hope so.'

Everything I toss around in my head feels like a lifeless animal. I know people who have had cancer scares, but luckily that's all it ever turned out to be. Scares. And they were older than Nick. I conjure my faint memories of him, washed over with layers of the preoccupations of my own life, and compare them to the grey man on the red sofa, his cropped hair like bristly feathers on his skull. No match.

'I'm sure he will,' I say. 'I'm sure he can beat this.'

'It's not about how *strong* you are, though.'

'No, of course not, sorry.'

Was Nick ill already when I met him at the zoo in March? Perhaps I should have seen something in him . . . If I look long enough, perhaps I can find an obvious sign I missed. Finding my own fault in this would help – I can't handle the sheer randomness, the unfairness of it.

The door creaks open behind us. Yuki and I both turn around, like teenagers caught smoking behind the school. The eggnog is untouched, warming up in my hand, seeping ice cubes turning the liquid grey. Nick is coming out onto the terrace, rummaging through his pockets. I can hear the jangling of his keys, almost familiar, and I'm awed by his presence, as if Death itself had walked through the door, scythe and all.

'Hiya, mate,' Yuki says perkily.

'Hey.'

He's wearing a sweater with a hood, zipped up close to his chin. Pasty bags line his eyes; his pale lips blend with his skin. I look away as quickly as I can, forcing a smile onto my face.

'Louise,' he says neutrally. 'Long time no see.'

'How are you?' I ask, flustered. 'You shaved off all your hair.'

Yuki looks like she's been stung. I can only stand there, unable to apologise because it would make it sound even worse (is that possible?), wishing the old wooden decking would splinter under my feet right now, which seems the most plausible way to get out of this embarrassment. I was trying too hard to act as if everything was *normal*, to say something somebody *normal* would say to another *normal* person, and now ...

'Lou,' Yuki stumbles, 'the treatment ...'

'I actually shaved it off before I started chemo,' Nick says. 'I kind of felt it would ... No, that's silly.'

'Go on?'

'Show the cancer I was game. I said it was dumb. Don't I look like a winner, though?' He bends forward, running his hand back and forth over his skull as if settling his grip on a rugby ball. To my surprise, he's chuckling.

'It's not funny,' Yuki says.

'No,' Nick replies, 'you're right, Yukes. It's not funny.' But he smiles, and when I catch his eye, my cheeks burning, he winks at me.

As I'm swearing to myself that I will take an eternal vow of silence, Nick opens his packet of tobacco and lights up a cigarette.

'You must be joking,' Yuki groans, clearly prepared to wrestle it off him, but she doesn't. Instead she stands on the wet decking and watches him, folding her arms across her chest. She hasn't bothered putting shoes on, and is comically hopping from one set of stripy toes to the other.

'Come on,' Nick says, 'it's hardly going to—'

'I kinda thought smoking made it worse.'

'Depends what you mean – make *what* worse?'

Defiant, his lit cigarette held in his lips, coughing a little, he leans back against the railing. His external shape is still that of a mountain climber, his bones holding together his outline. I wonder where the cancer is lodged, how it can be so devastating yet we can't see its presence, tearing at things, destroying vitals quietly from the inside while he is talking and joking.

'I'm not drinking, though,' he says, as if offering an olive branch.

Yuki shakes her head. 'Means you're missing out on my famous eggnog.'

He nods to my full glass of the stuff. 'Clearly a huge success.' Yuki goes to shove her elbow in his ribs, and he braces himself for impact, but she stops her movement. Nick sighs. 'And how are you, Louise?'

'I . . .' Nothing about me seems to matter any more. 'I'm fine, thank you.'

'Grand,' he says. 'Glad you're doing better than last time we met.'

Yuki's looking at me now, curious. 'Lou's been through some shit.'

They both stare at me, waiting for me to explain the *shit* in detail.

'My mum's orchid died,' I tell them.

'Fucking hell, Lou, really?' Yuki scoffs. Nick looks confused.

We stand silently for a bit while he finishes his cigarette and presses the butt down into an ashtray. I wonder whether it's smoking that is killing him. Such a waste.

That is making him sick, not killing him, I correct myself quickly.

'Lou hasn't had a boyfriend for ages,' Yuki says to Nick. 'She's so pretty, young, free, has that exotic French accent, and she's wasted all that time.'

'It's not necessarily a bad thing, Yukes, being single.' He turns to me. 'How are you feeling about it?'

I give a mortified shrug.

'Terrible,' Yuki says. 'Tell her, Nick.'

He slides his hands deep into the pockets of his hoodie, clearly amused. 'Tell her what, now?'

'You always give good advice. Tell Lou not to waste her life moping around, keeping herself unhappy.'

Now *I'm* hopping from one foot to the other; it's so uncomfortable having my life scrutinised like this. 'What does *moping around* mean? I don't—'

'It means Yuki's not being very sympathetic,' Nick says. 'Oh, you mean the actual word? It means ... let me think how to explain it ...'

'It means being le depressed,' Yuki says.

'Ah.'

'Don't worry, it's Yuki's tough love.' Nick is watching me

with concern, and the irony isn't lost on me. For the first time, I wonder if we could be friends.

'You should still tell her, Nick,' Yuki insists. 'Lou doesn't listen to me.' I look down at her feet. The pointy ends of her striped tights are soaked. She must be cold. I hope Nick won't mention the counsellor again.

He rolls his eyes, turns to me. 'Life's too short, don't waste it. Chase your dreams.' Then, to Yuki, 'There. Is that okay?' She nods gravely. 'But what about you, my dear?'

'Me?' She shrugs. 'All good.'

He grins. 'You're good, you *are* good. But you know who I think you should get in touch with?'

'Not this again . . .'

'Come on. Give Charlie a call – she could do with a friend. Or more.'

To my surprise, Yuki's cheeks flush, crimson spreading like teacher's ink. 'Stop, Nick.'

'In fact, I'll make it my dying wish.'

At this, we both stare at him in alarm.

'Don't you dare dying-wish me.' Yuki's eyes are wet. 'You won't die any time soon. You'll be fine.'

The glass in my hand is now slippery with condensation, and I worry I'm going to drop it.

'I'm sorry, Yukes, I was joking. Don't want to let you down.'

Nick looks contrite, and tired. He opens his arms to Yuki; she goes to him and he hugs her, and I meet his eyes over her shoulder, his half-apologetic smile for my benefit.

'And Lou . . . I know it's a cliché, and I was joking earlier, except . . . for what it's worth, seize your chances. Don't keep hurting yourself, if that's what you've been doing. You should be proud and confident. I know I for one wouldn't have the guts to start my life over again in a new country.'

I have no clue where the knowledge comes from, but as I look into his grey eyes, suddenly I know. I know he won't be okay, and that nobody around us is aware of it. It's like an intense whack to the back of the head.

Nick is going to die.

'I'll leave you to it,' I mumble, and I hurry back inside.

I stumble through the kitchen, the dining room, the lounge and 'Fairytale of New York' – too many people everywhere – and end up in the small hallway, half in, half out, not knowing what to do as panic grabs me. I take a sip of Yuki's disgusting cocktail, so diluted by now that it's a pale version of what it could have been; it goes down the wrong way, and I splutter. How do I know Nick is going to die? Am I just . . . ruining everything, always anticipating the worst, until all the negativity seeps out and I . . .

The threat of his death, its humbling immediacy, is making me light-headed, his words, and Yuki's, hitting hard. *Stop moping around.* I try to pause, think back to what Nick said, to hold on to his advice like a handrail. How would I start seizing my chances? What would I do differently? I now know there's nothing, nobody for me here. I've tried, and it didn't work out. If only I could go back, reply to Romain's text straight away. I would throw myself head first into that other path now I know the damage that fear, a moment of hesitation, can do. If only I could just . . .

But I can't. I'm stuck, and everything is wrong.

I've triggered something, and my breath accelerates out of control, as if there isn't enough oxygen in the here and now. In the lounge, 'Lonely This Christmas' starts booming out of Yuki's speakers. I steady myself against the door frame, my hands moving through air so thick it sticks my fingers together, wondering why they call this a Christmas song, and from the threshold I see that the whole party has frozen. *Lonely and cold . . . without you to hold . . .*

Mince pies floating in mid-air, hands putting mugs of mulled wine down with the caution of handling an unexploded bomb, uncomfortable glances stuck on the floorboards. All frozen, except Nick, at the edge of his last Christmas, who is standing right across from me on the opposite threshold. Our eyes meet across the space and he sends me a grin, eyebrows raised, before saying something to the room that sounds like it's coming from under water, while Yuki pushes past him in slow motion, fumbling with Spotify on her phone to skip the song.

Nick is going to die. Scenes from another time flash before my eyes, a wake in a pub not far from here: Yuki's sadness, my emptiness, despondency. *Life's too short, don't waste it.* I want Romain so much, so hard, it fills my brain, my ears, my eyes, as eerie, slow bells distort in the air. I can feel the promise of summer and new beginnings and a chance to fix everything waiting for me over the threshold, and I walk through the door . . .

*

We go back.

CHANCE 2

Saturday 15 July 2017

Déjà vu, unlike the nonsensical *double entendre* ('double hear'? Come again?), does exist in French, and means exactly the same. Something you've already seen, already experienced. This British summer, gentle, warm and perfect, seeps into me like a dream. Bees are busying themselves over the big terracotta pots, people are laughing, and my favourite jeans, which I ran home from work to change into, are soft and snug. I can feel the hard square of my phone when I walk, threatening to fall out of my back pocket, but I can't grab it because my hands are full, and I proceed slowly ahead, one foot in front of the other, hoping it will all come back to me soon.

'Lou! Over here!'

Through the smells of frying chips and spilled beer, I aim for Yuki's golden head, a beacon of light in the pub garden as she waves me over. It's her and Lucy. These legs might not be mine, the way my teeth bite into my lower lip, the weight of my tongue. Is this an out-of-body experience?

Yuki looks at me expectantly, and so does Lucy. I'm supposed to do something, but instead I'm gaping at Yuki's cropped top and soft tartan trousers. I know this outfit, loud and cool all at once, and very Yuki – she must have ordered it recently and shown it to me, before we moved out. She looks amazing, with her cherry-dipped fingers and her thousand-pin hairdo. She and Lucy are both staring under my chin, so I look down too. I'm carrying a huge, awkwardly wrapped present. It all comes back.

'Crap,' I say. 'Happy birthday!' They both laugh.

I know the enormous fruit basket is awkward, ill-chosen, but it's here now, and I hand it over with an apologetic shrug. Yuki can do with it what she wants, even leave it behind. Her eyebrows rise as she tears the paper, revealing its two-tiered empty practicality. She smiles, as Lucy says: 'Jeez, that's big.'

'Sorry,' I say.

'Ah, don't apologise, mate, thank you for the present!' Yuki attempts to give me a hug, but the basket stands between us, so I awkwardly tap the air around her.

I sit down, running my hand through my hair. Ah yes. I've just had a haircut to celebrate the end of the school year; new beginnings. It feels like discovering a forgotten fifty-pound note you sat on at the start of a game of Monopoly. I'm wearing my lucky shirt, and the tips of my hair are brushing my neck softly. The air is bright and mellow, and everything is so, so possible that I might get drunk on the excitement.

'How's it going at the new house? Are you all settled yet?' I ask.

Yuki shrugs sheepishly at the mention of her move, and it is Lucy who answers.

'Yeah, she's already started telling me off for the state of my plants, and she's buying a million cushions.'

I nod. 'A sofa isn't right if you can sit down without some prep.' Lucy rolls her eyes, and I catch Yuki's smile.

I'm feeling weirdly hopeful, but still a little stunned, and as more people arrive, as conversations and drinks start flowing, I breathe and take in my surroundings. England. The red-brick walls, the laughter, the pubs whose smell is so unique, so cosy. I remember the first time I walked through town, down St Peter's Street, past the Clock Tower and through the narrow passage, where I found myself in front of the imposing abbey. The shock, the beauty, the otherness and history – my heart leapt into another place and time. For a minute, sitting in the beer garden, watching it all through those expat eyes, I'm proud of myself. For a minute I appreciate the fact that perhaps attempting to start a life in a different country might have taken some bravery. I'm glad I did it, even if it didn't quite work out the way I imagined; but watching it now feels like a goodbye.

The main thing I feel, in the hints of citrusy aftershave in the air, is Romain. His presence is so strong in his absence. I'm expecting something to happen, I realise, a sixth sense, and this is why I'm so elated. This buzzing beer garden becomes a melting pot for change, for new beginnings. What are they seeking, these women who are overdressed for the flaky benches, holding out for something better? Who are they meeting, these men with gelled hair ready to plunge into the night like seals? Waiters waltz around carrying little baskets of mystery sauces.

My gaze falls on two people sitting at a table not far from ours, who look familiar.

'You're frowning, mate,' Yuki says next to me. 'Everything okay?'

'Yes, great, thank you.' I hide my face behind my glass as I take a sip of cider. A man and a woman. I've met them before, yet I don't think I actually have. But they look so familiar. Their heads are slightly bent towards each other; he's talking animatedly and making her laugh, she's hiding her mouth behind her fingers as she does. He's tanned, his shoulder-length hair coming loose a little, frizzing around his ears and chin.

Yuki is looking at them too. They are so good-looking, the two of them, even if the man is slightly scruffy. I'm about to ask Yuki where we know them from, but she startles, letting out a little cry.

'Something touched my leg!'

Our whole table cranes to look. A big Bernese Mountain Dog has appeared right by her, booping her knee with his snout, looking at her packet of bacon crisps expectantly.

'What a beautiful dog,' I say, bending to pet him, my fingers sinking into his fur as if they've been itching to do so for ages. It's wonderful. I can only reach his back from here, fuzzy and warmed by the evening sun, and a few black hairs get caught between my fingers.

'I guess,' says Yuki. 'It surprised me, that's all.' She's sitting tall and rigid on her chair, staring down at the dog, while others are crouching to stroke him. Yuki doesn't like dogs, especially big ones, the slobber and the hair.

'I'm so sorry.'

The man and the woman have approached us, the woman

74

holding a lead, fussing around the dog's massive head while he sits there patiently like a teddy bear. She has flawless skin and long, dark curly hair, and is wearing a crisp white shirt on which there isn't a single dog hair. How?

'Nick Harper?'

Nick. One of Yuki's uni friends, Max, has recognised him, his old school pal, and much beaming and shoulder-clapping follows. I feel like I'm watching the key scene of a film, something I missed when making a cup of tea and had to rewind for.

'This is my sister, Charlotte,' Nick says, but his sister doesn't smile.

'Sorry again.' She nods at Yuki, but Yuki is keeping her eyes firmly on the dog. She's acting like she's deeply annoyed, yet my instinct tells me there's something else to it. Is this embarrassment? Interest?

'Come sit with us for a bit, pal,' Max says to Nick, who looks at his sister. She says she must go back to London.

'I'll walk you to the station and come back,' Nick tells her.

She smiles, at him only. She doesn't seem to be wasting her smiles on anybody else. 'Don't be silly.' She points at the dog. 'I have my scary beast to protect me.'

They hug, and she speaks quietly, but I can hear because I'm the closest to them and the only one paying attention. 'Thank you for your advice earlier. You're the best.' Over her shoulder, his eyes meet mine. He blinks and looks away.

Almost immediately after Nick has sat down at the other end of the table, Yuki excuses herself. 'She'll be gone for a while,' Lucy says. 'That woman has the bladder of a great rhino.'

Perhaps I'm wrong, but it feels like Lucy wants to talk to

me about Yuki, now she's left; probably complain about her being a neat freak. Lucy is cool and posh and talks about air miles a lot. She was the one to insist she wanted Yuki to move into her spare room, Yuki and nobody else; she's a tricky one.

'Hiya, I'm Ben,' the guy next to me says, and Lucy turns away.

'I know,' I reply absent-mindedly. 'And I'm Louise, not Louisa.' This seems to make him immediately lose interest in me. Good. I move my chair a bit closer to the other end of the table, where Nick is talking. A story about the children in his Year 5 class.

'So last Monday, Ellie comes in and tells everyone her favourite chicken is dead.' Everybody around the table is listening, even Ben. 'All the kids are upset about Ellie's hen, who is called Millie, which is also the name of another girl in the class who Ellie has some beef with, and I'm pretty sure the name is deliberate. All their little faces are suddenly looking up at me, and I think, shit, I have no clue how to talk to kids about death, but I put on my reassuring teacher voice and start my speech: "I'm sure Millie is having a great time pecking worms in hens' heaven. She's in a better place now." I'm pretty happy with how it's come out, and all the kids seem to have accepted it and are getting ready for our lesson. But then Ellie turns to the rest of the class and says, "That's not true, though. Millie's not in heaven, she's in the green bin." At that point, five or six of them start crying and asking, "Sir, is my granny in the green bin too?" and I have to spend the rest of their maths hour talking to them about the meaning of life.'

They all chuckle at the story. 'Children are hilarious,'

lawyer Ben says, to general agreement, although several of them, who arrived earlier flustered and covered in baby sick, eyes riveted to the phone in case the babysitter called, also moan about how having a child is the end of everything you thought you were.

My phone buzzes, and immediately I *know* it's Romain. I open the text and stare at the words, which feel both old and new, like those smooth green pieces of glass I used to find on the shores of Lac Léman and collect like precious gems. I don't know what to think. I'm excited, and scared, familiar and confusing feelings; the main thing I know is that I have a chance to get it right.

'If you'll excuse me one sec . . . ' Across the table from me, Nick grabs his packet of tobacco and stands up.

He's headed to the smoking shelter at the side of the pub, a place that looks like it doubles up as the bin station, with a corrugated-iron roof. *Try me. I'm told I'm decent at giving advice.* Something is telling me to follow him; perhaps what his sister said when she hugged him. I want to hear what somebody neutral thinks, somebody who doesn't know Romain or me, who doesn't know my fears. I need someone who gives good advice, to spur me on. I get up and follow him.

He's selected a rolled cigarette and is in the process of pushing the packet into one of the side pockets of his trousers when I reach him. I'm not used to being this brave, approaching strangers and striking up conversation. It's scary, but the elation from the text helps to propel me forward, and I throw myself into it like a cold bath, lungs full, eyes open.

'Hi. Mind if I join you?'

'Hey, of course,' he says, fumbling a bit to retrieve his cigarettes, offering me one.

'No, thanks.'

'Okay.' He's clearly a bit taken aback that I'm not here to smoke.

'I'm Louise.'

'Nick.' He holds out his hand to shake mine.

'I know.'

His eyebrows lift, amused. 'Right.'

'Famous already,' I babble. 'I'll never forget Millie the hen.'

It's awkward, I sound like a groupie, but I don't care as much as I normally would. I'm emboldened by Romain's text, the door it has opened into my life.

Nick chuckles and brings the hand holding his cigarette to his face, wiping away a midge that has landed at the corner of his eye. His eyes are a little wrinkled, always shaped for amusement.

'Sorry,' he says, 'think I'm sleep-deprived, otherwise I'd have kept that ridiculous story to myself.'

'No, thank you for sharing it. It was good.'

'It's not that good. But glad to entertain.'

'Your sister is quite scary,' I say, out of the blue.

'Ha. She can be. But she's lovely, she really is. Don't let her intimidate you.'

'I'm always intimidated when people are so together.'

'And walk around with badly behaved beasts?'

'Oh no, the dog is wonderful.'

'Agreed,' Nick says. 'Sometimes I feel she got Chomsky for me.'

'Really? That's pretty nice.' If somebody got a dog for me, I would also love them unconditionally.

'Told ya. She's great.' He exhales, smoke filling the space between us. 'I, on the other hand . . .'

'You can't be that bad when you have Millie and Ellie and the others looking up to you.'

He laughs. 'Oh no. Ellie looks up to no one. The world will yield before her.'

Yuki is walking past us on her way back from the loo. She raises her eyebrows at me but doesn't stop. As I follow her with my eyes, I have a weird flash of her being here, in this space, snogging Nick. That can't be right, though maybe I could see them as a couple, their brightness, their matching friendly hugs and social ease. Her birthday table has depleted; Ben starts talking to her, his hand on her shoulder, while my impractical, enormous birthday present sits between her and Lucy like an unwanted child.

I take out my phone and bring up Romain's text. The screen glows white in the darkness. Nick squashes his cigarette into the ashtray, pushes both of his hands into his pockets, steps in a little closer to me. The bees have gone to sleep now, and the night is falling fast around us, like a silky dark bedsheet.

'This is a little random, but can I ask your advice?'

'Sure,' he says, looking surprised. 'Is this why you followed me out here?'

'Yes,' I say, pretending to joke while being earnest, which is a perilous exercise, 'of course. Why did you think I came?'

'I don't know. I thought perhaps you were looking for a high-school-style snog against the recycling bins.'

I'm glad it's dark, because I feel myself blushing. Romain's clever eyes. The lemon freshness of his neck – *who knows what life has in store for us.*

79

'No, sorry . . . ' I stumble.

Nick steps away slightly, smiles.

'Ah, Louise, sorry for making you feel uncomfortable – forget I said that, okay? What did you want to ask me?'

Saturday 22 July 2017

'How is Mum?' Marion asks. We are hurrying along the promenade, in the warm kiss of the sun. On this hot holiday Saturday, Vevey is busy both on land and water, with crowds ambling along the shore eating ice cream, or jumping off their pedalos. As we push our way through the melting-pot sounds of happy chatter, water splashes and duck quacks, I notice that the mountains across the lake are incredibly clear today, almost at an arm's reach. I long to extend my hand and pat them – their form and texture have the reassuring familiarity of a cat's spine.

The beads of Marion's necklace, fossilised grain or something, clatter as she walks. I've opted to wear something I hope Romain will like: my perfect girl-next-door outfit of a flowery dress and short denim jacket, which is a little too hot for the Swiss Riviera in July, but not wildly inappropriate for a traveller freshly arrived from Britain's misty moors. I'm going for that *je ne sais quoi* of sophisticated otherness.

'Mum's all right,' I say, wondering if it's true. This morning I came into the kitchen to find a half-plaited *tresse*, the white brioche loaf she always makes for breakfast when I visit. She told me long ago how Grandma made her practise the plaiting with tightly rolled kitchen towels, and that's how she got us to learn too. Mum was nowhere to be seen – she had gone to check on Grandma. The dough looked soft and vulnerable, left in the open. I glazed it and baked it and ate a few warm slices alone at the kitchen table.

'I haven't seen her much, to be honest,' I say to Marion as we approach the old town, its maze of narrow cobbled streets and old buildings, shops and boulangeries below and bright, colourful shutters above.

'I know,' she says. 'Looking after Grandma is starting to take its toll. Remember how well stocked her fridge used to be? Now she comes home exhausted in the evenings and eats a ready meal for one – when she eats, that is. I'm trying to help, but she says she's fine.'

For the first time, I realise how tired Marion herself looks. We hardly ever talk about Mum without arguing, so this is rare. I realise I haven't yet asked her how she is, *truly* is, and I open my mouth, but she catches herself. 'Nearly there,' she says. 'I can't believe you begged me to come with you to his bloody thing.'

At this, I startle. I thought she always got on with Romain. It's too late to worry. A bead of sweat runs down the length of my back, and I know I can't take off my jacket now, because I would look a damp mess. I'm nervous to be here, and I'm not sure whether I'm making the right decision – this feels like completely uncharted territory. Why have I come? I think back on Nick's encouragement, a week ago, to fuel my courage.

'Sorry,' Nick said when I showed him Romain's text in the smoking shelter. 'I can't read French – I got an E at GCSE.'

'I thought everybody got a C,' I said, and he looked a bit hurt. I hurriedly tried to rectify my mistake. 'Sorry, I don't mean ... That's what everybody says. Don't worry, an E is great.'

At this, his face relaxed and he chuckled. 'You mean everybody *wants* you to believe they got a C. Wankers.'

I translated the text for him, gave him some context. The moment had the strangeness and ineluctability of two worlds colliding.

'So this guy dumped you out of the blue?' Nick asked.

'I guess I'd missed it,' I told him, 'how he'd been feeling for a while. But he stayed in touch. He wrote me all those letters, and we had this ... thing when I went back home at Easter.'

'*Letters*, bloody hell.' Did Nick look slightly amused? Hard to tell.

'Yes, pen on paper. Romain is so clever, you know, and he's a writer back home. In his way, he's a little ...' I flustered a bit, patting around in the dark for the right word, and all I could find was French, '*décalé*, do you know what I mean?'

'Does it mean hipster? Because it sounds like it.'

'No,' I said, 'Romain's not a hipster. More like a thinker. A little old-fashioned, maybe. And anyway, you can talk.' I pointed at his tattoo in the dark.

'Why, this old thing?' He waved the subject off with his

hand, his second lit cigarette zigzagging like a Bonfire Night sparkler. 'Never mind me. You were saying?'

I couldn't believe he was still listening, asking me questions, that he didn't say we should go back to the table. He was an almost stranger, yet there I was boldly saying the words as and when I thought them, their soft prints dissipating in the air without my brain trying to catch them in a panic.

'The thing is, I think I didn't *try* as hard as I could have. I was so happy to have him, I ... He said I relied on him too much,' I explained. Nick nodded. 'And when I felt him start dropping off, I panicked and clung on even more, the opposite of what I should have done, and when he broke up with me, I kind of ran away.'

'Ran away?' Since his joke about us snogging, Nick had kept a respectful distance, but the darkness made me aware of the heat of his body, the smell of fresh smoke in the air.

I shrugged. 'Well, I moved here. Signed up on a teacher training course. Romain said ...' I tried to remember what he had said, but it kept escaping me, a memory twice removed. Had I really moved away for Romain? Hadn't it been because I knew that if I stayed, I would have withered and worse?

'And now you want to go back,' Nick said. He waited a bit, then: 'Do you think this time will be different?'

I didn't try to explain. How it all felt so tremendously important, like an actual second chance glowing neon in the night. That this time I had to hang on to it and not let it pass me by.

'I'm thirty ... huh, thirty-one now,' I said, a bit appalled that I had to stop and calculate my own age. 'I was twenty-eight when Romain and I got together. The first time.'

'A baby,' Nick agreed, and I started to worry he was making fun of me, that the whole thing had been one massively ironic conversation.

'Are you teasing me?'

'Not at all,' he said. 'I agree we don't have a clue in our twenties. We're there to fuck things up.'

'Did you?' I asked, suddenly aware that we'd spent all this time talking about me, about my life, and that I knew nothing of his.

He hopped away for a second to the ashtray, ignoring my question. 'But you're great now, Louise, I can tell. You've got this.'

I felt awkward again. 'What should I do?'

He thought for a moment, pretending to read the future or something. 'I think you should go to the exhibition.'

'Book launch.'

'Book launch, then. If you don't go, sounds like you'd always wonder what *could* have happened. Got nothing to lose, have you?'

I knew in my heart that I would happily lose my future as it currently stood for the mere possibility of change.

'What do I say to him, though?' I asked. 'Romain?'

Nick was watching me. 'Just strut up to him like you strutted up to me and pick up where you left off.'

Strut up to Romain? The thought makes me shivery with nerves as Marion and I walk across the small square. The bookshop has tall windows framed in wood against the cold grey stone front. Both floors can be seen from the street, hooked together by an elegant line of stairs. Shelves and piles of books, everywhere, tumbling over each other like a cornucopia of literature. The fountain at the edge of the Rue du Lac gave the shop its name, and the gentle flowing water sounds like music today.

'Why are we stopping?' Marion asks.

'I'd forgotten it was so gorgeous,' I say.

She laughs at the word I've used, *magnifique*. 'England is making you cheesy.'

The door of the shop has been propped open, and there's a sign inviting everyone to come in for the reading and book signing of Romain Bailly's *La Tentation d'Henri Debonneville*, with the tagline 'Mountains of darkness: a novel about the human condition set against the sinister backdrop of crime in a luxury ski resort.' Romain started writing the book when we were together, continued to tell me about it in his letters. It was something we shared privately for a long time, and it's about to be unveiled.

'Shall we go in?' Marion asks, scowling at the blurb.

'I saw that,' I say.

'What?'

'That face you made.'

She shrugs. 'Sorry, but − *mountains of darkness*? Come on ...'

'It's okay,' I say. 'You don't have to like it.'

'Don't worry,' she says. 'I'm sure I won't.'

There's no time to linger on my sister's snap ruthless judgements on people − she's clearly in a grump, which is no wonder given her level of tiredness. I take a deep breath as we enter. On his photo on the poster, Romain stands collar up against a snowy slope mottled with tiny red, blue and green skiers and a ski lift. He's so handsome: a straight nose, stubbly, slightly round cheeks, messy hair the colour of butterscotch fudge. His intelligent eyes pierce the stark frames of his glasses. He looks like a poster for the Swiss CSI, if such a thing existed (it doesn't). I keep jolting with fear that he might have forgotten me, that there might be a woman here with him, that he might think me pathetic; I have to remind myself it was only last week he texted me, only in April I ended up spending two weeks in and out of his flat. I have to keep my fears in check constantly, telling them to behave.

We shuffle to the back row.

'We were nearly late, see,' I whisper to Marion, because she made her reluctance to be my plus-one known every step of the way.

'Because you kept pausing for dramatic effect.'

Romain is here. Actually here. He's at the front of the room, talking to the owner of the shop. If I stare at him, he'll see me; I want and don't want this at the same time, so I try to look at him sideways while pretending to be listening to Marion, my face a pantomime of expression.

He stands with one hand in the pocket of his dark jacket, the other holding his fancy bronze fountain pen, the one he always writes his letters with; it dances in the air, sparkling in the evening light. I'm suddenly transported elsewhere, standing in a darker, more intimate space with another man, but I hurry to come back to the here and now.

I fluff my hair, adjust the shoulders of my jacket, sink into the back of my chair. It creaks, but it doesn't break. *I'm ready, you can see me now.* I think of *that* scene, when Elizabeth Bennet rescues Georgiana Darcy from humiliation and turns the pages of her music, and Mr Darcy looks at her from his seat, and she looks back, and they have the most sexually charged moment ever shown on the BBC. *I'm here, Romain. I'm back.*

'Are those elbow patches on his jacket?' Marion asks, but I shush her. The reading is starting.

'Well, that was *magnifique*,' Marion says, as everybody stands up and starts making their way to the other end of the room, where glasses of local white wine are set out on a table. Exactly as I pictured it; I've been thinking about this so often that it budded in my brain and grew roots into reality. Another table is waiting there for Romain, covered in neat piles of his book. He has hung back, and Marion pushes me towards the wine.

'You really think so?' I ask as we take a glass each, and select an adequate corner to stand in.

'No. It was bullshit.'

'Ah.'

'What did *you* think?' She's watching me as she takes a sip, almost confrontational.

'I thought it was well written,' I say.

'Perhaps. He sure knows a lot of . . . words. So many that I didn't get much of the actual meaning, to be honest. But that girl's murder left unpunished, it gives me the creeps—'

'That's what happens in real life, though,' says Romain's voice behind us. 'Not all crimes are solved.'

Damn. It wasn't supposed to happen this way – I'm so, so glad I was non-committal as usual. I need time to process the book, which has turned out very different to what I thought Romain and I discussed.

'Marion,' Romain says, bending a little to kiss my sister three times on the cheeks. Even when he does this, I feel jealous. Marion lets him do it like a queen allowing a peasant to kiss her gloved hand. 'Louise.' He turns to me, and we smile at each other for a second before he bends forward.

Kiss. Kiss. Kiss. I note with relief that he's slower with me, and his cheeks are stubbly, which makes the *bise* incredibly tactile, and he still smells of lemon and that fabric softener whose brand I never managed to find out. If I could go back in time, that's what I'd do – open his cupboards to put a label on the smell. 'You came,' he says. Is it me, or does he look a little surprised?

'Because you asked me to,' I say, attempting to make this flirty. It suddenly feels like I'm an idiot, hanging on to a text he sent me years ago, but it wasn't years ago. It was last week. *Last week*.

'Now I didn't ask you to, I asked you *if*,' Romain says.

He's smiling, his eyes lingering on me like they used to, as though we are the only two people in the bookshop. And at once I'm the shy girl by the Tacitus section again, the bookshop employee processing his book at the till, gob-smacked that he had noticed me. 'Still big on semantics, I see?' I tease him.

'Always.' He clinks his glass against mine. 'And always glad to see you. I didn't think you'd come. What an honour. Listen, I need to go and sign some books, but make sure you come and find me again later.' He bends forward and kisses my cheek again. He didn't need to do that – it's not part of the protocol, and it warms me up from the inside. From the corner of my eye I catch Marion making a face as she drinks her wine.

As Romain goes to his table, I pull her further into our corner. I have a feeling she's about to say something I don't want to hear.

'What he just read, Lou ...'

She doesn't finish, and looks at me with concern rather than defiance, which makes it much worse. So I do what I do best when I disagree with her, and sulk for a bit. When Marion and I argue, I always feel like I'm a teenager again. From the age of twelve, she was always right. She was right not to cry, she was right to get on with it, she won all our bets because she never lost confidence in her opinions, in her skills, whereas I was clumsy and constantly unsure.

You're the hard worker, my father told me once, *and Marion's got the charisma*. I wish that now, as an adult, I could laugh at the ridiculous comment this man made in passing, this man who left his wife and two teenage daughters to start another life on a vineyard in Australia. What did he know? But I can't deny Marion has something I wish I had, something that would make a man like Romain stay, perhaps. A no-*merde*-to-give approach. To my knowledge, she's never been broken up with, nor had her heart broken. I hate the fact I still look up to her.

The queue has died down; Romain is getting up from his signing table, wriggling his fingers, screwing the lid on his fountain pen. I watch him stroll to the drinks, stopping to receive congratulations on the way, picking up two glasses. I don't care what Marion says. I want him. My heart thumps in my chest, a *kukong, kukong* à la Patrick Swayze. What will we say to each other? I wipe my hands on my skirt as discreetly as possible, just in case our fingers touch when he hands me the glass.

He's on his way over to us when someone calls out to him, catches him by the elbow, and he stops. I watch in disarray as she says something, laughs and takes the glass from him, pretty and bashful and smiling the smile of the contented hunter.

'What's going on?' I feel like what I've seen is much bigger than it seems – he's only talking to somebody who's here, whom he clearly knows, but there was something so intimate, so assured in her gesture.

Marion glances over. 'I know that girl – Aurélie something, she was two years below me at school.'

'She's too young for him,' I groan.

'Ha,' Marion snorts. 'Sure. Shall I call the police?'

My cheeks are red, and I'm mortified that he might look in my direction and notice it, but I can't take my eyes off them. This can't be happening. Romain bends forward and Aurélie Something pushes her long hair aside so she can present her ear to him, pearly like a cute seashell. He's not coming to me any more. He's been hijacked.

'We need to do something,' I say to Marion.

'You didn't *actually* want to get back with Romain, did you?'

'Why did you think I came?'

'I don't know.' She shrugs. 'I assumed it was to remind yourself you're better off without him. To look like a cool expat, show off a little bit about all the . . . Shakespeare you've been reading. A moment of feminist win.'

I haven't read Shakespeare. Not a single word of it. I've seen *She's the Man* and *10 Things I Hate About You*, though I'm not sure Romain would want to discuss them.

'Well, I think we can both say it's gone really well.'

Marion moves in a little bit. Her face is concerned. I think she's seen that my eyes are filling. 'Sis,' she says.

91

'He *did* ask me to come. He said he missed me, and now he's flirting with someone else. Look.'

I fumble to show her Romain's text. As Marion reads, her frown deepens under her fringe. Her skin is more tanned than mine, and she has more freckles, gathered on her nose.

'Bastard,' she says. 'That clearly wasn't an *if*. He got you here, even gave you that extra cheeky kiss, and now . . .'

I'm so close to crying. I feel rejected, and worse – humiliated. The shame stings – that I was naïve enough to have hoped.

'Help me out, please,' I plead.

She nods. Marion can't resist such an injustice; she's unstoppable when she puts the world to rights. I follow her as she splits the crowd, aiming straight for Romain's companion.

'Aurélie, hey! It's been so long, how are you?'

When I join them with more wine, Aurélie and Marion are chatting, reminiscing about people whose names only ring a distant bell. Romain is sipping his drink at the edge. I'm a little worried, but he looks rather amused, so I place myself in the space Marion has left between them, and pretend to be following the *retrouvailles* with cool, semi-detached interest.

'You found me,' Romain says to me. 'And how are you, Louise? You look well.'

I bring the back of one hand to my cheek. I still feel a little flushed; perhaps that's what he means by 'well'. From cold to hot, I'm now completely exultant, tipsy on the ability to take things into my own hands rather than letting them string me along, like Achilles with Hector's corpse. I explain this to Romain, spinning it as a new, independent life overseas, in a city that's only nineteen minutes away from St Pancras by train. *Just strut up to him, Louise. You've got this.* He seems genuinely impressed.

'You sound different,' he says. 'I think England suits you.'

My mind flutters to what he said when he broke up with me, and I wonder if his has done the same. I wonder if what I'm seeing on his face, this interest, as if I'm now part stranger, is what we've both needed.

'But you,' I say, 'you, look at *this*! You did it, congratulations.'

He tilts his head, and as he does, Aurélie excuses herself. She's meeting friends in town for some drinks, and would Marion like to go with her? To my surprise, my sister accepts. When she triple-kisses me goodbye, which she never normally does, she takes hold of both my upper arms. For a moment, I think she's going to give me a pep talk, but she throws us a satisfied smile and leaves.

Slowly, the bookseller who is rearranging piles of books, the local retirees who come to every event for the free wine, and the general Vevey intelligentsia fade away, and only Romain and I are left standing amongst the shelves. The bookshop smells of wood wax, old paper and words so long they would wrap around your tongue like sour sweets. As the sun dipping into the lake sets everything on fire, a slow and steady burn, we begin the cat-and-mouse game we're accustomed to. I browse, stroking the glossy book spines as I do, picking some up and pretending to read the blurbs, but all the blurbs say: *He's looking over your shoulder, so close you could lean back against him.*

I do lean back, and he's there to catch me. My body relaxes against his warmth, his cheek pressing against mine to read the back cover of one of those deeply self-absorbed novels. I want his arms to wrap around me like they used to, his hands to caress my collarbones. But not yet.

'I'll sign my book for you.'

I follow him through the space his body has just left. He picks up a book from the pile, inspects it for flaws, whips out his pen and writes. 'It's a little strange, I suppose, to be signing my book for you,' he says, but the R of his name comes out weirdly assertive. He hands the book over still open.

To Louise — to new beginnings, he's written.

'Careful. The ink needs to dry.'

I hold the book open, unable to take my eyes off his, and I'm acutely aware, almost pained, that I'm his, that he could do and say anything to me right now, in this universe of mahogany and paper. Goosebumps grow on my arms, as though my skin itself were reaching tiny tentacles towards him, pulling me closer. My hairline is tingling.

'Listen,' he says. 'We need to catch up properly. The next few days will be quite busy with the book: a bit of promotion, the reviews and all. How long are you staying?'

'I'm not sure,' I tell him, when the answer is really *as long as you want me to*. But I don't want him to know that. I've changed, after all. I'm not so needy any more.

Friday 18 August 2017

'You should eat something, Mum.'

Marion and Fabio are hovering on the threshold of Mum's kitchen; Fabio's forehead is glistening, but he's wearing his dark suit jacket, and Marion's black shirt dress is still perfect, uncreased by the trials of Grandma's funeral. I noticed that Mum didn't eat anything at the wake; now we're back home, I want to take care of her. I want to show Marion that I can.

I rummage through the fridge and bring a few Tupperware boxes and glass jars out: Parma ham, stinky mountain cheese, lots of gherkins seeping with vinegar. Mum's favourites.

She shakes her head. 'Not hungry.'

'Ah, come on.' I'm using my teacher voice. I'm tired, I'm hot, I'm still traumatised by Auntie Sylvie's yellow dress. I came across a tad too firm, perhaps. 'You haven't eaten all day, you should—'

'Let her be, Lou. It's okay, Mum. You don't have to eat if you don't feel like it,' Marion says. She's playing with her car keys, clearly wanting nothing more than to take off, but instead she utters the dreaded command: 'Lou, a word?'

We leave Mum and Fabio to the silence and emptiness of the cool, dark kitchen, and go to the balcony. It's early evening, golden sun peeking through the departing thunder storm, the traffic below made louder by the wet pavements. I can see the white twinkle of a very small portion of lake through the trees of the park opposite.

'What's up with you?' Marion half whispers, half hisses. 'Why are you being so forceful?'

'Maybe because I care,' I say.

'Well, Mum is grieving, so maybe you're caring wrong.'

It feels like she's slapped me. Whatever I do, Marion will find fault with it.

'You've been pushing her around since Grandma died,' she continues.

Perhaps I *have* been pushing Mum a little. I can't help but watch her constantly, looking for signs of what is going on inside. A drooping plate, an aura of defeat. I have to keep fighting against the notion that things will never be the same, that we have lost more than our grandmother. My family is changing, all at once, and I don't think any of us is ready. I don't think Marion realises to what extent either.

A striking, ominous bird cackle rings out from the trees, soon drowned by the sputtering of a moped.

'Do you remember when Grandma used to take us to the zoo?' I ask Marion.

She rummages through her bag to find her lip salve, and starts applying it thoughtfully. It's something natural, coconut- or beeswax-based. Marion doesn't wear make-up. She doesn't need to.

'Yeah,' she says. 'You were obsessed with the capybaras. I liked the ponies. That was the one time in our lives I was more mainstream than you.'

She means more boring. I can't help but laugh. 'You were always running ahead too. I stuck with Grandma because I was worried I'd miss the ice cream.'

'You always thought you were destined to miss the good bits.'

'And Grandma always made sure we got the good bits. Both of us. The home-grown raspberries, the vanilla pretzels, the capybaras. All of it.'

'Yes,' Marion says. 'She did.'

We smile at each other, then my phone vibrates in my pocket. Since the book launch, I've been carrying it at all times. I check the message.

Dear Louise, sincere apologies
for my silence. Would you per
chance be free now for a drink? It
would be good to see you. R

'Are you coming?' Marion asks, holding the balcony door open for me.

'Yes. And actually, could you drop me off in town on your way back?'

Romain walks into the bar on the Place du Màrché, a narrow grotto full of old men and wooden panels darkened with scalp oil, wearing peacock blue. I wish he had chosen any of the other bars around here – perhaps Le National, with its funky terrace and lanterns. My funeral clothes are a little too formal for a Friday drink with a friend, a little too hot for the warm evening, and I'm hoping he'll notice and ask. In the silence of the car, on the very short journey with Marion and Fabio from Mum's to the town centre, I indulged in walking through the perfect evening with Romain, step by step, allowing myself to feel every emotion throughout the process. How he would look at me and see my sadness, tend to my open wounds; how the Muses would sprinkle our conversation with wit and emotional depth. We would effortlessly connect. I'd keep saying, *Wait, what's the word in French?* Because French is too rational a language, and my true feelings are increasingly untranslatable. And Romain, not an English speaker, would pretend not to be impressed, but would invite me to his flat, where we would find that absence distils longing into the best sex.

'Hiya,' I say, rising from my chair.

'Hi,' he says, bending to kiss my cheeks. After a month back home, I'm almost used to this ritual again, but there was so much of it today at the funeral, so much breathing in old ladies' heavy perfume, that even Romain's *bise* isn't as good as it normally is. He's distracted too, a bit brisk, and I immediately turn on my sensors to identify his mood. He's grumpy. What have I done now? Shouldn't *I* be grumpy that he took so long to contact me?

'What would you like to drink?' He sits down and gestures to the waiter.

I order the same as him. The waiter goes to the bar and Romain leans back, puffing air through his lips.

I wait for a little bit, but he's looking at me as if I had invited him here, so I ask, 'Everything okay?'

'Ah, Louise, where to start? Things have been intense.'

'Tell me about it.' His eyes stop on me, as if trying to figure out whether I'm joking. I nod, encouraging him to carry on.

Two glasses of red wine are placed in front of us, and a bowl of peanuts. He is silent, quickly pulling his phone out to check the screen. I'm a bit uncomfortable. I'd forgotten grumpy Romain and I'm not sure I have the energy for him tonight – it's a novel feeling, this lack of patience for his moods. But he's here, handsome as ever, his eyes dark and brooding, and he asked to see me. This is what you wanted, Louise. This is who you wanted. I know I can cheer him up – I used to do this routinely. I just need to distract him with a random topic of conversation. Because I'm me and my brain is classy, I settle on pee in peanuts.

'It's a myth,' Romain says.

'Like Jason and the Argonauts?'

Romain isn't a classicist, but he loves Jason. He bloody adores him and can't fail to be cheered up by his golden fleece and his ship. I used to keep the best stories for him, things I would uncover during my PhD research, and enjoyed digesting them and reworking them until they were funny, and entertaining, and gross. Romain always pretended he was above it, but I know he secretly loves the Greatest Hits. Theseus is another one. I used to write some snippets in my letters, and he would critique them, help me improve my style. It was this private joke we shared.

'Every single man I know washes his hands,' he says.

'That's a relief.' But how does he know? Does he check what people do in urinals? Does it ever come up naturally in his conversations with other artists and university types who wear long scarves and drink ironically in claustrophobic, unattractive bars? I find myself thinking back to the conversation with Nick in the smoking shelter. He would have something funny to say about this topic.

'How's your book doing?' I ask.

When I read the copy Romain signed for me, I was pained that I didn't appear anywhere in the novel, but it didn't come as a surprise, my mind always running a sentence ahead, as if I'd read it already. There were no clues to my existence in his psyche, none whatsoever. The savagely raped and murdered ski lift operator was blonde, demure, in her twenties. There were no other women except the detective's saintly mother. In Romain's universe, I wasn't even featuring as a corpse. I kept hearing Marion's sarcasms in my head as I read. The humour she injected into the whole experience was actually quite welcome.

Romain puts his phone face up on the table, starts playing with his keys, jingling them between his fingers. I'm struck by how endearing this gesture is, by how deeply it echoes. I've always loved Romain's hands – there's a certain idleness, an elegance about them. I imagine them prising precious things open: jars of pesto, oysters or heavy dictionaries.

'Not great,' he says. 'I hope you haven't read the reviews. They're . . . '

Finally the source of his grumpiness becomes clear. It doesn't have anything to do with me. That's a relief – I can work with that.

'I haven't read them, and I bet nobody else has either,' I say.

'Good,' he snaps, and drinks some of his wine. 'This is quite crap, isn't it? Might as well be drinking vinegar.' I briefly feel guilty, until I remember he was the one who chose it.

'Well, I've heard of some restaurants serving vinegar as drinks, you know, to balance a dish out or something.'

He's not listening. He's still on the subject of his detractors. 'I mean, one of them called Henri a conceited arse who would be more suited to being a creepy 1950s school teacher in a small valley than a police inspector in our modern country.' For a minute, I wonder if this was Marion writing to the newspaper. 'A conceited arse. *Conceited!*'

I know his outrage is my cue to speak – our little dance of him being down and relying on me to cheer him up is second nature. 'Isn't it better to have them write something about it than ignore it completely? At least people are going to want to check it out for themselves.' Sensible, supportive Louise. The thought comes briefly that this is why I have been summoned. I wave it away.

'Henri has high expectations,' Romain continues. 'He might not be *relatable* because he has ideals and sticks to them. He doesn't play the game, doesn't compromise. I wanted to show the struggle. And now the publisher might not want this to be a series after all.'

I used to love listening to Romain talk about his novel, or read about it in his letters. 'Critics always take themselves too seriously,' I say. 'Don't worry. You're the one who has written a novel; that's an amazing accomplishment. I'm sure your publisher won't listen. They signed you because of your talent.'

At this, he brightens up. In one smile, I'm reminded why I am here. How his features relaxing bring in a glimmer of sun in the doom. 'You think?' he asks.

'Of course.'

My phone is in my pocket, and a message arrives, the

vibration cutting through the mood. I fish it out to transfer it into my bag, glancing at the screen in passing.

> How was today? Funerals are
> tough. Hope you're okay

Funerals *are* tough. Am I okay? Nick and I have been texting occasionally since July. Checking in, or sharing random tweets and memes we like. I told him about Grandma, but I didn't think he'd remember. His increasingly familiar friendliness, coming through this text, makes me want to wrap myself in a blanket and watch elephant videos on YouTube.

I startle when Romain takes my hand.

'Sorry,' he says, contrite. 'I got a little carried away there. Apologies for being boring.'

In shock at his contact, I let go of my phone, checking with my nerve endings that I can actually feel Romain's hand closed on mine. Intense nostalgia, mixed with hope of new beginnings, crackles through our fingers. I know I have successfully managed to cheer him up, and I feel proud, and useful.

'Not at all,' I say. 'You're never boring.'

'So how are you? How are *you* doing, Louise?'

'I'm great. I'm perfect.'

My name sings in his mouth, and it all comes back: why I so desperately loved – love – him. His intelligent eyes fix on mine. I am here, I am worthy – my energy, fizzling out in all directions before, can pour itself into him, find its purpose.

We sit and talk until the bar closes. At first I felt we had years of our lives to catch up on, but this isn't true, there is no big news, no disasters, so instead we dig together into the minutiae of Romain's days, his successes and hopes.

When it is time to leave, my phone buzzes again. I couldn't care less, but because hints of my other life seemed to catch Romain's attention earlier, I let his hand go and check the message in a very obvious way, leaving my phone flat on the table. This time it's from Yuki.

Mate, just checking in, haven't heard
from you in a while. Brunch soon? x

Romain has been reading the text, but I know English isn't his forte, and that it grieves his scholarly ego.

'You're popular tonight,' he says as I put the phone away. He sounds surprised, and I am too. It's a nice feeling, having friends checking on you. 'With your life in London and your cool new friends, you're too good for us now.'

In the drabness of the bar, he looks almost contrite, almost vulnerable. It must be hard spending years writing something only for critics to pull it apart. Romain needs me to support him. I can reply to Yuki later. This is when I feel at my best, when I'm the most comfortable in my life. Perhaps England has served its purpose and it's time for me to move back. Mum could do with help too. It might all be working out.

I laugh off the ridiculous notion that I might be too cool for Romain, and I tug his face towards mine and kiss him. It's a pleasant, soft and warm kiss, brimming with memory and quite chaste. When I retreat, I wonder at how daring I've been, with a pang of dormant lust.

Romain leans back a little, and for a dreadful second, he doesn't say anything. 'So that's why you came back.'

I hope he can't tell that my cheeks ignite immediately.

'What? No, of course . . . Please don't think . . .'

He laughs. 'Why, Louise, don't fret – I'm teasing you.'

We stand up, gathering our things, and his arm is suddenly wrapping around my shoulder, and we're walking out of the bar, in the direction of his flat.

Friday 13 October 2017

'You told me to sit down, so *I sat down*.'

My whole Year 11 class is roaring with laughter, except for Fern Moreland, whose head is bent over her textbook, her dark fringe a thick curtain around her face. Tom is, indeed, sitting down, but on his table, facing the back wall. Even like this, he's taller than I am.

'Very well. Let me rephrase. Could you sit down on your chair with your knees and shoulders facing the front, Tom, thank you.'

He turns around, slowly for comical effect, and I'd love to pull the chair so he falls on his backside. It's not professional, but I've had dreams that Tom turned into a fly and I, an honest mistake, splatted it on the desk with a book. It felt amazing.

'Thank you. Now, open your books, everyone.'

There are three students who try in the class, three out of twenty-seven. Fern, who thinks my bad behaviour management is ruining her future and reminds me through a permanent display of eye-rolling; Chantelle who is easily led but doesn't want to let anybody down; Johnny, who lost his mother recently and wants to be in a rock band and is on track for a promising 6. Sometimes (most lessons) I give up on the rest and teach only those three, just so I don't feel that their time spent in my classroom was truly wasted.

'We're covering healthy eating today, and I have a worksheet for you,' I tell the class, as though I were announcing free sweets and Mario Kart. I'm pretty sure that the loud fart following my exciting lesson objectives isn't real. 'You can choose to spend the lesson filling in the sheet and I'll leave you alone, or if you want to work on verbs and tenses, which you'll need for your GCSE, you're welcome to follow what's going on at the front of the classroom. Up to you.'

I got up at five to make this worksheet, and it took me more than an hour (the length of the lesson) because I wanted to make sure that it would contain everything they needed to learn for today. I differentiated, built up the knowledge progressively, gave them grammar in speech bubbles spoken by *Love Island* contestants, and because it was early and I felt slightly drunk on excitement at how pedagogically good the sheet was, I added lots of memes and funny pictures. I'm rather proud of it and it was a shedload of work. Of course, I won't let on how I feel about it, as they won't even look at it if they know I care.

I throw the worksheets around, thinking that I must be reaching the limits of our department budget because photocopying is frowned upon, but needs must.

I can see that Tom is assembling his mob at the back, having slapped some poor boy's hand off my precious worksheet. They're looking at something on their phone. They're quiet. Okay, it's a silence that doesn't bode well, but this might give me ten minutes of teaching. *Choose your battles.* I've taught for little more than a year, and I know this is the mantra of the profession.

Johnny, Chantelle and Fern, right in front of the white-board, like the Trois Mousquetaires, are the only ones who have been sticking to the seating plan. I set Fern an extension task, which I also planned before six this morning, and spend some time with the other two until we're all satisfied that they can describe to people what those very people are eating and drinking, which of course does come up a lot in real life. *You eat fish. She drinks water.* After a few minutes, Chantelle starts drawing on the inside cover of her textbook, which is school property and already littered with profanities, but as she is drawing flowers on top of them, I think she's doing us all a favour.

'You're different today, miss,' she says.

'No, I'm not,' I say. 'Now you can't give up, Chantelle – look, just translate back into English, okay, "I take the tomato soup", "the" because it's the one on the menu, you see—'

'Yeah, miss,' Johnny says, 'did you get a haircut?'

Fern rolls her eyes. She's already copied all the vocabulary from the textbook into her exercise book, which I didn't ask her to do, because she knows it already, but she wanted to show me she was bored.

'Fern, how about you now try to put these sentences into the perfect tense,' I suggest.

'What's the perfect tense again?' Chantelle asks.

'The past tense.'

'Ah. So why don't you just call it the past tense, then?'

'It's called the perfect tense because it's perfected, fin-ished,' Fern says.

Chantelle stares at her.

'That's right,' I say. 'Well done, Fern.'

'You didn't get a haircut,' Fern informs me. 'Not since the twentieth of September. But I agree you're different.'

Something's brewing at the back of the classroom. It's too quiet there. Unsettling. But I just need to get to the past-tense revision, then I'll feel that my top three students will have learnt something. We whizz through the main verbs, working against the clock.

'OMG,' Chantelle giggles. 'D'you have a boyfriend, miss?'

'That's inappropriate,' I say. My go-to word. Can't count how many times a day I use it. Same for 'defiance', because it sounds so serious that it improves students' behaviour by 10 per cent.

Chantelle is now drawing a giant heart on the first page of the textbook, the only one that was previously untouched. 'OMG, I know, is your boyfriend *Swedish*, miss?' she whispers.

Fern snorts. 'Why Swedish?'

'Well, miss is Swedish, aren't you, miss?'

'Close,' I say, for the millionth time since I started teach-ing her. 'I'm Swiss. And again, please don't talk about your teachers' personal lives, not now or ever. Now, how would you make this sentence even more interesting, Fern?'

'It's about lettuce, miss, I don't think it can get more interesting.'

I raise my eyebrows at her, trying to find a gap in her fringe. Fern moans but starts to write something down.

'Do teachers talk about us? I bet they do, all the time,'

Johnny says. I look at his work, and he's been using the wrong word order all the way through, so I take his pen and gently draw an arrow across his first sentence.

'She's not answering, Johnny,' says Chantelle. 'I bet they talk about us all the time in the staffroom and the pub and stuff.'

'No offence, guys, but we're not interested,' I say.

They all whoop as though I'd attempted to deliver a massive burn.

'Whoa, miss, you don't joke about usually.'

'Something's definitely up then,' Fern says. She's finished the sentence in her book, written across the back page very neatly, and it's perfect and I think she's on track for her 8 and I'm so proud I want to cry.

This is the first time I realise I'll miss them, these three, when I leave in December, never to return. The international school called me yesterday to tell me that I'd got the job, starting in January. I'm handing in my notice today, just before the half-term deadline. I'm going back home, where a nice school flat awaits me, not far from Vevey, not far from Mum and Romain, and the relief of leaving this classroom has made me feel giddy all day.

Just as Fern looks up at me with the classic look of a half-smug kid who wants to appear uninterested in what their teacher thinks of their best work, we are all hit with a flurry of arrows, which, I quickly discover, are my worksheets turned into aeroplanes. It hurts more than it should, not only because of the time and effort I put into them, but because the mob have spiked them with a box of paper clips, stolen from my desk. Johnny immediately grabs as many as he can and starts to retaliate, Fern drops under her desk with her

109

textbook and Chantelle covers her head with her hands and squeals, and the lesson is, thirty-six minutes in, truly over.

Later, I ring Yuki's doorbell. I'm a little nervous, as we haven't met up in a while. She's been trying, but I was busy, swamped in the return to school, the job application process. Now I need to tell her I'm leaving, and I want to do it in person. She lets me in, greeting me like a soldier returning home.

'Your hair's getting quite long now,' I say as we move to the lounge. With a sigh of relief, I sink into the battered red sofa and she takes the tartan chair. The coffee table is velvety with dust, and somebody has been putting glasses or mugs down without using coasters, which in Yuki's world, as far as I know, is a crime against furniture. *Culaccini*.

'Yeah, Ben likes it long, so I thought why not? Feels weird, though,' she says. She rakes her fingers through it, and they catch towards the ends. In the twilight, in my mind's eye, I see another Yuki, with short, shiny hair like a ferret coiled around her head, her cherry-dipped fingers, her joyful eyes. How did I not see this before, this change in her? I have been busy with my own stuff, a foot in Switzerland, a foot in school, wrestling unimpressed pupils and a relationship, and I missed it.

'How is it going with Ben?' I fold my legs under me, hoping the weird foreboding will settle quicker than the ambient dust.

'Good.' I must have looked at her funny, because she laughs, and it's reassuring to hear her laugh. 'Honestly, it's kinda fine. You know what it's like. No, wait, *you* have a long-distance boyfriend, so you have the best of both worlds.'

110

'Well,' I say.

'Well?'

'Speaking of—'

Yuki immediately folds forward, pressing her hands on her knees.

'What, he didn't *propose*, did he?'

'No, of course not. But I handed in my notice today.'

She claps. A real clap, loud and enthusiastic.

'Ah, matey, that's great news. No more pricks ruining your lessons!'

I laugh. 'Not sure insulting fifteen-year-olds is appropriate.'

'Has their bullying of you been appropriate? I don't care, then.' She's properly gleeful. 'Little shits.'

'*Yuki*,' I scold, but I'm grinning. 'But you're right. Good riddance.'

'Let's drink to that.' She disappears into the kitchen and I sink a little further into the sofa, soothed by the sounds of her rummaging through the fridge. I'm leaving the UK. I should feel relieved. Do I?

Yuki brings a bottle of white wine, two glasses clinking in her other hand.

'Lucy's in Barcelona, so I'll make sure I replace this before she gets back. I forgot to go and buy some. Congratulations, matey. So what are you going to do now? Apply to a better school? Change jobs entirely?'

'I'm moving back home,' I say.

Yuki stops her glass halfway to her lips.

'*Home* home?'

'Yes. I got a job near my mum's. In an international boarding school. They called me yesterday.'

111

She takes a big swig of wine.

'When do you start?'

'January.'

'That's soon.'

'Yes. Incredibly soon, actually.'

I want to tell her I've enjoyed our friendship, how much it's meant to me, explain to her why I'm leaving. How I couldn't make it work here, that it's only a matter of time before I disappoint her. Mind you, she does already look a bit let down.

'Everything okay?' I ask her.

'All good, mate. I just hadn't realised you'd be *leaving* leaving. But listen, congrats, that's *fantastique*.'

'Thank you.'

'Things going well with Romaan, then?'

'Yes.'

A certain smile creeps onto my face every time I think: *I have someone.* The last weeks of my summer holiday were spent in Romain's flat, and it was wonderful and intense and familiar all at once. I knew what he liked by heart; I felt like I'd spent years making mental notes of what to do this time. I spurred on his writing, I laid out meals of spiced chicken and colourful salads when he came back from the library. I made sure the freezer was stocked up with Mövenpick's Caramelita, his favourite ice cream. More expensive than a bucket of gold when you're on a UK teacher's starting salary, but totally worth it for the look on Romain's face as he closed his eyes and put his arm around my shoulders, a spoon in his mouth. 'I could get used to this,' he said.

'Could get used to *me*, you mean?' I asked.

'Yes. I think I already am. Falling back in with you is easy.'

I knew he needed independence, so I went out some

112

evenings, to keep Mum company or walk along the lake, quiet moments to pinch myself that it all seemed to be working out this time.

Sex was kind of nice too. It was more grown up, more real than I remembered it. I thought of sexy scenes from Greek mythology, as they helped me get into the space quicker, to match Romain's immediate bursts of need. Jason's brawny muscles rubbing against Medea's lustful skin. Galatea's marble breasts becoming soft flesh under Pygmalion's caresses. I didn't share these thoughts with Romain, of course.

'I'm happy for you,' Yuki says. She doesn't quite sound like she is. I'm not sure what she wants me to say; I feel like I'm missing something, and this, this is our default position, our little habit.

'How is it going with Ben?'

'You've already asked, mate.' She picks up her phone. The screen is broken, a long, splintered crack running across it. 'So, what pizza do you want?'

It takes us some time to order, trying to work out how we can use the offers with a combination of toppings, meaning we can both eat some of each other's pizza and not miss out. After that, the silence comes back. I know I need to break it. I want to . . .

'Listen, Yukes,' I say. Yukes? Since when does anyone call her Yukes? 'I wanted to thank you for being there for me. It hasn't been easy for me over here, and I'm so lucky to have had you as a housemate.'

I'm pretty pleased with this speech. Only missing the dramatic Hollywood background music.

'But . . . ?' Yuki asks.

'What?'

113

'Sounds like there's a "but" coming. Sounds like you're, I dunno, breaking up with me.'

Does it? Am I? What about when *she* left *me* for Lucy?

'Sorry,' I say. 'I'm not ... It's, well, you know ...'

'Yeah. I was there when you needed me.'

The doorbell rings and we both look at each other in surprise.

'Can't be the pizza already,' I say. 'We only ordered five minutes ago.'

Yuki disappears to open the door, while I sit in my discomfort. But I'm leaving, I am, and she has her life here, I didn't think it would make so much of a difference to her. A male voice, mixed with Yuki's, comes through to the living room, the ruffle of a coat, and lawyer Ben enters.

'Hi there, Louisa,' he says, wiping rain off his forehead.

'It's Louise,' Yuki says, on her way to the kitchen.

'Louisa's fine,' I say, and Ben looks at me like I'm not making any sense.

'I guess I should try and get it right, as you're friends with my girlfriend,' he says.

Yuki calls out something from the kitchen, but because it has to travel through the dining room, it comes to us all muffled. It sounds a bit like she said, 'She's leaving anyway.'

'I guess so,' I say to Ben. 'Hi there.'

'I was out with my mates from the tennis club,' Ben informs me, sitting down on Yuki's chair, attempting to rectify the way his wet blonde hair falls back on top of his head, which makes him look, in my humble opinion, like a young rat who got overly excited in the bins. 'But it was tipping it down, and I thought I'd call it a night. Sorry if I'm interrupting your girlie evening.'

'It's all right,' I say, repulsed by the way he uses the word 'girlie'. 'The more the merrier.'

'Your English is very good,' he says, making it sound like a question or a deep, deep surprise.

'Ah, thanks.'

Ben doesn't like me, doesn't want me here, and it is reciprocal. I've known for a while that Yuki was dating him, since they made out on the 'epic night' of her birthday in July. I knew deep down that it isn't a good idea, but the extent of this is only coming to the fore tonight, the first time I've actually seen them together.

Yuki comes back, pours Ben a glass of wine before dropping next to me on the sofa.

'It's good to be home,' Ben sighs.

'Where do you live?' I ask, to remind him that this is not his home.

'My flat's in Hampstead, but since I spend most of my time here ...'

'He's always here,' Yuki says. 'Can't get rid of him.'

The atmosphere is a little muggy. Although it's cold and damp outside, the unsaid feels sticky. The window is steaming up. Probably Ben's tennis sweat, which I'd rather not think about.

'Lou was telling me about her boyfriend in Switzerland,' Yuki says. 'She's moving back there in January.'

I give her a look to signify that I don't fancy sharing my personal life with Ben, but she ignores me. She starts chewing one of her nails; they are bare, and she looks like a lost little girl.

'Great,' Ben says. He shuffles forward in his seat so he can take his jumper off. Cashmere, I bet. 'I love Zermatt. I go skiing there every year with mates from work.'

115

'Never been,' I say.

Everything feels reheated, but only to lukewarm. Suddenly I worry for Yuki. I would never have thought she would need my concern. What else have I missed? What else am I going to leave her to? It makes me think of Nick. I wish they'd met properly on her birthday; how, between the two of us, we could advise her, watch out for her. Shield her from *this*.

I consider being clumsy and spilling my drink on the jumper Ben has carefully laid out on the arm of the sofa, thus invading Yuki's and my space, but the doorbell rings again.

'Are you going to get that, Anna?' Ben asks.

Anna? Avoiding my eyes, Yuki slips out of the room. I don't want to ask Ben about this – I want to ask my friend.

Ben and I sit in silence, but he breaks first.

'I would take her,' he nods towards the door, 'skiing, I mean, but she's never tried. She'd have to go on the baby slope while we go on the, you know, decent ones.'

'I don't think Yuki would enjoy the cold and the falling over,' I say.

'Yeah,' he says, picking up his wine and downing it. 'It's a real shame. I always pictured me and my wife on the slopes, with the kiddies following, doing the snowplough.' Is he trying to sound cute? Did this chat work for him when he was on Hinge or something?

'Look, pizza!' Yuki returns, whipping the boxes from behind her back with a flourish. She nearly drops one.

'Jeez, be careful,' Ben says, snatching them off her.

'I'm sorry, love, we only ordered two,' Yuki says. For a minute I picture Ben having to eat a dry piece of toast, but she continues, 'Lou and I can share hers, and you can have mine.'

116

But your stuffed crust? I want to ask. Yuki always has stuffed crust and mine is a plain one.

'Works for me.' Ben grabs the box. 'Better for you to be sharing anyway, ladies, wouldn't want to ruin your diets.'

We eat in silence, until Yuki breaks it. 'You can see we're keeping your birthday present well fed,' she smiles, nodding to the fruit basket overflowing with brown bananas and dry satsumas. She didn't tuck it away in the kitchen; she's presented it in the middle of the coffee table like a piece of art. 'Thanks again, mate. I love it.'

'You gave her that for her birthday?' Ben snorts, munching.

'Yup,' I say. 'Why, you don't like fruit? Something against vitamin C?'

He shakes his head. 'Yuki's got so much tat. This place is too cluttered. She doesn't need to be encouraged. Those bananas belong in the bin.'

Yuki's smile fades. I pray for Ben to choke on a cheese string, and Yuki quietly pats under the coffee table for the remote control and turns the TV on. She doesn't bother changing channels, leaving what is on to fill the silence. It's a panel show, and watching five men and a woman throw jokes around only highlights our own cold atmosphere. Steadily the evening falls into a coma, until I can't take it any more and I make my excuses to leave.

'I'll walk you to the door,' Yuki says. Ben nods goodbye at me and turns Netflix on. In the tiny hallway, I put my coat on slowly, tuck my hair into the collar, fish around in my bag for my umbrella.

'Can I ask you something?' I say.

'Yeah, sure.' Yuki's voice is quiet. She looks back at the door to the lounge, and gently pushes it shut.

117

'Why does he call you Anna?'

She shrugs. 'He doesn't like Yuki. He says it sounds fake.'

'But isn't that your name?'

'My preferred name, yes. It's my middle name – I chose to go by it in Year 9. I . . . Listen, it's a little complicated. Well, not that much, but . . . '

'Tell me.'

She sighs, glancing at the door again, then picks up her coat and calls, 'Walking Lou to the bus stop!' Without waiting for an answer, she practically pushes me out, slamming the door behind us.

'You know I'm walking,' I say, reassured to see that she still has a little rebellious spark in her.

'I know.'

For the first time, she tells me of her Japanese grandmother, Yuki, immigrating to the UK as a pregnant bride with her US marine. Of her alcoholic grandad, who died young, and how her grandmother dealt with her isolation and vulnerability by assimilating as much as possible to her new culture. She talks so much, all at once, and I realise she might not have been asked about herself for a while. That I never actually asked her about her name, her heritage.

'She made friends with other, older widows in her street, who taught her to cook shepherd's pie and Yorkshire puddings,' Yuki says. Indoors, she was almost harassed, whispering; now she breathes the October air deep, a mix of toffee and woodsmoke. 'That's what she'd cook for me when I was little, never anything else. My dad was brought up like any other English working-class kid. Nana died when I started secondary school, and I got angry that we never spoke of our Japanese heritage, so I decided to use

118

my middle name. I was a rebellious teenager, trying to make myself different, kinda. It was silly, I'm only a quarter Japanese, but it stuck. I don't really care what people call me now.'

She looks exhausted. And tearful. I've never seen her like this.

'I get it,' I say. 'Being a bit torn.'

'I'm not torn. I know who I am.' She raises her chin, and I wonder if it's a lie. If Yuki only knows who she thinks she ought to be, if that's how she ended up with Ben. I'm scared for her suddenly, at the contrast between this Yuki and the one who tiptoes in his presence. Really scared.

'Ben should call you what you want to be called.'

'Lou, just leave it, okay. He's right: I'm more an Anna than a Yuki, after all. It doesn't matter.'

Does it not? Doesn't Ben secretly dream of dating an Anna Johnson who is a skiing pro and prefers skinny pizza? Yuki could do with a friend, a real one. What is Lucy doing, how is she helping her through all of this? The thought brings back something someone said long in the past. It must have been Nick, but when? *Charlie could do with a friend. Or more.*

'Do you remember Charlotte?' I ask.

'Charlotte who?'

'At your birthday at the Five Horseshoes.'

'When Ben and I got together? Well, I never thought *that* was going to last.'

'Yes, that night. Remember the woman with the big dog that scared you?'

'Ah, yeah.' She blushes. 'Barely. Why?'

'Wasn't she . . . ' I want to say something, but *wouldn't she have been better for you* doesn't make any sense. Why did I

119

even think of her now? Was it in a text of Nick's? I'm pretty sure it wasn't.

Nick texted me earlier. I've been trying not to think about it. He offered to meet up for a drink. We haven't seen each other since I came back, because I always had a good excuse not to, but we have carried on texting. I don't know exactly what has been holding me back, if he's such a good friend, but it feels like the worst timing. I have chosen my trajectory, and I am fearful of anything that might divert me from it.

Yuki frowns. 'Is there something you're trying to tell me?'

'Not unless there's something you'd like to hear.'

She laughs, and stops walking. We have come halfway, and I know she's about to turn back. I don't want to leave her. 'You teachers are so weird. Always batting questions back. Listen, we'll make sure we have a proper evening together before you leave, okay?' A car rushes by, a little too close to the pavement, making Yuki jump. I know the proper evening together won't happen. 'Mate, well done on your news. Really *really* well done.'

'Sorry you didn't get your stuffed-crust pizza,' I say.

I hug her before we part; her hair smells of cheese and her breath on my cheek is winey, acidic, a little sad.

Sunday 24 December 2017

When we're told that time moves forward and every week, day, second lasts the same, we're clearly being deceived. I flew back to Switzerland straight into a dimension where my mother had aged ten years in four months. When I made her a GP appointment, she refused to go, and she's ignored all my suggestions to see a counsellor, telling me my insistence is stressing her out.

Marion says she is going to get better by herself, that the past couple of years have been hard on her, with Grandma's health deteriorating, that she is grieving her now she's gone, but I know she won't improve without help. I'm relieved that I won't be leaving again, a desperate idea that if I keep an eye on her, I won't see her get worse, as though her illness were a weeping angel, only moving when I turn my head away.

'So, where's Romain?'

It's Christmas Eve, yet it doesn't feel like Christmas. There is no piano, no snow, and Mum hasn't bothered with decorations or a tree. Marion and I are standing at the sink. I've only been allowed to dry up because I don't wash thoroughly enough. I don't do the outside of bowls, apparently.

We've left Fabio and Mum in the living room, in the safe company of home-made Christmas biscuits. Mum mentioned she would not make any this year, because they had always been such an imposition on her time. It's hard to realise that all the traditions I love have become such burdens in her eyes. I pleaded with her to teach me, and eventually she complied. I sat down with her and helped her make Grandma's favourites, the vanilla pretzels, crumbly sweet lumps of sand. Mum went through the recipe, to the cadence of my what-nexts, while I handed kitchen implements over to her, sometimes turning my attention away to skip a track on Spotify. I thought that if I played greatest rock hits from the seventies, Mum would cheer up, but most of her favourites suddenly seemed to make her sad.

'Romain's with his family.'

'Don't you think—' Marion starts.

'No, I don't.'

In 2014, the only other Christmas Romain and I spent as a couple, he didn't want to come over, didn't invite me, and we fell out for two weeks. I cried for most of the festivities. I thought it might be different this year – after all, I have moved back because of him – but he's still the same. I said I understood (try something new) and find I don't care as much. I focused on baking instead, and decided that Romain would not get to eat any biscuits.

Perhaps, knowing that my neediness might have been a factor in our first break-up, I've trained myself to act more detached, and by practising, I have become it. It might be due to the past four months of being together but physically apart. I'm so careful with Romain and my feelings towards him that sometimes, especially when Marion probes me, I struggle to bring our relationship together in my head, to feel its threads and knots. I'm scared that the net has been made of thin air and wouldn't catch me or anything else thrown into it.

It is going well, though, considering. I spend the night at his on a regular basis, and we speak on the phone every evening if we're apart. He does things for me such as buying tea bags or those green chocolate pastries I like, *caracs* – Yuki used to say you can tell a man is committed when the contents of his fridge start to change.

Marion is elbow deep in the soapy hot water, and it reminds me of those photos of us having our bath as small children. She'd always throw soap into my eyes because she liked clapping bubbles off with her pudgy hands. I pick up a lump of foam on my index finger and blow it into her face. She shrieks. I haven't heard Marion shriek since she turned ten and started looking at the rest of the world as really immature.

'Stop it! Behave yourself! All right, let's change the subject, no more talking about your ghost boyfriend,' she says, wiping her cheek with her forearm because her hands are wet. 'Teaching?'

'Next.' This is a game we play sometimes.

'Brexit?'

'Yuck. Next.'

'I'm thinking of getting married.' This stops me. I put down the plate I was drying, still wet. She glances at it but doesn't comment.

'To whom?'

'Ha ha. Good one.' She's clearly not amused. 'We've been waiting for things to calm down with Grandma – for Mum to get better,' she continues. 'But we want kids and we'd like to get started soon, so it's a good first step.'

I'm surprised, and I realise it's been a long time since I've been surprised – the emotion grinds like a rusty cog. Marion really has mellowed with me since I spent last summer at home then decided to move back.

I nod. 'Congratulations. That's great, and, well, I'm here now, so maybe I can help Mum a bit, you know. So you have more time to plan it all.'

'I think it *is* good you're back.' The emphasis makes her sound unconvinced. 'As long as it's really what you want. Time will tell, I suppose.'

'I guess it will.' I slam the cupboard door a bit too hard after putting the plates away.

'How was it anyway, leaving your school?' Marion asks.

'Great. Highlight of my time there by far.' And I'm not lying. I received some thank yous, and even a home-made card from Chantelle, Johnny and Fern, which they made from a page torn out of Chantelle's exercise book. Johnny had drawn the three of them as stick figures in black biro, including an electric guitar and some extra muscles for himself, and Fern had added arrows with their names, in case I was too stupid to tell them apart. Chantelle had drawn a French flag and a message that read: *Au revoar! Enjoy Sweden!* and although there was at least one spelling mistake and one factual inaccuracy in there, I nearly burst into tears.

'You never really wanted to be a French teacher,' Marion says. 'Perhaps you weren't meant to be.'

'Well, that's not great, given it's what I'm still going to do.'

124

'You know what I mean.'

'No, I don't know – what *do* you mean?'

'Why are you so defensive? Mum said you called her in tears at least once a week during your training. Don't tell me you're cut out for it.'

I am, yet again, amazed at how everything, to my family, is final. *You're made for this – not made for that.* Sink or swim. They never thought I might stick at it, get better at it, earn the kids' trust until my tutor group stopped slamming the door in my face every morning. I mean, it never seemed to get better, but it could have. If I'd had more time. They don't realise that I miss England too. Nobody seems to mention it any more, as if normal life has simply resumed. But I do miss it; it's not that simple. I miss the rows of red-brick terraces and the rickety Tube and London's infinite possibilities. I miss roast dinners, and the freedom that only distance gives you to reinvent yourself.

We're interrupted by a commotion coming from the lounge. Marion drops the sponge, and we hurry towards the noise, her still wearing dripping washing gloves, me scrunching up the towel in my hands, to find Mum sitting on the sofa quietly insulting herself.

'What an idiot, I can't believe this, I can't do it any more, I'm such an awful . . .'

'What's going on?' Marion asks Fabio. He's picking up biscuit crumbs off the floor.

'I think they might have salt in them instead of sugar,' he says quietly.

'I can't believe I'm so useless,' Mum moans. She's actually shaking. I look at Marion, but her face is closed, and she takes the plate of crumbs out of Fabio's hands.

'It's okay, Mum,' she says. 'No big deal. We'll throw them away, that's all.' Mum opens her mouth, and for a minute, I fear she is going to wail, but then she closes it again.

'Which ones?' I ask, hovering over the biscuit platter Marion put together so beautifully, rows of perfectly innocent-looking treats.

'Those.' She points at the vanilla pretzels. I start to remove them all, placing them on the plate Marion is holding out for me. 'I told you,' Mum is speaking to me directly this time, 'you forced me to make them, I didn't want to, it stressed me out.'

I flinch, look to Marion for support, but she is staring at the plate.

'Don't worry, Mum, honestly,' she says.

'I don't like when people expect things from me. I don't like it one bit,' Mum continues. 'I cared for you since you were born, I did everything by myself since your father left. Is it too much to ask not to have to make you biscuits now?'

'Okay, Mum,' I say, but it comes out too harsh. A headache is growing in my skull like a tightening iron bar. I feel like I should have known about this, anticipated the disaster, but I didn't. A memory comes of something that hasn't happened, another first Christmas without Grandma, subdued and blue, when we didn't get Mum involved and Marion, Fabio and I made food that tasted almost right and pretended there had never been any biscuits made for Christmas. What did I do differently this time (*this time?*)? I tried to help Mum stay anchored in our traditions and I made it all worse. I'm helpless and wanting the very person who isn't able to comfort me.

Mum didn't use to be like this. I used to think she was

126

the strongest person I knew. I never saw her cry. She had friends she would go out for dinner with, or meet for coffee in town on Saturday mornings before the weekly shop at Migros. Every time Marion and I came home from school, there were cakes or biscuits baking in the oven. The flat always smelled of toasted hazelnuts and care. I don't know how quickly she became this different person, but it seems now that it happened in the blink of an eye, or worse: when I wasn't paying enough attention.

'Excuse me,' I say, avoiding Marion's glare telling me I always run away at a time of crisis. I take the plate of salt biscuits, drop them all into the kitchen bin, and go to my room, closing the door behind me. Out of the window, mountain side, I stare at the steep and overbuilt slopes. I have a shiny new job, I have Romain, Marion and Fabio want to get married. It should all be fabulous. Yet joys are being ripped from my body like plasters and I don't know what I should do for them to stick. I miss England. I shouldn't, but I do.

Perhaps I should call Romain. Isn't he the very person who should listen to me and cheer me up? But I'm unsure. I quickly play our potential conversation in my head – I think I would sound silly, even needy. I go to unlock my phone, and see that I have a message.

> Hey, happy Christmas. You celebrate
> on Christmas Eve in Switzerland
> dont you? Looked it up :) Thinking
> of you hope all is well

Nick. I hadn't heard from him in a while. Warmth shoots through me, as if I'd just drunk some mulled wine, making me realise how cold I've been feeling in Mum's flat. I have a sudden urge to see him, to sit with him on a pub bench, in the cosy smell of a wood burner. I think he would understand, and I open a new message to reply, but nothing I type makes sense. *I feel like I've lived through this Christmas before, yet somehow I've managed to make it worse. I feel like I ought to be so, so much happier than I am.* In a moment of madness, bravery, yearning, I press call instead.

Nick's voice as he picks up, even from miles away, is deep and textured, like wool. It wraps me up completely.

'Hiya,' I say, embarrassed. 'Sorry, I know it's Christmas Eve . . .'

'Lou, I was just thinking of you, that's grand.'

'I hope I'm not interrupting anything?'

'Ah, not at all. I'm just round my parents' with Charlie, mainly keeping the dog from eating the Christmas cake. What about you? Are you having a nice time at home?'

'Oh, I'm not sure. My mum is having a bit of a meltdown, I think.'

The sound of a door being shut.

'There,' Nick says, 'I'm all ears.'

'Your parents won't be angry you're missing out?'

He chuckles. I'm transported to the smoking shelter, in the intimate darkness, the light of his cigarette a much better Christmas sparkle than what Mum's flat has to offer right now. I wish I could go back. 'Ah, my mum will. She's quite protective of our family events, you know, quite fierce.'

'She sounds great.'

'She is. But tell me about yours – what's going on?'

I tell him everything. Everything Christmas used to be, everything it's failing to be now, my worries about my family, about where I belong. Nick listens to me until darkness starts to fall outside, the Wi-Fi connection a frail, invisible Christmas garland linking Switzerland and England through the night.

Sunday 18 March 2018

Romain's chest is so hot, it's not comfortable to cuddle him too close. In this mid-morning liquid haze, my eyelids are heavy but my brain is awake.

Something has been making me hyper aware for a while. I keep noticing little ways in which things aren't quite right, such as Romain's body temperature, his complete lack of interest in dogs. Our relationship has slowed to a halt as I try to adjust what I do and say to get it moving again. I stand in front of my wardrobe every morning, taking longer and longer to decide what to wear, every single small decision carrying weight. I feel responsible for Mum, for Marion's happiness, for Romain's state of mind. I'm running low on my own resources. *This*, this life I'm in right now, is not the way I had pictured things, and I can't fathom what I've done wrong.

'What would have happened if I hadn't replied to your text?' I ask Romain.

He likes to sleep in at the weekends, while I lie awake

next to him, missing Yuki's early fry-ups. I wasn't on duty at school, so I came to him, because I have less space to feel lonely in his physical proximity. Although the flat I've been allocated on school premises is nice, it doesn't feel like mine, merely borrowed – which it is, I suppose. Romain's doesn't feel like mine either. I opened the fridge last night to find no milk there. He bought tea for me in December, but hasn't replenished it since it ran out.

His answer is a sleepy moan. 'What text?'

I roll away from him, propping my head on my hand so I can look at his face. It's a tricky balance. All of this. Sometimes I just want to give up and fall backwards.

'The one you sent to invite me to your launch.'

'I didn't invite you. I informed you.'

I've heard this before, and today I have no patience for it.

'Okay, well, regardless, you said you missed me. And look at us now – it *worked*, you lucky man.' I probe his foot with mine playfully, but it is limp. 'So what would have happened?'

He has one eye opened now.

'You know I don't believe in fate or destiny or—'

'I know, but . . .'

'I guess I would have simply met somebody else by now.'

Ah. This isn't the reassurance I wanted – I should have known not to go there. I think about the young dead woman of his book, about Aurélie Something at his launch, pushing their hair away from their ears to listen closer.

'Would you rather have?'

He laughs, and his hand finds my knee under the duvet. It burns. 'Listen, perhaps you shouldn't ask questions you know you won't like the answers to.'

131

'But would you?' I don't push his hand off, but I'm not sure I want it there. I don't know what exactly I'm trying to stir up with this conversation.

'Would have, should have,' he says. 'What's the point in wondering? We only have one life anyway, and the fact is, I'm here, right now, with you.'

I attempt once again to count my blessings, so that they don't suffocate under everything else. I've found the pressure at the international school hard, the constant blurredness of work seeping into life, but I am getting through with the help of many spreadsheets, there's a photocopying budget, and the challenging students are more discreet, more under-hand, so I can pretend I don't see them snigger. Marion and I go and see Mum at least once a week, and I think Mum might appreciate it, though it's hard to tell. Marion asked me the other day who in the family would be more likely to suffer a nervous breakdown. We both said each other, and laughed. Things could be much worse.

Romain's hand moves from my knee to my thigh, higher and higher. I think of snapping it away, but I'm worried the rejection might be impossible to come back from. With him, I've learnt, little things can turn a room for ever. I think of telling him I'm going to make coffee, and getting up, but he's into his stride now, and suddenly he's on top of me. He kisses me and I kiss him back. I can get into this. I just need . . . a bit more time? What do I need exactly? I have everything I ever wanted. My brain is running away, anywhere but the now. Back to when I fantasised about Romain, because I couldn't have him. I don't remember sex with him being like this. I don't remember needing so much time to get into it – I don't remember minding when things moved on so fast, when we were clearly going to have sex but by the time he took care of it I wasn't quite there yet, quite ready in my head. Why do I mind now? *Are* we clearly going to have sex? Is my presence in his bed on a Sunday morning really enough as a sign of consent? I don't remember, before, choosing the option to retreat inwards as far as possible and wish it over quickly. Medea, playing dead.

After, he says I should choose something to do today, so we go to the Roman Museum. I've heard of the new exhibition there, called 'Archaeology of Us', imagining what future archaeologists will make of our lives, which I've been excited to check out. Nick thought it sounded cool, despite not being into museums, when I mentioned it to him. We talked for a bit about what objects we'd like to leave for posterity. He suggested a hoodie, and I mentioned his keys. It seems like me calling him at Christmas gave us some kind of permission, and we have been speaking on the phone regularly since.

Examining each artefact is like stepping into the same tiny existential loop. Computer circuits covered in soil; 'Children's game, pawns missing, circa 2000'. I weirdly find some comfort in the message: the dizzying scale of the future annihilates who I think I am right now. A little bit of perspective, helping me to deactivate some of my immediate worries that things aren't what they ought to be. It's also rather witty – I find myself chuckling at a broken Fitbit labelled 'Ceremonial bracelet', while Romain yawns next to me. I know he'd rather leave and go to the café, but I've been pretending not to notice because I'm enjoying myself.

The next artefact is a 'Votive figure': a broken Barbie, naked, soiled, staring at me with one scratched eye.

'What happened to you, Barbie? What's your story?' I muse, and Romain frowns.

'It's a plastic toy.'

'What do you mean?' I ask him, instead of agreeing. I can tell he wasn't expecting to have to explain himself, but he's making me grumpy now. Nick and I decided that my satchel would be the best object to represent me, because it has carried my entire life back and forth between two countries. I know leather wouldn't last, unless I ended up in a bog, I'm not an idiot. But those things, the objects we wear and carry, Nick's tattoo, his casual clothes, the grey of his eyes, the *materiality* of us, are far from pointless.

'Well, all these silly things to remember us by. I'd trade them all for a single good book,' Romain says.

'Wasn't *she* in your last book, though?' I gesture to the soiled Barbie, trying to keep my voice nonchalant, but fighting the urge to break her out of her glass coffin to bash Romain on the head.

'What?'

I find it impossible to back off. Something has come over me. I think it was thinking of Nick, and finding myself here with moody Romain instead.

'The dead girl in your book.'

'I don't even know how your brain works sometimes.'

'I think you quite like women to be dolls,' I say.

That was harsh. Harsh, but . . . it was like the words had been ready for me for weeks, and I had refused to acknowledge them. And now they're out.

Romain steps forward, resuming his visit, which is more akin to a straight march towards the exit, one hand stroking his quiff.

'You're being ridiculous,' he says as I follow him. 'If you're calling me a player ...' I scoff, and he looks even more offended. 'Is this what you think my book is about?'

Are we doing this? Have I started this? Where's the reset button? Panic rises, struggling against a sense of intense frustration – even, if I'm really honest, anger.

'This is not about your fucking book,' I hiss, and he stops dead in shock.

Present Louise is running ahead, leaving past Louise behind. Past Louise is pale with worry, wringing in her hands the severed head of a Ken doll. It's like another time dimension has opened and suddenly I see what I have been refusing to see. Romain did act this morning as if I only existed for his satisfaction, and he's been using me like this for ever. As far back as we go, in fact. The shape of our story has tilted on its axis, offering itself from a different angle. Romain approaching me at the library when I was lost and directionless, making me need him then scolding me for being too needy. His telling me I had to grow a life to become more interesting. Editing my writing. Pretending he hadn't invited me to his launch, then waiting a month to text me again when he had said he would. He would never see me, whatever I did. It would always all be on his terms. And I thought I wanted that, because it was easier to be told what to be than decide for myself and get it wrong.

'So you hate my book,' Romain says.

'No offence, but I didn't completely like it.' I'm imme-diately annoyed at my own words for being so tame. I can't see myself giving him a lesson about consent, about respect, in the middle of a semi-ironic exhibition about the future of humanity. It's pointless anyway.

He stays very calm, stroking his hair with both hands.

'I'm not surprised,' he finally says, 'given the crap you normally read.'

Romain has no idea what I read, because I now read in English. He's only noticed the colours of the book covers, which make him classify them immediately as 'commercial'. He has no idea what I enjoy, no idea who I am. I moulded myself around who he needed me to be, but he didn't give me a choice if I wanted to be with him. And I thought I did, until the broken Barbie.

'All the critics have said the same, though,' I tell him, sour berries on my tongue. 'It's not about taste, it's about . . . using women's bodies like that – that obsession with a defenceless, pure woman who can never expect to be listened to, who can never expect to be rescued at Christmas—'

'It's fiction, Louise.'

'Well, it stinks. In my humble intellectual opinion.'

A tear in the fabric of the argument, a moment when we both freeze, and I realise past Louise would have grabbed her sewing kit and desperately set off to repair the damage she had caused. But I want to keep ripping.

'*You* can talk about women's bodies.' Romain stops in front of the shop, lowers his voice, almost hisses, 'You hardly know you have one.'

'Excuse me?'

'When we . . . have sex, you just – you know – lie there, you're clearly not interested.'

I'm shaking, and I don't know if it's with rage or humiliation. There is a pause, when even he knows he has gone too far, and the venom drains away, leaving his voice neutral and businesslike. I steady myself. I want him out of my life right now. What a disaster.

'I can't be with somebody who doesn't support my writing,' he says, another adamant meerkat.

'I don't think you should, no,' I say, once I've regained my composure. 'And I can't be with somebody who'd rather fuck a doll.'

'Don't be crass,' he snaps.

I bury my hands deep in my coat pockets. We walk through the shop to the exit and emerge into a pale, drizzly March afternoon. There we both stop a couple of steps away from each other, shoulders up, blinking in the natural light.

'Male and female book holders, broken up, circa 18 March 2018,' I say. I'm much calmer now. It's happened. Again. Yet it's still the same day, the same sky.

Of course, Romain is still furious too. 'Whatever, Louise. Perhaps don't come to my next book launch.'

'Good luck. I mean it,' I say. With those reviews, it's unlikely there will ever be another book launch.

And because he's Romain, he claims this new dramatic ending for himself and walks away first. Signature move. I would have been going in the same direction, to take the same bus. This new Louise, purified with fire, stands awkwardly between space and time for a while, cold droplets of rain falling right where her hair parts.

I wait a bit longer for something to happen, for my consciousness to be snatched away from this disaster, unable to cope, for the realisation and loss to hit me hard, but I'm not distraught. Just a little empty. I can still feel the shape of past Romain and past Louise, like those Pompeii casts, the prints of bodies that have long dissolved. I have invested so much in the archaeology of Romain and me, and now that it's over, it actually feels right.

I open WhatsApp to text Nick, to distract myself. I want to tell him about the exhibit, about the magic powers of zooming back and forth in time, of Fitbits.

Are you at the zoo?

What YES. How did you know?

Yes, how did I know? I didn't even think, I just . . . I could scare myself with my psychic knowledge.

Didn't you tell me? It's the right depressing Sunday for it.

Depressing? Want me to go and say hello to any of the animals for you?

This makes me smile. I want to say capybaras, but something tells me otherwise. Something.

Otters, please.

Just a sec

I don't have anywhere to go right now, so I stand on the pavement. Some cars whoosh by, but Sundays are pretty dead in Switzerland, even in cities. I long for the constant bustling of St Albans, the open cafés, the many shops where you can always buy a funny card or a scented candle in exchange for your weight in gold. A few minutes later, a photo pings through. It's a selfie of Nick in front of an empty pen of murky water and rocks.

Evil bastards ran out of the shot

I type, *Only you can make me laugh in these moments*, delete it as another feeling grows, stronger and familiar. That I might have missed something very important, because Romain was holding me hostage in my own life, because I wasn't paying attention to the right things. And now I'm free from him, clear-headed for the first time in years.

Romain and I broke up.

> Shit Im so sorry, its fucked up.
> After you moved back for him
> and everything. Bastard

It's okay. I kind of feel it was
mutual in the end.

A pause.

> As long as youre okay

I am. That's the weird thing –
I feel relieved. Romain was
always in such a bad mood.

Always baffles me how some people can
be such drains to others. Thats why Im
pleased I've been single for so long.

He's ended it with a winky smiley face.

Sometimes I worry about it.

About what?

Being a drain. One of those people.

Nick's response comes after a while, during which I worry
he thinks I'm right.

You're not Lou that's the thing. Youre
sensitive and goofy and kind. Listen,
Ive been meaning to say for a while,
our conversation that night in the
smoking shelter stuck with me. Id
been feeling shite, I dont know. And
there you strutted up to me all full of
questions – you brightened me right up

My heart starts pounding in my chest. I'm here, in
Lausanne, not at the zoo. A residential street with blue
parking spaces, lined with square coral buildings, the wrong
types of number plates. The wrong place.

WhatsApp says Nick is still typing, so I wait. More rain
falls on my skull. He is typing for an awfully long time.

140

Listen, I know its not great timing
but just going to put it out there and
you don't have to do anything with
it. What Im trying to say Louise is I
like you. You should come back to
the UK and go to the zoo with me

How long has it been so obvious that I should be with
Nick? Because I like him too. And I'm floored by this feeling of certainty that he and I have already missed our best
moments, that there's not enough left, not enough time. That
I wasted all of it on Romain.

If only ... if only I'd seen that option. If I hadn't been
blinded to it – that I was meant to be with Nick. I wish it so
hard, I want it so much, that my breath freezes in my throat.
I gasp – a vaguely familiar feeling, reality losing its grip on
me – and start slipping through. I press my hands on my ears,
vaguely aware of some people stopping alongside me to ask
if I'm okay, but the world has slowed down. I push my way
toward the threshold, the museum's door opening up for
me, beckoning me back inside, where time is a melting pot
of dust and uncertainties and possibilities and broken objects
that can be mended. I'm leaving Nick hanging on the phone
to meet him again, try again, do it right this time ...

*

We go back.

141

CHANCE 3

Saturday 15 July 2017

'Are you with us, Lou? You've kinda been grinning like mad since you got here.'

Yuki and Lucy are staring at me. For the past ten minutes, I've been relishing the sour fragrance of vinegar and ale. I feel dizzy. Am I about to hyperventilate? Everything tingles, from the tips of my fingers to the cavities of my ears. I feel like I've been deprived of air for a bit too long, like I've arrived from a place of regret, straight into the sun. I have a growing certainty that I've been here before. It's mind-boggling, but I also know in my heart that there's nothing I left behind that I'll miss. As I stand there, all I feel is relief and incredible, incredible luck: it's Yuki's birthday and everything is fine, *still*. I want to embrace it. I'm ready for what could be.

'Sorry,' I say.

'Whatcha holding there?' Yuki asks.

I'm clinging on to the fruit basket so tightly that the

wrapping paper has torn over the edges. I present it to her, emboldened by the memory of it taking pride of place in her lounge, with the excitement of a warrior bringing treasure back from the dragon's lair.

'I thought you'd fancy one of these,' I say as she tears the paper off. 'For your new house. Sorry it's a bit bulky.'

'Thanks, mate!' Yuki says. Lucy's eyebrows rise. 'That's awesome.'

It strikes me how happy and *Yuki* she is, with her skilfully pinned hair, the cheerfulness of her clothes, her glowing skin. I want to hug her, so I do.

'Happy birthday,' I say.

'This is the most Yuki present ever,' Lucy scoffs.

Yuki tells her, gleeful, 'You'll have to put away all your rotting satsumas!'

'I thought – storage space and cleaning and bees and such . . . ' I trail off.

'What now?' Yuki asks. Then, to Lucy: 'What is she looking at?'

A few tables away, a handsome man is making his sister laugh. The fibres of my heart start stretching towards him. I know his name is Nick, and I want nothing more than to get closer – I need to meet him. I've learnt, though the why and how are blurred and unclear, that he's all I want – kind, funny, caring. That it's not *any* relationship I want, but a relationship with *him*; that I got so, so close, and somehow missed it. Well, not this time.

He looks at ease. Tan, messy honey-streaked hair, grin and all. I watch the muscles of his arm roll as he picks up his glass, holding my breath halfway in my lungs as he drinks, as if he were performing some kind of fire-eating trick.

I don't hear what Lucy says to Yuki, but Nick's sister has spotted me, and she bends forward to whisper something to him. I can see in his smile to her and the tilt of his head that he's trying not to look my way. Oh no. He's acting as if he doesn't know me, and it dawns on me that if we have really jumped backwards, if there's something strange happening with me and my timeline – and I suspect there is, some kind of glitch in my existence – all he'll see is a stalker with a lunatic grin. Everything, I realise, must happen tonight exactly as it did before, at first at least, or else it could go disastrously wrong. I flush and force my attention back to my drink; in my haste, the bubbles catch in my throat and I splutter. Yuki taps me gently on the back.

'Steady there, matey.'

There should be a dog, I remember. The dog is key, but key to what? When I've managed to expel the sticky liquid from my lungs, I try to hide behind my hair and steal another glance. I find a stunning Bernese lying under the woman's bench. My eyes meet hers again, then Nick's, and it's like I've touched an electric fence. It's not good. They're staring now. This wasn't supposed to happen – I must do something. *Just strut up to me . . .* I get up and walk to their table.

They're both waiting for me to say something, but I don't know what I could or should say.

Nick breaks the excruciating silence. 'Have we met before?'

'Excuse me,' I say. 'Sorry to bother you. Is it okay if I say hello to your dog?'

Nick looks amused, but his sister is stern. The awe I feel in her presence is familiar too.

'Ah, yes, I suppose,' she says. 'Go ahead, if you can reach him.'

147

She bends a little to check on the dog, and I crouch down so I can locate which side his snout is – it's hard to tell as he's currently so flat. I plunge my fingers into his thick fur, coarser on his back than the top of his head and his ears, trying to ignore the worry that I'm not merely a safe observer any more. Things will be different, but I don't know what was supposed to happen exactly. I'm a navigator in darkness. All I know is Nick.

'I told you she wasn't looking at me,' Nick tells his sister.

I blush and focus on stroking the dog.

'To be fair, Chomsky's much better-looking than you,' she says. For somebody so self-assured, so aloof, there's something pleasingly gauche to her teasing. It lasts for about a second, and she's back to herself, staring down at me, clearly worried I might be a dog thief.

'He's gorgeous . . .' I stumble.

I know there's only so much cuddling this sleepy dog can take before I appear to be way too clingy. The proximity of Nick is distracting me. I need to get him to the smoking shelter. The smoking shelter? How do I do that?

'Do you both live here?' I ask.

'Oh no, Charlie lives in Finchley. It's rare for her to venture beyond Zone 3.'

Charlotte doesn't seem inclined to answer herself.

'What about you, Nick?' I ask. He looks surprised. Damn. What have I said now?

'I moved here two years ago. I work at the primary school around the corner.' I already know all this, but he's unaware. I suddenly feel despondent; as far as he's concerned, we've just met.

'Are you still with us?'

148

I've missed something he said. I was running ahead with my worries into the next minutes, days, months. Suddenly wondering how anyone ever gets it right. *Every single small decision you make can spoil it all.* I've had this thought before, haven't I?

'Sorry?'

'I asked if you're from Switzerland,' Nick says. 'Sorry if I'm wrong – I thought you had a Swiss accent.'

'I am,' I say. 'But people usually assume I'm from somewhere in eastern Europe, when they don't think I'm French.'

'Or Swedish,' Nick says. We smile at each other.

'I'd better be off, Nick,' Charlotte says, checking her phone. She gets up, retrieving Chomsky's lead, adjusting the strap of her handbag on her shoulder.

'I'll walk you to the station.' Nick has got up too, as has Chomsky, and the four of us are now awkwardly standing between tables while they wait for me to leave. I glance back to see Yuki and Lucy talking to Ben, the people around them chatting, oblivious. Chomsky stretches, and I long to gently boop him in the direction of Yuki's chair, but Charlotte is watching me like a hawk, so I daren't go anywhere near him. I can't let Nick leave.

'Just come and say hi to my friend Yuki on your way, then, it's her birthday,' I try, sounding utterly pathetic.

Nick's eyes are amused, and Charlotte's impatient, and I reach for the lever that can shut down the cringing part of my brain, otherwise I would probably torture myself with this moment for the next hundred years. I'm pleased to find there is a lever now, a way to keep going rather than retract in awkwardness.

'I really must be off,' Charlotte says.

'I think you know someone at our table,' I tell Nick.

'I think I might. Hang on, Charlie ...'

Luckily, bored Chomsky appears to have found a dusty chip by Yuki's foot.

She shrieks, turning around, half standing up as though she's been bitten. Ben laughs.

'He's only a dog,' Charlotte snaps.

'Nick Harper?' Max says.

'And what if he bites me? What if I'm scared of dogs? You should watch him,' Yuki snaps back.

Relief washes over me as it all unfolds, two scenes superimposed on the same reel. While Nick and Max engage in a heart-warming reunion, Yuki and Charlotte stare at each other, waiting for the other to blink.

'He's friendly,' Charlotte snaps, pulling the dog back to her heel.

'Kinda doesn't look it,' Yuki says, as Chomsky drops down on the floor and offers her his belly for stroking.

There are holes in my instinct that are making me uncomfortable. Big gaps in what will, or could, or should not happen. Yuki and Charlotte should meet properly, Yuki should stay away from lawyer Ben, currently looking like he's sucking lemons as her attention has been taken away from him. Right now, this all appears to be important, and although I should feel powerful, it is utterly terrifying that I could still make the ripples spread in the wrong direction. That I probably already have. Too many lives intersect here for me to keep tabs on them all.

'Chomsky, sit,' Charlotte says, and he does. She turns to Nick, tugging at the sleeve of his T-shirt. I imagine her as a little girl, doing what adult Charlotte still does without thinking. It's endearing. His tattoo's there, I catch a glimpse of it. Longboats on a beach? 'I'm going,' she insists.

'Wait a minute, I'll walk you,' Nick says, pausing his conversation with Max.

'No, that's fine. You stay.'

'Are you sure?'

'Nick, the station's ten minutes away, and I have my ferocious beast to protect me.' She gives Yuki a pointed look.

'All right, if you're sure,' he says. 'Text me when you're home safe, okay?' He squeezes her, both his arms wrapping around her shoulders.

I hear her mutter against his T-shirt before she leaves: 'And listen, Nick, it'll happen for you. It will. Just you wait.'

Butterflies take flight in me, from the deep.

Somebody offers to shuffle along so that Nick can sit between Max and Yuki, and I get back to my seat, miraculously still free.

I've done it. I look at Yuki, who is a little flustered. Avoiding my gaze, she gets up and leaves. The bench's edge gnaws into the back of my thighs. I could ask her what's wrong, but I also know that her leaving is part of how things should go. This evening is the hardest thing I've ever done, juggling glass balls in the dark, steering events towards what? All I know is Nick. I blush when I think of him. *Our conversation that night in the smoking shelter stuck with me* – but the conversation hasn't happened yet, and what does *this* Nick want? Is he the same Nick? Will he like me too? I finally gather enough calm and courage to look at him.

It appears that Yuki's exit has focused Lucy's attention onto him. I was expecting him to be entertaining the whole table with his stories, but now he seems to be talking to Lucy

151

only. She doesn't need to bend in quite so much to listen to him; I can hear their conversation from where I sit.

'What about you, Lucy,' he asks. 'What do you do?'

She combs back her thick, wavy hair. Her bangles clink together as she lifts her wrists. She explains her boring job, clearly trying hard to make it sound fascinating.

'You must travel a lot,' Nick says. *Travelling is always a good topic on a date.* A date?

'Oh, you know.' A flick of her shoulders to indicate that yes, but it's no big deal. 'What about you?'

'What, as a primary school teacher?'

She laughs. 'No, of course not, I mean in your many holidays. You look like you travel too.'

'No, not really,' Nick says, and I love the fact that he doesn't pretend, doesn't dig deep to find common ground.

'Why not?' Lucy asks.

'Dunno. Money mainly. Don't have the energy to plan it all either.'

'You don't always need to plan. Buy a plane ticket. Go on an adventure.'

Lucy's kitchen surfaces might be neglected, but she isn't an adventurer. I know from Yuki that she mainly travels for work and stays in five-star hotels in Barcelona and Dubai. There hasn't been a single spark of backpacking spirit in her since, let me guess, she had that incredible festival experience she secretly hated; not a single fibre of that green green grass stuck to her silk top and suit trousers. That's how I know she's trying to impress Nick, attempting to be a person she imagines would attract him, and it scares me.

Nick shrugs. 'I went backpacking in my twenties,' he says. 'Thailand. Wasn't for me.'

I watch as Lucy's hand travels across the table to rest a few inches away from Nick's wrist. The guy sitting next to me bends forward at this very moment, blocking my view.

'Hi, I'm—'

'Not now, Ben,' I snap.

He retracts immediately and has no other choice than to try and join Lucy and Nick's conversation, but of course Lucy won't let him. I notice with relief that Nick has drawn his hand away, fiddling with his packet of tobacco and lighter.

'Lucy,' I call. She doesn't want to hear me. I try again.

'Yes?' She turns to me, clearly annoyed.

'Yuki's been gone for a while.'

'Yuki's always ages. That woman has the bladder of a great rhino,' she says, and turns her gaze back to Nick.

'Actually,' he tells her, 'all mammals pee for about twenty seconds, no matter their size.'

I smile at him. I knew he would have something interesting to say about pee.

'Do you think we should go check on her?' I ask Lucy. I'm desperate; I don't know what else to do to get her away from Nick.

'She's fine. But if you're worried, by all means, yeah, go and check.'

Nick's eyes are on me. He gives me a sympathetic smile, and returns to Lucy listing all the places in the world he *must absolutely visit* before he dies. I gathered from Yuki that Nick would be the kind of guy Lucy might have a secret fling with, someone she wouldn't publicly claim. Not ambitious enough, too scruffy. A bit of fun.

When I stand up, my legs are shaking. I can't stay and

listen to them now I've pretended to be worried about Yuki. I grab my empty glass and walk to the back door of the pub, dragging my body and my mind in my heels. I was so happy to be back, and I've somehow derailed it all within an hour.

The world inside the pub is warm and dense and loud. I stop dead on the threshold: Yuki is standing between the ladies' and the main entrance, all the way across the room, talking to Charlotte. They're both leaning on the ledge along the wall, Yuki's right forearm laid out towards Charlotte, her palm open as she speaks. They can't still be arguing about dogs. They're only talking, a pair of gorgeous human bookends, yet I feel like a voyeur. Of course. Yuki and Charlotte. The chemistry is obvious even from where I'm standing.

Hovering between inside and out, I look back to our table. Nick and Lucy are still chatting, and the fact that Ben looks left out and offended is hardly enough consolation.

My pocket buzzes, sending a shock of surprise up to my chest. Romain. I open the message, which I find already branded in my subconscious, and hit reply. I have to keep blinking, as I step aside to let two lads walk past me, loud and drunk. *Oi, don't get messed up.*

> No, I won't come. I don't think
> you actually miss me. And
> commiserations in advance for the
> reviews. They will be terrible.

I hit send, put my phone back into my pocket and press my fingers on my eyelids.

'So what do you think is going on there?'

154

Nick has joined me on the threshold, looking past my head at Charlotte and Yuki.

'You all right? No offence, Louise, but you don't look it. It's Louise, right?' he asks, suddenly uncertain.

I nod. I'm all right now, because he's here. He studies my face for a split second.

'Would you mind helping me with these?' He's carrying about five empties, and I take a couple off him. It's a tricky handover operation, and he thanks me as the glasses clink between our bodies. He nods me forward and follows me to the bar, where we drop our cargo.

'What are you having?'

I ask for one of those sickly-sweet strawberry ciders and he gets a pint of lemonade for himself; he doesn't roll his eyes or comment on my teenage drinking habits. I'm bracing myself to follow him back outside, to Lucy and the others, but to my surprise, he moves a little further along the bar, where there's an empty space, and I follow him. He nods towards Charlotte and Yuki, winking.

'Are we really doing this?' I feel giddy, and I haven't had any of my sugary drink yet.

'What do you think we're doing?' His grin. Goodness.

'Spying your sister and my friend.'

'Would you rather go back out there?' he asks, pointing. 'Because I saw you shut down that lawyer creep.'

'Ben?'

'I guess. He looks like a Ben.'

'No, I don't want to go back out. What about you?'

'What do you mean?'

'Lucy? You were planning a holiday?' I hope I don't come across as jealous. Well, I am jealous. In a burning, devasting kind of way. I pick up my drink and swallow about a quarter of it in one go; the taste is so sweet that only the ice-cold bubbles make it bearable. Delicious.

'She's nice,' Nick says. 'But I'm more interested in finding out why my sister's still here.'

'And I want to know whether my friend is going to make the right decision this time.'

'The right decision? This time?'

'Falling for somebody who doesn't . . . ' I blush, searching for the right words, '*drain* her.'

'Right,' he says.

I bury my face in my glass again and turn to watch Yuki and Charlotte. Yuki is clearly being her charming self, locks of hair falling out of the pins and brushing her face, and Charlotte hides her mouth as she laughs. I can't see Nick if I'm turned towards them. I don't know if he's looking at them too, or at his drink, or the back of my head. In this small space, in the boisterous atmosphere of a Friday night in July, I'm deeply aware of his presence, notes of leather and cotton and sun, and the warm, almost electric distortion around the edges of his body. I fizz with it.

'Charlie isn't usually a giggler,' his low and amused voice says close behind me.

'Isn't she? Why is that?' I've only ever seen Charlotte being aloof, or sad. I have a vague recollection of an Instagram profile, of a bay window.

'She thinks it makes her mouth look weird. Don't get me wrong, I love her to bits, and she has her moments. It's just . . . ' He nods towards them again, without the need to explain.

'I know,' I say. 'I haven't seen Yuki like this for ages either.'

This is both true and untrue, and I drink some more so that my head doesn't explode. 'Actually, this is quite nice.'

'You mean having a drink with me?' The grin again. Allowing myself to grin with him feels amazing. 'How did you know my name, by the way?'

And just like that, the sun disappears behind a cloud.

'When?' I ask, trying not to meet his gaze.

'Earlier. When you talked to us. You knew my name.'

'Your sister must have said . . .' I let my voice trail off, hoping it'll make some kind of sense. 'You knew my name too.'

'So I did,' he says. 'I must have overheard. Heck, let's do this properly, shall we? I'm Nick. Nice to meet you.'

He offers his hand, and the déjà vu is so strong that I fear I'm going to fall off the bar stool. I hesitate, then shake it, quick and skittish. It's only a hand, Lou. Bones and tendons under skin. Breathe.

For a little while we talk about teaching and our common experiences. I slowly let go of the worry that there are right and wrong things to say, that I have to steer the conversation a particular way, and relax into our chat. This is Nick, after all, and I know he liked me even when I wasn't trying.

We confer and chuckle like the worst spies in the world, Nick sometimes glancing over my shoulder to give me updates ('Charlotte's touched her hair, and Yuki too. It's that *mirror* thing, isn't it?'), until, out of the blue, he stands up.

'Shit. Charlie's leaving, Yuki's coming back. If she sees us, she'll know we were snooping. Come on!'

He presses his palm on my wrist and I want to catch it, anchor it there, I want him to linger, but he hurries out and I follow, around the side of the building to the smoking shelter. It's night, a curtain drawn on the outside world while we were in the pub. The air isn't much cooler and the tables are still full. In the shelter, however, it's only Nick and me.

'Think she didn't see us,' he says. He produces his packet of tobacco and opens it, fishing out a rolled cigarette. 'Do you mind?'

'Not at all. So what happened, with Yuki and Charlotte? I missed the end.'

'You're the worst spy in the world.' He lights a cigarette. In the darkness, which is only cut by a weak orange lamp on the external wall of the pub, his face is glowing. Warm, close. 'Looked like they swapped numbers.'

I shriek.

'Shh,' he laughs. He nods towards Yuki, who is gliding past, not noticing us in the slightest. She drops back onto her chair to the exclamations of her friends – *What the hell were you doing all this time?* – and I think that not one of those friends went to look for her, but the proximity of Nick soon diverts my thoughts.

He's holding his cigarette in the wrong hand so that his body protects me from the smoke, and he's laughing and coming closer ...

My phone starts ringing. Nick steps back and looks at me expectantly, so I pull it out. The screen glows grey-blue in the shelter, cooling everything down. Romain is calling. Actually *calling*.

'Aren't you going to ... ' Nick asks.

I never bothered to set up a voice mailbox; Romain will soon realise this. I pray for him to hang up now, but the phone buzzes and buzzes in my hand. I can't remember which button to press to cancel the call, and I'm worried I'll accidentally pick up. He's insistent. He must be furious at the text I sent him.

'It's . . . it's my ex,' I say to Nick. 'He texted earlier that he missed me.' Dammit, Louise. Why would you say that?

'Wow,' Nick says. He steps away to squeeze his cigarette in one of the ashtrays. I want to kick myself. 'And do you? Miss him?'

'No. I wish he'd leave me alone.'

The phone is still ringing. Nick takes it from my hand, presses the green button. I gasp.

'Hello,' he says. 'Louise's phone.'

Romain says something, and Nick's face melts in horror and hilarity. He places his hand on the receiver, turning to me. 'Shit. You didn't tell me he spoke French.' He appears to concentrate deeply, lines creasing his forehead. He's so handsome, my fingers are tingling. '*Je suis désolé, Louise elle est* . . . busy.' Pause. He's avoiding my gaze. '*Ouais. Très* busy. Yeah, that's right. Bye.'

Clearly proud of himself, he hands my phone back to me. 'Sorry, I only got an E at GCSE. How did I do?'

'More like *what* have you done?' I'm laughing, worried that if I punch his arm and scold him for his terrible French, we'll forever be mates and history will repeat itself over and over again, but Nick walks forward, one single step, and leans in. His hand reaches me first, under my ear, pressing my hair against my neck. His mouth is warm and smoky and he's still smiling as he kisses me, both hands cupping the sides of my face, and I smile too and melt into his warmth, our giddiness, this glorious moment of something missed that has finally, *finally* happened.

Friday 18 August 2017

'And then Ellie says . . . ' Nick shifts a little to pull me closer.

'She's not in heaven, she's in the green bin!' I say. His nose is pressing on the top of my head; I feel his breath catch as I realise I'm not supposed to know this.

'How . . . '

'I'm sure you've told me before.'

We have these moments often, when my knowledge bursts out a step ahead, confusing the both of us. Although our relationship feels new, I often stumble into patches of the known. I haven't told Nick that he has been familiar to me from the start. The more I care for him, the more flashes I get, of things he said, winks, grins, in a different life. I'm so happy with him.

'Anyway,' I say, 'won't we be late?' We're meeting Charlie and Yuki at the pub. Since they started dating in a way only *they* thought was discreet, Yuki hasn't stopped smiling. Charlotte, on the other hand, is still Charlotte. Nick says he's never seen her happier, but I can see no difference; she always looks like her job is to stand very still in a fridge. Yuki won't mind if we're late, because she'll have Charlotte to herself for longer; Charlotte, on the other hand, will think I'm getting between her and her brother. I'm trying not to let this bother me, telling myself she will accept me eventually.

I wait to see if Nick will believe that he's told me the story before. Technically, of course, it isn't a lie. I've thought and thought about it, and all I know is that something is happening with me, with the universe, with my timeline. Impossible, but happening. To only me. What else can he do but believe the most believable? He releases me, dropping his head back into the pillow, smiling.

'We won't be late,' he says, and it's clearly not true, but I don't care.

I'm still drunk on happiness. So tipsy that I'm muddling time. These lazy, deliciously slow summer weeks (teachers' holidays, take *that*, lawyer Ben), Nick and I have made a nest of our beds: happy tangles of sheets he never straightens when we leave, the broken springs of his mattress, the new dip on mine, where his body has started to burrow its shape. We have gone for occasional walks and coffee breaks, have cobbled sustenance together and eaten it hastily, holding a fork in one hand, the other maintaining unbroken contact between our bodies.

A message comes through. I glance at the screen and flip my phone onto its front on the bedside table.

'Don't you want to reply?' Nick asks, while I notice, once more, that the shape of my head has been sculpted to fit precisely into the space between his chin and shoulder.

'Not really, no.'

'Your phone's been buzzing all afternoon. I don't mind.'

'Just my sister.'

'Are you okay?'

'I'm perfect.'

'Is your sister okay?'

'Yes, Nick, Marion's fine. I'll reply later.' I think of propping myself up on my elbow, but I'm a dreadful liar. He shouldn't see my face. The top of my head will have to do. Not that it's a big lie, but I'm feeling dreadfully guilty about my family, missing Grandma's funeral and ignoring Marion's calls. I have to keep walking ahead. I know why I'm here, rather than there. My time with Nick is too precious.

Nick's hand is tracing my shoulder, drawing out the softness of my skin. Now and again I have flashes of sex with Romain, the rashness of it, where my body was nothing more than a machine whose buttons nobody had time to press. With Nick, I feel like I have been healing. I discover new materials I'm made of: silk and velvet and Velcro. Sometimes when we've finished talking and making love and he's fallen asleep, I lie there listening to his quiet presence and think I've found it. The elusive *it*.

Nick's room is what I've always experienced men's bedrooms to be like, and I can't get enough of it, of being here among the evidence of him. Functional and bare, with a few dusty trinkets making no sense at all. He moved into a furnished flat share when he started his job, therefore hardly anything is his. The metallic bed frame is cheap and low to the ground, the flatpack wardrobe's door constantly ajar. Of course, there's no lighting ambience, and we've resorted to turning his desk lamp on as a signal that one of us wants to instigate sex – more of a joke, really,

162

after I complained about the surgical brightness of the bare ceiling bulb.

The bookshelf is half empty too, folders of paperwork and resources from his teacher training at the bottom, *National Geographic* magazines in random piles that have lost their shine. The middle shelves serve as a pocket emptier, scattered with his keys, loose change, old receipts, bills, bank statements. I count four lighters, all in bright colours like sweets. At the top, a couple of faded birthday cards and unframed photos: Nick and Charlotte together on the day of their university graduation, flicking each other's mortar boards off, and one of a younger Nick standing in front of an island bursting out of the sea, overgrown with vines.

I sit up a little so I can take it all in once again. I've been staring at his belongings for weeks now, looking for clues about his past, and his future. I always come out empty-handed. Today I need to distract both of us from my phone ringing.

'I thought Charlotte was younger than you,' I say, nodding to the graduation photo.

'She is.' He follows my eyes. 'Much. Makes me look like a grandad.'

'But you graduated at the same time?'

'Yeah. When I was twenty-eight. A mature student, but not nearly mature enough. Charlie got me to sign up when she did.'

It's a bit unusual, and I want to ask more, but he gets in there first. 'Tell me about your PhD, though. What happened?'

I shrug. 'Not much. Not enough, in short. I thought I was good at academia, but turns out I mainly liked reading the stories. All the critical work was making me anxious. I was petrified about getting the wrong end of the stick.'

'You're good at telling them too, those stories,' Nick says. 'I loved hearing about Aeneas; the way you told it, it was like watching an episode of *EastEnders*.'

'Thank you, I guess,' I say, raising my eyebrows. Romain always said the way I had fun with those retellings was cheapening the source materials.

'What I mean is, you're funny. You know how to make them relevant. You educate me,' he says, with a flourish.

I turn back to the bookshelf.

'What about this photo?'

'Which one?'

'The one with the island. The travelling one.'

He shrugs. 'Right. Thailand. I was backpacking. A place called Railay. Incredible beach. You can only get there by boat, from Krabi, if I recall.'

'Sounds great.'

'Yeah.'

There's something there. A twitch. Am I imagining it?

I get up and go to the bookshelf, picking up the photo. Because it was leaning against the books in a slight stoop, it has a fine layer of dust on it. My thumb prints a round, darker spot on the side.

'When was that?' I ask.

'The eighteenth of March 2008,' he says.

He didn't have to think about it at all. If you asked me exactly when I spent a summer in Berlin, which was the main adventure of my early twenties, I would have to do the maths. Let alone know the exact date of a picture. Flashes come back, of a freezing bench, my phone in my hand, the

164

date on the home screen, a selfie of Nick in front of a murky empty pen. The eighteenth of March . . .

'The zoo,' I say. 'Do you always go to the zoo on the eighteenth of March?'

A beat. 'How do you know?'

'I just do.'

'That's strange. Well, I go and check on the baby elephants.'

'The baby elephants?'

'Yeah. I visited an elephant sanctuary in Phuket. They took in rescue elephants, orphans and so on. The bloke who was showing us around said calves can die of loneliness if they don't manage to bond with the herd. So that's just a thing I do. I know it's weird.'

He shrugs, and I stare at him. *Baby elephants can die of loneliness.* Something is trying to resurface. Something I don't want there.

In the picture, he looks like a different Nick, thinner, perhaps jet-lagged. He's standing on the beach and he's not smiling. Or am I reading too much into this, because he seems reluctant to tell me about the trip? You would have thought that after a month spent in each other's pocket, we would have covered all the basics. I've answered lots of Nick's questions about myself, but there's so much I still don't know about him.

I ask, 'Will you tell me about Thailand? Looks amazing.'

'I thought we were late? Shouldn't we be going?' He's smiling again. I can't stay away when he's smiling at me. I leave the bookshelf and quite literally throw myself at him. I mean to be all seductive, but it's more of a happy puppy tumble. 'Wow, easy,' he laughs as he catches me.

I kiss his neck, kiss his cheek. 'We're very late.'

'Shit, yes. Charlie will go berserk.'

'Berserk?'

'Angry. I think it might have meant wearing a bear coat or something.'

I'm delighted at this. I'm delighted at all the animal facts, the new layers of meaning and playfulness Nick is bringing into my life.

'I wish Charlie would like me,' I say.

'Ah, give her time,' Nick says. 'I know one day she'll love you like I do.'

I blush, and we look at each other. Did he really say, mean . . .

'I love you, Lou.'

Love for Nick has been slowly permeating my conscious-ness for a long while. He is acting all casual, leaning back against the pillow with his hands tucked behind his neck, his hair up in a messy bun, half a smile on his face, but I can see he's nervous. And I am too. I'm nervous to be finding myself, for once, exactly where I want to be. And taken aback that the nerves are still there, even when everything is going so well.

'Take your time,' he teases.

'I love you too.'

The moment stretches, and I wish for time to come to a halt.

'Perhaps you could kiss me, then,' Nick says.

I laugh and comply. His mouth is delicious and alive. I feel so happy, I fear my brain is going to do it again, overheat or something and rush me away. I'm almost floating above our selves, seeing my messy hazelnut hair nestled against

Nick's naked chest, his tattooed arm around my back and shoulder, his eyes half closed, relaxed, happy. Our bubble of meant-to-be.

'We must really be off.'

But he won't let go of me, and I won't let go of him. He's holding me tight as I breathe in the scent of his neck, so him, so addictive, and we grow still, wrapped in the moment, as the clock on his desk ticks seconds away uselessly. I'm with Nick, and Nick is with me. Nothing is a rush and there's nowhere else either of us should be. Everything, all my wanderings, make sense now, finally.

Sunday 24 December 2017

'So good of you to join us for Christmas. I was starting to think you'd burnt your passport.'

Marion is washing, I'm drying. The few tasks she trusts me to do are as invariable as this Christmas. We haven't talked much since I missed Grandma's funeral. I tried my best to push the guilt to the back of my mind, but now that I'm here, I have to face it full on. I already know that being defensive doesn't get me anywhere with Marion.

'I deserve that,' I say. 'I'm sorry. I guess I've been wrapped up in, you know, Nick.'

Marion stops, looks at me.

'Yeah. That's good of you to admit,' she says finally.

'I'm glad you've met him now.'

'For what it's worth, we really like him.'

'You don't think I've stressed Mum out by inviting him?'

She shrugs. She's intensely focused on her task, stopping briefly to wipe her fringe out of her eyes, and doesn't look up from the dish. She's thorough, scrubbing even when it appears perfectly clean to me.

Mum hasn't changed her towels for a while – I notice it when the smell of mouldy cloth rises off the plates I'm drying. There are little pieces of fluff sticking to them too. I wonder if, by drying the plates, I'm actually making them worse.

'I need to wash these towels,' I say.

A long, long sigh comes out of my sister. There's another layer of time, several in fact, when we stood here, at previous Christmases or in other lives, and I wonder whether anything has changed for her. Are she and Fabio trying for a baby? Should I tell her what Nick said at the airport? Would she understand without knowing that the flashes I've been having, those intense bouts of foreshadowing, have become more frequent, more intense?

We were drinking coffee in the early hours, just a normal couple travelling abroad together for the first time. We both had had little sleep, and the coffee tasted hot and delicious and upset my empty stomach. Nick was excited to be going abroad and kept flicking through his passport, which he had had to renew for the occasion; he had said he hadn't been abroad since Thailand, and his tone had discouraged me from pushing him on the subject. Instead I said something about the stress of travelling with babies, that I didn't know how anybody managed. I'd been counting young families in the departure lounge, about eight on our flight alone. In my experience, babies always cried when travelling. Did they even get a passport, and how – didn't babies all look the same? And when did you change them, and what did you do with the pram? Nick smiled and said, 'You just get on with it.'

'Well, you don't have to,' I said. 'You can choose not to travel with a small baby, that's much easier.'

'But wouldn't you want your family to meet our kid?' he asked. 'Wouldn't you want to bring our baby to Switzerland for Christmas?' And I stopped watching other families to bring my focus onto Nick, and me.

'Do you ...' I half choked on my coffee, the bitterness finding its way into the fabric of my throat. 'Do you want kids?'

'Yes,' he said, 'of course. What about you?'

'Well,' I said. 'I never really ... I don't ... Maybe, I guess, but ...'

'Too soon?' He laughed, watching me grab my shovel and attempt to bury the conversation I had started. 'Calm down, Lou, breathe, everything is fine.'

'I *am* breathing,' I said.

'Thing is,' he continued, 'I've always wanted at least one. You can't plan for it, I suppose, there's no guarantee, but when you know, *you know*, you know?'

He tried to take my hand, but I picked up my disposable cup instead, because I didn't want him to find my skin all clammy. He looked surprised.

'It's not that I don't want them,' I said.

'But what?' He wasn't pushy, but curious. Casually digging into the truth. 'Come on, Lou, tell me what's going on in your head.'

I couldn't tell him what he had just triggered, the impending doom I'd been trying to push aside for months let loose by his plans for our future, my subconscious fears taking shape like a monster unleashed by some kind of spell. Did we really have a future? Did Nick have one? Was the growing anxiety all in my head?

They opened boarding; Nick took my empty coffee cup and went to drop it into the bin at the other end of the lounge. I watched his PE teacher elastic jog, the square of his shoulders under the battered leather jacket he called his winter coat, which wasn't suitable at all for December in Switzerland. He negotiated the crowd with ease, and I wouldn't have been surprised if he'd made friends on his way to and from the bins. Babies turned their heads to look at him and squealed with delight when he waved. I was pinned in place on the plastic chair, overwhelmed with fear for him. I tried to mop up the beginning of tears quickly with the sleeve of my jumper. Why did I feel that our time together was limited?

Marion starts drying her hands with the mouldy dishcloth, staring into the distance. The washed plates and pots have been carefully piled up on the side. Something is dripping. I remember when she was thirteen and she got so angry that she punched her hand right through her bedroom window. She was angry because Dad hadn't believed that a teacher had been bullying her. She hadn't meant to break the window, I don't think. She'd punched it back to close it and her hand had gone right through it, like a superhero. Dad had taken her to hospital and she never talked to him about what bothered her again. That wasn't long before he left us for his dream to manage a vineyard in Australia. Mum called it his *crise de la quarantaine*, his midlife crisis, but he never came back, and over the years he slowly lost interest in us. It's not like we could see him for tea on Boxing Day anyway. He sends us those ridiculous email Christmas cards of him and his new family, his two blonde boys. Dad thought of himself as a misunderstood rebel, but he plunged straight into another settled life, just not with us. I know Marion never forgave him for it, and I don't think she should. Mum worked twice as hard until she retired, still baking for Marion and me when we went back home on Sundays, pressing jars of home-made jam in our hands when we left, pretending everything was fine.

'Nick wants kids,' I tell Marion.

She startles. 'Seems a bit early to bring that up. You haven't known each other that long.'

Technically she is right. 'I guess not, but I guess we're getting old.'

She doesn't deny it. 'That's a lot of guessing you're doing. Do you even want kids? You've never mentioned it.'

She puts a pan of water on the stove, setting out Mum's teapot and throwing a couple of sachets of Twinings into it, the best black tea you can find here, whose only possible brewing degree is 'weak'. We stand on either side, listening out for the water to start boiling.

'I'm not sure. Not for a while anyway,' I say.

When we bring the tea into the lounge, there's palpable relief that we're here. I open the biscuit tin, instructing Nick and Fabio to arrange the vanilla pretzels on a platter, as if I were talking to absent children, the next generation, who will display biscuits in flower and sun shapes, eating half of them in the process; what Marion and I used to do with Grandma. Our family is like a plant running out of water. That's why the conversation with Nick at the airport was so difficult.

172

'Who made Grandma's pretzels?' Mum is confused. She sounds upset. My heart sinks.

'Me and Nick,' I say. Nick looks at me.

Yesterday we sat in the kitchen and made a batch while Mum slept in her room with the blinds shut on the feeble sunlight. I knew somehow where Mum kept the recipe, hand-written on yellowed lined paper preserved between the pages of a Betty Bossi cookbook. Nick didn't ask any questions; he rolled up his sleeves, and as he pressed the dough together, there were creases on his forehead. He joked about how un-Swiss his clumsy pretzels were. I could have kissed him. I did.

'I wanted to learn a Swiss Christmas tradition, Mrs Saudan.' My last name in his mouth makes me tingly for a bit.

'And didn't we do a great job?' I ask lightly.

'Lou says these are your favourites,' Nick says to Mum. 'I apologise for not doing them justice.' I translate for Mum, and she seems flattered and placated by Nick's charm. I don't even know what the problem was. I still seem to have no ability to anticipate what might set her off.

I feel for Nick, parachuted into this strange, silent Swiss family. He is sitting forward, his elbows on his knees, showing something to Fabio on his phone, and he looks up and smiles, his grey eyes twinkling. I smile back. We haven't chipped at him yet. I wish I felt better about telling him I could maybe imagine having a baby in a couple of years. A couple of years. The thought shortens my breath. I picture swollen bellies, the hard plastic chairs in examination rooms, nurses rushing about with solemn faces, delivering good news or catastrophes. I see us sitting on those chairs, waiting for our disaster. And panic grips me. As soon as we're home, I'll talk to him about going to the doctor. Just a general check-up.

We all sit and drink our tea and eat the biscuits, and for a moment, it looks like a perfect picture of family Christmas peace. I'm so relieved the biscuits were edible, which strikes me as the relief of a worry I didn't even know I had. Nick squeezes my knee as he relaxes into the back of the sofa in that way he has, casual and perfectly at ease, talking to everyone about the dog he used to have when he was little, called Dog.

'A dog called Dog?' Marion isn't impressed.

'Yes.' He grins.

'My niece always calls her cat Cat,' Fabio says.

'Yes, but Julie is four, and she can't say Confucius,' Marion says.

'My sister's dog is called Chomsky,' Nick says. 'Pet philosophers. Because pets are so much better than we are.'

'Pets have it much easier than us,' Marion tells him. She always has to argue back, to have the last word, but she's smiling.

'Maybe,' Nick says. 'But I don't know a single bad dog, do you?'

Fabio shakes his head vigorously.

'Are you spending tomorrow with Fabio's family?' I ask both Marion and Fabio.

'As long as Fabio's sister doesn't give birth overnight,' Marion says. We all marvel at the thought of a Christmas Eve baby, the pleasing aesthetics of it.

'We'd still go even if she did,' Fabio says. 'Mum would have Julie to look after, and it'd be a lovely Christmas anyway.'

'I don't want that.' Mum's voice cuts through the conversation, firmer than any of us would have expected.

'What don't you want, Mum?' I ask.

We all turn to her, and she visibly braces herself. She places her teacup down on the coffee table – one of the few remnants of our parents' wedding service, incredibly fine and fragile, tinkling against the saucer.

'Grandchildren,' she says, as if she had merely turned down more tea. 'Looking after them – I don't want that.'

In the silence, Nick looks at me looking at Marion, and Marion turns to Mum. Now would be the perfect time for next year's Christmas card photo: puzzlement, worry and hurt, a perfect shot to send to Dad. Marion looks like she's searching for something to say, a way to take charge and make it better, but unusually for her, she finds nothing. Mum used to be a perfect future grandma. She used to mention it as a given, how she would keep Marion's room as it was for the grandkids. We used to laugh it off; we took it for granted.

'I'm sure Fabio's mum enjoys it from time to time,' I say.

Fabio nods bravely before engrossing himself in whatever is going on at the bottom of his cup.

'You don't want grandchildren?' Marion's voice is clipped.

Mum shakes her head vigorously.

'No. Small children are so much work. You,' she points at Marion and me, 'don't have kids, and it suits me well. Very well. I did all of that with you two, I don't want to go through it again.'

I see Marion scan the table. She picks up a full jug.

'I'll fetch more milk,' she says.

I can feel Nick's eyes on me. Part of me regrets bringing him here. With trembling hands Mum picks up the teapot, and because I was distracted and didn't manage to anticipate the disaster, she spills hot tea all over the table.

'No, no, no ...' She freezes, hot teapot in hand. Nick gently takes it from her.

'It's nothing, Mrs Saudan, don't worry,' he says.

I rush to the kitchen to fetch a cloth. I'm so exhausted. I lose track of the spillage, of how much Mum has said that has unwittingly hurt Marion or myself. I don't even know whether I've lived this before, or whether it's Mum's depression that keeps repeating itself in a loop.

In the kitchen, Marion is putting the dried plates away.

'Fabio and I are going to go,' she says.

'Already?'

She nods, her jaw tight. This time I remember when she was working as a barmaid, when she was at uni, and she slammed a guy's head on the bar because he'd groped her. Marion has done a lot of punching in her life, but I've never seen her more depleted.

'It feels like it's been going on for bloody ages,' she blurts out. 'When is it going to stop? When is she going to get better?'

'Not for a while, I think.'

'You don't know that.'

But I do. As far as I can see, we don't get our mother back. I try to keep my voice soft and soothing. 'My advice, for what it's worth, is not to wait.'

'Wait for what?'

'I'm talking about *your* kids. Don't wait for Mum to get better to move on with your own life.'

'How do you know? That we've been thinking about it?'

I shrug. 'Perhaps I listen more than you give me credit for.'

I expect a snarky remark about being a poor misunderstood expat, but she says, 'Perhaps you do.' We look at each other for a minute, and we're back in this same kitchen fifteen years ago, our teenage selves communicating silently over the dinner table as Mum busied herself at the hob, cooking more dinner than the three of us could ever eat, Dad's chair empty. Then Marion turns and opens the fridge. 'There must be something, though, we must be able to do *something*.'

'Yes. We can keep trying, and we will, but you don't need Mum to look after your children. Some people don't have their mothers around, and they cope.'

'It's easier for you,' she says.

Here we go. We can't get out of this conversation, it seems.

'You can go back there and do whatever you want. You've already given up on us.' She gestures in a vague direction that I'm pretty sure is the Italian Alps.

'Ah, sis, not again, please.'

'But it's true.'

'It's not as easy as you think, okay? I'm not running away. Perhaps I did, a long time ago, but now I'm trying to get on with my life, build a version of it I actually want to be in. I'm not trying to forget about you and Mum. If I could do anything, I would. We've told her so many times to go and see someone, and she won't. Even if we made her an appointment, she would refuse to go. What else can we do?'

'But Dad's not around either, and he won't care.' To my dismay and surprise, she starts crying. 'Remember how you and I spent all that time with Grandma, going to the zoo, eating bircher. I want my kids to have that.'

I don't know what to say to make it better. Her children might not have that. I see, suddenly, how lonely Marion feels. Little Marion running ahead at the zoo on her pudgy legs,

177

safe in the knowledge that there would always be somebody to catch her if she fell. She's built a carapace around that person, but deep down, that's still who she is. I walk towards her and hug her. She's rigid at first, because we never, ever hug, until her back and shoulders relax a little.

'Well, your kids will have two awesome parents, okay? And the coolest English aunt. I'll take them to the zoo and fill them up with ice cream, don't you worry about that.'

At this, she smiles through her tears. 'Sugar is so bad for children.'

A knock on the kitchen door, and Nick's head appears.

'I'm afraid we still need that cloth,' he says. 'Everything okay, you two?'

Friday 16 February 2018

'How is it going?' Yuki asks.

'All right, I guess.'

'Come on, matey. What's up?'

It's the last real day of half-term, Yuki had the day off, and she suggested we remind ourselves of the pure joy of sitting in a café for breakfast on a weekday. Being part of a quiet, smug club while everybody else is at work. I usually love British cafés; with their mismatched whitewashed tables and chairs, and their pictures of chickens by a local artist, they are Peter Rabbit's living room, but this one is failing to make me feel calmer and safer. I turn my cup of chai in my hands, trying to read my fortune in the cinnamon patterns. I don't want this break to end. I don't want time to pick up and move on. My heart is sinking in slow, slow quicksand.

'Charlie says you and Nick have been arguing,' Yuki continues. I haven't seen her by herself in a while; it's always the four of us. Now it's clear she's summoned me to quiz me.

'What?'

Yuki's face is soft, her hair brushing her cheeks – in fact, the whole of her has looked great for months, that elusive glow. People were staring at her when she sat down earlier, following her with their eyes like spooky paintings. I'm happy for her, and sad for myself, and I think of what I would give to be living her life, not mine. Not mine, with the awful flashes I've started to have. What started as a vague panic surrounding doctors' offices and beeping machines has morphed into glimpses of Nick's shaved head, of his funeral. I've been struggling with these since the new year: our conversation about future plans at Christmas opened some kind of Pandora's box. I think ... I think Nick might die. Soon. But I'm not completely sure if they are memories, or made-up fears; I keep trying to reason with myself and my anxiety, and it is driving me mad.

'Charlotte knows everything about me, then.'

'Ah, don't be like that.'

'Sorry.' I pick up my spoon and swirl and swirl. The cinnamon doesn't melt into the milk, it congeals in lumps. In fact, I don't know why I always say yes when asked if I want it. Cinnamon is powdery and sticks in your throat, and I can't keep going back to saying yes if it's unpleasant, can I?

'We care about you, both of you,' Yuki says.

'I know.'

'But Charlie tends to worry about Nick since ... '

'Since what?'

She shrugs it off. 'I think he kinda struggled to find his way.' Her eyes flick to mine before she continues. 'Charlie feels responsible for him somehow. You know, she supported him, got him to pick himself up, apply to uni ... '

'That's weird. She's his little sister. It should be the other way around.'

'Don't call my girlfriend weird.' Yuki pretends to be offended, but says the word *girlfriend* as if it were caramel in her mouth.

'Perhaps she should let go, though. Nick is an adult. She's being a little overbearing.'

'Ha, that's exactly what she says about you. You two have much more in common than you think.' She ignores my scoff. 'So, what's been going on? You and Nick are so good together.'

What has been going on is that I've asked Nick to go to the doctor's and he hasn't yet. Every day I hope he'll come home and say, *by the way, I made an appointment*, but he doesn't. He keeps refusing to talk about his health, or about his feelings, or his past. Small things, really. So small I can't sleep or eat or think of anything else. When I try to fall asleep next to him, I worry about the pattern of his breathing, the heat of his body I swear I can feel across the bed, surely a sign that he's fighting something off, something trying to root in him. We had another argument a couple of days ago, and I can't stop thinking about it.

Obviously I knew Valentine's Day wasn't the best time to bring up his health again, and I fought with myself hard. In the end, the words weighed too much, and they tumbled out all over the lovely meal Nick had cooked for me in my studio, *not* burnt and *not* smothered in barbecue sauce and showing so much effort and thought. The happier I get, the more I obsess over losing him.

'Perhaps we should eat a bit more healthily,' I said.

'Lou, please.' Nick's fork was suspended in the air, over the rare steak, the oven chips, the garlic butter. 'Not now.'

It was the first time he'd taken that sharp tone with me; I'd pushed him one time too many. I knew immediately that I'd ruined the evening. I still feel it in my bones now, that something broke, perhaps my stupid idea that because Nick is kind, his patience with me would be endless.

'It's important, though, Nick. You don't realise how important it is. We should ... What if—'

'What if. All of your what-ifs.'

I could see him being torn between letting his annoyance run free and bottling it up. He played with his fork, tapping the teeth of it on his plate. It dragged on until we both lost our appetite and gave up on the food grown cold.

'I'm going out for a smoke,' he said, getting up. And before I'd had time to say anything, he snapped, 'Please, don't.'

Petrified, silent, I watched him grab his coat and walk out. He always smoked on the pavement, by the traffic lights, and I could see him from the window. I watched him watching the traffic for a while, inhaling all those toxins. I felt so helpless.

I was relieved that he came back in afterwards, took his coat off. He had never snapped at me before, had always adopted a kind of deflective approach to my worries.

'Lou, perhaps you're the one who needs a little check-up,' he said, kind again, gentle. He went to my desk and wrote something on a piece of paper. 'Here. Maybe you should give this woman a call.' Because I was so scared of what the argument was doing to us, of the fabric of our relationship changing, I took the paper. *Eden Lubinski, counsellor, CBT*, and a phone number.

'Am I this hard to deal with?' I asked, my voice flat.

'It's not like that,' he sighed. We sat on the edge of the bed, in the studio too small for a sofa. He took my hand and pressed it in his, and there was a tremor, but I'm not sure which one of us was trembling.

'How do you know her?' I asked. 'How do you have her details?'

He didn't answer, and I was too apprehensive of where the conversation might go to probe any further, so I said, 'Okay. I might give it a try.'

We spent the rest of our Valentine's evening in a fragile state of flux, tiptoeing around each other and planning our trip to the zoo next month. The note with the counsellor's details went through the wash the next day, still in the pocket of my jeans.

'I'm feeling a little worried, that's all,' I tell Yuki.

'Ah, matey.' She is thinking, her eyes two dark pins over her silk scarf. 'Anxiety ruins everything.'

The word 'anxiety', in my world right now, is overused, a pale avatar of the truth I throw at people when I need to explain myself. I want to shout at Yuki: is it still anxiety when you're pretty sure that the worst is going to happen, and you can't do anything about it, because nobody would believe your thoughts might be real? Or is it called the worst fucking nightmare?

'How is it going with Charlie?' I force myself to ask.

'Kinda great.' Yuki beams, and I hate the jealousy I feel. Because they can enjoy their time together, having so much of it. 'I mean, she's something else. She's so sensitive. Loyal. She doesn't lower her standards. Makes me raise my game, you know.'

183

'Your game's always been pretty high, in my opinion,' I say.

'Ah, thanks, mate.'

'What do you think Charlie would say about you?'

She thinks. 'She might say I chill her out a bit. Lighten her up. Getting her to enjoy stuff more, you know.'

'She's able to enjoy *anything*?'

'Ah, come on. Give her a break.'

'If she gives *me* a break.'

I'm teenagery now, all sulky, and I try to stop myself.

'You and Nick have everything,' Yuki says, 'and I mean *everything* you need to be happy. We wouldn't want ... I wouldn't want ...'

'What?'

'For your brain to ruin this for you.' She picks up her croissant and dunks it in her coffee. 'I've seen what your brain does. It's like a dog with a bone sometimes. I know it's easy to say, and probably insensitive, but try to let it go. You have to trust that everything's gonna be fine, okay? What choice do we have anyway?'

I want to scream at her, and the violence of the impulse scares me. Yuki doesn't deserve it, and neither do the few obviously retired ladies around us, sipping their tea, and the mother with her little girl in a lime-green jumper. I wish I were able to follow her advice, live in the moment. Nick feels fine. He feels grand, he says, again and again like a broken record. Never better. All I have to do is believe him, yet I can't.

'So Nick's been talking to Charlotte about me.'

A dog with a bone. Now that I'm finally trying to do something, I'm banging my head against a wall. Repeatedly.

Yuki puts her cup down on the saucer. I think of all those croissant crumbs, dissolved into mush at the bottom.

'Well, sure. They're very close.'

'And Charlotte has been talking to you.'

She folds her arms now. 'Yes, and?'

'Why is everybody talking about me behind my back?'

There's a flicker in Yuki's eyes, the possibility of annoyance, but instead of telling me off, she taps my wrist with her finger. Her voice is that of a nurse, not a friend.

'And what do you think I'm doing right now, Louise?'

If only I could tell her what has been going on, but of course, I can't. It would not only make me sound deluded, it would also take Yuki's agency away from her current happiness. Make it sound like a complete coincidence, as if she could equally have ended up in an abusive relationship with lawyer Ben. The thought makes me uneasy. The possibilities would rattle anybody, the what-ifs. Exactly the way they're unnerving *me*.

'Point taken,' I say.

'*Le point*,' she beams, then seems to hesitate, as if unsure she can cross over to me the way she used to. We both know our significant others are the main bridge between us now.

She leans against the back of her chair, drinks some coffee, her face puzzled as she gets towards the grainy bottom of the cup. I take in the watercolour of the St Albans Clock Tower above her head, remembering how elated I felt when I first arrived, walking among the sloping pretty buildings of the town centre, my heart brimming with possibilities. Possibilities are much easier than making something of a real relationship.

'Listen, matey,' Yuki continues, 'I'm not really supposed

185

to say, but I think you need to know. I mean, I don't know the details, but Charlotte alluded to something serious happening to Nick.'

My heart jumps into my throat. 'Soon?' I ask, without thinking.

She stares at me. 'No, silly, in his past. Nick might have had an accident when he was backpacking in Thailand.'

'What kind of accident?'

'Charlie wasn't clear. I think she said he took too much Sara.'

'What's Sara?'

'I really don't know. I assumed it was some kind of Thai recreational drug – I think Nick used to be a bit of a party animal. I'm sorry. I just think that's why Charlotte worries so much about him, why she's so protective, kinda.'

That photo on his bookshelf, Nick's haunted, emaciated look. The elephants on 18 March. *We don't have a clue in our twenties. We're there to fuck things up.* Is that what he did? Fuck up his health, all that way back, where I can't reach him? And he won't tell me anything about it. My eyes dampen with frustration.

Yuki sees my face. 'Ah, Lou, I'm sorry. Maybe you should talk to him.'

I nod, but I know I can't ask him. He made it clear he doesn't want to open up, and I can't nag him any more. I have pushed us to the point where we might lose our balance. Nick has to decide to talk to me, and it's devastating to have to wait and not be able to do anything about it.

'Seriously,' Yuki says, examining the bottom of her cup, 'we've got a good thing going on. Both of us. If you think back a year, things are pretty great now. Your teaching is going better, you found a great guy ...'

And despite everything, I have to agree with her. I feel a bit more settled here in the UK, in my job – well, if I ignore my students' sarky comments about how having a boyfriend has made me chill out (I think some of them saw us in Tesco) – and being able to share difficulties and behaviour management tips with Nick has helped too. He is wise – he really is very good at giving advice. I must stop messing it all up with my worries.

Sunday 18 March 2018

Nick does love the zoo, Charlotte said. Or did she say he *did*? Past or present? Things are coming back to me more frequently now, in violent waves I have no time to brace myself for. As I walk between the animal enclosures, Nick's hand around mine, here I am again, wondering whether he's the real Nick or if his hand is an extension of my imagination, something my brain has made up entirely. The more I think, the more I seem to lose my grip on reality, and the more panicky I become.

'Are you okay?'

I swear this is all Nick ever asks me these days. I know it's not right, that this should be a joyful, fun occasion, but I can't stop it. Today is a bad day, one of those when my brain feels sticky. Fragments of memories and fears glued together, a stringy mess of cheese fondue in my head.

Since our conversation on Valentine's Day, I've tried hard not to mention the GP, not to be overbearing. 'Sometimes it's not about what you say,' Nick keeps telling me, 'but a vibe you give off. It's hard for it not to rub off on me, Lou.' And that is totally out of my control. The fear I have for his life is rising dangerously close to the lid I'm pressing down, and I'm exhausted.

'Yes,' I say. 'I'm okay.'

I realise I've been standing in front of the map for a while, looking at nothing. Somebody has drawn goggly eyes on the meerkat. Have I seen these eyes before, or am I making it up? Why would they be different, and how come they're exactly the same? Perhaps Nick is never going to be sick. If my brain can make me believe I've been here before, on this very day, it can also make up the imminent death of the man I love.

'Come here.' Nick's hands on my shoulders gently pull me away from the map and towards him. 'Bad day?' he asks. I let myself be drawn against his chest, breathe. His smell is definitely real; after he's been walking in the cold air and the drizzle for a while, something like rain-perfumed skin. Unless . . . he smells distinctively sweet. A little too sweet? Didn't they tell me on a first aid course that this is what diabetics' breath smells like? I think the guy said pear drops. I wasn't sure what he meant, but everybody around me nodded knowingly. I wriggle away from Nick, get my phone out. A quick google to reassure myself, that's all it'll take.

'Lou,' Nick says. I nod to indicate I'm listening. I'm not. 'You're not with me.'

'Sorry.' The search says it's a sweet smell. That's not helpful, Google. Here it is, though, straight away. Indicating high blood sugar.

'How about we go and see some animals? *Any* animals?'

They say it can also smell like nail varnish. What kind of country is fond of sweets that smell like nail varnish?

'Lou, we agreed this would be a nice date.'

I don't paint my nails, but I did live with Yuki, so I should know the smell. Perhaps Nick dies of diabetes after all; perhaps that's what it is. The symptom I've been looking for.

The landscape around me slowly sinks into the panic in my brain, the rush of scrolling through the pages as if the answer is going to spring out at me. Breathe, Louise. I try to steady myself. Only Nick can calm me nowadays, and he's the very source of my distress. Perhaps I should sniff him again.

But Nick isn't here any more.

Crap. I run to the elephant paddock, not far away, but he's nowhere to be seen. I go back to the map. The otters – he suggested the otters. Didn't he? Just now, or . . . ? I try to get my bearings, but my brain refuses to orientate itself. I don't know right from left, north from south, before from after. It takes me a while to find a sign. I run past a family with a tiger-faced little boy and a girl in a green jacket, until I get to the otters' small enclosure, panting and hot under my coat.

Nick is there, standing a little distance away from a gang of children pointing and laughing at a small bored mammal sharpening a stone. I can tell from the way he's rolling the edges of the map between his index finger and thumb that he would love to be smoking. He is typing on his phone, but as I approach, he puts it in his pocket. Please don't be texting Charlotte about me, I beg him silently.

'Hey,' I start, but he grabs my arm as soon as I'm close.

'Look!' He's pointing at the unimpressed otter, who, I

realise, appears to be doing some kind of juggling, throwing a pebble in and out of her armpits. 'Look, Lou!'

I can't help but squeak with excitement. One of the children, the tallest one, looks at us with disgust.

'I heard they could do this – I've never seen it before!' I tell Nick.

'Smashing stuff.'

One of the children bangs on the partition and the otter scampers into its burrow. Nick and I stand for a little while longer, the smiles fading on our faces. I turn to him, but he's still watching the empty enclosure.

'I'm sorry,' I say.

'Right.'

'But—'

He sighs. 'Please, Lou, no buts.'

'Listen,' I say.

'That's all I ever do.'

'That's a little mean.'

'I don't want to be mean to you. Ever, okay? But I keep listening to your ... your insecurities—'

'Is that what we're calling them now?'

He shrugs.

'Nick, they're not—'

'Anxieties?'

'No ...' I'm getting so muddled up, afraid of saying too much, and not saying enough, helplessly caught up in this torrent of fear washing me away. Every day I spend with Nick, I worry, try not to act on it, and fail.

'I don't know what to call them,' he says. 'All I know is you're not getting help.'

'But Nick, if only you—'

'Don't, Lou, not this again.'

'If only you'd go to the doctor.'

He's pale and silent, looking at the water in the otters' enclosure, a mockery of a wild river, a shallow mirror littered with twigs and duck feathers.

'Lou . . .'

It's too late. I've opened the door again, and my heart won't let me shut it. It always feels better going down the rabbit hole than resisting it, but I know the relief will be short-lived.

'You said you would— you said you would get checked out, but you haven't, I can't just forget about it, Nick. It's not that hard to organise yourself, pick up the phone, but you never do it.' He's silent now. 'You know I need you to do this, you know it's important to me, but you still won't.' What am I doing? I am no better than these boys who are kicking the fence, than the little girl in green who threw the biggest tantrum in the world.

Nick's phone beeps. I imagine Charlotte at the other end, tucked in a Shoreditch coffee shop with Yuki and Chomsky, the three of them shaking their heads: *Lou's done it again, ruined Nick's day, she's so controlling, how Nick still has patience for her, I can't think.* I can't remember feeling this alone, ever. I need to get through to Nick.

'You say you want a future with me,' I carry on, 'you say you want to move in together, have a family, but how can we have that' – I see him wince, and I hate myself so hard for a second – 'if you're not able to do that one small thing, and if you won't tell me why not, or be open about how you feel.'

He's walking away from me again. I can't lose him. I simply don't know what I'd do. I start running after him.

192

We get to the central point, in front of the restaurant and the small train station, and he stops.

Relieved that he's still here, I immediately search for feelings on his face. I realise now how tired and yellow he looks – is the sickness draining him already? It dawns on me that perhaps it's my behaviour. Perhaps I've done this to him.

'You're right,' he says.

'What?' I stare at his handsome face, trying to work out what is happening, what I'm being right about, my brain struggling to be both two steps behind and two steps ahead. I'm full of hope, suddenly, that the argument has been worth it, that he's agreed to pick up the phone, will be diagnosed early, and cured, and *voilà*.

He sighs, brings both hands up to his head, squeezing his skull as though it will stabilise his thoughts.

'It's a lot. It's too much.'

'What? What's too much? Nick?'

'Listen, I get it, anxiety, I really do, but it's like . . . ' He stops.

Tears are coming. My throat is closing up on me.

'It's like that's all we are now, isn't it,' I say.

The way he looks at me. My heart. Memories of a previous, unspoilt version of this start blooming like ink in water. How can my heart still be beating? Nick's chatty texts, the way he understood everything I typed, despite my lengthy foreign sentence structure, the words he would never use himself. His bad autocorrect and the absence of punctuation leaving his door constantly open. *You brightened me right up.*

For a minute, I still manage to hope we might be okay; because in this moment, we both understand where we stand, the damage that has been done. I imagine swallowing all my worries and, out of love for him, pretending to be

193

happy and carefree for ever, even if it destroys me, quietly, from the inside.

'I do so much already,' Nick says.

He's put his hands deep in his pockets, a gesture that scares me more than his words.

'So much?'

'So much to keep it from happening again,' he says. 'I watch my sleep, I don't drink much, yeah, smoking is bad for you, but it calms me down. I try to keep my life quiet and stable.'

'Keep what from happening again?' I ask.

He looks away, his shoulders tightening.

'Nick, what happened in Thailand?'

'I ... It's just not working.'

'Try me,' I croak, my throat and lungs suddenly empty. I've offered my hand to him. It doesn't quite stretch far enough to touch him, but it's there for the taking. He doesn't move. The panic intensifies. 'We can talk it through if I know what you worry about. I can change, I ... *Try me*, Nick, please.'

'I think we have. Both of us. We have tried.'

'*Please.*'

There's so much sadness in the way he looks at me that I know I've lost him. He won't open up to me. He's leaving me for good.

'No, Lou, no,' he mumbles. 'It's bloody heartbreaking, because I know we love each other. But we can't carry on like this. We're not good together. I seem to set you off, and you ...'

'Sorry,' I whisper, and I try to repeat it, but I'm crying too much. I can't breathe, let alone speak. If I spoke, it

194

would come out in French, something vestigial, deep, like a howl.

'I'm sorry too.'

I'm vaguely aware of his arm around me, of him walking me out, and all I can think of is that he's going to do the right thing and get me home, and perhaps he will change his mind along the way, or perhaps we need a little distance, and he'll miss me and will call me and we'll laugh about it. We'll try again, and we'll have learnt. I feel it, the tug of time, and regret, and terrible pain and loss and guilt, but Nick's arm is propping me up, and I keep telling myself that there's still hope, that he just said he still loved me, that it is worth hanging on to.

Thursday 23 August 2018

It's been me and her for an eternity. The balcony's blinds are down, the French windows shut so we don't hear the cars, the ever-worsening traffic, which distresses her. The sun is pressing its hot, sticky hands on the outside world; inside, the room is eerily cool. The tips of my toes are cold, the skin on my bare arms too. It's three in the afternoon, we should be warm. We should be enjoying the sun. But I can't move.

Mum takes the remote, stares at it for a bit then pushes it towards me.

'Can you change the channel,' she asks. I don't try and get her to do it herself any more. This time, I have found her company almost indifferent, depression neutralising depression.

Easter and the summer term passed in a daze, still carried by the hope that love would be enough, and that the next day, I would wake up to a text from Nick. I set a lot of project work at school, so I'd have to lose myself in tedious marking, into nights getting shorter and shorter. The stretching of the world itself was teasing me with all those hours made for barbecues and flirting in pub gardens.

When school finished for the summer holidays, with the loss of my routine, I found myself one of those cartoon characters who keep running up in the air over the cliff – I was finally plummeting. I did the only thing I could and flew to my mother. I've spent most days sitting here on the sofa, trying to remember how to breathe to the rumbling of the trains below, the too-cheerful jazzy notes of black-birds in the park, my only escape being painful trips to the supermarket, wandering amongst familiar yet uncanny products: green packets of nutty biscuits, saffron brioche, dried beef, all screaming at me in a cacophony of French, Italian and German.

'What would you like to watch?' I ask Mum as I flick through the channels. She shrugs. I struggle to find something she would describe as non-threatening, before settling on a 'France from the sky' documentary, a sleepy voice-over describing endless rivers and chateaux. I can't tell any more whether I'm selecting this for her benefit or mine. The list of banned programmes (documentaries about endangered species, suspense, the news) being much longer than what we can watch, every day we engage in a delicate negotiation with the remote.

My phone has been nothing but a reminder of emptiness this summer, so excruciating that some days I leave it off, go back to check it, turn it off again, and so on. The last text I received was on 30 July, when Yuki asked me how I was and sent me a GIF of an otter. I had to hide in my room to cry. There was no use in telling her how very much not okay I was. She has gone quiet now, and the hope that Nick would reach out has fizzled out. I have come to the realisation that to him, our break-up must have been a relief.

I've also had to let go of the hope of going back in time. That crazy, silly idea that magically I could be pulled out of my pain, travel to Yuki's birthday and start again, get it right this time. If I'm honest, though, I don't know what I'd do differently. I'm still here – still still *still* – and I've started to question my sanity, question if I ever did go back. I tried everything. I tried to hold my breath, to hyperventilate. I tried to sob. I took scalding showers followed by ice-cold bursts of water. I feel numb, bereft of power and agency.

'Hello?' The front door opens and Marion's voice reaches us. I swear my sister was made in an explosion of colours and sound, a goddess dunking her by the heel into a vat of fireworks. She drops her tote bag on the tiles – is it filled with cogs and tins? The beads around her neck clatter as she moves deeper into the room, huffing and puffing and sighing deeply.

'My, it's nice and cool in here! So dark . . .' She glances at the blinds, and although her voice is cheerful, her disapproval is palpable.

'Hi.' Mum accepts the kiss Marion plants on her cheek with great stoicism.

'Hi,' Marion says to me, before looking at us both, not sure whether to sit down.

'We're not contagious,' I say.

'Ha ha.' She perches on the edge of the sofa next to me, throws a handful of her possessions on the coffee table. Mum winces.

'You're looking well,' I say. And it's true. A summer spent doing her own thing while she knew Mum was safe with me has done Marion a whole lot of good. Her shoulders and cleavage are tanned, her skin radiating heat. I can't help it, I stretch out a hand towards her hair, glowing in sun streaks.

'Oi!' She bats my hand away. 'What are you doing?'

'Your hair,' I croak, sounding very much like a zombie moaning, 'Brains.'

'What about it?' She combs her fingers through her thick, healthy auburn waves, throwing their mass over the shoulder furthest away from me.

'It's so shiny.'

'What the f—' She glances at Mum, stops herself. 'You're weird, Louise.' She takes in the television, which is now showing us the castle of Chambord from all possible (aerial) angles, and the two untouched glasses of water I poured about three hours ago. 'When was the last time either of you went outside?'

Mum shuffles uncomfortably. 'I might meet someone I know, might have to make conversation.' Marion looks at me to check she's heard correctly. She frowns, and shrugs.

'Okay, Mum. But what about your vampire daughter here?'

I shake my head. 'Too hot.'

'Oh dear,' Marion says, putting on her Louise voice, which is nothing like mine. *'It's too sunny! My little English head can't take it! Bring back the rain at once!'*

'Whatever,' I say.

She stands up, snatching back her phone and keys. I have a dreadful feeling she came here with a scheme.

'Come on,' she says to me, and me only, 'let's go.'

'Where?'

'Outside. Anywhere but here. I'm getting you an ice cream.'

Déjà vu hadn't happened for a while. I was cautious, keeping myself away from triggers, or so I thought. But this was what Grandma used to say when she coaxed us into getting out and doing things. Ice cream is one of the few things Mum and I still like to eat. You don't have to chew it, and the sugar rush is always nice. We're a family of *becs à bonbons*, sweet teeth, and Marion knows our bait. Although Mum is a lost cause, my sister clearly hasn't despaired of me just yet.

'I'm too tired,' I moan.

'For fuck's sake.' Marion doesn't check her language this time – I look at Mum anxiously. She does so much wincing at the moment: mopeds on the road below, tense music on TV, the way I pour *tisane*, cut apples.

Marion pulls me up and starts ushering me out of the flat.

'Okay, but I need to be back for tea,' I say, glancing at Mum.

'Sure. Suit yourself. You might need sunglasses, though, or you'll go up in flames.' She takes the glasses off her head, perches them on my nose and kicks my shoes towards me.

It's a weird kind of world, I think as we sit on the promenade in Vevey. We're in the Jardin du Rivage, a lovely park area where kids paddle in big two-tiered octagonal fountains, or swim in the lake, and the air is gorged with suncream, happy shrieks and, sometimes, the *woo-shum* of a Belle Époque boat gliding past. Marion bought me my favourite ice cream without asking, Mövenpick's Stracciatella (she doesn't like it and calls it Tragitella), put it in my hand and sat me down on a bench, slightly dipped in shade so that I won't burn straight away. My feet are in the sun, though, and the heat is sizzling my skin, reminding me that I'm alive and that this is my present. I don't want it to be. I'm still waiting for a time door to open, for something to pull me out of now.

'You finished work early today,' I say, almost accusingly.

'Yup. I'm trying to be more flexible with my hours.'

'And they're letting you?' Marion is a social worker, and although she is supposed to work flexibly, her bosses always try to guilt-trip her into cancelling her leave. She's too good at dealing with their trickiest cases for things to tick along without her.

She shuffles a little on the bench. Her skirt brushes my ankles. I might combust from these surroundings: the heat, the sun, the people, the simple joy. Marion, eyes closed, is soaking it all in and radiating it back.

She shrugs. 'I've told them about the situation, and they're being understanding.'

'What situation?'

'You know what situation.'

'Mum?'

'Yeah,' she says. 'And you.'

I flinch. 'I'm not a situation.'

The ice cream has started to melt through the bottom of my cone. Swiss efficiency only goes so far, apparently. We make the best watches in the world, but aren't even capable of designing ice-cream-proof cones. Dammit. I lick my fingers with rage. It's delicious.

Marion's hot shoulder bumps into mine.

'Come on, Lou,' she says.

She never calls me Lou, except when talking about me to others. Normally she simply orders me around. *Please wash this, use this towel, not like that.* You would swear, seeing us together, that she's the elder sister. She has an air of authority, a slight jadedness. I'm smaller, my cheeks are rounder, my hair finer and straighter, and I dress like I'm aspiring to live in a New York autumnal romcom, wrapped in polka-dot dresses and pastel cardigans. I'm the one people assume needs protecting. And they might be right.

'You're right,' I say.

I can feel her resisting turning and looking at me. This is a rare moment, me agreeing with her, and she's enjoying it hugely.

'Right about what?' she asks innocently.

I grind my teeth. 'It hasn't been easy.'

'Finally,' she says.

'I feel ... it's crazy, but I feel I understand Mum better now, you know?'

She thinks for a moment, bending down to pull a thread from her hem.

'Don't you wish you didn't, though?'

'What do you mean?'

'I mean, I don't think it's been good for you at all, being here.'

'What about Mum?'

'Listen, I've had some time to think this summer. It was great being able to step back from it all. I know I used to nag you, because it was easier to have someone to blame. I'm so grateful to you for giving me that time, but I'm sorry to say I don't think anything will help until Mum sees somebody. Grief therapy. That's what she needs. And to be fair ... ' I dread what she's going to say next, brace myself, 'you could do with a little bit of help too.'

I turn to look at her. Her features are calm, not a bead of sweat sticking her fringe to her forehead.

'I'm not ready. You can't make me.'

'All right, Mum,' she ironises.

I was geared up for an argument, the same one we always have, in which she hints that I'd rather run away than face my problems, like Dad, but her response deflates me. I look at my feet. There are small pebbles on the concrete, probably brought here by the swimmers. I push them around a bit. Since when have I turned into my own mother? The thought is frightening.

'Wasn't it results day today, by the way?' Marion asks. 'How did the kids do?'

'They did okay.' Fern got an 8 and Johnny and Chantelle both a 6. It's nice that I didn't mess up their grades by staying and teaching them to the end, and that I still care about them and their unlikely French pop band formation ('We could be the Fantastiques Baguettes!' Chantelle was always very good with franglais).

'Maybe—' I start, but Marion stops me.

'Shit.' She's staring at the promenade ahead.

I follow her gaze. Romain is walking in our direction. Our eyes meet. Oh no. Not now. Aurélie is by his side, and she's spotted Marion too, her old school friend. If they decide to avoid us now, we'll all know it, but they carry on, Romain's brow furrowed, Aurélie sunny and radiant.

His life has continued without me, of course it has. I don't care about Romain, but I feel sick to think of Nick doing the same, that he exists somewhere on this earth, going out with Yuki and Charlie, rolling his cigarettes, checking the sky like he always does. Like a bear looking for rainbows. My eyes are prickling.

'Do you want me to pepper-spray them?' Marion whispers to me, a hand in her bag.

I shake my head and go back to shuffling dirt.

'Hey,' she says, pointedly to Aurélie, not Romain.

'Afternoon, Louise,' Romain says, and at this, I'm forced to look up. Aurélie is clinging to his hand, the only woman in the world who had the skills to tame the wild mythical artist. I want the ground to open and swallow them both.

'Hello,' I say.

'How are you?' He asks me.

They're all staring at me now, relieved that the burden of conversation has been placed on my shoulders.

'I'm fine,' I say, and the lie is obvious, but I don't care. I find myself examining Aurélie's perfectly manicured toenails to avoid meeting Romain's eyes. 'How are you both?'

Marion's hand is hovering above my wrist, as if she is prepared to pull me out of a stormy sea.

'We're amazing.' Aurélie laughs, and I wonder how Romain can bear to be around such smugness. Easily, is the answer, because he's the source of it. As far as he's concerned, he is her King Midas. I think of Romain's cold, petrifying touch on my skin.

Marion snorts. 'Good for you, to have found each other.'

'Why, thank you,' Aurélie says. 'It really felt like fate, you know – to think we went to the same school, though obviously quite a few years apart, and the day of his launch I was just walking past the bookshop and I went in on a whim ... He was early, and said he recognised me, so I stayed, and the rest is history ... But what about you, what have you been up to this summer?'

Thankfully she's asking Marion, not me. My eyes are now fixed on a sailing boat in the distance, to avoid looking at Romain and his quiff that I'd like to light up with a blowtorch. Marion is saying something about work and festivals and Fabio, and Aurélie can't hide that it doesn't sound, to her, as good as lying awake in the heat of summer listening to Romain's snores.

'What about you, Louise?' She suddenly turns to me.

'Oh, I'm—'

'You don't have to answer that,' Romain interrupts.

'Sorry?' Now I'm confused. We all turn to him. What the heck?

'Listen.' He takes his glasses off and starts cleaning them with the bottom of his shirt, revealing a slice of pale, hairy belly. 'I know *this*,' patting Aurélie's hand on his arm, 'must be hard for you. I'm sorry, we didn't know you'd be here. It's rather awkward.'

Does he think I'm still into him? Does he think I've spent the past, what, year (or more) pining after him? The thought of past Louise doing exactly that makes me cringe, but above all, I'm shocked that Romain is so full of himself, so unattractive, and that he is set on thinking of me as a desperate creature who only exists to enhance the life of others. Despite everything, despite losing Nick, I'm so happy that's not what I am any more. That I got a taste of something better.

'Not sure what you mean,' I say.

He nods. 'Of course. Sorry if I've made it worse for you.'

And then I remember: didn't I send him a vengeful text, after he invited me to his launch? And then Nick picked up the phone. Romain never forgets anything. He's making me pay.

'I've had other things on my mind for a while, believe it or not.' My indignant tone cuts right through the laid-back afternoon.

'Okay, Louise,' he says, glancing at Aurélie, who looks a little shocked. 'It'd be better for all of us if we could keep it civil.'

All I feel is how much I miss Nick. Nick and I will never get to be like this, a smug couple parading their happiness about the lake. Anger erupts into my numbness. Feeling this is weird, after months of nothing. It's pumping some energy back through my veins. I don't know if Nick is sick, whether he knows, whether he's doing anything about it. Every day brings me closer to never seeing him again. And Romain wants to take public credit for my misery?

'Louise is fine,' Marion says, in the voice she uses at work to deal with middle-aged men who call her 'young lady'. Looking at me, and being reminded of my general state, she's forced to add, 'And if she's not, I'm afraid it's got nothing to do with you. At all. Sorry to disappoint your ego.' Marion. My fierce sister, my protector. I wish I'd realised earlier how much stronger we are together.

Romain briefly glances at Aurélie, who now looks nothing but outraged. 'Come on, Marion . . .'

'Well, it was interesting seeing you,' I say. 'Enjoy the rest of your walk.'

And miraculously, they go, leaving us on our bench, immediately clinging on to each other. Marion watches them stride away. I don't.

'Well,' she says, 'I always said he was a complete jerk.'

'You didn't say anything when we were dating.'

'Didn't I? I did think it, though.'

'*Great*,' I say.

'It was good seeing you angry.'

'It was good feeling something.'

'I think you should go home.'

'Ah, okay,' I say, and go to stand up. She stops me.

'I mean England. I think you should go back. I think it's become your home – more than here.'

'But Nick—' I say, and she interrupts me again, her hand on my wrist. The gesture is so intimate, so rare between us.

'You got your heart broken,' she says. 'It sucks. But Nick was still better than anything else you've had here. I mean, look at that creep.' She nods in the direction of Romain. 'I think you're wildly unhappy here, and were for a while, even before you left. Most of your life, in fact. I know it's not easy, but we can both keep trying to help Mum, from our different places, in our different ways. I haven't always felt like this, but I'm getting used to the idea of not having you here. As long as you come back and visit, and Mum-sit sometimes. I'll need some breaks, I know that now. Otherwise I'll turn into a harpy. I've had a brilliant summer, but being here doesn't suit you. It doesn't have to be either me or you. We can both hope to be imperfectly happy.'

At this, I have to pop Marion's sunglasses back on.

'I do miss you, you know.' It comes out small and strangled.

'I know,' she says.

I want to tell her what I'm bracing myself for. A phone call, a message telling me about Nick's illness. Instead, I tell her how much her nagging me, pushing me forward, has meant over the past few years. How grateful I am that she looked out for me when I was at my worst, helped me stand up to Romain. How much harder I'm going to try to be there for her, even at a distance. She's right. Nick or no Nick, home has shifted. I know I'm not moving back here, and for the first time, it feels like something I've decided, something I can carry forward that stemmed from the presence of me and not the absence of somebody else. And I didn't realise how much I needed my sister's blessing.

Thursday 28 February 2019

> What a loss. Such a genuine and generous lad.
> Love to all the family. Will miss your smile so
> much, and all your wise advice. I'll never forget
> your help xoxo

I'm staring at the vaguely familiar messages on Nick's Facebook, hiding at the darker end of the pub even though I know they've all seen me. The lights are on, the bay window a square of greyness. The air is dry with radiator smell, but my fingers are so cold I can't hold my glass. A long time ago, another life, another season, like a presence you can only feel at the bottom of the sea, I suspect I was here, that this is what has been haunting me, but the extent of the hurt is entirely new, and scathing, and it takes my breath away, and every fibre of my body wants to rebel against the pain.

Yuki keeps turning around to glance at me, her eyebrows rising like an apology. I was going to leave after the service, but she caught me up and, all hushed, asked me to come to the wake. She said I should be there, but so far she hasn't come over. The space next to me at the bar feels warm, as if she has just left it, as if part of her from lives ago still exists there, a presence not quite embodied.

I can still hear Yuki's voice on the phone, in December. I had started to hope it would never happen, but one evening, her name flashed on my screen. 'Lou,' she said. It was the way she said it, vibrant with tears, after a long absence. I knew. 'I thought you should know, I'm sorry if . . . '

She waited for some pleasantries from me, but all I could say was 'It's about Nick, isn't it? Please tell me.'

'Yeah,' she said. 'Nick is sick,' and although I had been expecting the news for a long time, I felt so weak I had to sit down, bow my head to my knees so I wouldn't faint. Ants running up and down my arms, my jaw, my spine.

'Oh,' I said. Perhaps it would be different, milder this time, treatable. But it was December. So, so late. 'What . . . ' I began, but my vocal cords weren't doing their job.

'Pancreatic cancer,' Yuki said. She was crying.

'Is it . . . ' I tried again.

'It's uncurable. They found it late. He waited . . . He didn't want . . . Charlie's so angry with him. She's so scared, Lou.'

I realised I hadn't taken a breath since she said 'Nick', so I made myself inhale. You knew this, I told myself, you should be prepared. You're the only one who knew. Why didn't you manage to do something about it? 'Yuki,' I said.

'Yes?'

'I'm so sorry, it's all my fault.'

'What are you on about? It's not your fault.'

210

'I'm ... I kind of knew ... If I hadn't ... If I had ...'

'Stop,' she said. 'It's awful, it's the worst, but there's nothing ...' She sighed. 'It's shit, but it's not you, okay. I need to go now. I'm so sorry, Lou.'

I spent the day trying to go back in time again. Trying to hold my breath until it made me dizzy. Sobs came in waves, slicing through my breath, bringing my chest to near explosion.

In the evening, when nothing had worked, when now was the same as before, and the future looked its bleakest, for the first time in eight months, I called Nick.

It rang three, four times. Nick, like me, doesn't have a voice mailbox. Didn't. He would answer the phone for everyone, robots and scams and all.

Charlotte picked up. She didn't tell me if he was there, if he could hear me. To be polite, I asked her how she was, but she didn't reply. She told me she couldn't let me speak to him and I shouldn't call again, that I shouldn't expect him to comfort me because he was dying. That he was in no state to speak to me. She hung up.

I wish Charlotte would stop turning around to look at me now. I try not to stare back, and concentrate instead on Nick's Facebook. Surely even *she* understands that I couldn't miss saying goodbye. When is Yuki going to come and speak to me? I want her here, at my side, so desperately. I miss our friendship, lost in the meanders of my relationship with Nick and his family.

I wanted to feel Nick's presence one last time, be in an environment where I could fool myself that he might walk into the pub, grin and say, 'I'm here, everyone. Sorry I'm

211

late.' Every time my heart remembers what my brain knows, that he isn't here because he's in the dark and damp casket now deep in the ground, I feel like . . .

> Such a beautiful soul. I met Nick in Thailand in 2008. I've never met anybody quite like him since. Glad I was able to help, so blessed that we continued working together, and devastated that his life had to end like this. My thoughts are with you all, and with him. Eden

Eden Lubinski? The counsellor?

'Hey, Lou.'

I startle, nearly falling off my stool. Yuki's here. My heart sinks to see that she's brought Charlotte with her, in the long black coat lined with faux fur around her neck that she hasn't taken off. Charlotte's mascara is all clumped, making her eyes look like Man Ray's *Tears*. I understand why she's cold. I have no more blood in my veins, nothing left to warm me. I'm not sure what to say to her, what good Yuki expects to come from this.

'Hi,' I say.

'I thought you two could do with a bit of a chat,' Yuki says. She looks unsure now, but she's trying to smile. I don't know if it's for Charlotte's benefit or mine.

'You really don't have to,' I say, more to Charlotte than Yuki, and Charlotte appears surprised, irritated, doesn't attempt to hide any of it.

Yuki gives both of us a small encouraging nod. 'The thing is,' she says, 'things were said that weren't, I dunno, the most helpful . . .'

Charlotte glares at her, and she stops.

'I know you want us to get on, but I'm not apologising for not letting her speak to him.'

Ouch.

'You don't have to ... I understand,' I say. I'm trying my best here. I wish Yuki hadn't asked me to come to the wake. I wish Charlotte wasn't standing here in front of me. I can tell by the way her body is rigid, her eyes fixed on the bar behind me, that she's gearing up to something. It will be horrendous.

'You *don't* understand,' she says.

'Charlie ...' Yuki extends her hand, trying to stroke her arm, but she's fobbed off. 'Lou loved him too.'

'Don't,' Charlotte snaps. Yuki looks as if she's been slapped. 'He waited months until he went to the GP. *Months.* They said he might have been saved if they'd caught it earlier, before it spread. But he fucking waited, and I know it's because you nagged him so much when you were together. He was depressed, so low, he didn't even tell us he was feeling sick.' I'm shocked, hearing my own thoughts pouring out of her hard, hurt mouth. She seems to attempt to contain herself, and comes a bit closer, lowering her voice. 'And now ...' She gasps, unable to continue.

I don't know what to say, because she's right. Meeting me made everything worse for Nick. Charlotte doesn't storm off, doesn't sit down. She stands there, her breath ragged, and I'm aware of the rest of her family staring at us. I don't think they can hear us, but I know they hate me. I've never felt worse in my life. I briefly meet Yuki's eyes, but she looks away.

'Charlie, I'm so sorry.'

'Don't call me Charlie. I miss him so much, I'll never be

happy again. We all do. It took one bad relationship, *one*, to take him away from us. After all he'd been through. Fucking hell. I wish you'd never met.'

She stops for me to say something, but I can't. In her anger, I hear the devastating accusations I've tried to keep at bay. They stack up and they're too heavy and it's like the ceiling is caving in, about to bury me alive, and all I can do is wait for it to happen as it fills and fills ...

Nick's sad playlist, coming out of the pub's speakers. My body, on autopilot, brings a hand to my forehead, my voice says, 'I think I'm going to be sick,' and Charlotte walks away, her body fading into an outline. Nick is dead, he really is this time, and it's all my fault. I tried to make it work, I forced myself into his life, and he was all the worse for it. I just want ... I so desperately want him alive, happy ... I wish we'd never met.

The pain is so huge that I stumble on my feet and I know I'm going to crash down right here, in the middle of the wake, but there's also huge relief at the familiar door opening, finally, *finally*, and I run through ...

*

We go back.

CHANCE 4

Friday 18 August 2017

The pub smells of beer and deodorant, the atmosphere thick with it. I find myself surrounded by dark wooden stools on floorboards, pints of beer popping up everywhere like mushrooms, a pool table, laughter erupting in a giddy, drunken kind of way. People speak English, and as I wait, I listen avidly to the twangs of their accents. This is a new reality, a garish Disneyland version of a pub, with details like curly fonts that are deeply foreign. Even inside, the dark air is buzzing, not with bees but mosquitoes – I pull the cuffs of my trousers down, because the bastards have feasted enough.

It's another hot evening, but it rained violently and briefly on my walk down. I've got used to my light clothes, long sleeves and cotton trousers, sticking to my skin. I walked along the road to Ao Nang's centre, narrowly avoiding being run over by mopeds. The hills were green and lush with waxy leaves. Through whiff after whiff of coconut pancakes cooking on improvised stalls, I reached the street lined with an army of colourful signs screaming at me. *Beauty Salon Massage! Tattoo! Happy Hour!* In blue, orange, purple and some extra neon for emphasis. The Irish pub is the dark open mouth at the end, gobbling up all the tourists who are too scared of the local bars – those who travel to stay as close to home as possible.

I wish she hadn't chosen this place of all places – I feel like I'm in a drugged dream of my past. I chose to sit at a small table near the balcony upstairs, surrounded by lanterns floating around like big golden balloons. I'd rather be outside, on the beach; away from the water, it can get rather stifling.

'Don't get messed up by a Brit. Listen to me. Don't.'

I turn my head sharply. Two girls and a boy are chatting at the big table. They're all in their twenties, all drinking shots, acidic blue and pink like sweets. One of the girls moans and bumps her head repeatedly against her hands. Her friend strokes her back compassionately. I can't see the boy's face, but my heart skips a beat: he has shoulder-length hair tied back in a messy bun and is wearing a long-sleeved maroon hoodie. It's not him, Lou. You've left him behind. I try to focus on my pineapple shake. A group of inebriated bare-chested lads come in and sit down at the other end of the big table, drowning the conversation in banter that makes me cringe.

A month ago, on Yuki's birthday, I immediately knew it had happened again. The bees, the terracotta pots. I also remembered where I'd come back from, the coolness of ghost tears on my cheeks. I've had some time, in Asia, at a safe distance, to think about it all; in my hotel rooms, draining the Wi-Fi, I've researched the power of mind over our perception of time, trying to make sense of what has been happening to me; I've read articles about habits, about synapses growing stronger through repetition, neurons firing. Nothing exactly like this weird loop, the time seizures I'd been experiencing, but patterns. Little pockets of light that seemed to make sense, with how my memory worked, at least. How I seemed to remember more every time I went back. Going through the same motions again and again was making everything clearer. Too clear, too painful.

This time, I didn't want to be there; every fibre of me refused to go through it all again, and to save Nick, or at least give him a chance, I knew I couldn't meet him. I avoided looking at Yuki, or towards Nick and Charlotte's table, the wound of Charlotte's words at the funeral still fresh. I shut my eyes tight, breathed. The last choice left, Louise. You've tried everything else. I turned around, 180 degrees on my heels, opened my eyes and ran.

The fruit basket was still in my arms, huge and cumbersome. I narrowly avoided a barmaid with a tray full of plates, and as I swung around her, I crashed into somebody else. The shock of seeing him alive took my breath away, and I stumbled and fell to the floor. People turned around, gasped, laughed. 'I'm so sorry, so sorry,' he said. 'Didn't see you coming.' I couldn't speak to him. If I spoke, I would not leave. I looked away, stared at the pub's threshold, to the street beyond and the way to my empty studio flat, another pain that was more bearable than this.

I would sit down, close the blinds and book tickets. I'd go somewhere for the summer. Further away than I had ever gone. I'd delete Facebook and any other kind of social media where I could find Nick, then keep running.

'Are you okay?' he asked, helping me up, picking up the fruit basket, which had rolled a few paces away, wounded and dusty, white ribs emerging from the wrapping paper. 'No offence, but you don't look it.' At that, he stopped, as though he had confused himself.

I didn't allow myself a last glance. I said, 'Keep the basket, it's a present,' and ran again. This time I was unencumbered, and I made it out.

'Hiya.' A perfectly tanned tornado of blonde hair and piercings drops onto the stool opposite me. 'Gosh, it's a li'l bit stuffy in here, isn't it, mate?'

'Are you doing your London accent again?' I ask. When Lauren tries, she says *mate* as if it has three syllables, definitely a twang, more of a dissonant mandolin. She doesn't have a great ear – the first time we met, she thought I was Scottish. I miss Yuki's singy, unaffected tones.

'Yeah,' Lauren says, placing her Guinness on the table, and her phone, which she has to wrestle out of the back pocket of her tiny shorts to sit down. 'Was it better this time?'

'It was grand,' I say without thinking. Nick's words in my mouth, like the memory of a kiss. I wash it away with a large sip of my drink.

She chuckles. '*Grand.*'

Lauren, from Oklahoma and twenty-three years old, works at a small international school in the area, teaching soccer, PE 'and whatever else'. We've been hanging out for a few days now, and I don't know if she likes me or just doesn't think to question our alliance, this weird kind of travelling relationship, both close and devoid of real intimacy. She has taken to using the pool in my resort in the afternoons while she recovers from her hangovers. I was starting to get a little lonely, to speak to myself in the mirror in a croaky voice in the mornings to see if I still could, so I'm grateful for the arrangement. These past few days, Lauren's excited chatter, the sea and the sun have finally started lulling me into a sense of temporary relief.

'So, girl, you're still here,' she says. 'I thought you said you were moving on. Didn't think you'd still be around when I messaged you.'

I shrug. 'Well, this place has lots to offer, clearly.'

'Ha ha,' she says. 'British sarcasm. But I think it does. It's the best place on earth, nothing like the local nightlife.'

I was on the move: Vietnam, Cambodia, Bangkok. I kept landing, peeling myself off again, from hotel to hotel, staying hardly long enough in each place for my laundry to dry; it was dizzying and numbing how quickly and easily borders could be crossed.

Things eventually came to a halt here. In Ao Nang, you can take a boat to Railay. I now realise that's what I've been doing, sleepwalking my way here, towards the edge of Nick. After weeks of distance, the presence of his memories, the place coming alive with the promise of a pale, faded hologram of him, of a past he never spoke of but inhabited, is tantalising.

'You always look like you're so, like, down.' Lauren's bluntness reminds me of Marion. This time Marion was the one telling me not to interrupt my trip for Grandma's funeral, that she understood, and she sounded sincere. In July, remembering her tanned skin, her shiny hair, I'd planned a stop in Switzerland first; I gave her a week of enforced rest before I flew out to Asia. And with the memory of her coming to my rescue still fresh, how she was there for me when I was at my lowest, I opened up to her. As we walked along the lake, I told her I'd had my heart broken, that I needed to get far away from England, that I was sorry and grateful for all she was doing. She listened, and I felt the remnants of our old resentments melt away. Her anger at being abandoned, my guilt at living another life. I've made a conscious effort to keep it up – that connection – to make myself worthy of her trust. Replace physical presence with emotional support. I've kept checking on her and sharing my adventures with her on WhatsApp – I've stopped using other social media because I didn't want to come across Nick. I check my watch. They must still be in the church. I'll call her when it's evening, when she's back home with Fabio.

'Oh my God, you have a watch!' Lauren makes it sound like it's the silliest thing in the world. 'What do you need a watch for here? You're on vacation. Look.' She jiggles her own wrist, covered with pub-crawl, nightclub, friendship bracelets. Lauren is a rainbow of colour in the darkness of the bar.

I smile. 'Boats to catch, you know.'

'There's always another boat. There's always tomorrow. You know where you should go next – Ko Pha Ngan, the full-moon party, have a little fun.'

'No, thanks,' I say, but I smile.

'But seriously,' she continues, 'you still haven't told me about the sadness. Come *on*, we're all friends here.'

I glance at the boy I'm now inclined to call 'fake Nick', sitting a few metres away. He's moved a bit to make more space for the loud lads, and I can see his profile now. He isn't as handsome as Nick, his forehead is bigger, his nose too straight. His beard is a bit pathetic too – it looks like it's been glued onto his baby face.

'Same old story,' I say. 'I got my heart broken.'

'Aw,' Lauren says. 'Me too. My boyfriend dumped me on graduation day, can you imagine? I found the job here, and *voilà*. I'm great now.' She gestures to the rowdy pub, a glittery queen waving at her subjects. 'What happened to you?'

What happened to me? I mean, in which of the many chances I was given and managed to mess up?

'He died.'

Lauren's face falls. 'Shit,' she says.

'Yeah.'

Nick died, yet he's still alive. I don't know why I chose to tell Lauren this truth instead of the easier one, that I've been dumped too – we could have shared a consolatory piña colada. Perhaps I needed to hear it aloud, to remind myself why I'm here.

Lauren thinks silently for a minute. The pub is getting a bit rowdier; some of the bare-chested lads walk past us on their way to the bar, turning to admire Lauren's back on the way, the perfect slice of tanned skin between her shoulder blades, emerging from a complicated criss-cross of tops. Her hair falls in almost dreadlocks, tangled by sea, sex and sun.

'That's why you haven't moved on,' she says.

'What do you mean?'

'From here, Ao Nang,' she says. 'You're hoping that if you don't make it to the next stop, you won't have to go home eventually. Be there without him.'

I think about my job starting again, the staff training on 3 September. I haven't booked my ticket back yet. I told myself I didn't know where I'd be flying from, but Lauren is spot on.

'So stay,' she continues.

'I can't,' I say. 'I'd run out of money. I wasn't minted back home, it's not sustainable. I only have enough to last another two months, perhaps.'

'Shh ...' She indicates that she's thinking, pressing the little umbrella that was in my glass against her lips, like an artist with a pen, visualising the next stroke. 'Oh my *God*, of course, how did I not even think about it before? It's so perfect! Girl,' she's tapping my wrist with the point of the umbrella now, tap tap tap, 'there's a job at my school.'

'A job?'

'The French girl, Alex – no, Alix, "wiz an eye, not an euh" – she dropped out, went home for the summer and said she wouldn't come back. We all got an email from the head being all, like, hey, do you know anybody, we're in deep shit, kinda need to replace her for the start of term ...'

I flick the umbrella off my wrist, straighten a little on my stool. The streets outside are flooded in pink, green and blue, as if the whole town is painted in broad neon strokes. I feel drunk: all these colours are too bright, too artificial, like a tantalising plastic version of what my life could be.

'Wait,' I say, 'slow down. Your school's French teacher has dropped out?'

'Yeah, I can't believe I didn't think of it earlier. They're desperate – we start in a week. It's destiny!'

Through Lauren's enthusiasm, I'd almost believe that such a thing as destiny exists, that I could have made all those mistakes before just so that I'd end up here, in this dark and hot bar, surrounded by sweaty lads engaged in a surreal imitation of back home.

'Hang on, I have a job. In the UK.'

'So tell them you're quitting. That's what Alix wiz-an-eye did.'

'I have a term's notice to give, I—'

'Girl, what are they going to do?' she asks. 'For real? Fly all the way out here to get you?'

The opportunity, the decision, although huge, doesn't feel that daunting. I want to be far, far away from the UK. I'm prepared to be reckless. Indeed nobody will fly all the way here to get me. Especially not the person I want. And perhaps it's time I learnt to be okay on my own.

I want to have a serious conversation with Lauren, ask her more questions about the school, but she turns away, squeaks and, to my dismay, reaches across and tugs fake Nick's sleeve.

'You're back!' she shouts, hugging him tight. 'You didn't DM me, you jerk!'

'Back today,' fake Nick says, smiling a crooked smile, running a hand through his hair, which is now untied.

'Louise, Josh, Josh, Louise,' Lauren says. He smiles and shakes my hand. He's young; his teeth are so white they radiate in the dark like a glowstick. 'Josh works at the school too,' Lauren explains, or enthuses. 'Louise is a French teacher from the UK – Josh, you *have* to tell her to come and work with us, isn't she perfect?'

'I guess,' Josh says.

'Guys, I know, let's go on a pub crawl together! To new beginnings!'

In Lauren's world, that's when the piña coladas come in, I suppose.

Josh's smile isn't directed to me, more like a moth flut-tering from light bulb to lantern. A pale duplicate. A pale duplicate of . . . I must stop thinking that this life is the failed version, like a child's drawing, of something better. The something better left me so bereft that I ran across two continents to get away.

'Whatever,' I say. 'Let's do it.'

Lauren throws her arms around my neck and Josh's, jumping up and down and singing along to 'Girls Just Wanna Have Fun', which has just burst out of the speakers. We barge our way through the pub, through the boys messing girls up and the other way around, through the blue and pink neon night.

Later, as I collapse in my stuffy hotel room, full of alcohol and drowsiness, and the bed immediately starts spinning like a fairground teacup, I realise I've forgotten to call Marion. Not again, I can't let this happen again. I open WhatsApp, clumsily pressing to send a voice note. I don't know what time it is back in Switzerland, I'm too drunk to calculate. 'Sis, listen, I'm sorry I didn't call earlier, but I was thinking about you, and Mum, and you know what, you need to go for it. The wedding, the baby, whatever – if that's what you want, don't let anything stop you ... Life is too short ... ' I blabber heartfelt clichés until I'm repeating myself on a loop and the phone falls out of my hand.

Sunday 24 December 2017

And I snog him behind the bar, in the warm darkness of Christmas Eve, to the distant rumbling of waves and bass, like a twenty-year-old tourist on Kho Phi Phi. The Santa hat falls off my head. His mouth is a tad too eager, tastes of palm sugar mixed with alcohol. The party roars in the bar beyond, and the sea lies ahead with her arms crossed, silently judging me. I'm tipsy too, but only a little – tonight I'm perched at the edge of almost: almost drunk, almost enjoying myself, almost not homesick.

He pulls back slightly, and his breath is warm on my cheek. He's taller than me, broader than I thought at first and, thank goodness, he got rid of his ridiculous travelling beard as soon as term started.

'This is kind of a surprise,' he says. 'A nice one.'

'It's a surprise for me too.' I can't see his face; we've snuck into the shadow of the wall, away from the cheap golden fairy lights. The skin on his neck is flecked with grains of

227

sand. He laughs and bends towards me. We kiss again in the drumming heartbeat of the music, and I give in to the excitement of his proximity, a body offered to explore, this novelty that trumps all. Loud, shouted singing rings out from the bar, where what is left of our colleagues, the ones who didn't go home for Christmas or haven't collapsed yet, are dancing into oblivion and spilling sticky sweet cocktails on the sand.

'I never thought you fancied me,' he says. 'We didn't think you were into anyone.'

'*We?*'

With my arms around his neck, I feel his shoulders shrug. His physicality is intriguing because I don't care much about any other part of him. 'Me, Lauren, the others.'

I shrug too. What does he want me to say, that I've been silently fancying him for months? It's not like that at all.

'Lauren, well, she said your, y'know, ex died, so I didn't think . . .'

I step away from him. Damn American bluntness. It burns like alcohol on a wound.

'We'd better go back.'

Since I've started at the international school, the days have lined up all the same, like faded beads of equal size – smooth and blunt. The school opened only two years ago, so the classes are small, the textbooks brand new, the students eager and polite. I've been able to teach the way I've always wanted to, and they're listening. For the first time, I feel skilled and confident. The senior leadership team keep banging on that we must prove ourselves through our first set of results, so the teaching staff find every way to blow off steam as soon as they're off duty. They're all tanned, in their twenties, able to survive on about three hours' sleep, even in term time: the Lauren and Josh gang, a crew of Americans, Australians, a few Brits. And me. It's been way easier to slot in there, to pretend I belong, than I would have thought.

'Wait, Louise.' Josh's grip on my arm is half-hearted. I could easily slip out if I wanted to, but I stay. Nobody calls me Lou here. They've all adopted Louise without even trying to shorten it. I miss the intimacy of Lou. Sometimes, when I talk to Marion, when she's tired with worry for Mum, she says *It's hard, Lou*, and ice breaks off my heart like those melting icebergs, exposing the core of me a bit. My true shape. *You should come and visit, sis. You deserve a break*, I keep telling her. 'I meant no offence,' Josh says.

'I don't want to talk about it. Ever.' I'm starting to unlearn the *I'd rather not, if that's no bother* that punctuated my needs in the UK. I'm starting to revert to a more Latin directness, under American guidance. It feels quite refreshing to be able to say *I don't, no, absolutely not. Are you out of your mind?*

'Okay,' he says. 'Sure.'

There's an awkward pause, in which I wonder if he's going to kiss me again. I'm not sure what I want.

'Oh my God, guys, you're here!'

Lauren has found us. She tornadoes into our world, the gem stickers on her cheeks and the tinsel around her neck flickering furiously, accompanied by her current fling, an Italian bloke on a gap year.

'I thought you'd gone home, girl. I'm so happy!' Everything makes Lauren so happy. 'You both need to come and dance with us. *Right. Now*. George is so wasted, he's stolen an elf costume.' She slurs happily, sways like a palm tree, her hand open to tug us with her. Josh follows, and I'm about to when my phone starts ringing. It's Marion. I FaceTimed her a few hours earlier, when she was at Mum's, and it's not like her to call me twice in a day, even at Christmas.

'Everything okay?' I ask immediately, aware of my breath catching a bit, hobbling clumsily on the sand to get away from the noise. 'Is Mum all right?'

I'm not sure whether the signal is bad, or whether Marion isn't saying anything. Oh my God. Flashes of Mum in an ambulance, of Marion in a hospital corridor.

'Marion? Are you there?' I try again.

'Yes. Yes, sorry. I'm fine, we're all fine. I just ... I just thought I'd call to wish you a happy Christmas.'

'We spoke a few hours ago,' I say. Is she upset? There's too much else going on around me, whoops of cheer when Mariah Carey starts vocalising, but something is definitely wrong. 'Are you sure Mum's okay? If you're trying not to worry me, it's not working.'

'It's not Mum, Lou, it's me,' she snaps. 'It's me, I ...'

'What? What's going on?'

There's another pause, then her voice sounds a bit calmer. 'I think I'd like to visit you,' she says. 'You're right, I bloody deserve a break. That's what I wanted to check with you. I have some annual leave left to take. All of it, actually. How about February? Around half-term?'

'Sure,' I say. I'm relieved Mum hasn't had an accident, or a stroke, and I'm delighted Marion is coming. I think she'd love it here – in my world of glowsticks and fluorescent cocktails, we can have some fun together for once; she can leave her worries about Mum behind and enjoy a change of scenery. 'Of course. Looking forward to seeing you.'

*

Later, our little group huddled up on two beach sofas we've pushed together, we watch the sunrise. The sky burns to life in streaks of orange and pink, as if a hand has stroked across the horizon with fingers dipped in paint. There are only a few of us left, lost children on a desert beach. George is sprawled on the floor at our feet, the half of his face I can see dusted with sand. He's snoring gently, the torn elf outfit – I still don't understand how he got his hands on it, and I don't want to know – draped around him. Lauren and her Italian are dozing off, her head on his lap, her feet resting against my leg. He's doing that thing 'real men' do, propping himself up to pretend he's keeping watch, although his eyelids keep closing. Lauren's hair is tangled, and she's lost a shoe somewhere on the beach. I feel protective of her, an odd Disney princess covered in glitter, drunk and peaceful with her mouth slightly ajar.

I'm awake. It's Christmas Day. Music is still playing through the speakers. I think, a while ago, George convinced the bar staff to relinquish their sound system and plugged in his phone. They've all left us now. I'm listening to Portishead, Elliott Smith, Fleetwood Mac as they seep through the early morning like musical mist. I can't sleep, partly because of the proximity of Josh, whose head is lolling off the sofa's cushion. In the faint coolness of dawn, the heat of his sleeping body reminds me that I'm a little bit cold, with goosebumps on my forearms, but I'm alive.

The next song change brings Johnny Cash's expectant guitar chords out of the speakers, matching the waves. Roll after roll. Lauren sighs and her foot presses briefly against my shin. The music has melted into everyone's sleep, but for me, it conjures Nick. Nick and his playlists, men and women and their raw voices, haunting. 'Hurt' was one of his favourite songs.

As the guitar wraps its long chords around my chest and neck, I feel it again, for the first time in ages. The thread through time, not linear, perhaps, but not confused either. The thread linking me to my other selves, all my regrets and hopes and failures. The huge, huge gap where Nick has been.

But also, the space for myself in that gap. From the beach, alight with reds and oranges and blushed pinks, I can see her across the sea, the timid, broken girl from before. The Lou too afraid to fail. The insecure friend, the sister unable to show up, the woman paralysed in love. All those endless waves of anxiety, her brain twisting on itself, reliving and regretting and worrying at every possible outcome. Perhaps I haven't been weak; I have, with each one of these loops, been trying, and this might be something to be proud of. This time wasn't, perhaps, merely running away, but giving myself the space to let go of Nick. To mourn him and what could have been. To accept his loss and to discover who else I can be.

I move my legs slowly away from Lauren's, bring my knees up to my chest, wrapping my arms around them. The song talks about starting again, a million miles away. My empire would be an empire of sand. Sand is broken, basically; isn't it made of pieces the sea has chipped at? Or an empire of water, which always changes, yet always appears the same, which never starts nor ends completely.

I miss Nick. I miss him so, so much, yet we made each other unhappy. As the song fades, I keep my face hidden in my elbows and knees, swallowing the sobs like silent sips of water.

I feel stirring next to me and try to still my shaking shoulders. A hand knocks on my left upper arm as if it were a door.

'Are you cold?' Josh whispers. I shake my head. 'Hey, what's up?'

I have to look up at him.

'Oh,' he says.

'Sorry,' I whisper, the British conditioning resurfacing in my hour of need.

He looks away for a minute while I try to dry my eyes with nothing but my fingers, which are salted with seawater and sandy and splashed with alcohol, not fit for purpose. We live lives of immediacy here, no handbags, no tissues, no lip balms, no nothing. A few banknotes in the back pockets of our shorts.

My eyes sting. I want a shower. Josh looks so awkward, such a lost little boy. I want to be alone.

He is looking around, and I wonder whether he's going to crawl away, pretending he has to go and pee or something, but he shuffles a bit, and takes his T-shirt off. This is so out of the blue, so ridiculous, that I scoff. There's a certain type of lad here who thinks their bare chest is the answer to everything.

'Why don't you use that,' he says.

I look at him, finally understanding his kind gesture, and I feel so bad for misjudging him that I take the shirt and delicately dab my cheeks with it, like a silk handkerchief.

Josh puts his arm around my shoulders, and I fold towards him, backwards, like a tree hit by lightning. His chest smells of sand, faintly of sweat and deodorant, but it's not unpleasant. He doesn't move. I can't see his face. I imagine he's watching the world alight too, the round, fluorescent ball of sun bouncing off the surface of the sea, listening to 'That Look You Give That Guy', to 'Between the Bars' and 'The Chain'.

The world is so vast. I must be able to find my happy in it, in other kinds of kindness. I must be able to move on, stop defining myself and my worth by my relationship to others. Good or bad. A swing hanging from a tree dances in the slight breeze towards the invisible next mass of land across the sea, a million miles away.

Friday 16 February 2018

'Tonsai beach is better than Railay,' I tell Marion, trying to sound like I know my rocks. I'm a couple of metres off the ground, trying to find my next hold. Below, Marion is belaying me under the supervision of Aran, our instructor, a handsome guy in his mid twenties with a crooked smile and a full head of boyish black hair. The air is muggy, and I can feel the sweat running down my back. Marion seems happy, though. She's been chatting to Aran all the way to the limestone cliffs, and I can't help but notice that she was pretending to be less experienced than she is as he kitted us out: 'And should this be *this* loose, or tighter?'

When Marion walked through arrivals at Krabi's small airport on Monday, she looked perfectly at home, in her white linen shirt, her yoga pants and her huge rucksack. She had lost weight, though, and my heart squeezed in my chest as I waved at her. Something was wrong – I knew it wasn't my anxiety shading the picture before me; this time it was simply that I knew her.

'Lou!' To my surprise, she hurled herself at me. Our hug lasted a while, and I could feel her ribs under my hands.

'Welcome to Thailand,' I said.

'That was three different plane journeys.' She extricated herself, readjusted her backpack straps. 'Could you not have stayed in Bangkok?'

Part of me was annoyed that she'd immediately teased me about my choices; I was also relieved that she was still her usual abrasive self. It was a familiar feeling, that impulse to start bickering with her, and I was grateful for it.

'Wait until you see Ao Nang. You'll like it there,' I told her.

She waved a Routard guide right in my face. 'I've been planning, and we're going to do some sightseeing. I'm ready for a bit of adventure.'

I laughed, plucked the guide out of her hand – 'Oi, not so close to my face!' – then, curious, opened it at the page she had marked. *Plages de Railay.* The book slid out, dropped on the floor.

'Great start,' Marion said, 'throwing our guide away.'

I didn't want to joke any more. There was no way we were going to Railay, I'd make sure of it. In all this time, I hadn't gone, trying hard to leave Nick be.

'You're not too bothered by the heat, are you?' I asked, to change the subject, as I steered her towards the white bus with the neat dark blue writing. She threw her head back to tie her hair up in a ponytail. Some of her locks were sticking to her neck, and she prised them away with the tips of her fingers. She suddenly seemed so vulnerable.

'Nothing bothers me much any more,' she said.

Despite her alleged thorough planning, so far Marion has been happy to go along with me as a tourist guide. I've been showing off my knowledge of the country and its ways, navigating tips and insider transport routes with an efficiency I'm a little amazed at. It seems that without fearing others' judgement, without the pressure of proving my worth, settling into a new country has been much easier. Marion also hasn't told me why she's here, why she suddenly decided to travel halfway across the world to see me, when every time I mentioned that she should visit me in England, she was too busy, too much in demand back home. I've taken her island-hopping, hoping eventually that Railay would sound like just another beach and lose its attractive shine, despite the almighty praise of the Routard. We visited James Bond Island, went snorkelling, and now we have booked a private climbing instructor in Tonsai.

As I make my way further up the rock face, clumsy and clearly lacking any kind of elegance or technique, I think: this is fun. Through trying to please Marion, I'm also getting out of my comfort zone. I could never have imagined myself rock-climbing, but look at me now . . .

'You need to pinch for this next one,' Aran calls to me. 'Just there, on your right.'

I look down, and he gestures to me, demonstrating. Marion says something to him, quietly, and they both laugh. Is that her hand on his shoulder? What is going on? My fingers slip, my gripless weight pulling me away from the rock, and I find myself dangling about three metres above the ground. Marion is still chatting to Aran.

'A bit of help, please?' I call out, feeling like a strapped ham, and they finally pay me some attention. Aran grabs Marion by the harness to stabilise her as I abseil down.

'Lower your . . .' he starts.

'Your bum, Lou!' Marion calls out.

'Wait until that bum of mine lands on your head,' I call back to her.

After Marion and I switch places, Aran asks us to wait and walks a few paces away to get some water. I lean in and whisper to her, 'What are you playing at?'

'What?' she asks innocently.

'Flirting with our instructor.'

She shrugs. 'He's super cute.'

I want to say more, of course, but Aran is back, and now we all focus on Marion's climb. She struts confidently up to the rock, turning around to smile at Aran. 'Like this?' She's clearly experienced, and her form is perfect. He nods, and she begins to ascend.

While my sister climbs, methodical and graceful like a rock panther, I consider the rope in my hands tying us together, yet I've never felt more estranged from her. There's something going on, and I don't know what – I don't know who this flirty twenty-two-year-old-style version of Marion is. Marion who I've barely seen look at another man since she met Fabio three years ago. I resolve to talk to her – when we're alone.

'Lou?'

I look up. She is much higher than I was; she's hugging the rock, one hand desperately patting above her, finding no suitable grip. Aran tries to guide her, but her fingers keep slipping. She brings them back to the lower holds.

'Come down,' he tells her. 'I'll show you a better route.'

'Lou, I'm stuck.' She's not talking to Aran now; she's talking to me.

'Just abseil down,' I say. 'You know, lowering your bum and all.'

'It's not funny, I think I'm ...'

I realise that her shoulders are shaking. She's completely out of reach.

'It's okay,' I say. 'I've got you.'

She shakes her head, staring at the rock face like she can't bear to look back. 'I can't breathe, I don't know why I can't do it.' I can hear her panting louder and louder.

I see her standing in Mum's kitchen, her profile against the wintry light of the window, the straight, fine nose I'm so jealous of, drying and drying and drying already dried plates. Her sadness, her helplessness. *I want my kids to have that. When is she going to get better?* I'm usually the one who can't cope, the one who stalls, gets stuck.

I turn to Aran. 'I think I have to get up there and help her.'

'I'll go,' he says, but I shake my head. We can hear Marion panting from here, her raspy, shaky loud breaths. Aran whistles to his colleague, who was standing by looking after the equipment. Between the two of them, they make sure both Marion and I are belayed, and I start climbing.

Of course I'm not as good as her, and I don't quite manage to get to the same height, just a bit below her, finding an easy enough grip with my right hand, my left hand not too far from Marion's waist. I glance over my shoulder at Aran and his colleague; a slice of glowing turquoise sea is visible through the trees, monkeys circling abandoned belongings on the beach. It's so bloody high, so bloody hot. I pause, listening to my breath, pressing my cheek against the rocks, then turn to her. Her eyes are shut tight, her knuckles white, her whole body trembling.

'Marion . . . ' I start.

'I just can't do it, Lou,' she pants.

'Course you can. You're like a professional at this climbing thing,' I say.

'I don't mean the climbing.'

Checking my footholds are secure, I let go with my left hand. All I can stretch to touch is Marion's calf, so that's what I hold.

'I've got you,' I say, the best I can do right now.

'I told Fabio I wanted a break,' she says. Her breathing is still shallow. 'I don't want to talk about it. I just wanted . . . Well, now you know.' She opens her eyes, and one glance stops me from asking why. It feels like everything around us is crumbling – the rock face dissolving into sand, the sand falling into the pit of the sea, shaken by the totally new, unexpected concept of her and Fabio not being together. I realise how much I've been counting on some things to remain the same, selfishly, while I pulled apart the bricks of my own constructions. Now it is my hand, on Marion's calf, that is holding her up, safe while she crumbles.

'Okay,' I say, 'but you can't spend your whole holiday in Thailand here on this rock. The monkeys will come and mug you.' She snorts. 'Listen to me. You need to let go. Nothing bad will happen. We've got you. Just let go of the rock and grab the rope. That's it.'

Little by little, Aran and I coax her down, until she finally reaches the floor, her legs shaking under her. Immediately she composes herself, fluffing her long wavy hair over her shoulder, and Marion is back.

'I have a headache,' she tells me and the guides, as if that was the problem all along. 'Does anyone have any painkillers?'

I don't, but Aran rummages through his first aid kit.

'There,' he says, handing Marion a white and pink sachet with a familiar name on it. *Sara*.

She thanks him, takes two tablets with water. I take the empty sachet out of her hand, my mind spinning.

'Sara?' I say, to no one in particular.

'Painkiller,' Aran replies, busy putting the first aid kit back into the rucksack. 'Like paracetamol.'

Charlie wasn't clear. I think she said he took too much Sara. Yuki's words come back to me, how angry I got at Nick for doing drugs, being reckless. For not telling me about his past. Sara isn't a mystery Thai party drug. It's paracetamol. And if Nick really took too much of it, could it mean . . . could it mean he *meant* to take too much? Meant to . . . Oh, Nick. He always closed off when I asked him about Thailand – I always knew there was a part of him he kept out of sight. Now I understand how deep it runs, what he might have been trying to keep at bay.

'I need to drink another coconut,' Marion announces. 'I think I'm addicted, but I don't care.'

I nod. I'm elsewhere, searching memories for a time that to all my companions here didn't exist, trying to figure out everything I have missed. My blood beats in my ears, in my jaw, thinking about Nick.

241

'And by the way,' Marion's voice reaches me through the climbers' calls to one another, the distant happy shrieks of children on the beach, 'I've booked us a hotel in Railay tonight. It's all so close together – we can easily go back and get our stuff, then take one of the late boats, right?'

Oh no. The Marion I know. Bossy, impossible. *You have no idea what you're doing, what Railay means to me*, I want to call out to her. At the same time, what I just found out urges me to go, as if the place holds some of the answers about Nick's past. Marion walks off towards the bar, her legs still shaking, and I think about the toddler version of her at the zoo. If I'm with her, I think I can try to face my demons.

In the early evening, we whoosh across the sea, deep green like it's made of glass. Cool white droplets splash up the sides of the boat. Marion stretches her arm over the side, her fingers grazing the waves. We haven't talked about Fabio, I haven't asked, because I've been feeling sick with apprehension about this trip. As we rushed back to my room to pack overnight bags, I reviewed every possible kind of excuse; all I wanted was to crawl under the duvet and think about Nick, ten years ago, so close to where I now find myself. 'Some time together,' Marion said as I flaked, pleadingly, once she had had her coconut and was mellowed. 'Not dangling from a cliff. Please.' I couldn't say no to her.

The boat ride only lasts a moment. As we approach Phra Nang beach, I'm relieved that from the water, it looks like we could be anywhere – golden sand, a few quiet bars. I've read that everything here is more relaxed, more hippy than Ao Nang, and I suspect this is why Marion wanted to come. Our wooden boat slots nicely into a row among all the others, with their low purple roofs, their festive rainbow ribbons floating in the breeze. Marion hops off, drops her rucksack, runs a few paces inland like a little girl, whirls and whirls, her arms stretched wide.

'Lou, why aren't you looking?' As I join her, bringing her backpack with me, stubbornly refusing to face the sea, she grabs my shoulders to orientate me, as if I were a telescope. 'Good old Routard was right. It's stunning!'

I've looked at this view many times through the screen of my phone. The dramatic rock face on the left, a gaping giant shark mouth engulfing the sea, stalactites drooping off it, and further to the right, the mossy stone island in front of which Nick posed all those years ago. I knew he wouldn't be here, but his past still is, superimposed on my present as a dusty photograph.

The boats come and go, and there are still plenty of people lying on towels although it's reaching evening. My heart beats fast. I wish I were alone. To do what, Louise? Sniff for his presence in the air, which has been washed over many times since?

'The sea is so . . . ' I say, aware that Marion is expecting a better reaction. She lets go of my shoulders.

I'm away, breathing in another timeline. I walk closer to the shore, mesmerised by the photograph coming to life. I think *that's* the exact angle. Except that without a central subject, the sea appears awfully empty.

'I want to relax while we're here,' Marion says. 'Your life is one drunken party, it's exhausting.'

'It's not like I'm on holiday all the time. I've been work-ing. Even if it's hot and sunny . . . '

'You're not fooling me. I've met your colleagues. Josh and

Lauren and George are never "working". And by the way, we'll have to talk about "Josh" and what's going on there.' She's punctuating her statement with finger speech marks.

It was so easy to adopt this lifestyle. It attracted me because it required so little thinking, no projection backwards or forwards. I needed it, I think. To shed some of the burdens that held me back. Abandon the things that once triggered me. And I've finally been able to reflect on the person I want to be. I know, like Marion does, that I'm not meant to stay here for ever.

'Do you think this was all the same ten years ago?' I ask.

'What?'

'Do you think any of those molecules' – I gesture to the sea – 'were the same then?' I look at the rocks and think of the erosion, all the particles that were lost because I'm here ten years too late to meet Nick, and I feel crushingly sad. I was hoping for something delusional, a clue to what happened to him. Perhaps some kind of connection, an ability to suddenly, in the right location, understand what he's never told me.

'I don't know.'

'It . . . ' I forget she's here for a moment, and try to voice my feelings. 'It feels like something is missing.'

We stand there for a while, silent, until I hear what I think is a hiccup, bringing me back to the here and now. I turn to Marion. She's crying.

'Sis, what's going on?'

'Nothing.'

Like the little Marion I knew when she had scraped her knee and refused to stay down, she's standing tall, defiantly wiping her eyes with the sleeve of her shirt.

'I know it's not nothing,' I say. 'Please tell me. What happened with Fabio? I'm sorry I've been distracted. I'm listening.'

I drop down on the fine white sand and she eventually does the same. I try not to look at her, giving her time. Her ragged breathing mixes with the to-and-fro of the waves.

'I had a miscarriage,' she says. 'At Christmas.'

Delayed seasickness washes over me. I plunge my fingers deep into the sand, find some coolness, try to steady myself. My little sister.

'I'm so sorry.'

I wrap my arm around her shoulders and some time passes. We watch a monkey wrestle a little girl in a green swimming costume for sweetcorn on a stick. The monkey wins, the child wails, and Marion continues to cry.

'How long had you been trying? I didn't realise you were,' I say.

'Since August. Things had been really hard with Mum, then there was something you said, a voice message – I think you were smashed, to be honest. But it made me want to stop waiting for things to be perfect. I got pregnant in October.'

'Why didn't you say something earlier?'

'Oh, don't tell me off on top of it,' she snaps.

'No, of course not, sorry, it's just . . . I would have wanted to be there for you.'

'And you have been, as much as you can. I guess that's why I'm here. I've just not wanted to talk about it. No one can do anything about it anyway.'

I don't know what to say. I feel wretched. 'I'm sorry you were the one who had to travel all this way.'

'That's why I needed a break from it all,' she says.

'Suddenly it was so hard to be around Fabio. And looking after Mum.'

I look down at the handful of sand I'm holding. All those rocks, those shells, crushed to nothing, unrecognisable.

'I've always thought you two were good, that he was nice.'

'He *is* nice.' She starts drawing swirly patterns on the sand. 'But he also doesn't say anything. Fucking ever. I'm fed up with him not talking about it – the baby. Our loss. All he ever does is make me tea and make sure my feet aren't cold and look at me like a golden retriever puppy.'

'Sounds like he's trying, Fabio style,' I say.

'Yes, but Lou, I'm so done with *nice*. The way I feel, I'd rather someone who would scream, or someone who'd drive me around on his motorbike with no helmet on. Like my ex, you know, Fred.'

'Which one was he? The one who also lived with his gran?'

'He lived above his gran's garage.' But she's smiling now. 'And he used his toenail clippings as toothpicks.'

'It sounds like Fabio is a better prospect, everything considered,' I say. 'Maybe you're the one who needs to scream. To let it all out.'

'Maybe.' A pause. We listen to the sea, its constant music, the sound of two hands rubbing one another, of millions of grains of sand falling into an hourglass. 'My God. I've done what Mum has done, haven't I? I've shut myself away from him. I've refused to face it.'

'You're not like Mum,' I say. 'You're here. You just needed a break. I'm sure Fabio is waiting for you, if you want to work things out with him.'

'And you're not like Dad. I used to be so angry with you,

246

for leaving us like he did. I didn't think you'd stay away, I thought you'd be back after a few months, a year maybe. But you didn't come back, and it broke my heart again, just like when he left. And then losing the baby …'

'Marion …' I squeeze her closer, unused to this new proximity of our bodies but unable to let her go.

'I'm glad we're not our parents. Thanks for being here,' she says, wiping her cheeks, leaving a streak of golden sand on her skin. When she speaks again, her tone is lighter, and I know she wants to move on. 'Talking about useless men, you're clearly wasting your time with Josh.'

'I just needed to have fun,' I say.

She nods sagely. 'Oh, I know. But he's as deep as a cardboard cut-out. Your life here has no substance, and I know you need substance. You thrive on it.' She grips my hand. 'Lou, I'm serious. I need you nearer. I don't mean Switzerland, England will do, but not *here*. Not on the other side of the world. I don't know what you were running away from, but I hope it wasn't from me. I need you.'

I look into my sister's lovely moon-shaped face, and I know I'm ready now. Ready to show up for the ones I love.

Later, we leave our very nice hotel on East Railay ('We're not twenty any more, we're not savages,' Marion said when I praised her choice of accommodation), and go for a stroll along the cement strip bordering the mangrove beachfront, lined by bars and stalls. I get a bottle of Coke, and Marion a fresh coconut that she nurses along with her, sipping from it through a straw. We stop at the end of the path by a bar with a climbing wall advertising a free bucket of alcohol to anyone who can get to the top. In silence, we watch lad after lad slip and fall off the wall, in a moment of shared sisterly *Schadenfreude*.

There's a family sitting at a table – father, mother and two children in their early teens, though it's past eleven and everybody is getting drunk. They are all blonde, all with long hair. One of the teenagers would clearly love to have a go at climbing.

'Go on, Klara,' the rest of the family encourage her, in Swiss German.

Marion and I smile at each other. Grandma's name. And a Swiss family. What are the chances? Unfortunately, Klara is a little too small, and she doesn't manage to get higher than about a metre above the ground before having to give up to the consolatory cheers of her family of clones.

'Hold this,' Marion says, slurping the end of her drink very loudly and handing me the empty coconut, her purse and her phone.

'You sure?'

She nods. For the second time today, I watch her being harnessed and clipped in. Then she starts climbing. In no time, she reaches the top, tapping the last, highest rock, and as everyone in the bar explodes in cheers, she throws her head back and screams. A long, whooping, lung-emptying, tension-releasing howl.

As she throws herself down, backwards, a different woman from this morning, so much more herself, I think about how I've grown here too. How I've learnt to put myself out of my comfort zone – have some fun without worrying too much about the future. But I think I'm done – I'll finish my year here, then I'll go back. And I'll start by being more *there*, in every way I can, for the important people in my life, and also for myself. No more hiding, no more fear. I connect to the bar's Wi-Fi to download Facebook and Instagram on my phone again. It's time Louise came back to reclaim her life, tell the world that she exists.

As Marion gets unclipped, and condescends to high-five pretty much everyone in the bar, shaking her head at the offer of her free bucket, I open the app I haven't checked since July. I have one new Facebook message.

18 AUG 2017, 21:35

Hello there. First of all I know Im a stranger but I'm not a stalker just to reassure you. I wanted to apologise for crashing into you and sending you flying like that at the Five Horseshoes. Its only a few days ago that Yuki commented on an old photo of you on here and I realised you're her friend, the Lou who never turned up for her birthday. I assumed the fruit basket was for her, hope that's okay, she loves it and will keep it well fed. You probably know but Yuki and I are together now, so I don't want you and me to start on the wrong foot. So yeah I wanted to apologise for ruining an 'epic night out' (Yukis words) and I hope when you come back the 3 of us can go out for a drink. Yuki misses you actually but shed kill me if she knew I said that. Also you looked so so familiar even then but I couldnt place you. Did I know you before? Nick

Sunday 18 March 2018

The taxi drops me off in the main car park, and I walk through the underpass to the zoo, trying to push aside the memory, much clearer than I would like, that I have been miserable here; the worst version of myself. I don't want to face my own ghost, but not coming here today wasn't an option.

I booked my ticket in advance, making sure I would be here for opening time. I wriggle to extract it from my travelling backpack, which is half full and strapped up tightly, ready for the airport tonight. A few people are waiting by the turnstiles, almost all exhausted parents with excited marshmallow children. No Nick yet. I don't know when he'll appear. I hope it's soon.

Even though holograms of past painful scenes keep popping up at the corner of my eye, I'm proud of my boldness. It was the messages that did it. At school, I told the head there had been a family emergency and I had to fly back to

Europe for a few days. Marion's visit had prompted me to act, like the protector I was always meant to be, but never dared: somebody who climbs up mountains or jumps on planes to make sure that the ones they love are okay.

Josh hardly noticed my goodbye, cradling his Singha, laughing with George. Lauren, however, hugged me as if it were the last time. 'Aww, girl,' she said, then seemed to stall.

'I'll be back in a few days, you know,' I said. 'I'm finishing my year, don't want to let the school down, not like Alix wiz-an-eye.'

'Who?' she said, then blew me a kiss.

On the plane, the thought hit me that she and Josh might have started sleeping together. Would she tell me? I imagined their tanned, perfect limbs intertwined, Josh's hand grabbing Lauren's wild hair, something animalistic yet pleasingly symmetrical. I found this picture more arousing than having sex with Josh myself. We both knew we were never enough, not even close.

After buying the biggest chai latte the café can make me, I head all the way across the zoo, towards the otters' pen, to wait for Nick. My memories of being here with him are patchy, but sadness has printed this place in my mind, and the morning mist ripples with his presence. I know I was overbearing, that delicate constructions crumbled under my clumsy, grasping hands. Strangely, I don't miss the Thai sun; the cold, the greyness is invigorating. I should introduce myself to the otters, ask them to be my lucky charms, to intercede in my favour with the gods of rotten fish and fake rivers (*panta rhei*, everything flows, I would joke with them, if they cared), but they're nowhere to be seen. Probably still snoozing.

The frozen wetness of a nearby bench permeates my jeans immediately. *I'm told I'm decent at giving advice.* Flashes of Nick's grin make the longing almost unbearable. I get my phone out, return to Facebook and WhatsApp to stare at the messages again, despite knowing them by heart.

I didn't sleep at all that night in Railay, kept reading and rereading Nick's message, sent six months earlier. Yuki hadn't told me anything; I had left her behind too, and we hadn't really kept in touch. As I wondered whether they would still be together, an image formed in my mind: Yuki kissing Nick in the smoking shelter, buried under layers of time and experiences but strong enough to instil the idea that perhaps it was meant to be, he was better off this way, no matter how much it hurt me. In the early hours, Marion looking peaceful, asleep in the other twin bed hugging her pillow like when she was little, I read the message yet again, trying to convince myself it brought some sort of closure.

Then, a couple of weeks later, a WhatsApp came from Yuki.

> Lou, something happened. I mean I did something so dumb. Pls can we talk? I know you're miles away and you prob don't care but I messed up massively and I would really really appreciate talking to someone who hasn't been around. I know it sounds kinda weird but can I call you?

Even after so long without speaking, I heard the call of our friendship. I phoned her a few hours after she texted me, during my dinner and her lunch break. She sounded cheerful at first, and I wondered if I had misinterpreted her message before understanding that she was in the office. As she moved out of her colleagues' earshot, she fired filler questions at me about Thailand, and we talked like the two distant acquaintances we had become. Then there was the sound of a door shutting, and her voice came much closer to the receiver, shockingly direct and intimate. Its texture echoed another time, the chopping of lawnmowers, giving me goosebumps. 'What's going on, Yukes?' I asked, my concern for her resurfacing but also my concern for Nick.

'Yukes?' she asked, startled. I winced, because I knew that was what Nick called her.

'Your text seemed urgent,' I said. 'What happened?'

'It's all been shite . . . it's all fucked up,' she said. 'I'm sorry to bother you. I know we haven't spoken in a while, but I really needed to talk to somebody neutral.'

'Is it because I'm Swi—' I tried, but she spoke over me.

'I'm well aware I'm the one who messed up, by the way. I've been feeling terrible. It's just I can't exactly talk to Charlie about it, and she's the only person I'd . . . I have no one, nobody left to talk to, and I feel so awful.'

There was a silence, in which I remembered I wasn't supposed to know who Charlie was, so I asked.

'Ah, mate,' Yuki said. 'Where to start.'

Listening to her story was like having sleep paralysis: watching an unfolding disaster, unable to do anything to stop it. How she'd met a guy called Nick at her birthday, how they had grown close, eventually started dating. 'I knew,' she said, 'that neither of us thought it was quite right, but he was so nice, so kind, you know.' (*I know*, I wanted to shout back at her.) She met his sister at Christmas and they started going to art galleries, the two of them, because Nick wasn't into art, until what Yuki described as 'the inevitable' happened. 'I think we were so focused on lying to ourselves about where it was going that we actually allowed it to happen. I shut my brain down, I know Charlie did too. It was terribly selfish, pretending that only what we wanted mattered, that there would never be a next day.'

That all this had happened while I was living my life in Ao Nang, that it could have actually unfolded without me somehow *feeling* it, having some kind of hunch, was mind-boggling. Should I have anticipated it? Did I have any responsibility in this disaster?

'What happened – with Nick?' I finally managed to ask.

'We told him straight away,' Yuki said. 'We couldn't lie to him, Lou. You don't know him, but he's such a good guy. We should have stuck to being mates. He's . . . he's kinda disappeared since. Won't reply to messages, pick up the phone, nothing. Charlie tried his school, but they said he was signed off. She went to his flat, but he didn't open the door. She's losing it.' Her voice broke. 'She's so worried, and now she's refusing to see me too. It's all my fault – I can't sleep, can't eat, I keep thinking there must have been another way for me to meet her without messing her brother up, it should have all been different. It isn't fair.'

There was a soft semi-silence indicating that Yuki was crying. I wanted to be compassionate, but I also felt so much anger.

'Yuki, listen,' I said, not managing to smooth the snappiness from my tone. 'Let Charlie try to find Nick, okay. She'll know what to do. I'm afraid I need to go now. Sorry. It's the end of my break. Evening duty.'

After a pause, her voice came through. 'Okay. Thanks for listening. Sorry to bother you when you're busy.'

'No bother,' I said. What I wanted to say was: *You hurt the man I love because you can't make up your mind who you really want to be with. You live a different life every time, depending on who comes along and wants to be with you. He was going to be happy this time, peaceful. This is so messed up, Yuki.* I hung up.

I thought about 18 March, the significance of the date, what I had started to suspect. Nick in Thailand, pockets full of painkillers. Charlie's bottomless despair – *he was depressed, so low.* Could it happen again? Filled with dread, I looked up his Facebook profile, but it was set to private, and there was nothing there I could access. Nick was grinning on his picture as if nothing had happened. It seemed I wouldn't ever be able to have a life now entirely free from feeling entangled in his fate. I knew I had to know he was okay, and there was only one day, one place where, as a stranger who used to know him, I could hope to find him.

The zoo is getting busier, despite the weather. I start walking around to warm up, making sure I keep sight of the otters' pen. It's now one o'clock. Where is he? Something isn't right, and I don't know what I'm supposed to do.

As I stalk the area like a freezing big cat, I try to remember a conversation Nick and I had in a different life. It exists in my head in the shape of a cloud, but if I try to isolate an element and zoom in, everything dissipates. It is so frustrating. I try again and again to look at the memory from all possible angles. *The zoo is my happy place.* Happy place? For me, it's full of ghosts. *Please, Nick, don't leave me.* Did I say this, or think it? At the time, or now? *It's my thing. I go and check on the baby elephants.*

Oh no. Of course, Nick isn't here.

I pick up my rucksack and break into a clunky, numb-legged run, to the hilarity of the otters, who have finally decided to come out, peeping over the barrier. I know now that they're in fact demons, who have been happily toying with me.

I run across the path, nearly ending up under the wheels of a big 4x4. Behind the windscreen, the mother yells something, the father gesticulates at me. I catch a glimpse of a small person in a green jacket on the back seat. I hold my hand out to apologise and spring forward, past the *Asian Elephants* sign.

The paddock is huge, at the edge of the park, and the public can walk up to it from every direction, or sit on one of the many benches. I don't know where to look, panicking that I've missed him. *Always playing catch-up, Louise.* I try to calm down, to examine the visitors again, one by one, counting and discarding them, until I stop.

He is here.

He's standing by the barrier, looking into the paddock, the flow of passers-by parting and closing around him. Like me, he isn't wearing enough layers, only his battered leather jacket on top of a hoodie. Loss and lust crackle in my jaw. He's alive. I imagined . . . I thought . . .

My legs are bending like Plasticine, so I drop on a bench a little way behind him. I must wait until my breathing calms down, which will take some time, so I watch Nick watching the elephants. His back is a little stooped, and he stands out because he's alone. If I weren't the random former housemate

256

of his evil ex, I would run to him and throw my arms around his chest to prop him up. It seems the natural thing to do, despite the two people at war in me, two different Louises, both making decisions fit for a different set of circumstances.

There's a smaller elephant in the herd. She's clearly young, but not quite a baby any more. My heart melts that Nick and I are both watching how she sticks to the bigger ones, while constantly exploring with her trunk, theirs in turn patting her head for reassurance. Nick's right hand, down by his side, is fiddling with his keys. With his other hand he checks his phone, puts it back into his pocket. It's such a peaceful scene, him watching the elephants, the families walking between us on the frozen ground, the accents I've missed as they bicker over sharing prawn cocktail crisps and Cadbury's Dairy Milk. I've missed it all – England jabs my heart, the greyness and warmth of it. I know I'm home.

He shouldn't be standing there alone. I'm going to walk up to him, tell him it's okay. Perhaps I could help him, like I know he tried to help me all those chances ago. If I stay on this bench any longer, thinking about the fact that he's here, breathing the same damp English air as me, there's a chance my heart might keep accelerating to the point of no return. I need to do it, I must be brave *now*, or another chance will pass me by.

I'm getting up when he turns around and looks in my direction. Our eyes lock. Nick's eyebrows rise, his face opens, he takes a step forward, then stops as a familiar figure hurries towards him. Charlotte. She's running in her delicate boots, her fur-lined coat. She appears clumsy, tiny without Chomsky at her side.

She stops a few paces away from Nick. Then she does what

I've been aching to do: she hurls herself at him and squeezes tightly. His body, from here, looks rigid in her arms as her shoulders shake, against the backdrop of placid elephants going about their day.

At least Nick is going to be okay. For now. I push the thought away, ignoring the yellow tinge of his complexion. I tighten the straps of my backpack, try to wriggle my frozen toes in my trainers. On my way out, I walk past Nick and Charlotte as close as I dare. She's sobbing and saying how sorry she is, how worried she's been. He is silent, but he's crying too – his face and eyes glisten in the grey light.

Thursday 23 August 2018

'Hello. You're here.'

'Hi, Mum. I guess I am.'

I gently kiss her on both cheeks, nod to my bags.

'Is it okay if . . .'

She steps aside after some hesitation. Has my mother actually forgotten that I was coming back to stay with her for two weeks? But perhaps it's the space her body is taking up she is unsure of. I drop my backpack and my suitcase in the corner of the living room. Mum considers the evidence of me for a moment, as if trying to make sense of the whole affair. She turns to me.

'You look so different, Louise,' she says.

My name coming out of her mouth is such a relief.

'I was in Thailand, Mum, of course I look different.' But I know there's more than the tan and the long hair, bleached by the sun. I know I hold myself differently. I feel different too. Stronger.

'Must have been awfully hot.'

I fuss around her for a while, in organising mode, which I have learnt is the best way I can deal with the shock of seeing her smaller, frailer. I do the dishes, put on a load of washing, make the bed in the guest room, organise my clothes in the empty wardrobe. It still smells of IKEA plywood, all those years after my adolescent presence has been worn out. It was Mum who used to put furniture together; she had a methodical way of going about it, and it used to drive me mad, watching her counting screws and lining them up by type before getting started. How much I would give for her to take on a project, any project, now.

Finally, when I can't find anything else to do, I make us some tea and sit down with her in front of the TV. The sunlight glows orange through the balcony blinds, projecting sturdy and unmoving shadows.

'How was your flight?' Mum asks.

'Fine,' I say. 'Long.'

We watch the millionth replay of *Murder She Wrote*, while the tea cools slowly, untouched by either of us, and I think of everything that could be said in this silence.

'Wouldn't it have been more practical if you'd stayed in England right now?' Mum asks. She seems to play back what she said, and adds, 'Sorry. You're welcome here.'

'That's okay.'

But it's not okay, is it? She's already talking about me gone. I want her to reassure me. I want to know that she's proud of me, that she has my back no matter what. I wonder how different my choices would have been if I had felt that reassurance. You have to carry on without it, be your own person, but it stings. It's like walking a tightrope without a net.

'I meant it would have been more handy to stay with your friends,' she continues.

'I don't have friends in England,' I say.

'What about your Japanese friend?'

'Yuki and I aren't talking any more.'

'Oh. When are you starting your new job in London?' Mum says *London* as if the thought of it gives her the shivers. In her world, London is full of smog and Jack the Ripper.

'The seventeenth of September.'

When I returned to Thailand in March, I realised that time had indeed paused, that Marion was right: it wasn't me, it was a phase of me – sure, both useful and temporary, but it wasn't home. Despite the tiny risk of bumping into Nick or Yuki, I decided I had as much right to be in and around London as them, and I started organising my return, propelled forward by this new efficiency I'd discovered in the most foreign country I could imagine.

I secured a job as a bilingual content manager in a marketing firm. There were lots of words in the job description I had to look up, and I was gobsmacked that I could be hired in the UK as a non-teacher, something I hadn't thought possible before. I'm moving into a flat share in Barnet. It's all sorted, weird how easy it's been. This is my chameleon life: without the fear of getting it wrong, I have learnt I can adapt, change my colours and try out all the paths to see what suits. From the pink, blue and green neon of Ao Nang's nightlife to the silver mirror scales of London's inner-city skyscrapers.

'Will you be taking all your stuff with you?' Mum asks, the only thing that matters to her.

'I don't think I'll manage all of it, Mum, but I'll try

261

my best. I can always pick up more when I come back at Christmas. How's Marion?'

Marion and Fabio have just come back from a road trip to Italy, clearly a sign that they have been trying to patch things up. As I considered what to do with my own summer, I gave in to the guilty fear of spending my time alone with Mum, catching her low mood as if it were a cold. I was high on my new sense of independence, of freedom, of self-reliance. I took some more time to explore Laos and Malaysia before making my way back to her.

During my travelling, Marion and I communicated more than we ever had when we lived in the same country, and I thought about what it actually meant – *keeping in touch*. Not sending drunken inspirational voice notes, but being present, reaching out with honesty. I've learnt so much about what she needs, how to read between her lines. I can't wait to see her tonight, for the whirlwind of her clattering necklaces and many tote bags, our quest for Mövenpick's Tragitella. Meanwhile, I don't think Mum has any idea what has been happening, either for Marion or for me. I don't think she's ever asked.

'She's been busy, I think.' Mum shrugs.

'And Fabio?'

She shrugs again. 'Nice young man. Just like ... What was his name again?' She frowns, but I know exactly who she means. 'Your writer.'

'Not mine, Mum, never was,' I say, keeping my voice as kind as possible, but I want to scream. I don't know how I'm going to spend two weeks here, around her. I change the subject to better memories. Something that might make her smile.

'Do you remember when Grandma used to take me and Marion to the zoo to see the capybaras when we were little?' I ask.

'I wasn't there when she took you.'

'I'm sure we have some photos.'

It's true. I don't remember Mum ever coming with us to the zoo; she was always busy. I get up and go over to the cabinet along the wall. There's a big drawer in there where our family photos are kept. Mum stuck all of them into albums. Sometimes I would pad into the living room in my pyjamas, finding her peaceful, focused, hard at work at the dining table, under the golden lampshade, sorting, organising, dabbing the photos' glossy backs with glue, carefully placing them down. The loops of her handwriting. *Vevey, juin 1992.* I want to meet that version of her again, escape into her carefully compiled notes of a time long gone.

But the drawer is empty. Mum has stood up too; she's checking on her orchid.

'I can't find the photos,' I say.

'Yes.' She's poking at her pet plant's yellow leaves, and my heart sinks.

'Where are they?'

'I tidied up.'

'But where have you put them?'

'I threw them away.'

'You what, Mum?' I stare at the drawer, which only contains a few sad, useless items, as if I can somehow conjure those three decades of family history into being. When I turn back to Mum, I'm not trying to hide my disbelief.

Mum knows she's in trouble. Her face hardens. She presses

263

her hands together, interlacing her fingers, bracing for an imaginary impact.

'I ... I didn't like all this clutter any more.'

'You kept the *napkin rings*.' I'm waving one at her like hard evidence. 'You never even use them, and you kept them.'

'You never looked at the photos, either you or Marion. You're never here.'

'I ... But doesn't Marion come to see you every week? Do your shopping?'

She nods. Her hands are trembling.

'There were photos of your father in there, of Grandma, and I ...'.

'Mum ...' But I don't know what to say. I've been away too long, that's true. You drop one glass ball and they all crash.

'My orchid is dead,' Mum whimpers, staring hard at the stems of the plant, the exact same colour and texture as the supportive twigs.

I wonder if she's going to wash off, dissolve in the moment. She seems to be about to. Her eyes flutter about the room. Our lives, our childhood, Grandma, Dad, the idea that things were once okay, once balanced and safe – all gone. Thrown into a landfill somewhere amongst vegetable peelings and dirty nappies.

We stand there looking at each other, two strangers with shaking hands. Matching bookends, circa 2018, until I can't contain it any more.

'I don't care about your bloody orchid,' I hiss. 'You threw it all away – all our memories. I can't believe ... I can't believe how selfishly you've been acting for so long. Marion and I *exist*. It's not only about how we make you feel – how do you think *we've* been feeling?'

I hate to see her recoil, I hate myself for my unkindness. All I want is for my mother to hold me, but my mother, as such, is no more. There is a stranger I love in her place, a stranger who starts crying.

'It was so hard when Grandma was sick,' she whimpers. 'She said I didn't do it right.'

I sigh, press my fingers on my temples. 'What do you mean?'

'When I got her to hospital ... She was so mean. She wanted to die at home, she said ...' She doesn't finish, because she's pitching on her feet, opening her mouth wide around a silent wail, immediately bringing up both hands to contain it.

It's the first time Mum has spoken about it, the toll it has taken on her, and my anger starts draining out, my arms dropping to my sides. Caring for Grandma. Three small words, evidence of something I never really thought about, that I took for granted, the only tiny tip of her story she lets us see. I think about everything she doesn't show, how deep she's had to dig herself in to manage the sadness, what her subconscious decided to sacrifice so she could merely survive.

I want to run away, to reset, but I don't. Instead, I go to her. I become the mother, and she the child who sobs inconsolably. I feel in my arms how brittle her body has become, and I fear that her big, raspy sobs will be too much for either of us to bear. Caring until you break. I consider silently the points where my mother's life and mine have started to intersect, without our knowledge, consider the urgent need for me to harden myself, to preserve my sanity. And I hang on.

Saturday 15 December 2018

Throwing myself out of the drizzle into the welcoming cosiness of the Five Horseshoes, I find Yuki at a small table in the corner. It's mid afternoon, and everything is temporarily quiet, the fire crackling in the big log burner. The air smells of mulled wine, sizzling bacon and winter spices. England at Christmas – how I've missed this. I fold my coat and place it on the comfortable bench next to me with my handbag, patting them briefly as if they were small dogs. I wish. Yuki is already sitting on one of the wonky chairs opposite; she didn't take the bench like she usually does.

'Jeez, I nearly didn't recognise you. What happened to your faithful satchel?' she asks, her tone light and conversational.

'Not suitable for the office.'

'I kinda liked it. It was very you. I don't think I've ever seen you in a suit before, even when you were teaching. You look so smart.'

I know she's nervous, and I am too. We haven't met, or reached out to each other, since our rather cold conversation on the phone in March, when she told me what she'd done to Nick. I've been angry with her since. I wasn't sure whether she wanted to meet to have it out with me, but she appears civil, if slightly self-conscious, fiddling with her metal straw. Her nail polish is unusually flaky, like the paint on those neglected houses by the seaside. As I notice it, something clicks into place, the cogs of a machine that immediately sends a pain signal to my brain, but I have hardened myself to memories, and I shake it off.

There's so much good in my life now. Marion and I text or speak most days. I feel this new patience, this new understanding of Mum's situation. I've been enjoying London, walking out of Bank Tube station and under the Gherkin on my way to work, pinching myself that I'm here, a little Swiss in the City. The job is going fairly well, as nobody makes paper aeroplanes with the content I've produced. I'm 'the French girl' both in the office and in my house share, navigating Friday post-work drinks with a new kind of social ease imported from Krabi's bars. When colleagues and I share retellings of epic nights out at the coffee machine, or I watch iPlayer alone in my room, I feel safe and distant. Now, seeing Yuki, remembering our friendship of the Food Network and fry-ups, I have a whiff of longing, and I wonder if I may have fallen into this version of my life like an ant into amber.

That's exactly what I was worried about. I don't want to be unsettled again when I've worked so hard to find some kind of balance. When Yuki texted me out of the blue to ask to meet up, she was almost pleading. It opened something:

the need for closure – always a risk. Yuki and Nick have been two ghosts with unresolved business whose haunting I've kept at bay, but I know I can't really move on without confronting them one way or another.

'You said you wanted to ask me something,' I say.

'I want to ask many things,' Yuki says. 'Like where did you buy that shirt? Never mind. I'm sorry . . . '

Her voice trails off, and I say, unable to stifle a smile, 'Come on, spill the beans.'

'*Les beans?*' she offers tentatively.

'*Les haricots.*' I can't help but give in to our little game, and she appears to relax.

'Have you met someone? You're wearing make-up, and your hair is so sleek.'

I automatically bring my hand up to my hair. I grew it in Thailand, have started looking after it more. I've started looking after *myself* more. A bit of Lauren's influence, a bit of focusing on myself, having the chance to do that away from everything else, I suppose. 'It's not always about dating somebody, Yuki.'

'You're right. Sorry.' As quickly as it was spurred, the excitement settles back to awkwardness, like flakes in a snow globe. She's wearing a linty jumper with a distressed collar; the roots of her hair have grown brown. Her nails are bare, chewed right to the edge of the flesh. I'm suddenly afraid that she has found her way back to Ben – a trauma buried deep.

'How is Ben?'

'Who?' She's confused. 'You mean lawyer Ben? I dunno. Why do you ask?'

'Just popped into my head.'

'Are you asking because you want me to set you up, now that you work in the City too?'

'Oh my God, absolutely not.'

'Ah, mate,' she smiles, 'it's good to know that even if you've been, you know ...' she gestures to the shirt, my straightened hair, the handbag next to me, 'you're still weird. Lucy's always rated Ben, but I think he might be a bit of a twat.'

She still knows me, and she's figured Ben out too.

'How is Lucy?' I ask.

'I dunno.' She shrugs, pressing her straw so firmly between the tips of her fingers that they turn white. 'I moved out. She was awful to me after ...' She hesitates, seems to decide that it's okay to go ahead. 'That's what I wanted to ask you, actually. I was wondering if you'd consider sharing a flat again, with me. You know, now you're back. We used to have fun, didn't we?'

That's the last thing I expected. Where I live now, house-mates pass each other like ships in the night. There is always evidence of cooking in the kitchen, yet I never meet anyone there. One moved out last week and was swiftly replaced by another with the exact same shirts and haircut and even smell, whose name I might not know for another while. I assumed it was independence, a hardened, strong kind of solitude that has become second nature.

'I don't know, Yuki.'

She appraises me, her disappointment obvious. 'Are you mad at me? I understood why you didn't stay in touch much when you were away, but finding out you were back through Facebook ...'

'I'm sorry, I didn't mean to upset you.'

269

'It's not about what I did to Nick, is it? I know I messed up, I said that when we talked on the phone back then – I made a huge mistake, and believe me, I'm still paying for it. I thought you wouldn't judge me.'

'Because I don't know you as well as your other friends? Because you think I don't care?' Bits of what I used to read between Yuki's lines, in other lives, put pins in my mouth. Prickly, uncomfortable.

'The opposite. I kinda thought you did still care. Despite you moving away. I thought you'd still be there for me. I'm so sorry about Nick – you don't even know how sorry I am.'

I want to say, how could you do this to him ... I don't know how he is, but the way Yuki presents, her haunted look, I know it's not good news. No miracle. She looks like she's about to cry, her dark eyes rounding up.

But I have to face it, be completely honest with myself: Yuki didn't know. She followed what she really wanted, for once, in the worst possible circumstances, the worst timing, unaware that Nick was going to get sick. She had no idea; it was a mistake, a moment of selfish recklessness. And anyway, what she did to Nick isn't for me to forgive.

'It's not about Nick,' I say, and that's true, though the truth surprises me. 'I can't just be there for you when it's convenient, Yuki. I don't want to be your last choice. Always coming after Lucy and the others. The one you call when you have no one else to talk to. And now you don't have a housemate, you're getting back in touch with me.'

'What about you running away from my birthday without a word, then fucking off to Thailand? Hardly staying in contact?'

We look at each other over our drinks. All this Christmas

270

music is giving me a headache. Or perhaps it's the gin. As I reinvented my clothes, I needed to reinvent my drink too. I take a sip of G&T, the bitterness making my taste buds recoil. I hate the taste. I hate the person Yuki's words are describing, someone who runs away from a friend, who judges their decisions harshly. What am I doing?

Before I can reply, Yuki continues. 'Listen, I'm sorry I moved in with Lucy and left you.' She starts fiddling with her earrings. 'No, really, I shouldn't have done it. I've never been good at saying no to people. I've had some time to think about it in the past few months. I've had to, when all my mates started bitching about me – it was entertainment to them, kinda. Whereas you . . . I know you were disappointed in me, and now I think I appreciate that you expected better of me. But back in March, all I wanted was for you to listen. I didn't ask you to tell me I was right, because I wasn't. Sometimes you're very bad at listening, Lou, that's a fact. But I'm the one who messed up, on multiple accounts. I'm trying to work on it now.'

The memories her speech unlock, washing over me with such force that I have to grip the table, are not of March. They are of that terrible place nestled deep in another time: Yuki and I standing together at the bar of another pub, her almost in tears, pleading: *Lou, please listen*. She was holding a funeral order of service, and I didn't hug her. A Christmas party, as well, when she kept me at her side, in the kitchen, and gave me jobs, because she knew how awkward I felt around strangers. All the while my carapace softens. I always thought she didn't need me, I ignored how many times she said she wanted me in her life.

I think about what we could have saved if we had

talked about it earlier. I still wonder at not seeing Yuki's vulnerability, her tendency to make bad decisions, which at the time seemed preferable to my natural inability to make any. Yuki is the one person, in all my chances, who has been tossed about by circumstances, including by me. I realise with a jolt of shock that I've been treating her badly too, using her according to my needs. I always operated on the premise that I was the awkward, unconfident one, somewhat wronged and weak. Neither of us is weak, but between the two of us we could fill bucket after bucket of self-doubt. Shame burns my cheeks as I promise myself to do better. Not next time, but now. Right now, and for ever.

'I'm sorry I didn't listen,' I say. 'Not only that time, but all the others too. I got into the habit of keeping some distance so I didn't seem too needy and wouldn't get rejected. Survival mechanism, you know, rock-bottom confidence. It's no excuse. I'm also sorry I didn't stay in touch. Your friendship mattered to me more than I realised.'

'Ah, mate,' she says. 'I think we both took our friendship for granted. I want to do better, I really do, for those things it's not too late to save.'

We look at each other, and her smile is so relieved, so vulnerable that I feel like bursting into tears.

'Yuki,' I say when the moment has lingered long enough, taking a deep breath. I have to hear it. The shell has been cracked open. I have to know. 'Too late ... What is it too late to save?'

Her voice wavers. In the Five Horseshoes, under the flickering Christmas lights, we are two people of clefts and breaks and rubble. 'Nick. It's too late for Nick. And it's all my fault.'

'Nick has pancreatic cancer,' I say.

Her eyes widen. 'They found it so late. Way too late. He was depressed, he ... Fucking hell, if I hadn't ... if Charlie and I hadn't ... But Lou, how do you know?'

We're interrupted by the barmaid. The density of Yuki's question, hovering between us, is briefly dissipated by her leaning over the table, the empty glasses clinking as she pinches them.

'Do you want another?' I ask Yuki, looking to buy some time. She shakes her head slowly.

'Nick used to ask after you, you know.'

'He did?' My voice is quiet. Yuki doesn't answer straight away, and I wait as Nick, his grin, his all-encompassing hugs, takes over, the volume of my longing turned up, up, up.

'Yeah. He saw an old picture of us on Facebook, I think; he said something about bumping into you at my birthday, here. Sending you flying. He asked how you were doing in Thailand, what you're like. When I tried to make sense of it, you just disappeared that night, and I thought ... It might be idiotic, but I wondered whether something had happened between you and Nick. If I'm honest, that's why I didn't tell you we were dating. I was worried about what I might find out.'

Nick's message. His eyes on mine at the zoo. He knew me. He thought I was important enough to reach out to me. The implications are too big – surely I can't just barge back into his life, not after so much time has passed. I take a deep breath. 'It's complicated, Yuki.'

'So there *is* something. I'm so confused. Please, help me out here.'

I hold my breath for a moment, poised at the apex of this

273

choice. *I've been stuck in a time loop, I've been travelling back in time, I fell in love with Nick and when he dies it breaks my heart.*

I would love to tell her, but I can't. I can't, because it's too much to ask of her – to believe me, to find out that her life has turned out crappy when it could have been so different. Sharing the burden would be selfish right now. She needs to move forward. We both do.

I see things more clearly than ever. Yuki and Nick hugging on the wooden decking, their sparky, healthy friendship. Their kiss in the smoking shelter, the one that tortured me so much in Thailand, wasn't meant to be, wasn't something I'd snatched away from them. I kept expecting them to know more than me, be wiser, a step ahead. I've been angry a lot, with everyone, this time around, but I'm the only one who deserves my anger, bitter and bubbling in my throat like my G&T, for running away from all of this, all of them. I left everything behind, hoping people would sort things out for me, write a version of life I could be happy in, where I wouldn't hurt anyone, wouldn't suffer, just exist. I don't want to wear suits and have to name my butter in the fridge and be the French girl. I don't want not to have Yuki in my life. I miss Nick like hell. I'm angry at all the time it's taken me to realise that I need them, that I want to show up for every imperfect moment with my loved ones.

'Ah, nothing much,' I say. 'We'd met before, on a teachers' night out, had a snog in the smoking shelter. I guess it was weird seeing him again. I was a bit spooked – you know me, I'm skittish – but there's nothing for you to worry about. It was nothing, really, and then I went away anyway.' The words of my lie are thin and watery, like skimmed milk. They slide down my throat leaving absolutely no trace. I tried to say what would help Yuki most, put her mind at ease.

She starts rearranging the beer mats so they align perfectly, like tarot cards.

'Did it help?' she asks eventually. 'Thailand? I've thought about running away, somewhere far. Starting afresh.'

'No. Yes. I guess – it helped me with *me*. With my confidence.' It's so weird. That conflict. Knowing I've done wrong by those I love but right by me, somehow. Prepared myself for greater things. Built my armour, my resources. I'm ready now, finally, and I hope it's not too late. 'But listen,' I say, 'there are good things ahead for you. Great things. You deserve so much better than what you've settled for.'

She smiles. 'I've started seeing a counsellor. I'm really trying to understand how I came to fuck up the way I did. She's helping me unpick it all – I know now there were things I couldn't have known. I never had all the cards. Nick doesn't open up much. As for Charlie ... well, I think it could have been a different story. I really wish.'

'Maybe it still could be,' I say.

'That's why I got back in touch. I worked it out in my sessions – I'm trying to reach out to the people who used to treat me well, you know, not like a rotten banana.'

I smile. *'Une banane pourrie.'*

'Oui,' she says, smiling back.

'Lonely This Christmas' starts playing, and Yuki visibly cringes. Then she leans forward, patting my hand gently. I freeze, not knowing what to do with her warmth, the offer of connection that I feel I don't deserve right now.

'You're right,' she says. 'Nick is dying. He refused treatment. He's been in palliative care at his parents' flat for a while. The nurses say he doesn't have long. I'm not saying you should do anything, but I think he would have liked to see you, deal with whatever unfinished business there is. Whatever you decided not to tell me, to be kind to me.'

We blink at each other.

'Thank you, Yuki. I have to go. I'll call you later, okay? About the flat? I promise I will.'

She nods. I grab my handbag, my coat, and run out, shouldering my way through Christmas shoppers on St Peter's Street. I run to the station, hop on the first train to Luton, searching my way through the town centre to Nick's parents' block of flats, following the recollections of a route he guided me through before, when we were together.

Somebody is coming out of the building; I run, and they hold the door open for me, I climb to number 8, on the third floor. I wait for my breath to steady, but not long enough that I'll lose my nerve. The doorbell rings loudly, like a drill in my brain. Any second, I could run away from this, back down the echoey stairs, but Nick is dying and I need to see him. He asked after me. He deserves an explanation, my apologies, more than anybody else before he goes. *Unfinished business.*

'Yes?' A nurse opens the door: young, petite, in her twenties, her brown hair pulled back. In her spotless blue scrubs, she exudes as much authority as a club bouncer.

'Hi, I'm here to see Nick, please.'

She shrugs. 'Wait here.' She shuts the door in my face. Not taking any chances. I can't hear anything going on in the flat. I can't bear to think about what lies behind that door. I can't bear to think I might not be allowed in.

The muffled sounds of two female voices draw near, and the door cracks open.

'What's going on?' Nick's mother asks. She's wearing a soft peach cardigan. Her hair is impeccable, her face deeply tired. A whiff of deeply mum-like, comforting floral perfume reaches me, and my eyes start prickling.

'Hello, Mrs Adeyemi, I'm a friend of Nick's,' I start.

'I don't recall meeting you before.'

I do. I carry with me the memories of her looking at me from a bay window, whispering something to Charlotte; of her disliking me because, first, I was an imposter at her son's funeral, then I let him down. Those memories are heavy, slowing me. I glimpse the nurse behind her, walking from Nick's bedroom door, which is now slightly ajar, to the kitchen. I hear the sound of the kettle being filled.

'I . . .'

'Nick is very sick.'

'I know. I'm so sorry.'

'We're extremely sorry too, love.' Her voice is strained.

I want to kick myself. But what else could I say? I feel around for the magic words, the ones that would open this door to me, if they existed. 'May I see him, please?'

'No, you can't, I'm afraid. Nick isn't in a state to see visitors. I'm very sorry. Have a good day.'

My eyes are filling, but she isn't looking at me. She starts closing the door.

'Please, Mrs Adeyemi, I know it's not . . . I know it's not ideal, but please let me see him. It's important. I've come all the way from . . .' All the way from where? St Albans? Nick's troubled past?

'I'm sorry,' she says again. The door shuts in my face.

I stand there pressing my fingers into my eyes. Then a loud, shrill sound erupts on the other side of the door – like an alarm, a panic button having been pressed. Oh my God, Nick. Maybe he's dying right now, on the other side of this door.

Maybe he dies every time.

I've hit the heart of it, and I lean forward, press my forehead against the door to consider the awful, hard truth: Nick dies every time, no matter what I do. The realisation is like losing him all over again, the very thing I've tried to avoid this chance around.

It doesn't matter if I shrink away from my life, if I answer Romain's text, if I run to Thailand, if I meet Nick at the elephants. Regardless of my choices, he always dies.

'I'm sorry,' I whisper to the door, 'I'm so sorry I abandoned you. I was such a coward – I was so, so stupid. I thought by leaving I'd make it better. I'm so sorry for putting you through this. But I know, now. I know that having you in my life, even for a short time, is better than not knowing you at all.'

I will the door to open, wishing too hard for what could have been, whispering that I'm ready, armed for what is ahead, coaxing it to let me in now I've shown up. Soon my words start mixing together, floating and dissonant, tumbling everywhere in the echoey stairwell, all the memories. Is Nick's mum opening the door to call me in? Is Nick getting up and walking out with me, straight out of the door into the sunshine, rushing through the summer streets because we're late, *but we can catch up*, lying in his old bed, my head nestling in the crook of his elbow; standing at the stove pouring mustard and barbecue sauce into the stir-fry, *it's burnt, we need to throw it away*, I say, *no it's not*, he's saying, *it's not too late, I can save it, just you watch*, and we both laugh

278

and scrape it all into the bin, and finally the door opens, it opens ...

*

We go back.

CHANCE 5

Saturday 15 July 2017

Bees rush in suddenly, my friends, the fuzzy softness of their sound making me dizzy. What I first take for coughing, wheezing is actually somebody laughing so much they choke on their beer. I flick off the remnants of darkness, tangled in the fingers of my brain like cobwebs. I'm so glad to have another chance. I will never, ever forget this feeling, I promise myself, this place where everything can start anew. I will enjoy it this time. I step out of the way and stay there for a little while, closing my eyes, breathing, patrons and waiters coming and going around me.

'All right, matey?' Yuki's voice sings behind me. I turn to face her, my heart tense with anticipation, but she's beaming, holding a pint in each hand.

'Happy birthday!' I drop my impractical present on the grass to give her the most effusive hug, and some cider spills on my back, soaking my shirt.

'Oops, sorry,' Yuki says, offering me one of the drinks. 'Might as well take it and drink it.'

I shake my head. I will stay clear-headed for this. 'Not drinking today – but can I carry it for you?'

'Don't worry,' she says, nodding to the fruit basket. 'Looks like you've got your hands full. What on earth is that?'

'Why, it's a present fit for the occasion,' I grin.

We go and sit at the table and she tears the paper open. 'That's incredible, I really *really* wanted one of those!'

'For Lucy's rotten fruit?'

Lucy scowls at me, 'Excuse me,' but Yuki's delighted.

'Yeah,' she says. 'Exactly for that.'

This is perfect. The sun is stroking my back, and I'm struck by how clearly I remember my previous goes, exactly as my past research predicted. The more I go back, the clearer it gets. I can see it all now, panes of glass lined up on top of one another, some bits matching perfectly and others completely different, and I'm giddy – Yuki and I haven't fallen out, and for the first time, I realise how precious this is to me. And also, of course, I know Nick is here. What would be different this time? Me. I'm different, and I can't wait to find him again. I can't look yet, because I want to enjoy this pre-moment of seeing him, in the warm safety of knowing what will happen next.

Yuki is admiring the fruit basket like a piece of art, while Lucy puzzles at it. There's something I must tell Yuki, but it is taking a bit of time to resurface in my excitement.

'Shame we were planning an epic night out,' Lucy says, nodding to my gift. 'You can't exactly drag this monster with you to the club.'

'Oh, shut up,' Yuki tells her, grinning. 'I'll ask the pub to look after it for me and pick it up tomorrow.'

Epic night out? It comes back to me. 'Yuki, stay away from Ben.'

'What?' She looks up from the basket. 'What about Ben?'

'Yes, what about him?' Lucy echoes Yuki perfectly. A flash of her jingling bangles brushing Nick's wrist, of her nasty gossip.

'He ... uh,' I say, finding myself at quite a loss. Nothing I can say would make sense to them.

'He's a good bloke,' Lucy insists. 'What do you mean, Louise? Are you playing matchmaker now?'

'Better than you playing travel agent.' She and Yuki look confused, but I'm proud that it makes sense to the people who can remember her pathetic seduction attempts in another life – I'm my best and only audience.

'Lou, I'm not wanting anything with or from Ben,' Yuki says.

'You did tell me you quite liked him on New Year's Eve, though,' Lucy says, 'so perhaps Louise does have a point, though I don't see what would be so bad in that.' As she picks up her cider, ever the meddler, the new sense of safety I felt, of knowing that nothing will ever happen in exactly the same way as it did in the past, shatters like a dropped pint glass. Everything is possible, and I want to find a way to help Yuki, encourage her back on the path she embarked on when we last spoke, finding what she really wants rather than who she's supposed to be with. I think I can do it all. I think I'm strong enough, insightful enough now. It'll just take a little fine-tuning. But I also have Nick to worry about.

I can't hold it off any longer, and I look towards Nick and Charlotte's table. A quick turn of the head as Lucy teases Yuki about making out with Ben in a cupboard last New Year's Eve. I want to feel that surge of happiness at the sight of him, an addiction strong enough to transcend time travel.

Except he isn't here.

'See, Louise, not a chance in the world of that happening.' Lucy's sarcasm calls me into their conversation.

'What?' I stare at the empty table where Nick and Charlotte should be. Two lads arrive, carrying beers and puffy bags of crisps under their armpits, and take a seat. This can't be right. Where is he?

'Never mind,' Lucy says. 'You're clearly a million miles away.'

What if he . . . stayed dead? Or what if his heart stopped, or he got run over by a car on the way here? He knew me, last life, he seemed to know something about us; what else has he worked out? Perhaps he remembered I'd be here, perhaps he's the one who has decided to step away this time. To avoid meeting me. A new, fully formed fear takes over: Nick has met someone on his way here, I was never anything more to him than a helper, somebody who would nudge him toward his true life. That's what I wished for him last time, and it's too late to take it back. What a fool I was.

'Lou?' Yuki's face is concerned.

'Hey,' Lucy says, 'I don't know what I said to offend you, but . . .'

I shake my head. More people are joining us now, exclamations ringing in the air: birthday girl, thirty today, for ever – for ever – *for ever.* I sit for a moment in the midst of it all. The panic is intense. Because I had hope, certainty, that I would see him again, and now . . . I'm going to be sick, and I'd rather not vomit into the fruit basket.

I get up, fish my silent phone out of my pocket: 7.51. Somebody asks me about Brexit. I ignore them, mumble something about going to the bar, and walk past Nick's table, wondering what to do with myself. The two lads are munching through their crisps. These seats are taken, I want to say, but clearly they're not. There's nothing, no cardigan, no abandoned dog lead, not even any empties, no trace of the people I thought would always be there.

Inside, there's a free stool at the bar where Nick and I sat once to spy on Charlotte and Yuki. I sit down, turning away so I can scan the room. Perhaps they're inside. Perhaps Nick is, in this life ... what is the word – *frileux*. Sensitive to cold. Even French escapes me now, and it's not cold outside. My anchor in time, my mother tongue, my sense of self, my purpose. I want him so much that for a second I feel I could *will* him here, conjure him out of thin air, ready for this life I'm burning to start. With him.

'Excuse me,' a male voice says as somebody shoves their body against the bar next to me. The place is busy now, but still. The move is forceful, and unwelcome in my space of loss. I glance at him.

'Ben.'

He turns to me, surprised, and I catch it, how the transformation from a troll into a lawyer is a conscious one, a process he has to activate.

'I'm sorry ...'

'Louise,' I say. 'I'm a friend of Yuki's.'

'Oh. Of course, yes. Hi, Louisa.'

Some people don't change. They never, ever do. No matter how many chances they get.

He's waiting for the barman to acknowledge him. Clearly, being ignored bothers him. He's put gel in his hair and stinks of aftershave – his tangy smell is as invasive as his presence.

'So what are you doing sitting here by yourself?' he asks.

Talking to me is clearly a way to look like he's not been made to wait. It's only me and him in this room among lots of strangers, and Yuki is outside. I don't want him near her. And I'm angry with fate, or destiny, or whatever normally gets a capital letter but doesn't deserve one right now. If I can keep Ben from getting drinks for a little longer, perhaps Yuki will start talking to somebody else.

'Taking a breather, I guess. I was going to order more drinks, actually, but it's rather busy,' I say.

'Rather busy,' he repeats, mimicking my accent, and it takes all my scrambled-together sense of purpose not to smash a nearby empty glass on his head. I find myself wanting to whack men a lot these days. 'Where are you from?'

Memories and instincts come back in bulk, but this time I try to be Lauren, all relaxed and open. I pretend I believe Ben is the kind of guy who would own a chalet in Zermatt. I go through the motions, wondering how long I can sustain this, spurred on by the way Yuki faded when she settled with him, the *culaccini* on her coffee table, the dusty quality of her face and existence. I think back to our first conversation, when I was wondering how I never managed to get *those guys'* attention, and how little I care now. It's empowering.

Ben's eyes are on me, not on the barman any more – he looks like he's made a pleasing discovery.

'It's a good accent. Not quite French, but almost.' He smirks, shuffling a little closer to me. 'My last girlfriend was Spanish.'

'Ah,' I say, wondering what this has to do with anything.

'Carla. Sadly it didn't work out. You know the Spanish,' he says conspiratorially.

'No. Tell me.'

288

'Well ... *fiery*. Demanding. I mean, she was stunningly beautiful, but ...'

I wonder whether these people walking past us are here to see Yuki. They look familiar. If they are, surely that's enough seats taken, danger averted?

'That's a shame,' I say.

'Say that again?' He leans in closer. I have a quiet voice, I know that. But still. His overpowering cologne is locking me in. So thick I can almost see lime-green mist in the air around him, out of which I can't escape.

'Shame it didn't work out,' I lie. Good for Carla.

'Ah, that's okay. Like I said, I've decided to change what I go for, you know, in that department.'

'You mean, no more *stunningly beautiful*?'

He pauses, appearing to think deeply, his eyes on mine. I resist the urge to look away. Not when the only power I have left is to waste his time.

'I wouldn't put it like that exactly, but yes. Perhaps looking more for a girl-next-door now, somebody *sane*, you know.'

'That's so profound, Ben,' I say.

He laughs. 'You do have the cutest accent,' he says, placing his hand on my knee. 'Especially when you're trying to be all sarky.'

The urge to slap his hand off, to get up and go as far away from him as possible is excruciating. How ironic that I find myself knowing how to play this game now, after a life in Krabi's bars and wearing a suit in the City, yet care little for it. The thought that I ever needed these men to like me, that I ever let them influence my choices and my views of myself – all those books I didn't read because I knew Romain would disapprove, the stories I abandoned because of his silent undermining – infuriates me now. All that lost time. I wish I could meet those former Louises and shake them by the shoulders. Hard. I'm so lucky this time has been given back to me.

There's a clock above the bar. It's 8.38. By now, we should have met Nick, and Charlotte should have left with Chomsky. The timings of this evening are set in my brain, handholds of fire through the fog of the unknown. I'm reviewing the options of what to do with Ben's hand on my knee when Yuki walks past and catches my eye. Ben spots her too, but he doesn't acknowledge her, even when she sees his hand and pulls a surprised face. *What the fuck*, she mouths at me, but not in an angry way. She doesn't stop, makes for the ladies'.

'Yuki,' Ben whispers, close to my ear. 'You know, I made out with her on New Year's Eve. It's a shame she dresses as crazy as she does, she could look great. I like girls who dress more . . . *plain*, like you.'

'Yuki's great as she is,' I say. I'm about to say much, much more, but my pocket vibrates. A text. My heart does a little dance; it's Nick, I'm convinced of it. He must have found me, got my number, I don't know how, but it has to be him. As I lean away from Ben, shuffle to retrieve my phone, he drops his hand.

I'm so stupid. It's 8.42 – Romain's text. I had forgotten all about it. Last time, I deleted it straight away. Of course Nick doesn't have my number. Nick doesn't know anything about me, and now he never will. My eyes are getting blurry staring at the screen, checking and checking that I have read the name right, willing the letters to change.

'What do I need to do to get a drink in this shithole?'

Ben is shouting to the imaginary audience following him everywhere. I need to go. I'm pretty sure Yuki's safe from him now that she's seen him flirting with me. My deed is done, the only thing I could achieve tonight.

More people enter the pub, and I start worrying about the lack of space, why so many bodies have gathered precisely here, obstructing my escape. Ben's anger is bubbling near the edges, I can see it from the way his shoulders tense. He keeps wiping sweat off his forehead, and checks his phone over and over again. I get up, start moving away, but his hand grabs my upper arm.

'Stay with me,' he says, in a way that makes me freeze. My eyes fix on the door – the exit.

The door opens, and Nick comes in.

Everything slows. My breath catches in my throat. I try to move away from Ben, but he's holding me in place. His grip hurts. The barman finally starts pouring the drinks, places a pint on the bar. Nick pushes through the crowd in that friendly yet determined way he has, his PE teacher purpose, car keys in hand. He stops for someone stumbling in his way and looks right, left, scanning the room. I'm straight across the pub from him, but there are so many obstacles between us, and he must be looking for Charlotte, or Max. My hands start trembling, his name forms in my throat. Ben turns to me, as if to whisper something in my ear, too close, and with my free hand I grab the pint of beer and throw its contents in his face.

In slow motion, the pee-like liquid soaks his hair, his stupid shirt, coats his face with glistening rage. He lets me go with a shriek.

I push my own way through the crowd, to the gasps of

291

people who witnessed the incident, to Ben shouting that I'm a bitch. I have no idea whether it's me Nick is looking for, whether he'll stop for me; it takes all the time in the world as I walk through the many memories of tonight, until at last a giggling couple move out of the way, and I find myself standing right in front of him, and he sees me.

He sees me.

For a second, he doesn't say anything and I fear he's going to walk around me, but then he stops.

'Lou?'

I don't question anything. I jump towards him and throw my arms around his neck, and he receives my weight laughing, stumbling back. People around us moan at bumped elbows and spilled drinks, and there is a big commotion at the bar, where Ben is flapping hysterically, but we don't care. I press my face against Nick's shoulder and I hear his voice say, 'Sorry I'm late.'

Saturday 15 July 2017 (still)

Let it be now for ever. Let it never fade, never need to be lived again, because it won't ever again be as perfect as this. Before I knew Nick, I often had a dream. A dream that I loved and was loved and felt safe and known. A dream of one person whose eyes I would meet across a room, with the deep certitude that with them I existed in a space that was mine, where nothing I could do or say would ever be a mistake, simply a manifestation of me, and 'me' was enough. The feeling was so real, it spread through my bones, filled my heart like a balloon. Waking up afterwards, I would feel bereft with loss, call myself naïve and sentimental. Only in dreams . . .

I tell Nick I don't want to go to sleep, and he says I must. He says he'll still be here tomorrow, but right now, I refuse to consider tomorrow. Or the next day. I lie still against him, avoiding moving air or dust, so as to not precipitate time.

*

Earlier, we left the pub and ran to my flat, cutting through the town's nightlife, the pavements crowded with party-goers. For them it was just another Saturday night, but to me, everything looked new. The Peahen pub twinkled with golden lights and the sweetness of the air made me hiccup with suppressed sobs of joy. When we got to the flat, Nick waited a step behind, while I tried the lock three times before I could manage it. The street light outside drew long shadows on the parquet. We stepped in and out of them as we kicked our shoes off; I threw my satchel on the floor, then we stood still.

All I could hear in that moment was our breathing, Nick's a little shorter than mine, a touch more rugged, until the rhythms started synchronising. There was only the space of a step between us, and I took it, trembling with the antici-pation of him, but he slipped away. 'Is this okay?' he said, walking to the lamp I keep in the corner by my bed.

'Sure,' I said.

He switched on the lamp, stood for a moment with his back towards me. I looked at the shape of him, his back, his biceps tensing as he briefly leant both hands against the wall and took a deep breath, as if trying to make sense of it all. I tried to resist the urge to run to him, stayed still, quietly on fire.

'I'm not sure,' he said, turning to face me. 'I'm not sure I entirely know what's going on.'

The moment stretched, half lit, while I feared I wouldn't find the right words to keep him here. But he walked back to me, placed his warm hands on the sides of my neck, studying my face, frowning at first.

'Did you really throw a pint at that creep?'

I smiled, said nothing.

'You legend.' His closeness was so familiar and intense that it liquefied my body. I closed my eyes briefly, enjoying his touch like I never had before, basking in it. Nick. 'I know you, don't I,' he said. His grin spread, and I thought, you're so fucking beautiful, I can only swear. Because it's all too clichéd and fragile otherwise and I want this moment to be as strong as it can possibly be.

'What do you . . . ' I stopped, chewing my lip so I couldn't say the word *remember*. Not now.

'What do I what?' His mouth so close, his fingers tucking a lock of my hair behind my ear, his voice saying, 'Have you cut your hair? I remember it long.'

It was long in Thailand, I thought. I tugged his face gently and he kissed me again, and again, a dance instinctive yet new, and more intense than I ever remembered it to be. His T-shirt fell on the floor, then my blouse, and we stood in the middle of the room, skin against skin, taking our time. I'd never been so aware of every place our bodies met, the firm and tender pressure of his hands on my back as he held me. I kissed his shoulder, the nape of his neck, his tattoo, faded on his bicep; he held me as if he were worried I'd dissolve into thin air, anchoring me. We were finally here, a moment we had stored for a long time, that had been taking root inside us. That dream. I wasn't *dreaming* of being loved. It was real, waiting to be revived.

Now I don't want to go to sleep, and I feel almost angry with Nick for dozing off. The blinds are open, I can see all the textures of the outside world: asphalt, the bark of a tree, some grass grey and thick like the furry back of a sleeping

295

creature. I place my hand between Nick's shoulder blades, feeling his lungs expand, his skin stretch slightly, willing his body to be kind to him.

'I felt shite, Lou, so shite, and then I walked in and saw you.' His voice isn't in the slightest tainted with sleep. He doesn't turn to face me. I focus on the sensations in my hand, the vibrations of that hollow space, the flip side of his chest.

'Don't you want to smoke?' I suddenly realise he hasn't had a cigarette since we met.

He laughs. 'I'm all right, thank you.'

Of course, technically it is now past midnight, Sunday 16 July 2017, but does it really count? It's not the next day until the sun rises, I decide, and there are a few more hours before that. If I count every second, it will be the longest time.

'Guess this is what they call an instant crush,' Nick says, his arm wrapping around me, pulling me close.

'*Un coup de foudre.*'

'What? I don't speak French, I only got—'

'I know. It's like a lightning strike. You know, at first sight.'

'Right. Love at first sight,' he says. There's a pause, our thoughts growing towards each other like tendrils reaching for the light. What exactly do you remember, Nick? Do I want to know?

We stay close like this as the night turns into early morning, both struggling to fend off sleep, because being awake means we are together. I don't want to think about how much time we have, but I'm going to be there for every minute of it.

Sunday 24 December 2017

There isn't much to say when you are this happy. I thought I could stop time, but happiness accelerates it, and we already find ourselves at our first Christmas together. I try not to think about it all running away. I'm tired, mainly because I lie in bed every night refusing to sleep off any time with Nick; I want to spend every moment aware that he's alive, with me.

We've been here a few times before, but approaching Nick's parents' flat always makes me nervous. The echoey stairwell especially. As we climb, I brace myself for his mother to slam the door in my face, or to hear her voice reverberating off the lift cage, snapping at me that I shouldn't be here, that I should leave him alone. Although this time around, it is as warm and friendly a place as it could possibly be.

'Not so fast, please.'

I realise that, caught up in my haste to leave the stairwell,

I've been running ahead. Nick is a whole floor behind, and I wait, my hand on the handrail, to allow him to catch up with me.

'It's my back again,' he explains, wincing. He's out of breath and we are only two floors up. He doesn't even smoke any more. Don't think about it, Louise. Don't say anything. Against the familiar pull of panic, I plunge my hand into my coat pocket, feeling the reassurance of my phone, and through it, my connection to Marion, grounding me. I smile at Nick, who comes to stand next to me, and I watch him stretch as if he's just run 10K.

'Are you okay?' I ask.

'Grand,' he grins. 'Looking forward to seeing my folks.'

When his mother opens the door, she pretends to scold us. 'You're late.' She's talking to Nick rather than me, but she beams as she wraps him in a hug.

'Are you surprised?' Charlie appears behind her in the frame of the living-room door.

'I would love to be surprised with Nick not being late for once. Hello, Louise,' Mrs Adeyemi says, warmly enough. 'Come on in.'

She takes the bottle of wine I insisted on bringing and disappears into the kitchen. Nick throws his coat over the handle of the cupboard door, but I tidy mine away neatly. As I do, my hand brushes the battered leather of his jacket. I'm so grateful I'm here with him. Outside, the weather is only half bothered, cars slushing about on the road below.

'Come and sit with us!' Charlie disappears into the living room. Is it Christmas bringing out this childish excitement I've never seen in her? Nick and I stand still for a second, facing each other, in front of his childhood bedroom door.

The door is shut, keeping its secrets deep within. He opens his arms and I walk into them.

'It's good to be alive,' he mumbles with his lips in my hair, and my heart skips a beat.

'No time for this,' tuts his mother, who emerges from the kitchen bearing a roasted turkey in her pink oven gloves. 'Come on, lovebirds, don't make us wait any longer.'

'Wait, Lou, I . . . ' Nick says, but I giggle self-consciously, squeeze out of his arms and follow his mum. I feel she accepts me now – just about. Nick's family are so tight, so protective of him. I remember it intimidating me long ago, feeling I could only let them down. Now that I know what they've been scared of, I'm standing tall, telling them, *here I am, and I love him.* They'll catch up when they're ready.

'Lou!' Yuki springs up from the sofa, hugs me as if we haven't met for ages. Her hair, of course, is up in a thousand pins, and she's wearing well-behaved black leggings with her Christmas pudding shirt. I think of Ben criticising her style, and the sight of her shirt delights me.

'You look amazing, Yukes.'

'She really does,' Charlie says, and Abe, Nick's stepdad, sitting in his chair, looks up from his phone, over the rim of his glasses, and chuckles. 'All right, Dad.' Charlie goes over to him, holding her hand out for him to squeeze.

At the sight of her lean, crisp shoulders against the frame of the big window, her long arm stretched to her father, in a blink it's July, and she's crying. Grass and flowers and cats. I catch myself again.

Every other Sunday is Yuki and my pub brunch tradition; we go to the Five Horseshoes, curl up on the bench by the fire and catch up about our week. One time, early on, I brought Nick with me, at Yuki's request. They got on so well; later, as Nick and I debriefed, he agreed that she and Charlie would be perfect for each other. We set them up through a double date to an art gallery; both Nick and I found it boring, but Yuki and Charlie enthused about it, and that was that, the universe was set to rights. Needless to say, the brunch tradition has continued, but I've made sure that it remains something Yuki and I do on our own. The four of us have plenty of other opportunities to be together.

Yuki and Charlie squeeze together on the sofa, looking for a minute exactly like their Christmas Instagram post, Charlie's skin glowing in her perfect white shirt, Yuki's hair falling out of the pins, one by one, as they giggle. I sit at the other end. Nick brings over a chair from the dining table, and I find Chomsky's ear and rub it gently between my fingers, once again wishing time could stand still.

When Nick's mother brings in dessert, a dense fruit cake she makes every year, according to Nick, adapting Abe's mother's recipe from Nigeria, everybody quietens.

'Ah, Mum,' Charlie coos.

'It's a little burnt this year,' her mother replies, pouting.

'You always say that, and it's never burnt,' Nick says.

'Looks perfect, love,' Abe says, and he holds his hand out to her, exactly in the way that Charlie did to him. We watch them squeeze hands for a second, glance at their family, at their children and their two girlfriends, the furry beast drawing dangerously close to the cake tin. Seeing Nick's family united and happy makes me a little sad for mine, but deep down, I know this is the best I'm going to get, and given how much work it's taken, the work of five lifetimes, it's hard not to be grateful for it.

I video-called Marion earlier, before Nick drove us here. I've kept that going this time around – checking in on her regularly, chatting nonsense and support through WhatsApp and Facebook. She was surprised at first – to her, it was new – but I kept pushing, standing firm through her sarcasm until she knew I hadn't abandoned her. I made sure I was home in the summer when Grandma died, I stayed to help with the funeral arrangements. Nick flew over for it; we stayed with Mum for a bit to give Marion a summer break. I promised I would bring him over for New Year.

Marion's face on the screen was as relaxed as it could be. 'Mum's a little stressed,' she said, 'but at least it's just us.'

'Did she make vanilla pretzels this year?' I asked.

'No, she didn't, thank goodness – I don't even know why I'm saying that, because I love them. Usually.' Marion walked into the lounge, and I waved at Mum, who seemed thoroughly caught out by her prodigal daughter being presented to her on a small screen.

'Tell her to water her orchid, but only a little,' I said when Marion had carried me back to the kitchen.

'All right, chief gardener,' she said.

'And Marion, please take the family photos away.'

'What? What are you on about?'

'Do it,' I said. 'You know, that drawer with all our albums? Empty it, keep them safe.'

'Okay,' she said. No sarcasm this time. 'Happy Christmas, sis. And Lou?'

'Yeah?'

'Looking forward to seeing you and Nick in a few days.'

All families take work, but it's easy to forget when you're immersed in your own. Nick only recently told me one of his childhood memories, walking through town when Debbie moved them from their council house into Abe's flat – a single mum, she had met Abe soon after Charlotte was born, which Nick said had made it easier for Charlie, who hadn't known their dad. 'She's always been Abe's daughter,' he said, smiling with a melancholy that didn't escape me. He'd carried all his possessions in a child-sized backpack. He told me how bare his new bedroom had looked even after he'd emptied the bag. How he pined for his real dad to come and take him away from the big, echoey rooms with the model cars that weren't for playing with, and the TV so huge it gave him a headache. He told me how if he could, he'd go back and be a more grateful stepson, ignore his embarrassment when Abe would come to pick him up after school in his roaring Porsche, which wasn't designed for families, not correct the teachers when they assumed at parents' evening that Abe was his father. 'If I'd been Abe,' Nick said, 'I would have given up on me much earlier. But he's been there for me since day one.'

These memories were new to me, new to this version of us, and the more I learnt, the more I tried to give him space to share more. He told me he still said no to Abe's offers of financial help, even after Abe gifted Charlie the deposit for her flat. 'I feel like I would be taking advantage. If I'd been a nicer teenager, perhaps I would have said yes.'

'I can't imagine you ever not being nice,' I told him as I stroked his hair.

'I don't always like thinking about it,' he said. 'But I actually don't mind sharing that with you.'

We all eat the Nigerian cake, delicious and moist, Yuki,

Charlie and Nick chattering away while every so often Abe meets my eyes and winks. We are the quieter of the party, sharing a mute complicity. I wonder what Dad is doing. Probably eating cake with his new family, a glass of wine in hand, watching his vines in the smouldering sun. Whatever. I'd swap a father running out on his family to find himself for a stepdad like Abe any day.

'Nick looks good,' his mother says to me as she pours more tea into my cup. 'I think he's happy.'

'Ah, Mum,' Nick grins, 'please.'

'But it's true,' she says. 'Finally.'

Nick meets my eyes, and I give him my best shy smile. Finally indeed.

'Debbie, don't embarrass the boy,' Abe chuckles.

'Well, speaking of happy,' Charlie says, 'and given that all the most important people and dogs in the world are here, Yuki and I have something to tell you.'

She leaves a silence after this, in which we all stare at her and Yuki blushes deep crimson. Debbie gasps, bringing her elegant hands to her mouth. Nick looks surprised.

'We got engaged,' Charlie says. 'In fact, I have a present for you.' She turns to face Yuki, producing a small box.

'And here's yours,' Yuki says, doing the same. We wait until they've opened the boxes and put the rings on before we jump up and congratulate them. Many tearful hugs follow, and admiring coos at stones so shiny they even eclipse Yuki's golden manicure – effusions that seem to confuse Chomsky greatly, as he puppy-bows around us, hoping that somehow the fuss is all for him.

'Your dog's trying to steal your thunder, Charlie,' Nick says, holding her tight.

'Ah, whatever. He's such a diva, but I'm used to it.'

Once it has all calmed down and Abe has gone to the kitchen to look for more champagne, Debbie says, 'So, this might actually mean grandchildren soon? We need a new generation; Christmas isn't the same without little ones around.'

I'd rather we didn't talk about children. I know from a previous life that Nick wants them, though he hasn't mentioned anything since we started dating again.

'Come on, Mum,' Nick gently scolds her, putting his arm around her shoulders and squeezing. 'Patience.'

'Sure,' Charlie says. 'But give us a little time, okay. We might, I don't know, get *married* first.'

I know Yuki's always said she doesn't want children. But equally, she always said she hated dogs, so . . . I glance at her. She's even more crimson than before, turning her new ring around her finger. We're sitting next to each other, and as Debbie and Charlie engage in an intense discussion about wedding dresses, sleeves or no sleeves, and Debbie scolds Charlie for refusing to consider a dress without pockets ('It's a wedding dress, love, you'll have bridesmaids to carry your things'), I whisper: 'All good?'

Yuki nods.

'So when is this wedding?' Abe starts pouring champagne into flutes.

'August,' Charlie says.

'August?' Debbie says. 'That's a bit soon, don't you think?'

'Not this August, Mum. August the following year.'

Nick was reaching out to pick up his glass, but somehow, he must have miscalculated, because he knocks it over. The delicate crystal rim smashes on the table, fizzy liquid gushing everywhere.

'Shit,' he groans, before jumping up and jogging towards the kitchen. Chomsky starts barking and Charlotte pulls him towards her.

'Why are you all upset?' she soothes the dog. 'Hey, boy?'

Nick comes back with a tea towel, starts mopping up.

'For a PE teacher, Nick, you have shocking hand–eye coordination,' Charlotte teases. Now that Chomsky has settled, she's folded her legs under her and is watching Nick hard at work. Proper siblings.

'Ha ha,' Nick says.

'It's the excitement,' Abe chuckles. 'Are you all right, son?'

'Fine.' But he's pale. Nobody's looking at me, but I know I'm the same. Because I've never lived past July 2019. And more importantly, neither has Nick.

Late in the evening, in the car, I watch Nick's profile as he navigates intricate junctions and roundabouts. His steering is smooth, the leather of his jacket squeaking as he changes gears. He hasn't plugged his phone into the sound system as he usually does, so only the purring of the engine is keeping us company.

After the smashed glass episode, he recovered quickly, and the rest of the evening was lovely, but something has been on his mind since. I don't want to ask him what, because I'm scared that it's what I'm thinking. As the white markings on the road rush beside the car, whoosh – whoosh – whoosh, I imagine us stuck in this time loop for ever. It wouldn't be so bad at all. I know we're the happiest we've ever been.

The roads aren't too busy. In Switzerland, families would be travelling, like us, driving back from celebrating with loved ones. I remember spending long Christmas Eves in the car, counting the farms' lit-up trees along the motorway with Marion. Here, I think everybody might be down the pub. Marion and Fabio have surely left Mum's by now, and I paint a quiet picture of her silent flat on the car window, the backdrop of my face in the mirror. Mum is there, sitting on the sofa still, in the same self-conscious defensive posture she adopted on the video call. *You're not alone, Mum*, I silently say to her. *Happy Christmas. Sorry I'm not here. I love you.* My face is staring back at me, and I've never looked more like myself.

'Are you okay?' Nick asks, pressing my knee briefly before returning to the wheel. I have no idea where we are, I have no idea what route we're taking. He could take me anywhere, this man, he could ask me to do anything. I trust him, his decisions, his judgement, with all my heart.

'I think so,' I say. 'Are you?'

'I think I'd better go get another check-up,' he says. 'When I went in July, they said everything was fine, but ... I'm feeling grand, it's just ... I don't know. I could get an appointment when we're back from Switzerland maybe.'

'Sounds good.'

I want to say more but I have to clear my throat first. I put my hand on his knee, and squeeze.

'By the way,' he says, 'I love you.'

'I love you too. Always.'

Sunday 18 March 2018

The baby elephants are doing great. They're not exactly babies any more, but they're great. Just awesome. Everything is grand. Nick and I watch them in their paddock, their mischiefs of trunks and shoves, despite the cold. The bench I sat on last, the memory of Nick's pain shimmering at arm's length, is empty.

'Do you want to sit down?' I ask him.

'It's a bit chilly.'

Debbie bought him an actual winter jacket, a garment that looks like the love child of a duvet and a mattress, khaki and, of course, armed with a hood. Nick being Nick, he would have stuck to his leather jacket and piled on the hoodies. He's wearing the Fair Isle jumper Charlie got him at Christmas underneath. His scarf has come undone, one side hanging along his arm. I wrap it around his neck.

'All right, Lou,' he chuckles. 'Don't fuss. Treating me like I'm a delicate flower.'

'You wish,' I say. 'It's asymmetrical, it's annoying me.'

'Ah, I see. Nothing to do with you caring about me.'

'I bet you're happy to have a control freak in your life,' I produce a KitKat from my satchel, 'because I brought snacks.'

'You legend.' He might feel delighted, or sick at the sight. I never know at the moment. I thought it was worth a shot.

I tear off the paper. Its crackling sound is akin to the half-frozen puddles under our boots in the car park earlier. I know Nick won't be able to eat much, so I break the first bar off and offer him half of it.

'How generous of you,' he teases. I raise my eyebrows at him.

He wraps his arm around me as we munch, watching the ambling elephants. It's easy to forget how much weight he's lost since the surgery, because of all the layers he's wearing. But it's still him, as handsome as ever. My body fits perfectly against his, and I'm hoping so hard that this will remain the case, as we are bracing ourselves for a worse time.

Chemo is looming. I realise now that *chemo* used to be only a word, something thrown about in films that meant people disappearing and reappearing with a scarf on their head. It becomes real next week. A testing experience that I'd do anything to spare Nick from, yet the only thing that can save him. The worst that *has* to happen. Because I could ask a million questions of the oncologist and paint it all in my head in advance, I am finding myself in this strange comfort zone: an anticipated disaster.

'Was it in Thailand, Nick?'

'What?' He's still holding me, and his lips speak through my bobble hat. I thought for a minute that he'd fallen asleep as I felt his weight rest against me. It wouldn't be the first time.

'Was it in Thailand you found out that baby elephants can die of loneliness?'

'Yeah,' he says after a pause, and I think he's going to stop there, but he continues. 'I'm sorry I've never told you about Thailand before. It was hard, you know. I don't like talking about it.'

I say nothing. I wait, as we watch the youngest elephant half-heartedly kick a huge ball.

'I guess I had what you would call a breakdown,' Nick says, and my heart jolts.

'What happened?'

'Actually, can we sit down? Sorry.'

We go to the bench I watched him from last time. His ghost is still standing by the barrier, with that look of recognition as he sees me. Taking a step forward – something that couldn't be then, against the little miracle of today. The cold seeps through my jeans. I wrap my arms around Nick to keep him warm, the fur of his hood tickling my cheek.

'Well,' he says, with a weak smile, staring straight ahead, 'just the usual. After school, I'd been helping Abe with his business, but I was wasting time, wasn't good at it either. Katie – she was my girlfriend then – and I had saved up for a year travelling around the world. We lasted two months before she broke up with me. She was the one who'd wanted to travel, I'd followed her, but she got tired of it. And of me. We were different. She'd gone to uni, her parents were well-off – she said I wasn't ambitious enough, that we weren't going anywhere. She went straight back to the job in her dad's company she claimed she didn't want. I carried on on my own, became a little wild, I guess, too much alcohol and partying, even got this old thing,' he points to his tattoo, under all his layers, 'but all it achieved was to make me lonely, really messed up, and I ended up on Railay beach, ready to make it all go away.'

He stops then. He's frozen still, and I don't know if it's the cold.

'Did you . . . ' I start, hugging him tighter.

'I was going to. I sat on the beach and waited for it to get dark. I hadn't booked a hostel for the night, that's how sure I was. Then a British woman came up to me, asked me if everything was okay. She wouldn't leave until I reassured her, and I couldn't, so she stayed. She got me to sleep on one of the twin beds in her hotel room and flew me back to my parents herself.'

Everything clicks into place. It was all there, all the pieces, the panes of glass, lining up perfectly.

'Eden,' I say.

'Yeah,' Nick says, with a probing glance, 'her day job helped, you know – she had an instinct, spotted something wasn't right.' He takes a breath. 'And that's how a random therapist tourist saved my life,' he finishes with a kind of flourish. 'I continued seeing her back in the UK, she got me on meds, and I got better, little by little. What a lucky bastard I am.'

'*I'm* the lucky bastard,' I say. 'She found you, and then I was able to.'

'Think you'll find *I* found you,' he grins.

'What did it feel like?' I ask.

'What did what feel like? Finding you? Bloody amazing.'

'No . . . having a breakdown.'

He thinks for a bit. 'This is going to sound weird, but it felt like I was stuck in Groundhog Day. I was reliving the same day over and over again. Like no matter what I did, nothing could ever move forward. I suppose it felt like I had no future.'

My chest thumps with recognition. I've never felt more connected to him. 'I know the feeling,' I tell him, trying and failing to do this very feeling justice.

We talk quietly on the cold bench as people come and go, little girls in green jackets and boys with tiger faces: about Eden's trainers streaked with red mud, which, in Nick's confused mental state, he'd mistaken for blood. How she flushed the pills down the toilet and watched him all night. The next day, before they embarked on the small boat that would take them back to Krabi, the airport, Bangkok, home, she insisted on taking a photo of the beach, so Nick would remember there was always a next day to be lived. He describes his parents and teenage Charlie picking him up at Heathrow, how she's been his protector ever since.

'I do look back at that photo,' he says. 'And I come and check in on the elephants, every anniversary of the date. I suppose it's a way of doing something nice.'

'So today is the tenth anniversary?'

'Yeah, and these little ones seem on top form,' he says, pointing at the elephants in front of us.

'Yes, they do.'

'Proves that things *can* get better.'

'For the elephants?'

'Yeah. And for us.'

'But not for the otters, though.'

'God, no. Hopeless cases.'

311

'Good, because the otters are our next stop. We can walk there or drive to a closer car park. Do you need a break?'

I've planned our day carefully, taking into account the amount of time Nick can move around for, how often and much he eats, the cold, his energy levels. I don't boast about it in his presence, but I have a spreadsheet. He wouldn't be surprised, as he's already seen the map I took with us, with optimal timings and highlighted toilets, indoor cafés and car itinerary. Since he underwent surgery, I have channelled my forward planning abilities into supporting him. I have even started to drive his car so I can ferry him around, despite everything being on the wrong side. He gets a little bashful about it, and sometimes even grumpy. Teasing me is the best way for him to cut through the fact that he does need somebody to look out for him at the moment, but I know he's grateful for it.

'I'm fine – I can handle the walk. I'm not quite dead yet,' he says, but he's exhausted, I can tell. Talking about his breakdown has taken a lot out of him. However, I've learnt it's better not to mollycoddle him too much.

'It's not funny,' I scold, but I can't help but smile, because he's grinning at me.

His cancer was never caught this early before. I know it in my heart – in none of our previous chances did Nick visit the zoo on 18 March 2018 having recovered from successful surgery. Looking to start a six-month course of chemotherapy, which the doctors are optimistic about. In the appointments I've attended with him and his parents, the prognosis always seemed hopeful. I was the only one sitting there trying to remain cautious. I've decided to look at it as borrowed time, and I've embraced all of it. I've researched the unfamiliar

312

terms: oncologist, Whipple procedure, Folfirinox, Creon. In another world, miles and centuries away, Creon was a king who denied a deceased man his funeral rites, buried somebody else alive and lost everything for it. In the world I share with Nick, now, they're capsules that allow his body to digest food. A world smelling of hospitals, a well-oiled machine of tablets and drips and dressings, and many afternoons spent asleep on the sofa.

We walk to the otters, slowly.

'If we shared this zoo, as joint owners . . . ' I start.

'You have my attention,' Nick says. 'Please continue.'

'The first change we'd have to make would be to get some capybaras.'

'Giant guinea pigs who don't give a crap? Absolutely. Essential zoo residents.'

'We'd also need to move the whole thing to a river, and get more goats.' I think of Marion running ahead on her little legs, petting Pygmy goats along the flowing Aar.

'Lots of planning involved,' Nick chuckles. 'But then you're quite ambitious.'

'Really?' I think of my failed PhD, of my years of paralysed indecision.

'Yeah. You started your life over in a new country, learnt a new language, took a new job, all of it. That was incredibly brave, and I don't think you realise how driven you really are. You make me more ambitious too. About what my life could be. You brighten me right up,' Nick says. Then: 'Look!' He turns, pointing at the pen.

One of the unimpressed otters, clearly fed up that we weren't paying much attention to her, has started juggling.

'Cool!' I squeak. It's always exciting.

'That's smashing. Wait. Have we seen this before? I feel like we have.'

Yes, but not in this life. I don't say anything, because I don't want to lie to him. I've been balancing on tiptoes on this fine line for months. Learning to run back and forth, to make cups of tea poised on it, to console and cajole. He's opening up to me about his past, his mental health, but I haven't found the words, the right moment, to tell him what anyone would struggle to believe. That we have, indeed, both been here before.

Next to us, a gang of children are about to throw something into the enclosure. I bend towards them and hiss, 'Don't even think about it,' and they scamper away. My behaviour management has much improved since dealing with Ben, and my lessons aren't so disrupted now that I have taught these students again and again and know their sassy tricks. I've applied the lessons learnt in Thailand, and my newly found confidence coupled with Nick's advice has seemed to earn me more respect in the classroom. It's not perfect, but it'll do for now. I know there are better things in store for me – better jobs – but I don't want the distraction, not yet. Even through the heartache of Nick's illness, there is balance in this version of our life, and I'm feeling very protective of it.

'Maybe,' I say. 'Let's go and check on the red pandas.'

'I think I might shave my hair off next week,' Nick says.

'Show the cancer you're game.'

'Exactly. It's ... it's going to be shite, Lou, so shite. You need to be prepared.'

'Yes, it is. And I am.'

I can't say anything else, because he's the one who's going

to have to go through this: infections, mouth ulcers, nose-bleeds, nausea . . . The list is frightening, and that's only the common side effects. When I think how his veins are going to be on fire, I feel a spark of pain in mine, the match being lit at the edge of a network of gunpowder, and I wonder if I could, if I focused hard and well enough, take some of his future pain on myself.

He kisses the side of my head, and we watch the otters lounging around for a while. The families get bored and walk away. Various zoo noises rise to the sky, echoey, as if the whole place exists in a dome. Nick's stubbly chin is warm against my forehead.

'By the way,' he says, 'did you know otters only tolerate each other during the breeding season?'

I laugh. 'Evil bastards.'

He peels me off him so he can face me, cups my cheeks in his hands. They are ice cold. We need to go back to the car, back to his parents' flat; he's moved home, his mother guarding him like a lioness ready to pounce. He must be exhausted, and I don't want to worry Debbie, or to over-stretch Nick a week before his chemo is due to start. She thinks I'm overstretching him a lot – she frowns at my lists – but I know how important it is for him to be at the zoo today.

His eyes are two sparkling pools reflecting the snow-flurried sky. This time together is worth it. All of it.

Saturday 15 December 2018

'So how's Nick doing?' Yuki asks me in the kitchen.

Wham! and Mariah Carey. The ambience is familiar: a hint of citrus and the tinkling of bells. This kitchen is different, though, because Yuki now lives with Charlie in her flat in Finchley, tastefully decorated and impeccably clean. Guests are crowded together in every possible corner of the lounge, including Lucy, who is sipping mulled wine amongst some of Yuki's uni friends. No Ben, I note with relief. Charlie's crowd are more serious, and I wonder what they make of Yuki's stripy tights and the giant baubles hanging from her ear lobes. Chomsky's been doing his popularity rounds, and Charlie has had to beg people to stop feeding him.

'He's doing great, actually,' I say.

'Ah, mate, that's brilliant. I'm so pleased.'

Yuki knows everything, of course, every single detail of Nick's journey. She's seen me in tears many times over his course of chemo, and many times she's taken me out and plied me with hot chocolate and melted cheese. And for this I'll be forever grateful.

She was there too on 25 September, when Nick rang the bell at the hospital to signal the end of his treatment. He was exhausted and told me later that he worried he was going to throw up right there in the corridor, but he didn't. Everybody clapped and cheered, Abe was shaking all the nurses' hands, Debbie was sobbing in Charlie's arms, and Nick's expression was one of complete surprise to have made it this far.

I didn't cry. That day, for the first time, I actually thought: did we do it? Are we out of it for real? The adrenaline was still running high. I kept expecting something to go wrong, but since the end of chemo, Nick has been slowly coming back to his old self, like a balloon inflating almost to its original shape, and so has our relationship: we have been growing back into the couple we were meant to be. I've seen him grin and laugh openly at my jokes, his head thrown back and throat open to the sky, drinking in the moment and his happiness at being alive. This is enough. More than enough.

Yuki gets a golden plate and starts piling mince pies onto it. I'm pouring mulled cider into mugs.

'No Yuki's eggnog this year?' I ask.

'I didn't realise you knew about my famous eggless eggnog,' she says, but because she's drunk, her tongue gets muddled. '*Oh là là, le tongue twister,*' she giggles. 'Never mind, mate. Charlie says my cocktails taste like washing-up water.'

'Ha, and what do you say to that?'

To my surprise, she shrugs. 'Lots of things I do aren't quite right for Charlie.'

I stop what I'm doing and turn to her. *Yuki* means snow, apparently, and her ring is a delicate diamond snowflake kissing her hand. Charlie does have impeccable taste and exacting standards, but at what cost?

'Are you okay? Are you happy?' I've learnt to ask direct questions, but I'm not sure these are welcome.

'Course I'm happy,' she says. 'But you know, Charlie's so ... she's so perfect, and she has her life all planned out, with two-year timelines, whatever, and her flat is so pretty, and she doesn't let me buy new cushions for the sofa, and her dog hates me.'

'Chomsky doesn't hate you. But if he did, have you tried buying his love? With a juicy bone or something?'

Yuki snorts. 'Juicy bone. Mate, you kinda sound like you don't know anything about dogs. Well, me neither. Anyway, it's not about that.'

'What is it then?' I don't say, *You two are great together.* Because although it's true, I've been there. I've heard people say that to her while her nails were chewed down and she never got to eat her stuffed crust pizza. And I want to be a good friend this time. I think I've been managing quite well, but there's always the possibility of a slip-up.

Yuki downs the rest of her drink. 'Charlie wants a babyyyyy and a familyyyyy ... eventuallyyy.' Her drunken singsong is quiet. One of Charlie's friends walks into the kitchen, one of the fridge crew (cold and crisp and impeccable); they side-glance at Yuki. I nod to the glasses of cider, they help themselves and leave again immediately.

'That's hard, Yukes. Do you want to talk about it?'

'No,' she sighs, sounding much more sober this time. 'Thanks, matey, but I don't think it would help.'

When we go back to the lounge, Nick is standing in the middle of the room, his coat on. I go straight to him.

'Are you making a run for it?'

'Tempting.' He glances around the room. People with job titles we can't make sense of, for thrice our salaries, are picking at mince pies with the tips of their fingers, more of an exercise in deconstruction than *gourmandise*. 'I need some fresh air. I'm going to take Chomskers for a quick round of the park. To stretch our paws.'

He seems distracted, doesn't ask me if I want to come. 'I'll keep an eye on Yuki,' I say. 'See you when you get back.'

'All right. Won't be long.'

Something is going on, but I promised myself I was done catastrophising, and Charlie calls me from the other end of the room. She's sitting in the middle of the sofa, holding court. When I approach, she gestures for her friends to make space for me, and they dutifully get up.

'So this is where the Instagram magic happens.' I gesture to the room, the beautiful herringbone parquet, the dark grey mouldings. It looks like a spread from an interiors magazine. I wonder how she copes with Chomsky's abundant shedding.

'Ah, don't tease me.' I wonder if I've gone too far – I never know if I can tease Charlie – but from the way she pouts, I think I'm okay, and that she's tipsy too. 'Now Nick's gone, I wanted to talk to you,' she continues, and my heart sinks. She doesn't know how painful my memories of some of our conversations are.

'Go on.'

Let it happen, Louise. The more you fight it, try to avoid it, the more painful it's going to be.

'I'm so happy Nick found you,' she says, and the surprise is so great that I look up sharply, almost spilling my drink. 'Thank you for making my brother happy. Thank you for sticking with him even when he threw up on you.' She giggles.

I think of how shite – as Nick would say – the six months of chemo have been. Charlotte never got close to any bodily fluids herself. I want to tell her that the vomit wasn't as painful as when he was short with me, or when he coldly told me to leave him alone. It wasn't as painful as watching his pain screaming out through his grumpiness. We toughed it out, me working through the summer term, doing my marking on the train to see him at his parents' most evenings, waving my GCSE class off to their exams in a bit of a daze. They got their grades, though, Johnny, Fern and Chantelle. They were still fine, and even some of the others did better than expected. I think my teaching improved because the classroom wasn't the place where I had to prove myself any more. The little wins became more rewarding.

'You're welcome,' I say. 'It does seem funnier now than it did at the time.'

'Nick's had some hard times in the past.'

'I know.'

'You make him happy. You just do. Even if you say *I know* a lot, like a wise old tree,' she adds, finding it all hilarious.

I nod. We smile at each other.

'I didn't use to think that, between you and me.' She picks up her glass of wine and inspects it, as if expecting to find something floating in it.

'Think what?'

'I used to think you wouldn't be good for Nick. That it was all a bad idea.'

You don't say.

'I guess it was a risk,' I say.

'I expected you to be much more controlling, to freak out when . . . ' Still, now, three months after the end-of-chemo bell, she can't say it. She shakes her head. 'I don't know why I thought that, and I'm sorry if I was, you know, a bit of a bitch to you. I know I can be sometimes.'

I'm not sure which life she's apologising for exactly, but it's good to hear.

'I'm sticking with him whatever happens,' I say.

'Nick has been through so much. And before he knew you, he just . . . he was so guarded. He didn't ever get close to anyone. I don't think people understood, because he's so friendly – he always took an interest in them, and they never realised they didn't really know him.'

'It took me a while too,' I say. 'It's not easy being a decent girlfriend.'

'I was so worried he'd be alone, you know, lonely. I know he was, though he'd never have said.'

We sit for a while in silence, watching the rest of the party.

'But he's okay now, isn't he?' Charlie asks in a small voice. I see her in the church, at the wake; I imagine her squeezed between Abe and Debbie at the airport when Nick flew back from Thailand, her angst. I see her as my little sister too, somebody to be strong for. But Nick is going to be there now – Nick can do that. I don't need to.

'He is right now, Charlie, he really is.'

'Good.' She seems to be about to say something else, hesitates. I would nudge her, but I'd still rather be cautious with her. Not push her too much. She's like a fawn.

We sit side by side pretending to listen to the looped play-list while she turns her glass between her hands.

Eventually she mumbles, 'I could do with being a better girlfriend myself.' Her eyes are on Yuki, talking to Lucy at the other end of the room. Lucy is in her natural habitat, flicking her curly hair from one shoulder to the other. I wonder what gossip she's sharing this time.

'Don't be too harsh on yourself,' I say, though I'd like to tell her to back off a bit, because I know nothing is gained by exhausting your loved ones with demands.

'I do want Yuki to be happy, I do, but I've always wanted things to go a certain way. I'm not sure how to let go and still be satisfied, you know? Like I've gone too far, I can't go back and ... and compromise.'

'It's hard. And I understand why you might find it difficult to let go.' I know more, now, about love, and about all these people I've shared so many lives with. I also know that Yuki needs to learn to stand up for herself. 'But just listen to her. There's no need to push. Sometimes she needs people to give her space to figure out what she wants.'

When Nick comes back, his short hair and skin all cold from the outside, he asks me to slip out with him to the 'balcony', which is actually the fire escape. Because it's damp and uninteresting, we have it to ourselves.

We stand together shoulder to shoulder against the rail-ing, looking at the quiet residential road outside, lined with cars packed so tightly that if one person drove out, they'd all fall like dominoes. I can't believe we're here, on this day, with Nick being fine. Cured. After I'd thought, after I'd accepted ...

322

'This is lovely, isn't it? A great party.' I nod back towards the kitchen window.

'I wouldn't exactly call it a perfect Christmas party. Not enough cake,' Nick says. 'I saw you were talking to Charlie. She really likes you, you know.'

'And I her. Especially when she's tipsy.' I expect to see a smile, but he seems nervous.

'She could do with a friend like you. I'm chuffed you're getting on. That you can count on each other.'

My heart sinks. Oh no. I was right earlier. Something is up.

'Did you enjoy your walk?' I try.

'Yeah. Sorry I left. I just needed ... I just needed to clear my head. A bit of time to think.'

This doesn't reassure me.

'Did you want to tell me something?' I burrow my hand through the crook of his elbow. He's still wearing his jacket, warm and comfortable.

'I wanted to apologise for being a bit of a dick – I mean these past few months. You deserve better.' He doesn't look at me. It sounds like he's saying goodbye. I'm stunned, worry washing over me like a cold bucket of night, all poured out at once. Is he going to end things? I start shivering against him, and he pulls away, rummages in his coat. He hasn't smoked for ages, I want to remind him, I thought he was done.

'Out with it, Nick,' I say. If it all comes crashing down again, at least I'll know I've given it my best shot. I can't control how he feels about me, about ...

'I'm not sure *I* deserve it, Lou, but ... Now feels like the right time to ask. I guess I don't want to wait any longer.'

He stuffs a small box into my hand. A ring-sized box.

I stare at it, speechless.

'I'm sure this isn't the way I'm supposed to do it, I know I should kneel and open the box with a flourish and say, *will you marry me?*, but I know you don't like too much drama . . .'

He stops, looks at me, running his hand back and forth over his skull as if settling his grip on a rugby ball. 'I'm ruining this, aren't I?'

My hands are shaking. He opens the box for me. The ring glows quietly on the dark velvet.

'For the first time, I can imagine the future,' he says. 'And I want to spend it with you.'

I take in his face tilted towards mine – his crooked nose, which he broke in a fight when he was fourteen, his eyes like molten Lac Léman – and I lower myself into the hope of it, like a hot bath after the longest, most arduous mountain hike.

'I want to spend it with you too,' I say.

He laughs, clearly relieved, as I hurl myself into his arms.

Right on cue, 'Lonely This Christmas' starts playing in the lounge, reaching us through the French door, which we left ajar. Nick is holding me, and I'm holding him, and we start swaying slightly to the music, without even thinking about it. It's not really a dance, because we're both awful dancers, with a terrible sense of coordination. It's more of a delicious, clumsy moving hug.

'How is this even a Christmas song?' he whispers after a while.

'It quite literally says "Christmas" in the title,' I mumble against his chest.

'That's not enough, though. How is that good enough, Louise?'

Nobody scrambles to skip the song this time, because nobody is dying. I close my eyes against him, and I see another Nick across another room, the look we exchanged then, threshold to threshold, a lifetime ago, as people around him panicked and fussed.

'I can't believe this,' he says.

'What? Are you still on about the song?'

'That this is my life. That my life could ever be as good as this.'

'The power of a good spreadsheet.'

He chuckles. 'I'm serious, Lou.'

'This is the best my life has ever been too.'

His neck smells of fresh water and cinnamon and clementines. We sway slowly under Yuki's red and gold fairy lights, the metal of the fire escape clinking under us like a set of old pipes, against the backdrop of leafy, twinkling Finchley. We stay like this, on the best of all our best days, for ever.

Monday 7 January 2019

A lovely Christmas in Switzerland has passed, followed by a wonderful new year in England, celebrating our engagement with our families. I allowed myself to be happy, fully, wondering at how I have become able to do this: to let any potential worries rest in the corner of the room like a sleeping Cerberus. I have accepted that happiness makes things both worse and better, capturing the fragile balance of our existence in a suspended bauble. I can safely say I have loved every minute of my life since 25 September, a length of time that is my unbroken record.

Yet I have spent today carefully holding the bauble against my heart, in danger of shattering. Nick said he would text me once he got the results of his follow-up CT scan and blood tests, but he hasn't. We both treated it as routine, as if we assumed he would stay in the clear, but there is no guarantee. I was stuck in school for an inset day; Nick's appointment was at eleven this morning, and I've been checking my phone all afternoon throughout meetings. Nothing.

I stand a few seconds in front of my front door. Although Nick hasn't moved in officially, because the place is too small for the two of us, he has done in everything but name. He lives out of a sports bag of belongings thrown under the bed. He hardly owns anything, as if he always knew that— Stop. Stop, Louise. I clench my ring, its small stone denting my palm. This is the best timeline, when we did everything right. Part of me wants to stay outside the door, where I can keep telling myself this.

But I have to go in. I can see the whole room, and one glance shows me Nick, sitting on the bed, his back turned to me. Quiet music, his music, sad and slow, is seeping through the Bluetooth speaker he brought with him. His shoulders are shaking.

'Nick! Nick, are you okay?'

I drop my bag and rush to him, crouching on the floor, both hands on his knees, looking up at his face. He's crying.

'Please, can you give me a minute ...'

'What's going on?'

The fear isn't so much fear as dread. Because I know, however much my brain refuses to acknowledge it, what is going on. I clench his knee – his battered combat trousers, so soft and faded that they might as well have merged with his skin.

'A minute, Lou,' he snaps. '*Please.*'

That's what he was like at the worst of chemo. My instincts kick in again, to back off. With tremendous effort, I do.

'Sorry,' I say. 'Of course.'

I walk a few paces away to the shiny wall serving as a kitchen, set up our favourite mugs, take the tea bags from the 'Home Sweet Home' tea caddy that Debbie gave me for Christmas. While the kettle boils, I gather the estate agents' brochures scattered on the surfaces, pile them up neatly. I can't bring myself to put them in the bin, so I shove them into the cupboard under the sink, hiding them beneath the bags for life. Not this time. There won't be a lovely airy flat, perhaps even a maisonette, for me and Nick to share. I'd allowed myself . . . we had allowed ourselves to hope, and it's being snatched from under us once more. The unfairness of it makes me shake.

I'm pouring boiling water into the cups when Nick says, 'Actually, I'd better tell you now. Sorry for snapping.'

I wait, adding milk to my tea, a little sugar to his, stirring.

'It's back.'

The floor opens under my feet, and I cling on to the spoon as if it is my only connection to the room.

'Oh.' I try not to let anything spill. I go back to Nick and place the steaming mug on the windowsill in front of him. 'How bad is it?'

We sit shoulder to shoulder on the bed. The eternal night of January has fallen on the dark pavement outside.

'Dr Patel used the word "aggressive",' Nick says. 'They can't operate this time. It's growing around the veins.'

Now that he's stopped crying, he sounds worse. Resigned.

'What are they going to do?'

'They said I need to have another round of chemo, as soon as possible. To control the growth of the tumour. Buy me time.'

'Okay,' I say, trying to remain calm. Trying to be support-ive. 'When do we start?'

'Lou, *stop*. I'm not going to do it.'

I keep my eyes on the cars beyond the window, queuing towards the traffic lights, how they stop, wait and go. I wonder if on this date, at this specific time, throughout all my chances, it's always been the exact same cars carrying the same people, or if their lives have changed too, if they also had something to battle with – whether they were lucky enough, unlike me, to win the fight.

'What do you mean?'

'I'm not doing chemo. Not to gain a few months of life. It's too high a price to pay.'

'But Nick,' I gasp. I'm back to how I felt many lives ago, petrified that if I can't find the right words, Nick and I will fall out, miss out on happiness, go through lives of misery again. But I'm braver now, so I compose myself and try. 'What if there's a chance, even a tiny one ... We need to speak to Dr Patel again—'

'Lou,' he says, 'no.'

'You're going to give up and leave me,' I say. My fingers find my ring, clutch it hard. Nick's eyes follow.

'I don't want to. You know that's the last thing I want to do.'

'So? What?' I'm surprised at how hard my voice sounds, gathering strength for both of us.

'The thing is,' his eyes meet mine, liquid grey, 'I always die.'

Such a genuine and generous person. I'll make it my dying wish. RIP Nick Harper.

I know I don't look surprised. I don't even try.

'You know, don't you,' Nick says. 'You've been going back too. Back in time.'

We look at each other as the sorrowful notes of Nick's

329

playlist whirl between us, and I know that for the first time, we can see each other truly, the whole of our story, each and every chance for us. All the cycles of this we've struggled through. Together.

'I should have known,' I say.

I know it's been me all along, but I thought it was only about me. I've been pulling Nick back too, pulling him through it all. Of course. He knew who I was, he indicated he knew more and more every time. I just didn't want to see it.

'It took me a while,' he tells me. 'It wasn't more than vague dread at first, a bit like a hangover, but I realised I hadn't made it up. I had died before – it was there in my bones, in my brain, Lou. Last time threw me, when you weren't there and I spent all that time trying to figure out what was missing. Something important. I looked for meaning. I thought I was losing my mind. I made shite decisions, though I can't exactly remember what they were.'

'Nick . . . ' I start.

'All that déjà vu, messing with me,' Nick says, his English accent twisting the vowels like chewing gum. It's beautiful, and sad, the way he says it. 'And the more time passed, the closer I got to . . . Every time, things got clearer. I think death does that to you.'

I take a deep breath. I'm worried he's angry with me, but he deserves the truth. 'I think I'm the one who has those moments, you know, when we go back. I think they're triggered by me. They feel like . . . like a seizure, a point when a door opens to another timeline. Like a glitch. But I didn't think anyone in their right mind would believe me.'

'Makes sense.' Nick picks up his tea, takes a sip. He smiles sadly at me. 'But then again, perhaps I'm not in my right mind. Never have been.'

'Nobody else seemed to notice. Not Marion, Charlie or Yuki. Why you?'

'Don't know. I think our lives got more and more tangled somehow. I don't have an explanation for any of it, except that I fell in love with you, and you're the most stubborn person I know, so if anybody is capable of bringing me back to life, it's you.'

'Like a dog with a bone,' I say, and he chuckles softly.

He wraps his arm around my shoulder, and we sit for a moment, propping each other up, while we let the revelations of this conversation settle in the room. The song playing speaks of empires of dirt, of needles. I turn my ring around my finger, think of him walking into the Five Horseshoes, of us swaying under the red and gold stars on Charlotte's precarious balcony, in the dripping English winter, the best of all our best days. Behind us. I thought I could accept losing it all, but perhaps there is another way. Perhaps we can relive it again and again. Have even more of those perfect days.

'I know I'm going to die, Lou. Now I know it'll happen every time, whatever you and I do.' Nick's voice is kind, but firm. 'I'm not doing chemo again. I won't put myself through it. I want to spend every hour I have left with you, with my family, not sitting in a hospital chair. Not throwing up or snapping at you.'

'Okay,' I say. 'Perhaps you're right. We'll live through it together, as far as it takes us until we go back. Don't you see? It doesn't matter, because we can start again every time, get our two years together. We can find each other again for ever.'

I'm almost giddy now. Nick knows. It feels so good that we're both in this, that we are being completely honest with each other, sharing everything for the first time. No more holding back, no more running away. What does it matter that the date never goes past 15 July 2019 if every time we get to pick our story up where we left it?

Nick lets his arm drop off my shoulders, turns to face me.

'You're not listening. I said I always die.'

'And I always bring you back. You said that if somebody could do it, it was me.'

'I know,' he says. 'And every time you put me through it all over again.'

The giddiness ebbs away. I delve at once into the seriousness of his eyes.

'What do you mean?'

'When I'm pulled back, whether I actually died or came close to it, I remember it better every time. My body does too. It hurts, Lou.' He gently prises my fingers off his wrist. I hadn't realised how tightly I was gripping him. The cuff of his sweater is so soft, faded, washed and dried again and again. 'The operation, the chemo, dying ... fucking hell, it's unbearable.'

This isn't some kind of metaphysical experiment. Every time, Nick has lived it. His veins on fire. His body throwing itself up. His hair falling out by the handful. His lovely mouth eaten up by ulcers. The ache of nearing death, the delirium. I feel it through his words for half a second, and my body almost keels over with the shock.

'I never knew I hurt you, I thought you only remembered ... *me*, not ... just ... I'm so sorry ... ' I retch, pressing my hand against my mouth.

'Hey,' Nick says. I try my best to control myself. 'It's okay, neither of us knew, we're only just figuring it out. Together.'

He puts his arms around me and I cling on to him, not knowing where his emotions end and mine start, where his body starts and mine ends. So much time and energy spent to entangle us further, and now I'm going to lose him for ever? I thought I could do it, just enjoy the time we had, but I didn't realise I would love him more. More and more as time went on. From the giddiness of the start to something much deeper. Something so essential to my life that I might wither without it.

'But still, isn't it . . . ' I'm going to say *worth it*, worth being alive, but he stops me.

'No, Lou. You have to let me be the judge of this. It's my life. My death.'

'You're going to ask me to stop, aren't you?' I whimper against his hoodie, hoping he will say that he won't. He doesn't. 'But it's not like I control it, it was never a choice. It just happens to me, I can't breathe and things start fizzing, and all of a sudden I'm being pulled back,' and as I say this, it starts happening to me right here, right now. The outline of a door frame appears, a tantalising opening, and I'm going to . . .

'It's okay.' Nick's arms tighten around me. Only he can anchor me – what will I do when he's not here any more? I close my eyes.

'But how do I make sure it doesn't happen again, when all I'll ever want is to see you? Will you be angry if I fail? How much will it hurt you? I really don't want to keep hurting you . . . '

Sobs rise, wanting to wash away my words, and I try to

resist. I'm in danger of walking through again. I'm reminded of Charlie's words. *Don't expect him to comfort you because he's dying.* It's not about me. It's about Nick. Doing the best for Nick. I manage to compose myself a little, pulling back from him.

'Please can I have a minute,' I manage to say. I need to be alone to handle this.

He looks a bit taken aback. 'Right. Sure.'

He puts his coat on, kisses me on the forehead. 'I wanted to get some fresh air anyway. I'll be back in an hour.'

I hear the door close and watch him walk along the pavement towards the traffic lights and Clarence Park beyond, turning briefly to look back. He gives me a little wave.

A life without him. A whole life stretching ahead of me. I pick up my empty mug, try to focus on the weight of it in my hands. What fortune can I read in this, the empty vessel of a future without Nick? I've been given the one choice I didn't want to have to make. I don't want to go back. I don't want to do this to him, and I've learnt to channel sadness into anger, I've learnt its power . . . *Non.* I hurl the mug at the wall. It shatters.

At the noise of the explosion and the scattering shards of pottery, it all recedes. I have to choose to be here, the next second, and the next. Another crack in this previously pristine flat. I won't get my deposit back, but where would I go all by myself? I burst into tears and sob out my anger in my hands until Nick's playlist runs out.

'Lou.' Nick is sitting next to me, still in his coat. I've fallen asleep, I think; it can't have been that long. He's here, he's smiling, and for a second, everything is well with the world.

'What happened to your favourite mug?' he asks, glancing at the debris on the floor, and I remember where we are. Most importantly, when.

'I . . . I got a little angry, I think.'

He chuckles, smoothing a strand of hair out of my face. 'Fierce like an otter.'

I can't help but smile too. I push myself up to a sitting position, hugging my knees against my chest. I feel dizzy.

'How are you?' I ask him.

'You know, not too bad. To be honest with you, I was half expecting to be pulled out on my walk, to wake up back at the beginning, but I wasn't, so thank you.'

'I don't know if I'll be able to prevent it from ever happening again.'

He's thoughtful for a moment. 'Perhaps if you could try to look to the future. To look past me. It would help.'

'I'll be so heartbroken.'

'I'm the one who's going to die. You're stealing my thunder.'

'Nick . . .'

'Be fucking heartbroken then. Don't fight it. It makes it more flattering for me, actually. Make sure you write a great eulogy on Facebook. Make sure to mention the elephants.'

'It's not funny . . .'

'No, you're right, it's not. But there's a difference between sadness and regret,' he says. 'Please don't have regrets about this life. This one last chance we've had. I know I don't.'

Here he is. Nick Harper, the man in the smoking shelter, the man at the zoo. His handsome, earnest face, which has been through so much, coaching me through his own death.

'That's wise,' I say.

'Right. I'm told I'm decent at giving advice.'

'I'm glad I tried you. You didn't disappoint.'

'Neither did you,' he chuckles.

'Thing is,' I clear my throat, 'I've always been scared of the future. And now the worst is actually happening.'

'Won't it be a little less scary after the worst has already happened, though?'

I don't want to think about that, to explore the thought right now. It's too big. 'I think we both need to sleep. Or try, at least.'

'One last thing.'

He gets up, takes his jacket off and throws it on my desk chair. Then he picks up my notepad and writes something down.

'Here,' he says. 'Perhaps you should finally meet Eden. She can start helping you too, with everything.'

'Okay.' I take the page.

'And please don't wash it in your jeans pocket this time.'

I promise him that I won't.

Thursday 28 February 2019

'Hey, sis.'

'Hi.' Marion's face fills most of the screen. She adjusts the angle, combs her fringe with her fingers.

'How are you?' I ask.

'I'm good.' She squints at the camera. 'More importantly, how are you?'

I'm going to cry. I look over my shoulder. Everybody else is in the lounge, but I snuck into Nick's bedroom to take Marion's call.

'All right,' I say, finding nothing else.

'Oh no. Is it Nick? How is he?'

Marion knows everything about Nick's illness. She knows he's moved back to his parents' flat and is receiving palliative care. The word 'palliative' still gives me the shivers. Abe has taken over and has insisted on paying for a private nurse, Roksana, the strict young woman with brown hair I met last life. Nick didn't refuse his help this time, and Abe paid for everything. Nick knows he's going to need it, that his mother will too. They've planned everything, and although Nick has been deteriorating quite slowly so far, the new hospital bed arrived today. He hasn't slept in it yet – he insisted they keep his old one at the other side of the room.

'Nick is fine,' I tell Marion. 'I mean, he's okay, nothing new.'

He is still able to do so much. I can hear him laughing with his family, Charlie squeaking, teasing him. We're so lucky to have him. Yesterday, today, this very moment. So lucky.

'Ah, sis,' she says, with an intake of breath. 'I'm sorry, it sucks so bad.'

'Please can we talk about something else? Anything.'

'Okay. Well, Mum's great,' she says.

'Really?'

'No. I mean, she's all right, but if I tell you she's upset because her orchid died, it might be a bit . . . a bit insensitive.'

'Might be,' I agree. 'How about we move on to the next topic.'

'Let me see. Fabio says hi.'

'He speaks now?'

'Ha.'

'Tell him I love him too and he's a good boy for taking such good care of my sister. Next.'

'I saw Romain the other day,' she says.

'What?'

Laughter erupts in the lounge, reaching me faintly. How many months, even lives, has it been since I last thought of Romain?

'With Aurélie. With his girlfriend.'

'I know she's his girlfriend. What were they doing?'

'They were coming out of the station. They looked so smug,' Marion continues. 'They give me rage, those two, with their perfect lives. It's so unfair that they're parading their happiness like this when ... ' Suddenly the phone tilts and all I can see is the ceiling. I hear some clanging noises.

'Marion?'

'Still here,' her voice says, cool and composed. 'Making coffee.'

'You can tell me how awful they were some more if you want,' I offer.

'So bloody awful! Romain was walking her around like a handbag dog – I wanted to punch him so bad. I can't believe you were with him once, that Mum liked him so much. Lucky escape.'

'Ah well. At least he finally got the damning reviews he deserves.'

We rejoice in this for a while, as the cafetière boils, followed by the sound of espresso being poured into a tiny cup. Marion's face reappears. She sits at the table, and I realise how much I long to be with her, right now, in the tiny kitchenette lined with old tiles, its rattly window opening on to the *ruelle*.

'But enough about bastards and their groupies,' she says, sipping her coffee. 'How is your friend, the one who broke up with Nick's sister?'

'Next,' I say, glancing at the door, ajar behind me. 'Marion, please. This is hardly going to cheer me up as much as the thought of your fist in Romain's face.'

'I wouldn't have punched his *face*,' she says coldly. 'Do Abe and Debbie know yet?'

'That you dream of kicking men in the—'

'No, idiot, about the broken engagement.'

'No. I think neither Charlie nor Yuki wants to rock the boat at the moment.'

'Waiting is going to make it worse.'

'I know. They're just trying to figure stuff out, I guess.'

'Yeah, I get that.' I hear Fabio in the background, his presence only noticeable from the sound of pouring coffee and a slight clearing of the throat. 'Speaking about figuring stuff out,' Marion says, 'there's something we wanted to tell you.'

'We?'

She looks sheepish, almost anxious, her mahogany eyes gleaming under her fringe.

'I'm pregnant.'

It's hard handling big life events on a small screen, and Marion and I aren't quite experts at it yet. For a beat, I can't speak. I close my eyes, remembering holding her on a beach as she sobbed. *I had a miscarriage.* Not this. I can't handle this on top of everything else.

'I'm sorry,' she says. I want to reach across and hug her.

'What are you talking about? Why are you sorry?'

'Because it's such bad timing, for you, for our family, because of what's happening to Nick.'

'How far gone are you?' I ask.

'We just had the twelve-week scan,' she says, 'and so far it's all looking good. I know I shouldn't get carried away . . .'

Twelve weeks. That's a different timeline, a different baby, different circumstances. She doesn't want to tell me, and I don't want to hear, but I can imagine that Nick's fate might have made her and Fabio realise they didn't want to wait.

A different timeline. Some kind of hope, of happiness, for some of the people I love, at least.

'Marion, it's the most incredible news. I'm so, so happy for you, and Fabio, and . . . ' I catch myself. 'But you're right. Let's be *cautiously* blooming ecstatic.' She laughs. 'Have you told Mum?'

'No. I wanted to tell you first. I'm not sure . . . '

'How she'll react. I know.'

We both sit in silence for a little bit, while Marion stirs her coffee. 'It's going to be so hard,' she says, 'without her help. I mean, I know we're lucky still to have her . . . ' She stops. 'Sorry, Lou, I didn't realise what I was saying.'

'It's okay,' I tell her. 'Honestly, sis, this is the best news I could have hoped for. I know how much you've wanted it. And Mum will be pleased too, in her way. It might even help her. You'll see.'

After we hang up, I stay sitting on the bed for a little longer. The mattress protector beneath me is thick and rubbery. I know Nick is going to die right on this spot, and that I'm going to watch him go, and accepting it, looking to the future afterwards, will be the hardest thing I'll ever have to do. There's also an actual chance that it will go well for Marion and Fabio this time, that I'll become an auntie. Things are moving, on a conveyor belt, slow but out of my control. I should be happy, and I am, but there's also a deep melancholy to the news. I try to keep my sobs silent.

'Are you all right, love?' The door is pushed open, and Nick's mother appears. 'It's awfully quiet and dark in here.'

I can't reply, so I try to wipe my eyes.

'Oh no,' she says. 'What happened?'

'Nothing,' I say, 'it's fine. I spoke to my sister. It's all good.'

I don't want to tell Debbie that Marion is pregnant, because I know how much she wanted grandchildren herself.

She comes and sits beside me on the bed. The rubber squeaks a little as she does. She flattens it with her hand. She always smells so good.

'Louise,' she scolds, 'I know too well it's not all good.'

'Sorry, Debbie.'

'Anything I can do?'

She's doing so much. For Nick. She's holding him up, feeding him his favourite dishes, shielding the end of his life from the world.

'I just ... I miss my family,' I gasp, surprised that it's come out this simple, this obvious.

'Oh, love. Of course you do.'

'It's not ... it's not only the distance, it's ...' I don't know how to explain.

'I know. Nick told me about your mum. Must be really hard.'

'I'm sorry, Debbie,' I say. 'I know you have enough on your plate.'

We sit in silence for a bit, then she taps my knee and gets up.

'How about you come and live here with us for now. That way you can spend all your spare time with Nick. I know it's not ideal, but you can have Charlie's room.'

I stand up too. 'I ... Thank you. I don't want to impose ...' But there's nothing in the world I would like more than to move in with them, be surrounded by their love, even if it's not directed at me.

'That's settled,' she says.

When we go back into the lounge, Abe, Charlie and Nick are playing Scrabble on the coffee table, and Nick is complaining that Charlie chose a game she knows she's always been miles better at. Debbie and I sit in the spaces they left us and watch them, holding strong cups of tea, Chomsky demanding attention between our feet, and slowly the longing for my own mother, for Marion, settles to a tremor, and I don't feel like wailing any more. Nothing is normal, nothing is as it should be, but Nick grins and shakes his head when Charlie gets another seven-letter word, and I think of Marion kicking Romain in the nuts, and the future slowly starts feeling a little less daunting.

Date unknown

School gave me compassionate leave, a few weeks until the start of the summer holiday. Time wasn't so much made of days any more, but of one whole process of worsening, of the peaks and troughs of loss, the ill-advised hopes triggering vertiginous drops. Time lived in Nick eating less and less, smiling less and less, in his essence slowly dwindling as he was coaxed towards death. Time was never so much my enemy before, tainting every day with the same rust of helplessness.

I wasn't prepared for how messy his last few weeks and days of life would be. For how much Roksana, the blessed saint of palliative care, would need to do. In that time, he slid in and out of being Nick. I sat with Debbie in his room at night, taking it in turns to swap his old bed for the armchair at his side. Sometimes Abe would bring a chair in too, but he was mainly making tea, reheating ready meals. Taking Nick out for drives when he was still able to go. Charlie came over too, in the evenings after work. In a tacit agreement, she lent us Chomsky, who stayed with Nick, lying at the foot of the bed, or sometimes in the bed itself, which became roomier as Nick's body melted away. Nick's hand burrowing into the dog's thick fur would always make me feel better that he had that comfort at least. Charlie *did* get Chomsky for him after all.

The hardest thing was watching Nick's personality change with no chance of return. He became more withdrawn, frequently asking to be left alone. At times, he was irritable, annoyed by his mother's presence and mine, the way we moved around the room. He wouldn't say it openly, but would either snap, or pretend to be asleep. He would watch us cry at the loss of him, at his pain, with dry eyes. It was worse than when he was having chemo, because this time, every episode of aloofness robbed us of a few more hours with the real Nick. I still loved that grumpy, suffering man, with all my heart, but loving him stopped being so easy.

His insomnia was back, which Roksana assured us was normal. She was constantly tweaking him with meds, tablets and liquids and injections and pumps. We were all so relieved we didn't have to deal with this, yet I knew we all felt bad that we weren't, especially Debbie. We were getting all the good bits – mainly sitting beside Nick in silence, either on the sofa when he was still well enough to move around, or by his bed. Sometimes he asked me to tell him one of my stories, and I fished in and out of the *Metamorphoses*, thinking of all the iterations of us in our past lives. I cherished those moments sitting with him, our souls entwined in the same space, his smile or chuckle, our fingers meeting in

Chomsky's fur. I started writing snippets down when he slept, so I wouldn't forget.

Eden came and sat with him a few times, at his request, during his last weeks. She advised him to keep a notepad to hand and to write down anything that kept him awake at night. He never talked to me about his worries, but I knew too well they were there. I knew that he could not face his approaching death with his usual laid-back demeanour. Even though he'd gone through this before, this time would be final. It was the most terrifying thought, so much bigger than my brain that I couldn't grasp it or examine it – I drowned in it, and I knew Nick did too.

Neither Debbie nor I would read Nick's notes, but every morning he would work through them with us, telling us the ones we needed to help him with, things like 'make sure my hoodies go to Cancer Trust charity shops', 'ask people to donate to Macmillan at my wake – NO CARDS', etc. Those lists, which often repeated themselves and contained items that only made sense to Nick, ripped my heart out of my chest every morning. I could hardly bear to listen to them. Debbie wrote all his wishes down, and between us, Roksana, Charlie and Abe, we were able to make most of them happen.

Among all this, my heart burning, I stole some snippets of time to make my own lists. In my head, at his bedside, counting and counting my blessings. All the chances I'd had to earn this time with him, the bridges I'd finally managed to build, the part Nick himself had played, in teaching me to be more open, making me see my own strength. The texts that kept coming through from Marion (*How are you, sis? Speak tonight?*). Yuki appearing at the front door, despite

346

the awkwardness this must have generated for her ('I'm stealing Lou for a hot chocolate, Debbie, just for an hour or so'). The long hours spent with Charlie in Nick's room, our eyes meeting every so often, that look of connection, of recognition. I hung on to the list of the good things as the light flickered and faded.

Then there came a point, at the end of June, when Roksana gathered us in the kitchen, and told us in a kind but direct manner that she thought Nick didn't have long left. Abe's face stilled, and Debbie, who had been putting crockery away, crashed together the two mugs she was still holding. Abe sprung up and took them from her, wrapped both her hands in his. She shook so much she looked like she was trying to fight him off. He didn't say it was going to be okay. Charlie started sobbing and wrapped her arms around both of them. I hid my face in my hands, focused on my breathing. One breath after the next, to hold on to what I could, as the wave of helplessness crashed into me. What will life be like, after the worst has already happened? The only thing I could cling on to was: it's Nick she's talking about. He won't leave us this soon. He's always late for everything.

That night, in his room, my light sleep was interrupted by him stirring and gasping for air. I rose from his childhood bed, panic immediately clogging my throat, as though my nap had only paused it mid flow. He was restless, twisting his limbs, his breathing so irregular that I automatically tried to match it, to take the pain away from him, as if I could, and soon had to stop for feeling faint. I crossed the room to him. I could hear Debbie in the kitchen, boiling the kettle, putting things away at two a.m. I dropped into the armchair,

347

placed my hand on his forearm. Under the bed, Chomsky whimpered.

'All right, boys, it's okay,' I said, one foot patting Chomsky's flank and one hand stroking Nick's arm. Oh, Nick. The pain you must be in. How I wish you'd let me try to bring you back.

'Louise,' his voice said, husky and dry. I looked at his face; the little lamp on his desk was always on now, in case he woke up and couldn't remember where he was, which had been happening more and more often. I could see his features change as he opened his eyes slowly. 'Long time no see.'

'What are you talking about?' I whispered. I made an effort to smile. 'Do you want some water?' We always had to try and keep his mouth wet.

His face twitched. He was annoyed with me.

'You took your time,' he said.

I wasn't sure what to do. At least he knew who I was.

'Nick, I've been here with you the whole time. In this flat. Since February.'

'No, you haven't. You abandoned me.'

'Nick, I swear—'

'You buggered off to Thailand.'

He turned his head away, his eyes and brow all crunched up.

I couldn't stand him being upset with me.

'And to Switzerland,' he said. 'You keep buggering off.'

It was all mixing up, I realised. All our timelines. I'd thought my mistakes had been forgotten. I had thought that because I had finally done my best, my bravest in this life, I had earned the right to a complete reset.

'Those were other lives, Nick,' I said. 'This time I stayed. I stuck with you. I'm here.'

Please let it be the one that matters, the one he takes away with him.

He opened his eyes again, jerked his head to scrutinise me. He was emaciated, exhausted, but his expression was that of a child, unsure as to whether he believed me. It was a long time before his features relaxed. Chomsky sighed and stirred under my toes.

'I recognise your voice.' He spoke as if I'd just turned up. 'Your accent. Lou.'

'Hi, Nick,' I said, the tears making his name gurgle in my throat.

He closed his eyes, and I thought for a few seconds that he was going to sleep, but he spoke again. 'You said you could make it all better, you said you could take me back. Lou, I'm in so much pain.'

My breath caught. Was he asking ... What should I do? I was so ready to take him, to snatch him out of this. My breathing sped up, the immense weight of pain on my chest ready to be lifted. I was more than willing to lean into it, to hold Nick in my arms while we tumbled away to the beginning, where he would be spared this pain and we could be together. Two whole years stretching ahead of us.

But we would go through this again. And again.

'I know, my love.' I wiped my cheeks as discreetly as I could. 'If I could take the pain away for ever, you know I would.'

I looked to him for some clue as to what he really wanted, but he seemed to have dropped the subject.

I cried silently at his side while he drifted off. I tried to bargain, but I wasn't sure who I was bargaining with. It was easier sometimes to think that if I could find the right thing to trade, it would all work out. If I could create the right amount of the exact type of pain for myself, I would earn Nick back. At his mention of starting again, the time seizure had attached itself to my chest, like a small, soft octopus, gently tugging at my heart with its suckers. It was beginning – the real end. I tried to ignore it, dropping to the floor instead and hiding my face in Chomsky's neck.

The end stretches for an eternity of days, and the octopus grows, feeding on my distress, as Nick drifts in and out of consciousness, Roksana hovering above him like an efficient hawk, armed with various painkillers and syringes. When I doze off, the very sensation of relinquishing control wakes me with a start, a jolt of panic that I will fall into the arms of time and allow it to take me back to the beginning. This constant state of resistance is chipping at everything I have left.

Roksana only gave me one task: keep Nick's mouth moisturised. I apply some salve as delicately as I can to his cracked lips; sometimes I kiss them when I think it won't disturb his breathing. His breath smells sweet with drugs and blackcurrant squash, the only thing he can still absorb. He can't keep food down any more; the cancer has taken over his digestive system. They don't tell you, the bastards, they don't tell you that with this illness you die of starvation. When I stop and think that I'm watching Nick die of hunger, the horror of it is so immense that I think it could kill me too. There couldn't possibly be any *after*.

'Louise, Lou, wake up.'

Early hours feed into late hours and so on, until it is early morning again, and I open my eyes to find that I'm not alone. Debbie is sitting on a dining-room chair next to me, her hand shaking my shoulder gently, Abe at her side, and Charlie is kneeling at the opposite side of the bed, her face resting on Nick's right hand, the one that isn't in mine. Her curly hair spills over the mattress, her shoulders are shaking. Debbie is sobbing, the noise like semi-silent gasps for air. The bedroom window is wide open, because Nick always loved the coolness of the breeze in these hours, the silence of the town. His music has been playing too, softly, through the speakers, looping round and round as time merges into itself.

As my consciousness emerges, I look at him. He seems more relaxed than I have seen him for days, his face peaceful, the corners of his mouth slightly raised, as if he just heard a funny story. His stomach is not moving. I wait. I wait for his next breath, holding mine, the way I've done for the past few days. If you won't breathe, I won't. Another one of my little bargains, and he's always indulged me. But there is no next breath.

I gasp, clasping my hand to my mouth, and Debbie turns to me.

'He's gone.'

I want to howl, but nothing comes, not even the octopus of time, not even the bees. I cling to Nick's wrist, and Debbie's hand, like a shipwrecked sailor in the most horrendous storm. I don't think I've ever been in so much pain, fire sparking in my veins, igniting the whole of me, and I don't think it's the appeal of going back: only pure, unadulterated grief.

Nick is gone, for real, and I am deeply anchored in the

351

worst time of my life. I grab it with both hands and plant my feet deep into it.

If I can help it, he is never coming back. Because I love him.

Monday 15 July 2019

They say that change happens when something moves, but the church is silent and still. I step down carefully and make my way back to my seat, Marion gently shoving elderly ladies out of the way with her bump, handing me a packet of tissues and a water bottle. I don't even know what I said, exactly. I still operate at the knife edge of two timelines fighting to have me, and I'm tired, but people nod to me as I squeeze between them, so I hope what I said hasn't been too confused. I look at the notes I wrote, the paper torn and wet in places, the ink blotched in tiny tentacles. Something about the zoo, about mythical capy-baras, about Nick's keys.

A few rows behind, I see the beacon of Yuki's hair, the little wave she gives me, a tissue crumpled between her fingers. Eden is sitting next to her, wearing the chunky necklace and hiking trousers I've known all along, her dynamic haircut. She throws me a kiss, uncurls it on her palm like a blessing.

It was Eden who turned up the day after Nick's death, who came to find me in Charlie's room, where I had taken refuge. Still a sailor, still fighting against the storm. I was shaking with it, my breath rasping. She pushed the door, and I opened my eyes and said, 'He died yesterday, you're too late.' My defiance surprised me, but it didn't seem to throw her.

'I've come for you, Louise,' she said. 'How are you?'

She sat at the end of the single bed. I refused to leave my foetal position.

'I don't care.'

She watched me for a moment. 'You know you're allowed to breathe, Lou. Nick is dead, but you're still alive.'

'If I breathe, I might lose it.'

'No, you won't.'

She put her warm, dry hand on my cold calf. Although she didn't know what I was talking about, this was the anchor I needed. Under her guidance, I took in more air, like a fresh gulp of water, feeling immediately drunk with it. The fight was still happening, but I was slowly starting to see that I could turn from its victim into a warrior.

'Debbie and I thought you might want to see this,' Eden said. She waved Nick's notebook at me. 'He wrote it a while back but never showed it to anyone. Then we can continue breathing together, okay?'

I nodded, propped myself up to sitting, my back against the wall. My hands were shaking when I took the notebook, which she had opened at the last page.

Ask my family to make sure that the hen in the green bin
story lives on. It would make an awesome children's book.
Perhaps Lou can write it.

Tell Charlie to get back with Yuki.

This was crossed out, and there was another note, saying:

But the bugger will do what she wants anyway.

Remember to tell Abe that he's my dad. Tell Mum that
she's my rock. Tell Charlie that she's a pain. How much I
love them.

Tell Lou how grateful I am. For those conversations in the
smoking shelter (how many have there been? Does she even
know?). We kept going back to that point because we were
meant to save each other. I was feeling so shite, and now I
know it's because I'd died scared of having missed out. Through
wanting to keep myself sane after Thailand, I'd also avoided
love and joy. Lou, you saved me from all my old what-ifs.
Please, leave that space open, allow yourself to be surprised.
Take risks, like you took a risk on me. I hope what I've left you
will help. I hope you can take a little time out, figure out what's
next, what you really want to do, where you really want to be.

'You know he wanted you to move on,' Eden said.

'I can't really think about this right now, Eden.'

'Of course. He just asked me to tell you that if you want
to go back to it, to start again . . . '

'Start again?' I stared at her. Surely she can't mean . . .

'Your PhD. Was it in classics? He said he'll fund it, or
anything else you want to do – he mentioned some time out
travelling, perhaps.'

I laughed. 'Nick doesn't have any money.' He insisted his small savings went towards organising his funeral, didn't want Abe to keep paying.

'I'm talking about his life insurance. That's what he's telling you in his note, what he's left you.'

'What?' He hadn't mentioned any insurance to me.

'Lou, Nick took out life insurance two years ago. He's asked for the lump sum to be split between his family, a donation to the zoo's conservation projects, and you. There should be enough to give you a head start on your studies, or to have a couple of years out, just figuring what you want to do next.'

I looked up at Eden's face, so calm and kind, her chunky necklace of gold and green beads. I could see the tan line on her upper arms where her T-shirt sleeves had ridden up. I don't want the money, I wanted to say. I would pay triple the price to have Nick back instead. But I knew this bargain wasn't available to me.

'I know it won't bring him back,' Eden said, 'but he asked me to say that he wanted to gift you a little time to figure out what you really want, and that you're stronger than you know.'

I imagined Nick coming to on 15 July 2017, feeling like he'd been run over by a lorry, hating the aftertaste of death on his tongue, rushing back home while I glanced away, too caught up in my moment and all my hopes, opening his laptop, looking for a life insurance policy. Click, click, click. His handsome face, the tiredness on his features, his hand combing through his messy hair. Was that why he was late at the pub that night? I would never know.

'And if you need me, ever,' Eden said, 'if you want to talk, I'm here.'

*

The doors of the church have been propped open to let more people attend the service. I lower myself onto the pew, wobbly from head to toe. We all sit and listen to the Louis Armstrong song Nick chose, in the sad stillness of this warm afternoon. In the music, its peaceful notes, I hear his voice. *There's a difference between sadness and regret. Please don't have regrets about this life. This one last chance we've had. I know I don't.*

Debbie puts her arm around me, Marion presses my hand. Charlie's fingers brush my wrist. Baby elephants can die of loneliness. But not today.

Tuesday 16 July 2019

I wake up with an ache, a deep feeling of absence. I don't know where I am. I feel around with my hands, my palms and fingers sticky with sweat. I'm on a narrow bed with checked blue sheets. The sheets feel used and old and smell strongly of softener. The room is too empty. I review it: the bookcase of GCSE set texts, football club memorabilia, two discarded lighters, a desk that is empty except for a small green lamp, the photo of Nick on Railay beach. My hand brushes something on the pillow – a faded T-shirt of Nick's. I need to talk to him. I had such a dream . . .

Daylight is already pouring through the curtains. How long have I slept? I check my phone on the bedside table: 05:54, 16 July 2019.

I remember that Nick isn't here.

Today is the first time ever I've experienced this date, the day after his funeral, and grief is physically trying to tear me in half from the inside.

Yesterday comes back. The wake at the pub, how we all huddled together in the bay window. The garden full of scornful cats. Yuki's sheepish demeanour around Abe and Debbie. Charlie's coldness towards her. Eden holding both my upper arms as if she thought I needed propping up (I did). The steady stream of people who missed Nick. All the while, the constant tugging of the strong tentacles of time, trying to take me back to him. An hour in, I was exhausted. Abe, Debbie and I dropped Marion and Fabio off at the airport (she had snarled at her GP's suggestion that it might not be wise to fly at thirty-four weeks), then drove home. We didn't discuss where I'd be sleeping. Since Nick had died, they'd let me stay among his things. It was both a relief and a shock when the hospital bed was taken away and Roksana packed up all the medical equipment.

It's a new day, a brand-new one, and I'm exhausted. I need a drink of water ... I put a jumper on, stagger to open the door into the hallway.

Nick is here. I see him in his faded blue hoodie, hood up, opening the front door. Is he running away? My heart is sucked into my throat, beating there; the shock at seeing him again is so violent I have to grip the door frame.

'Nick?'

He stops trying to sneak out and turns around.

It's Yuki.

'What the fuck, Yuki?' I hiss.

She takes down the hood. Her eyes widen. 'Oh my God, Lou, I'm so sorry, so so sorry, I didn't think, I—'

'What are you ...' I pant, my breath accelerating, slipping out of control as the door frame disintegrates under my fingers.

She glances towards Charlie's bedroom door.

'Shh. Please, mate,' she urges, 'we'll talk another time. I need to go ...'

A raging pangolin of pain uncurls inside me. It's not fair, I thought he was back, I thought I'd dreamt it all ... The surprise was so great, I lost my grip on the present, and now the control I've worked so desperately to hang on to is slipping away from me. Black bees are flying right into my eyes ...

'Lou, matey, are you okay? What's going on?' Yuki's voice reaches me through the distortion of time, as the familiar door opens and sucks me in, full of warm air and buzzing. I want to run in, I try to look through the garden to find Nick. If I could just find him, speak to him, hold him one last time ... I crave it so much I'm shaking all over, and I think I might be losing ...

A crack, searing pain at the back of my head, then ...

Nick walks in. He's here, in the smoking shelter. It's dark, and I can smell him, his skin soaked with sun. *I thought perhaps you were looking for a high-school-style snog against the recycling bins.* His grin, the ring of his tattoo as he lights a cigarette. *You sure you're all right? No offence, Louise, but you don't look it.* Animal noises echo around us, calling against the grey sky, while I shiver with cold, Nick's lips against my forehead through my bobble hat. *Long time no see. I'll just go and stretch my legs, come with me.* I run to follow him, giggling, like the worst spy, then we're in the car. I watch his profile as he navigates intricate junctions and roundabouts, lit-up Christmas trees lining our path. *I'm so glad I found you*, I tell him. We hop out onto Charlotte's balcony, and he holds me under Yuki's red and gold fairy lights. *I love you too*, he says. *Always. But let's stop here.*

The best of all our best days. We've had so many chances, and the best chance of us. We have had it, have lived it, and I'm grateful for it.

Let's stop here.

Later, much later. This place is unfamiliar, filled with hushed voices and beeps, muffled behind separation curtains, smelling of antiseptic and lemon. I must have slept, but it doesn't feel like I have. I have no idea what time it is, what day it is, but I notice natural light coming in from the windows. I think I'm in hospital; there are doctors and nurses walking through the ward. I'm not at the pub. On the chair beside the bed, Yuki is asleep, her long limbs folded around her, her blonde hair escaping Nick's blue hood. I turn my head and feel the pain again. I probe it with my fingers, find a thick bandage on my temple.

'Yuki,' I rasp. 'Yukes?'

She opens an eye, blinks.

'You're awake.' She straightens herself in the chair. 'Mate, you gave us a fright. No, don't touch that,' she tells me as I prod some more. It hurts.

'What's the time? And the date?'

She smiles, scrambles to find her phone.

'Such a Swiss question,' she says. 'Always obsessed with watches. Glad to know you're still yourself. It's nine thirty, the sixteenth of July 2019.'

The sixteenth of July 2019. I stayed. I resisted it – like Nick wanted me to.

'What happened?'

'You just passed out on me. You banged your head on the door frame, it was wild. I had to go get Charlie, who got her

361

parents, but you wouldn't come back to consciousness, so we called an ambulance. They did lots of tests, but they couldn't figure out what was wrong, why you had that seizure, you were just . . . somewhere else. I'm so glad you're awake. How are you feeling?'

I try to smile.

'Glad. I'm feeling glad too, to be awake,' I say.

We both sit in silence for a little bit.

'So, you and Charlie?' I say.

'Ah, not now.' But the grin spreading on her face says it all. My best friend. How grateful I am.

'Thank you for staying with me.'

'Ah, you're welcome, matey. Any time.'

I need to call Marion, but as I pick up my phone – which Yuki said Charlie went back home to get especially, so I would have it when I woke up – it lights up in my hand with my mother's name. Yuki whispers that she'll get us some chocolate from the shop, and slips out.

The ward echoes with the sounds of buzzers and reception phones and anxious chatter and the *flitch flitch* of nurses' Crocs. My head hurts as I pick up.

'Hello, Mum.'

'Louise?' she says.

'Yes, it's me. How are you?'

'Oh, you know,' she says.

Her voice is so small in the receiver. I can't remember the last time she called me. I can't remember the last time she asked me anything. I know I should tell her I bashed my head, that I'm in hospital, but I can't do that to her, not when she can't do anything about it.

'How's Marion?'

'She's at work, I think.'

'Okay.' That wasn't really the question, but I guess it answers it. Marion is fine, and so is the baby. A silence.

'I wanted to . . . I wanted to check in on you. After the . . . yesterday. How are you?'

Tears come. I thought I didn't have any left. The wound on my head starts stabbing. Damn all those bodily fluids, our wobbly membranes.

'I'm . . . I'm okay, Mum. Thank you for checking on me.'

I think about her back at home, in the still, dark flat, the orange blinds on the balcony trying to keep out the sun. The lake glittering below, children and parents throwing themselves into its cooling arms, eating ice cream, far away. And in the living room, my mother's silent personal battle against her depression to dial my number.

'What's the weather like for you?' she asks.

'Nice. Sunny,' I say, checking out of the window. 'And for you?'

'Too hot.'

I feel my throat close. 'Mum. It's been so hard, losing Nick.'

'I know,' she says after some reflection. 'It's really hard. But you'll get used to it, you'll see.'

I start crying, because she's listening, because she's there. Because she understands.

I think of Grandma taking us away and feeding us ice cream. Of my mother disappearing for whole weeks at a time. I weigh up my next words. This is a moment of clarity. A moment of truth. There aren't many of those. 'When you were caring for us, and for Grandma, Mum. Thank you. I know how hard it's been. I understand now.'

She doesn't answer. I wonder if she's going to hang up, but

I find the silence, her presence a million miles away, quite comforting.

'Oh,' she gasps, as though she's just noticed something.

'What?' I'm sleepy and I feel myself slowly drifting away, but the current isn't pulling me back this time. It's pulling me forward. I smell the fresh scent of lake water, hear it lapping against the black rocks on the promenade. I feel Marion's cotton skirt brush my legs as we sit and eat ice cream leaking through waffle cones. Marion is holding her baby, Mum is cooing at her. I stroke the adorable fat rolls on my niece's wrists. Goosebumps. I'm loved. I'm seen. It feels real, so I continue trying, and it rushes towards me, the future – I can sense it for the very first time.

'Never mind,' Mum's voice says, reaching me through deep water.

'No, tell me, what's going on?'

'My orchid's back. I thought it was dead, but it's blooming again.'

18 March, in the future

'Miss, who's the fittest, Jason or Theseus?'

'How about that for a last question,' the school librarian says. He's taken off his glasses, pinches the top of his nose, in embarrassment perhaps, but I see him stifle a smile.

'They were both liars and cheats,' I say. 'That's not so fit. Perhaps a better question would be: who was the worst ex, Medea or Ariadne?'

One of the girls at the back rolls her eyes. Her fringe is thick, and she's wearing as many layers and colours of forbidden make-up as one of Van Gogh's self-portraits. 'Medea, no question, miss. Ariadne was just stuck on an island, but Medea killed her brother, her children, her ex's new fiancée ...' Then she stops. 'Or I guess it depends whose point of view you're taking.'

She reminds me of Fern. Fern, who recently got in touch on Instagram to tell me she was about to finish university and was considering training to become a teacher. *Thank you for teaching me and not giving up*, she said, and it made me wonder, a little voice in my head, whether I might get back to it. Proper teaching. Whether I might be ready soon.

'Thank you, Leanne,' the librarian, Mr Byrne, call-me-Aidan, interrupts her before she goes into full flow describing exactly how Medea committed her multiple murders. 'And I think that's all we have time for, unfortunately. Ms Saudan has a train to catch.'

I would flatter myself to think that I hear grumbling in this motley crowd of Year 9s, but some of the students do send a quick 'Thanks, miss!' my way as they flock out of the library.

'Well, thank you for your time. I think it went as well as one could have hoped,' Aidan says.

'Sorry, we spent rather a long time talking about whether each snake of Medusa's hair had to be fed separately . . .'

'Are you kidding? I haven't seen them that engaged in a long time.'

'That girl, Leanne, she seems to know a lot.'

'She's very smart and takes great pains to hide it. She's on our gifted and talented list; I wouldn't be surprised if she made it all the way to Oxbridge, eye-rolls and all.'

I smile. I wouldn't say that I wrote down my stories for secondary school kids in the first place. I wrote some after Nick died as a way to continue speaking to him. Then I wrote more for Klara, hoping that she would enjoy them when she grew up. I didn't think it'd get anywhere, but somehow, when I started sharing them and engaging around them online, taking small risk after risk, it did. A uni contacted me about a job doing classics outreach workshops in schools, and in the course of my in-and-out banter-full visits, I am enjoying my interactions with teenagers much more than I used to. After some soul-searching, I decided not to try and get back to my PhD. It wasn't for me. I've been thinking of putting my stories, my scraps of blog and papers, together for a while; I don't know if I do have a book in me, where it might all lead, but I'm enjoying the possibilities.

'Leanne will need a good stock of eye-rolls to get her through the next four years,' I tell Aidan as I pack my satchel, put my coat on and finish my coffee, which has gone cold. Aidan made it for me from his personal stash, with the kettle he keeps hidden in the small kitchen across from the library, and I feel too grateful for his gift to leave it.

'Oh, I wouldn't worry about her. The world will yield before her. I'll walk you back to reception,' he says.

It's break time, and we have to push our way through a great pupil exodus in the maze of corridors. I know now that I'll always feel a bit of stress in these situations, as boys in skew-whiff ties bump into me to shove each other against colourful anti-bullying displays: a slight jolt of the heart, a deeply engrained response from all my past teaching challenges. But despite that, I relish the intense emotional content, the high stakes; I like talking to kids, and knowing who I am now, having this confidence, makes the interactions so much better – enjoyable, even. I feel alive, imperfect, but whole.

I hand my badge back in to the receptionist and sign out in the visitors' book.

'I'm afraid I have to run,' I tell Aidan. 'It was great meeting you in person, finally, and all the students, of course.'

He smiles, a little shy, and attempts to wipe a stain away

from his shirt. There are several biro strokes he can't do anything about, and I notice that he is, under the shirt and the tie, surprisingly strong. For a librarian.

'Thank you for coming,' he says, shaking my hand. 'It was great meeting you, and I enjoyed our emails too. If you ... if you'd like to meet up for coffee, talk about Medusa's hair some more, you know where to find me.'

At that, he turns away, and is immediately engulfed by the pupil landslide.

I smile, push the door open, make my way to the gate. I have to get to the station. What time is it? I check my watch. *Crap.* I'm late.

The taxi drops me off in the main car park and I walk through the underpass to the zoo. Marion and Fabio are standing by the entrance, armed with more bags than you'd need to climb the Matterhorn, Marion clearly unimpressed. Klara runs towards me.

'Auntie Lou! I have an ice cream!'

'So I see. Hello, sweetie.' I hug her and cover her in kisses, expertly avoiding the smears of melted chocolate on her face, then turn to Marion.

'You came from St Albans, we came from Switzerland, and you're the one who's late!' she scolds me, stifling a smile as she kisses me on both cheeks. Kiss, kiss, kiss.

We run through the zoo to the elephant paddock, Fabio holding Klara by the hand, the two of them falling behind, Marion and I arm in arm.

Every day is the potential first day of the rest of my life. This March is mild, the mildest we've had in years. Daffodils and snowdrops and primroses edge the path we are taking, the grass looking sweet and edible like sorbet. Trees in bloom reach their branches to the limitless sky. My chosen home, England, with its cream teas and rolling countryside and soft hedgerows and London musicals and very bad Tinder dates. I no longer feel the need to justify my choices. I'm here, the sky is open, the future full of possibilities.

Under the *Asian Elephants* sign, we greet Yuki and Charlie, curled around each other like mermaids, their hair floating as one in the breeze, blonde and dark algae. Klara runs straight towards Charlie's daughter, Nicola, who is two years younger than her. Yuki and Charlie seem to have found a rhythm of doing things together, yet separately, over the years. I don't quite ever understand the shape of it, or what it'll be tomorrow.

'You're late,' Charlotte says, and I still have that second when I worry she's angry with me. 'Long live Nick's bad influence on you.' She smiles sadly, and I hug her.

Abe and Debbie kiss Nicola and Klara, dispensing biscuits and juice. I think of Marion and her lectures about sugar, years ago – having Klara has relaxed her principles somehow. Eden is here too, in her walking gear; she comes and says hi, then retreats, and I watch her walk to the other end of the paddock, wonder how she remembers him, what form he takes when she pays him homage, as we all are. She is a family friend, but also my long-time counsellor. There are delicate boundaries all around us, threads of relationships that grow stronger and more precious with every year. We're a family that was not meant to be, brought together by Nick, and even if we don't meet every day, we're here for each other.

'Thank you for coming,' I tell Marion.

'I'm glad we could make it this year,' she says. 'With Mum doing better, with Klara being older . . . I really wanted to come, you know.'

'I'm so happy Mum is still seeing her counsellor.'

'Oh, yes. Thank goodness we found someone she liked in the end. I think she'd never have stuck with it if you hadn't been seeing someone yourself, you know. She's even started talking about coming with us to visit you next time.' Marion smiles, but I can see how tired she is. It's been a tough few years.

She rushes to wipe Klara's chin: more chocolate. 'Shall we take this coat off, Boo?' she asks her daughter, and I watch her remove the garment delicately, revealing a green pinafore dress over a knitted jumper, bright as the tender new spring grass growing in the fields and hills around. The little girl in green. She's always been here.

I used to feel I was watching other people live the life I wanted; now I know I'm in *my* life, with its uncertain and exciting future: the studio flat that finally feels like mine, with my lucky outfits and my favourite commercial novels and the laptop on which I rewrite classical stories for teenagers. Nick's keys and hoodie and my engagement ring, safely tucked away in a drawer, will always stay with me.

Together we watch the elephants ambling about their business, and all at once, Nick is here too. Klara points at the smallest elephant, doing mischief with his trunk, and everybody stops, Charlie and Yuki and Abe and Debbie and even Marion, because Nicola grins, and she looks like Nick. In this very moment, in the warm kiss of the sun, she looks like him, and for a few seconds we stand silent, flooded in memories of him, how grateful we are for the time we had with him.

Don't worry, Nick, I report silently, aching as I know I always will. Don't you worry a bit. The baby elephants are on top form.

Acknowledgements

I'd never realised before how much goes into making a book, and this book is no exception: it's the product of many places and people and casual conversations and memorable events. When I upended my life in 2008 to move to England, I never thought I would become a published author, and for this I have so many people to thank.

The biggest thank you goes to my agent Olivia Maidment, who after reading the manuscript sent me the best email one could ever read just after a Year 11 French lesson, and has kept delivering after that. Thank you for your patience, your many texts and emails of encouragement, your insights, your incredible negotiation skills and for choosing to invest some of your precious time championing me and helping me develop my writing. I'm so lucky.

I'm so grateful to my wonderful editors Hannah Wann at Piatkus and MJ Johnston at Sourcebooks, who both took their chance on me and whose editorial insights made this novel. I'm blown away by the amount of time and hard work they have invested into Lou and Nick's story and their enthusiastic comments about Chomsky the dog.

Thank you also to everyone at Piatkus who worked on the book: Hannah Wood who designed the stunning UK cover and Jane Selley who had to deal with my non-native speaker punctuation quirks in the copy edits. I'd also like to thank Abby Marshall (production), as well as Henry Lord and Brionee Fenlon for publicity and marketing, and Jill Cole for her proofreading. I've been so lucky to be looked after by such a great team.

I'm hugely grateful to the fantastic team at Sourcebooks: Jessica Thelander for her meticulous editorial production, as well as Laura Boren on internal design, Deve McLemore and Michelle Denney on manufacturing. Big shout out to Anna Venckus and Cristina Arreola for their tireless work on marketing the book, and of course, to Steph Gafron and Kelly Lawler for designing the wonderful and dreamy US cover.

Many thanks also to the whole team at Madeleine Milburn Literary, TV & Film Agency for their support, and more particularly to Liane-Louise Smith, Georgina Simmonds and Valentina Paulmichl from the International team, and Hannah Ladds for film and TV. I'm so lucky to be championed by such an incredible, tightknit and highly skilled team.

Huge thanks to Charlotte Mendelson and Curtis Brown Creative. Charlotte gives the fiercest and most astute feedback as well as the best pep talks. Thanks to Jennifer Kerslake and the rest of the CBC team for their guidance throughout, their kindness and availability. When I got a place on the three-month course, it was the first time someone saw potential in my writing in English and it changed my life.

I have to mention the CBC writing crew, cheerleaders, workshoppers, storytellers and best literary chatterboxes down the pub – thank you all, and to Keaton, Parry, Francesca and Alex especially for their generous and thoughtful early critiques of my manuscript.

More thanks go to Jennie and Sue, dear friends and early readers, as well as my school colleagues, in particular Chris, Stephen and Kajal for being so ready to help me navigate two vocations and all-encompassing jobs. Thank you all for cheering me on so kindly.

Thank you to Hélène and Melissa, best sisters this sister could hope for, the masters of tough and unconditional love – you mean the world to me even across a (narrow) sea. To my parents, who watched the whole proceedings with a raised eyebrow, in true Swiss fashion, whose love and support I've always been so lucky to have.

We lost our beloved grandmother Dora Kislig to pancreatic cancer in 2015. The swiftness and brutality of the illness was devastating and I remain in awe of the sacrifices my mother made to accompany her own mother through her last months of life. I know there are too many people out there who have suffered similar losses, or who might be enduring the illness themselves. I have tried my best to do justice to the harrowing process of fighting, then losing somebody to it, and have found Pancreatic Cancer UK to be an incredibly useful source of information and testimonies, as was Macmillan for guidance on accompanying patients in palliative care. Thank you for all the work you do in helping families like mine – all mistakes in the book or misconceptions are wholly mine. I hope people will forgive me if I have taken some licence with timelines and medical plausibility. Though Lou and Nick's chances had a particular structure, I have tried my best to respect the suffering involved while raising awareness of this type of cancer.

As a typical sufferer of anxiety, I'm terrified of leaving anyone out, so here's to anyone who has encouraged me or asked me how the book was coming along, or just taken me seriously as a writer. My lovely friends Julien and Joseph, Irène and Steffi come to mind, and many others. It matters more than you imagine.

Last but not least, Luke, thank you. I didn't know that date at the British Museum in May 2016, looking for a secret door on our way to the exhibit, would change my life and I'm so glad it did. You're my partner in the best sense of the term and this book wouldn't exist without you.